PRAISE FOR *HALF-BLOOD BLUES*

"Assured, vivid, and persuasive . . . Impressively evocative of period and place, and an effortlessly involving and dramatically unusual second novel." —Sharon O'Connell, *Time Out* (London)

"Mesmerizing . . . Edugyan has a perfect ear for conversations and the confusions of human love and jealousy. . . . Moving . . . A remarkable novel." —*The Morning Star* (London)

"This is a wonderful, vibrant, tense novel about war and its aftermath. Its author has brought both the wartime past of a devastated city and its confident reinvention of itself in a new era to life with extraordinary assurance." —Susan Hill, Man Booker Prize judge

"With *Half-Blood Blues*, Esi Edugyan has written a truly beautiful novel. With perfect pitch, and brilliantly in tune with the diction, musicality, suffering, and dignity of black jazz musicians trying to survive in France and Germany during World War II, and to hold their lives together in the aftermath of horror, it is both taut and expansive, like perfect jazz. Exquisite language, throughout. And did I say beautiful?"
—Lawrence Hill, award-winning author of *Someone Knows My Name*

"Simply stunning, one of the freshest pieces of fiction I've read. A story I'd never heard before, told in a way I'd never seen before. I felt the whole time I was reading it like I was being let in on something, the story of a legend deconstructed. It's a world of characters so realized that I found myself at one point looking up Hieronymous Falk on Wikipedia, disbelieving he was the product of one woman's imagination." —Attica Locke, author of *Black Water Rising*

ALSO BY ESI EDUGYAN

The Second Life of Samuel Tyne

HALF-
BLOOD
BLUES

ESI EDUGYAN

HALF-BLOOD BLUES

A NOVEL

PICADOR
NEW YORK

www.picadorusa.com

www.twitter.com/picadorusa • www.facebook.com/picadorusa

Picador® is a U.S. registered trademark and is used by St. Martin's Press under license from Pan Books Limited.

For book club information, please e-mail marketing@picadorusa.com or visit www.facebook.com/picadorbookclub.

Library of Congress Cataloging-in-Publication Data

Edugyan, Esi.
 Half-blood blues : a novel / Esi Edugyan. — First U.S. edition.
  pages cm
  ISBN 978-1-250-01270-8 (pbk.)
  ISBN 978-1-4668-0284-1 (e-book)
1. Jazz musicians—Fiction. 2. Racially mixed people—Fiction. 3. Ex-concentration camp inmates—Fiction. 4. Reunions—Fiction. 5. Paris (France)—History–1940–1944—Fiction. 6. Berlin (Germany)—History—1918–1945—Fiction. I. Title.
 PR9199.4.E35H35 2012
 813'.6—dc23

                    2011044816

Originally published in Great Britain by Serpent's Tail, an imprint of Profile Books

First U.S. Edition: March 2012

10 9 8 7 6 5 4 3

for Steve

I

Paris
1940

Chip told us not to go out. Said, don't you boys tempt the devil. But it been one brawl of a night, I tell you, all of us still reeling from the rot— rot was cheap, see, the drink of French peasants, but it stayed like nails in you gut. Didn't even look right, all mossy and black in the bottle. Like drinking swamp water.

See, we lay exhausted in the flat, sheets nailed over the windows. The sunrise so fierce it seeped through the gaps, dropped like cloth on our skin. Couple hours before, we was playing in some back-alley studio, trying to cut a record. A grim little room, more like a closet of ghosts than any joint for music, the cracked heaters lisping steam, empty bottles rolling all over the warped floor. Our cigarettes glowed like small holes in the dark, and that's how I known we wasn't buzzing, Hiero's smoke not moving or nothing. The cig just sitting there in his mouth like he couldn't hear his way clear. Everyone pacing about, listening between takes to the scrabble of rats in the wall. Restless as hell. Could be we wasn't so rotten, but I at least felt off. Too nervous, too crazed, too busy watching the door. Forget the rot. Forget the studio's seclusion. Nothing tore me out of myself. Take after take, I'd play sweating to the end of it only to have Hiero scratch the damn disc, tossing it in the trash.

"Just a damn braid of mistakes," Hiero kept muttering. "A damn braid of *mistakes*."

"We sound like royalty—*after* the mob got done with em," said Chip.

Coleman and I ain't said nothing, our heads hanging tiredly.

But Hiero, wiping his horn with a blacked-up handkerchief, he turn and give Chip a look of pure spite. "Yeah, but, *hell*. Even at our *worst* we genius."

Did that ever stun me, him saying this. For weeks the kid been going on and on about how dreadful we sound. He kept snatching up the discs, scratching the lacquer with a pocket knife, wrecking them. Yelling how there wasn't nothing there. But there *was* something. Some seed of twisted beauty.

I didn't mean to. But somehow when the kid turned his back I was sliding off my vest, taking the last disc—still delicate, the grooves still new—and folding the fabric round it. I glanced around, nervous, then tucked it into my bass case. The others was packing up their axes.

"Where's that last record at?" said Hiero, frowning. He peered at the trash bin, at the damaged discs all in there.

"It's in there, buck," I said. "You didn't want it, did you?"

He give me a sour look. "Ain't no damn point. We ain't never goin get this right."

"What you sayin, kid?" said Chip, slurring his words. "You sayin we should give it up?"

The kid just shrugged.

We lined up the empty bottles along the wall, locked up real quiet, gone our separate routes back to Delilah's flat. Curfew was on and Paris was grim, all clotted shadows and stale air. I made my quiet way along the alleys, dreading the sound of footsteps, till we met up again at the flat. Everyone but

Coleman, of course, Coleman who was staying with his lady. We collapsed onto dirty couches under blackout curtains.

I'd set my axe against the wall and it was like I could feel the damn disc just sitting in there, still warm. I felt its presence so intensely it seemed strange the others ain't sensed it too. Its wax holding all that heat like a altar candle.

———————— ■ ————————

It was the four of us living here. Delilah, Hieronymus, Chip and me. Couple months before we'd spent the day nailing black sheets across the flat's windows, but damn if that grim sun didn't flood through anyway. The rooms felt too stale to sober up in. We needed to sweat it out in the fresh air, get our heads about us. Ain't been no breeze in weeks.

Hiero was draped in his chair, his scrawny legs dangling, when all a sudden he turn to me. His face dark and smooth as an eggplant. "Christ I feel green. My guts are pure gravy, man."

"Amen," I said.

"Man, I got to get me some *milk*."

"Amen," I said again.

We talked like mongrels, see—half German, half Baltimore bar slang. Just a few scraps of French between us. Only real language I spoke aside from English was *Hochdeutsch*. But once I started messing up the words I couldn't straighten nothing out again. Besides, I known Hiero preferred it this way. Kid hailed from the Rhineland, sure, but he got old Baltimore in the blood. Or talked like he did.

He was still young that way. Mimicking.

Something had changed in him lately, though. He ain't hardly et nothing since the Boots descended on the city, been laid up feverish and slack for days on end. And when he come to, there was this new darkness in him I ain't never seen before.

I gave my old axe a quick glance, thinking of the record tucked away in there. It wasn't guilt I felt. Not that exactly.

Hiero sort of half rolled onto the patchy rug. "Aw, Sid," he groaned. "I need milk."

"In the cupboard, I reckon. We got milk? Chip?"

But Chip, he just open one brown eye like a man half-drowned. His face dark as cinder in this light.

Hiero coughed. "I'm tryin to clean my stomach, not rough it up." His left eye twitched all high up in the lid, the way you sometimes see the heart of a thin woman beating through her blouse. "It's *milk* I need, brother. Cream. That powdered stuff'll rip right through you. Like you shittin sand. Like you a damn hourglass."

"Aw, it ain't that bad," I said. "Ain't nothin open at this hour anyway, kid. You know that. Except maybe the Coup. But that's too damn far." We lay on in silence a minute. I tossed my arm up over my mouth and man if my skin didn't stink of rancid vinegar—that was the rot, it did that to you.

In the bad light I could just make out the room's last few chairs huddled by the fireplace. They looked absurd, like a flock of geese hiding from the hatchet. Cause they was the last of it, see. This been a grand old flat once, to go by Lilah's stories. All Louis XIV chairs, Murano chandeliers, Aubusson tapestries, ceilings high as a damn train station. But the count who lent Delilah the place, he done urge her sell what she could before the Krauts come in. Seemed less bleak to him. And now, the flat being so empty, you felt only its depths, like you stranded at sea. Whole place nothing but darkness.

Across the room, Chip started snoring, faint like.

I glanced over at Hiero, now all knotted up in his chair. "Kid," I said thickly. "Hey, kid." I put a hand to my head. "You ain't serious bout givin up on the record. We close, buck. You know that."

Hiero opened his mouth, belched.

"Good mornin right back at you," I said.

He didn't seem to have heard me. I watched him heave hisself up on his feet, the chair moaning like a old mule. Then he sort of staggered on over to the door. Least I reckon that was his idea. Looked more like he heading for the fireplace, stumbling all about. His shoulder smacked a wall.

Then he was on the floor, on all fours.

"What you doin?" I said. "Hiero, what you doin, kid?"

"What you mean, what my doin? You ain't never seen a man put on his shoes before? Well, stick around, cause it's bout to get excitin. I'm gonna put my damn coat on next."

Hiero was wrestling his old houndstooth coat. It'd gone all twisted in the sleeves. He still ain't stood up. "I need me some daylight right bout now."

I pulled on my fob, stared at my watch till it made damn sense. "This ain't no kind of hour, kid. You ain't youself."

He ain't said nothing.

"Least just wait till Lilah wake up. She take you."

"I ain't waitin till my *foot* wake up, never mind Lilah."

"You got to at least tell her what you doin."

"I ain't got to do *nought*."

A soft moan drifted over from the window, and then Chip lifted up onto one dark elbow, like he posing for a sculpture. His eyes looking all glassy, the lids flickering like moths. Then his head sunk right back on his shoulders so that, throat exposed, it like he talking to the ceiling. "Don't you damn well go out," he told that ceiling. "Lie youself down, get some sleep. I mean it."

"You tell it, buck," said Hiero, grinning. "You stick it to that ceilin."

"Put that old cracked plaster in its place," I said.

But Chip, he fallen back and was snoring along already.

"Go on into Lilah's room and wake her," I said to Hiero.

Hiero's thin, leonine face stared me down from the doorway. "What kind of life you livin you can't even go into the street for a cup of milk, you got to have a nanny?" He stood under the hat rack, leaning like a brisk wind done come up. "Hell, Sid, just what you expect Lilah to do, you get in real trouble? She got a special lipstick I don't know bout, it shoot bullets?"

"You bein a damn fool, buck." Pausing, I glanced away. "You know you don't got any damn papers. What you goin do you get stopped?"

He shrugged. "I just goin down the Bug's. It ain't far." He yanked open the door and slid out onto the landing, swaying in the half-dark.

Staring into the shadows there, I felt sort of uneasy. Don't know why. Well. The Bug was our name for the tobacconist a few blocks away. It *wasn't* far.

"Alright, alright," I muttered. "Hold up, I'm comin."

He slapped one slender hand on the doorknob like it alone would hold him up. I thought, *This kid goin be the death of you, Sid.*

The kid grimaced. "You waitin for a mailed invitation? Let's ankle."

I stumbled up, fumbling for my other shoe.

"There won't be no trouble anyhow," he added. "It be fine. Ain't no one go down the Bug's at this hour."

"He so sure," I said. "Listen to how sure he is."

Hiero smiled. "Aw, I'm livin a charmed life, Sid. You just stick close."

But by then we was slipping down those wide marble stairs in the dark and pushing out into the grey street. See, thing about the kid—he so majestically bony and so damn grave that with his look of a starving child, it felt well nigh impossible to deny him anything. Take Chip. Used to be the kid annoyed him something awful. Now he so protective of him he become like a second mother. So watching the kid slip into his raggedy old tramp's hat and step out, I thought, *What I done got myself into.* I supposed to be the older responsible one. But here I was trotting after the kid like a little purse dog. Hell. Delilah was going to cut my head off.

We usually went all of nowhere in the daytime. Never without Delilah, never the same route twice, and not ever into Rue des Saussaies or Avenue Foch. But Hiero, he grown reckless as the occupation deepened. He was a *Mischling*, a half-breed, but so dark no soul ever like to guess his mama a white Rhinelander. Hell, his skin glistened like pure oil. But he German-born, sure. And if his face wasn't of the Fatherland, just bout everything else bout him rooted him there right good. And add to this the fact that he didn't have no identity papers right now—well, let's just say wasn't no cakewalk for him.

Me? I was American, and so light-skinned folks often took me for white. Son of two Baltimore quadroons, I come out straight-haired, green-eyed, a right little Spaniard. In Baltimore this given me a softer ride than some. I be lying if I said it ain't back in Berlin, too. When we gone out together in that city, any Kraut approaching us always come straight to me. When Hiero'd cut in with his native German, well, the gent would damn near die of surprise. Most ain't liked it, though. A savage talking like he civilized. You'd see that old glint in their eye, like a knife turning.

We fled to Paris to outrun all that. But we known Lilah's gutted flat wouldn't fend off the chaos forever. Ain't no man can outrun his fate. Sometimes when I looked out through the curtains, staring onto the emptiness of Rue de Veron, I'd see our old Berlin, I'd see that night when all the glass on our street shattered. We'd been in Ernst's flat on Fasanenstrasse, messing it up, and when we drifted over to the curtains it was like looking down on a carnival. Crowds in the firelight, broken bottles. We gone down after a minute, and it was like walking a gravel path, all them shards crunching at each step. The synagogue up the block was on fire. We watched firemen standing with their backs to the flames, spraying water on all the other buildings. To keep the fire from *spreading*, see.

I remember the crowd been real quiet. Firelight was shining on the wet streets, the hose water running into the drains. Here and there, I seen teeth glowing like opals on the black cobblestones.

<hr>

Hiero and me threaded through Montmartre's grey streets not talking. Once the home of jazz so fresh it wouldn't take no for a answer, the clubs had all gone Boot now. Nearly overnight the cafés filled with well-fed broads in torn stockings crooning awful songs to Gestapo. We took the side roads to avoid these joints, noise bleeding from them even at this hour. The air was cool, and Hiero, he shove his hands up so deep in his pits it like he got wings. Dawn was breaking strangely, the sky leathery and brown. Everything stunk of mud. I trailed a few steps behind, checking my watch as we walked cause it seemed, I don't know, slow.

"Listen. This sound slow to you?" I yanked the fob up and held the watch to the kid's ear.

He just leaned back and looked at me like I was off my nut.

As we walked, tall apartments loomed dark on either side of the street. Shadows was long in the gutters. I was feeling more and more uneasy. "Nothin's open this hour, man. What we doin, Hiero? What we doin?"

"Bug's open," said the kid. "Bug's always open."

I wasn't listening. I stared all round me, wondering what we'd do if a Boot turned the corner. "Hey—remember that gorgeous jane in Club Noiseuse that night? That dame in a man's suit?"

"You bringin that leslie up again?" Hiero was walking all brisk with them skinny legs of his. "You know, every time you drink the rot you go on bout that jack."

"She wasn't no leslie, brother—she was a *woman*. Bona *fide*."

"You talkin bout the one in the green suit? Nearest the stage?"

"She was a *Venus*, man, real prime rib."

Hiero chortled. "I done told you already, that been a leslie, brother. A *man*. It was writ plain as day all over his hairy ass."

"I guess you'd know. You the man to see bout hairy asses."

"Keep confusin the two, Sid, and see what happens. You end up in bed with a Boot."

We come round the corner, onto the wide square, when all a sudden my stomach lurched. I been expecting it—you need guts of iron to ride out what all we drunk last night. Iron guts I ain't got, but don't let that fool you bout other parts of my anatomy. My strength, I tell you, is of another stripe. I shuffled on over to a linden tree and leaned up under it, retching.

"You get to know this here corner a bit better," said Hiero, smirking. "I be right back." He stumbled off the sidewalk, hopped the far curb to the Bug's.

"Don't you be takin no fake change!" I hollered after him. "With you eyesight, the Bug like to cheat you out of you own skin." A white sun, tender as early fruit, stirred in the windows of the dark buildings. But the air, it still felt stale, filled with a grime that burned hot in you nostrils. I stamped my feet, then doubled over again, heaving. The goddamn rot.

A real racket started up across the street. I looked up to see Hieronymus yanking on the Bug's door like he meant to break in. Like he reckoned he got the power to pop every damn lock in this city. When it didn't open, what do he do but press his fool face up to the glass like a child. Hell, though, he was a child. Stupid young for what all he could do on a horn. You heard a lifetime in one brutal note.

He run on back over to me. "Closed," he said, breathing hard. "You reckon all these stores be closed? What time is it?"

"Half nine or so."

"Check you watch."

"Half nine."

"Don't make no sense." Frowning, he looked all around. A white car passed through the shady street like a block of ice skimming a river, its pale driver turning to us as we turned to him. I shivered, feeling all a sudden very exposed. That gent looked dressed for a funeral, all that black and white plumage.

"Hell, it's Sunday, fool," I said, hitting Hiero's arm. "Won't nothin be open. You got to go to Café Coup you want milk." On Sundays, the streets belonged to the Boots.

Hiero gripped his gut, giving me a miserable look. "Aw, man, the Coup's so *far*."

"You right," I said. "We got to go back."

He got to moaning.

"I ain't goin listen to that," I said. "I mean it. Aw, where you goin now? Hiero?"

I got a hard knot in my gullet, watching the kid wander off. I just stood there in the road. Then I swore, and went after him.

"You goin get us both pinched," I hissed at him when I caught up. I could feel my face flushing, my shoes slipping on the slick black cobblestones. "Kid?"

He shrugged. "Let's just get to the Coup."

"Coup's halfway to hell from here. You serious?"

He give me a sort a sick grin, and all a sudden I got to thinking bout that disc I'd took and hid in my case. I was thinking of it feeling something real close to guilt. But it wasn't guilt. I give him a quick look.

"Tell me somethin," I said. "You serious bout quittin that record?"

He didn't answer. But at least this time he look like he taking it in, his eyes dry and hard with thought, two black rocks.

Lucky for us, Café Coup de Foudre done just open. The kid slunk in gripping his gut like he bout to spew his fuel right there. Me, I paused on the threshold, looking. I had a strange feeling, not sickness no more, but something like it. The low wood tables inside was nearly empty. But the few jacks and janes here made such a haze with their cigarettes it was like wading through cobwebs. Stink of raw tobacco and last night's hooch. Radio murmuring in the background. At the bar it smelled, gloriously, of milk, of cafés au lait and chocolats chauds. The kid, he climbed up onto a flaking red stool and cradled his head in his hands. The barkeep come over.

"A glass of milk," I said in English, with a nod at Hiero.

"Milk," Hiero muttered, not lifting his head.

The barkeep propped his thick forearms on the counter, leaned down low. We known him, though, it wasn't menacing. He spoke broken German into the kid's ear: "Milk only? You are a cat?"

Hiero's muffled voice drifted up. He still hadn't lifted his face. "Ain't you a laugh factory. Bout near as funny as Sid here. You two ought to get together. Take that show on the road."

The barkeep smirked, mumbled something more into Hiero's ear. Something I ain't caught. Then I seen the kid stiffen in silence, lift up his face, his lips clenching.

"Hiero," I said. "Come on, man, he kiddin."

Going over to the icebox, the barkeep stare at me a second, then glance on up at the clock. I check my own watch. Five to ten. He wandered on back with a glass of milk, his voice cracking against the silence like snooker balls hitting each other. "But I warn you," he said. "You drink all the milk in France, you still not turn white." He laughed his strange, high, feathery laugh.

Hiero brought the glass to his lips, his left eye shutting as he drank.

A sad, hot feeling well up in me. I cleared my throat.

The kid, he suddenly reached back and touched my shoulder. "Might as well do another take," he said. "The disc ain't all bad. And my damn visas ain't come yet. What else I got to do?"

I swallowed nervously.

Then he give me a long, clear look. "We goin get it right. Just be patient, buck."

"Sure," I said. "Sure we will. But wasn't that last one any good, kid? *Good* good? Would it make us?"

The kid set the glass down on the counter, and pointing at it, hollered, "Encore!"

My stomach lurched, and just holding it together, I said, "I be right back. You ain't goin leave without me?"

In the basement john, I got down to business. I felt sick as hell, the bile rising in me. For a second I stood there clutching the filthy basin, yellow grime all caked up on its porcelain. Head down, just breathing. I ran the faucet and splashed my face with cold water. It smelled of hot iron, the water, making my face feel alien to me, like I ain't even in my own skin.

Then I could hear something through the ceiling, sudden, loud. I paused, holding my breath. Hell. Sounded like Hiero and the damn barkeep. The kid was prone to it these days, wired for a fight. I dragged in a long breath, walked over to the dented door.

I ain't gone out though. I just stood there, listening to the air like a hound. After a minute I reached for the knob.

The talk got softer. Then the whole place seemed to shudder with the sound of something crashing. Hell. I couldn't hear the barkeep's voice. My hand, it was shaking so bad the knob rattled softly. I forced myself to turn it, take a step into the stuffy corridor. I made it up three steps before stalling. The stairs, they was shaded by a brick wall, giving me a glimpse of the café without betraying my shadow.

All the lights was up. I ain't never seen all the lights up in the Coup, *ever*. I never known till that moment how nightmarish so much light can be.

The place went dead quiet. Everything, everyone, felt distinct, pillowed by silence. One gent turned to me, slow. He got creases like knife wounds in his face. I glanced under his table—only one leg. His hands gnarled like something dredged from a lake, they was both shaking like crazy. He was holding dirty papers. I watched ash from his cigarette fall onto his pants.

I looked around sharply. On every occupied table sat identity papers. A few crisp as fall leaves, others almost thumbed to powder. A young brunette slapped hers down so nervously she set it in a puddle of coffee. I stared at the bloating paper. She was chewing a loose thread on the collar of her heavy tweed coat, her jaw working softly. I remember thinking, ain't she warm in that.

The barkeep begun cleaning quietly, rubbing down the bar with a gingham towel.

There was this other chap, though. Sitting in the window's starched light, his expression too bright. A coldness crept over me.

Then the talking started again, and I glanced up.

Two Boots, in pale uniforms. Used to be just plain black: at night you seen nothing but a ghostly white face and an armband the colour of blood coming at you over the cobblestones. But Boots was Boots.

One was tall and thin, a tree branch of a man. The other, he short and thickset. With his back turned to me, I could see a fat roll of muscle at his neck.

I dropped my eyes, and like I was letting it occur to me for the first time, I looked for Hiero. He standing on over at the front door, staring at the Boots. Another kid stood at his side, Jewish I reckon, a look of terrified defiance on his face. The taller Boot was making a real show of thumbing slow through his papers, not saying nothing. Just licking his thumb, turning a page, licking his thumb, turning a page. Like that Boot could pass a summer's day doing it. I looked at his quiet grey face. Was a face like anyone's. Just going bout his business.

"Foreign," the shorter Boot was saying, his voice so calm and soft I almost ain't heard it. "Stateless person of Negro descent."

Hiero and that Jewish kid, they stood there with their hands dangling at their sides, defiant schoolboys. It ached to watch, the both of them so helpless, their hearts going hard. With the broad pane of glass shining bright behind them I couldn't see too clear. But even from here I could hear them. Their breathing.

The tall Boot done soften his voice, too. It was odder than odd: these Boots was so courteous, so upstage in their behaviour, they might've been talking bout the weather. Nothing like how they'd behaved in Berlin. There was even a weak apology in their gestures, like they was gentlemen at heart, and only rough times forced them to act this way. And this politeness, this quiet civility, it scared me more than outright violence. It seemed a newer kind of brutality.

"Foreigners," said the short Boot calmly. "Hottentot."

"Stateless," said the other. "Foreigner," he said. Jew, he said. Negro, he said.

I wanted to close my eyes. My legs was shaking softly, I couldn't feel nothing in my feet. Don't you drop, boy, I told myself, don't you damn well drop. Get you wits together, for god's sake, and go out there.

I stood there, rooted to the spot.

Hieronymus, he stared down them Boots. When their hard gazes forced his away, he look at the tiled floor. He never once look in the direction of the toilets, and I understood. Hell. *He*, of all people, protecting *me*. I couldn't let him do it.

But just then the Boots yanked wide the Coup's door, its chain singing. Taking Hiero's arm, they led him and the other boy out into the street. I stood there. Stood there with my hands hanging like strange weights against my thighs, my chest full of something like water. Stood there watching Hiero go.

The front door shut with a clatter. The lights was all still up in the café. Silence, no one talking at all.

Then that gent, the one I seen before almost smiling, he got up and walked to the bar. Counting out his francs, he stacked them on the mahogany bar. He said something in French to the barkeep.

The barkeep just swept up the damp francs and turned to put them into the register. The man skirted the tables, his heels scraping the worn floor. No one spoke, all of us watching. And then the door jangled cheerfully shut behind him.

II

Berlin
1992

Chip called to say he was dropping in and I told him Sure, brother, anytime.

I had all the lights on in my Fells Point pad, the thick shag carpet of my narrow living room drowned in clothes and folders and trash, the detritus of a life, all of it pulled out as I tried to decide just what to pack, when I heard his sharp rapping at the door. See, we was set to fly out the next day. I headed down the hall, past its stacks of browning newsprint, its crooked, black-framed photos. Forty-four years I'd lived here. Lola's father had bought it for us after the war, and when she died five years after our wedding, it come on down to me.

The door was like to stick now, so that I had to yank on the old brass handle till it give. And there he stood, my oldest friend, looking worn as a used mattress, his face all dry and pocked with pores.

He come in grinning. "Man, Sid, ain't you ever going to clean up? You live in plain disrepair." He crossed my bald welcome mat, his face dark against his gleaming shirt. He got this booming voice, and when he talked it overwhelmed the air, shoved it aside like oil in a cup of water.

A real feat, considering his size. Shoeless and hatless, Chip Jones stood just five feet four inches tall.

"You a fine one to talk of disrepair, brother," I said, taking his soft black coat to hang on the hatstand. "You seen your *face* lately? You look like an old lady's handbag."

"Don't I know it," said Chip, rubbing his cheeks with his huge hands. "On my walk over here a man tried to mug me for my face."

"Ain't you funny," I said, patting his back. "Ain't you hilarious. You already packed, I guess."

He shrugged. "A man's got to unpack first before he can pack." He glanced theatrically again at the mess on the floor. "I guess you know that though."

I got Chip settled into my chaotic living room and went on over to the kitchenette.

"What you drinking?" I called out to him. "Scotch?" When he didn't reply I leaned through the door and looked at him. "You want a scotch?"

He looked up. "What?"

"All that drumming catching up with you, brother? You going a little deaf?"

He smiled. "Aw, just a little. What you say?"

"Scotch alright with you?"

He licked his old chops. "I ain't never said no to one yet."

I was watching him there, feeling awful for him. I known that the state of his face wasn't only cause he tired. The drugs was finally taking their toll. See, he been on horse for decades, only kicked the habit about fifteen years ago. He been clean so long now I done forgot he'd used at all. I *still* couldn't get my head around the idea. If you'd known Chip in his youth, addiction would have seemed impossible. He was *proper* proper, straight-laced, hell, almost a prude when it come to illegal substances. Anyway, it shocked me, seeing a disease long-conquered showing up now in his features. It's like that, I guess, when the past come to collect what you owe.

I poured us two scotches neat, just the thinnest blade of ice in them. "You think the Hound'll still be there?" I said.

"Where? You mean in Berlin?"

I smiled as I sat down.

"Naw," said Chip. "There ain't nothing much left of all that. You won't recognize it."

"Well," I said. "I never much thought I'd go back."

Chip held up his drink.

"*Prost*," we said together, hitting thimbles.

"You seen the picture yet?"

Chip shook his head. "Caspars won't let no one see it. Not before the festival. How bad you think it can be?"

"Oh bad, bad. How you talked me into this, brother, I don't know."

He grinned. "It just my damned charming face, I reckon."

"Yeah," I said. "That must be it."

We was silent then for a time. I got to tell you how strange it was seeing Chip here. Even with his face falling apart he still hands down the nattiest thing in my house. He wore a navy suit of such beautiful tailoring I would've had to mortgage my place to buy it.

Chip used to say, you don't got blue blood in you veins, Sid, may as well dress like you do. Confuse folks. And so even when he didn't have the money, he stepped out in seersucker suits and shirts starched so stiff they left pressure marks on his wrists. Even onstage hitting the skins, he look like a croupier dealing cards. Only time you ever seen him untidy is after a fight, and what a sight *that* was: James Bond run through a blender. Though you known the other fella probably got off worse.

"The scotch is excellent," said Chip, setting down his glass on the sun-faded table.

"Aw, I know you used to better."

"It's fine." Chip glanced around, clearing his throat softly. Without thought or permission (when has Chip Jones *ever* needed permission?), he whipped out a titanium cigarette case engraved with his initials. Taking out what I known could only be the finest of cigarillos, he lit up. He held the case out to me.

"Naw. I start smoking the good stuff, I never be able to go back. Besides, got to watch my health."

"You ill?"

"No, sir. Just . . . retirement. Gets you thinking."

"What's coming is coming, Sid. It don't do a man no good to dwell on it." Chip smiled. "I'm surprised you retired at all. *I* can't imagine ever doing so."

I believed it. We was old as mud, sure, but even at eighty-three Chip kept up a hectic touring schedule. As like to be in Buenos Aires or Reykjavík as Baltimore.

Not me. No, sir. I been my own boss these, oh, thirty-one years. A medical transcriptionist for a couple different doctors—a group of stuffy, high-hat gents with faces worn as dishrags. I typed out the long, complex illnesses of their patients thanking god it wasn't me I was writing about. And despite the sickness around me I stayed hale, born under a lucky star, as my third wife liked to say with her face all screwed up. Don't know as she was right. Try waking up alone at eighty-two and deciding to stop doing the one thing you got to do all day. It's a job all on its own to keep the hours full. Not two weeks passed when I reckoned I'd start transcribing again. But see, something had already changed in me. I wasn't as drawn to the body's autumn—like I had some new awareness, some idea of my own frailty. I needed to keep it at bay. Cause once that invades you, you done for, friend.

Chip was looking uneasy at me, and I known he got something touchy on his mind. "So what is it, Jones?" I said. "Talk already."

He laughed all high up in his throat. "You such an old maid lately,

Sid. I so much as pick my teeth and you got to ascribe ten meanings to it."

"Your false teeth, maybe," I said.

He leaned forward in his chair, and picking up his scotch, downed it in one sound gulp. He got oddly thin lips, and with the drink still glistening on them, they looked like oysters.

"I *am* right, though, ain't I? You got something on your mind?"

Looking irked, Chip cleared his throat. He stared me plain in the eye. "Sidney Griffiths," he said.

I kind of half laughed. Old Chip here, he full of it.

"Sidney Griffiths," he said again. He held the cigarillo close to his lips but didn't smoke it. I watched the end burning down. "What I got to tell you I don't want to tell you. Cause you ain't going to believe me."

Chip reckons he's charming as hell, and who am I to poke holes in his theory. But what that means is that sometimes lies leave his mouth dressed like truth. He just can't help it.

"Sidney Griffiths," he said a third time, and then I known I was in for something. "You remember back to when the Wall fell? How I had to force you to put down the phone and go check the goddamn TV? This is like that, boy. Except bigger."

I laughed, irritated. It's true. I *hadn't* believed the Wall had fallen. He'd had to force me to seek out the TV in my bedroom. That old den had seen me through three other brides after Lola, all of them still alive and none as beloved as her. I remember it'd still been filled with my final wife's decor, polyester curtains and ugly knickknacks from her Roanoke childhood. I guess she hadn't collected them all yet. She's got them now, thank the good lord.

I'd sat on the bed and turned on the ancient TV. Hadn't been on more than ten seconds when I already thought, god strike me down. Cause what I seen, it ain't seemed real. How on earth. Folks with pick-axes hacked away at the Berlin Wall, that awful concrete with its rash of graffiti. Sprays of champagne flying. Screams and tears and cameras flashing like gun flare in the dark as people poured through cracks. Some went on foot, in worn shoes and speckled jeans. Some was in those toy-like cars, Trabis, the crowds buckling the roofs with their banging. I'd sat there like some monk locked in prayer, disbelieving. It wasn't no city we ever set foot in. Not that Berlin.

Now Chip sat forward in his seat, hitting with his big toe the empty scotch glass he'd placed on the floor. "You know what I mean, brother. You refuse to live in the world."

"Go on. Baltimore ain't in the world?" I shook my head. "And I'm going to Berlin, ain't I? Berlin don't count?"

Chip chuckled. He took pride in being the wiliest SOB this side the Atlantic. Always has, even when we was kids. He's just got this madness in him, this rash hot need to be contrary.

I told him so. Cause, see, I'd made *sacrifices*. On *his* account.

"See, now that's what I mean," he said. "Take this trip to Berlin. This documentary. That ain't something you done on my account. Least I hope not. You done it for Hiero. You done it for the history of jazz. You done it for *yourself.*"

I lifted an eyebrow at him. "Remind me to send myself a bill."

Cause they was real. These sacrifices I'd made to please Chip, they was damned real. See, about a year ago, he approached me excited as all hell over some documentary. Fellow by the name of Kurt Caspars—a half-Finn half-Kraut filmmaker famous for an expose on white slavery in Holland—he been commissioned by a German TV station to make the first full-scale film on Hieronymus Falk. Caspars was the natural choice, Chip had explained—his hatchet-fast visuals had a lot in common with the kid's playing. But like any artist, Caspars needed raw material to build his pictures out of. And we, my friend, was to be that brick and mortar.

Caspars wanted talking heads to blab for ninety minutes on every last shred of the kid's existence. We all know Buddy Bolden died nuts in the bughouse, and Bix Beiderbecke, he died of the DTs—but Falk? By all accounts he passed on right after getting sprung from an Austrian work camp. Mauthausen. Except no one knows how, or when, or where. Knowing he died after being in a camp ain't the same as knowing the nature of his death. If it was his suffering finally got to him or its sudden absence, the world strangely greyer afterwards with its safe, empty routines. Even less can you know what all it meant for him, if the end was a welcome thing, or the final outrage.

Hell, there wasn't even a grave.

I ain't had the least desire to be filmed last year, and even less to go see the damn picture in Berlin. It was only *after* Chip had Caspars arrange our tickets to Berlin for the premiere that he mentioned, just all casual, like it wasn't nothing, that the film would be debuting at a bigger festival: the Hieronymus Falk Festival. A weekend-long celebration of the great trumpeter's life. With the east now open, they could offer all kinds of walking tours of our old haunts. "Come on Sid," Chip had said. "Everyone's going: Wynton Marsalis, even old Grappelli. It'll be something."

I refused to go. Of course I did. Then slowly, over the last few months, Chip had talked me into it. The things you do for friends in old age. Maybe it's cause you know you won't have to suffer them much longer.

"So what is it?" I said. "Out with it now. I got a list of pressing things needs doing. My TV needs watching. Damn thing's been off a whole two hours. It's unnatural."

Chip shrugged. "Aw. You ain't going to believe me."

"I expect that's right."

He shuffled his feet. "I don't want you to take it the wrong way."

"You just stalling now. What is it?"

But I could tell something was in him, and it was big.

"You want to know? You really want to know?" He leaned in, his face going totally serious. "Sid. The kid is alive."

Seem like a whole damn minute passed. Then I let out a sharp laugh, my head swinging back to hit the headrest.

"I'm not kidding, boy," Chip continued. "He's alive and living up north Poland."

"This ain't funny, Chip."

"I'm serious."

"I mean it, it ain't funny. What is it, really?"

"I ain't lying, brother. It's the truth."

"Hell, boy. What's the matter with you? You jump back on that old horse again?"

His face darkened, and I known I'd gone too far. But I was angry now too.

"You don't got nothing else to tell me? For real?"

He just sat there, the empty glass in his hand. I watched him, the smile sitting dryly on my lips. A fly's dim whine surfaced on the air, like the sound of distant machinery.

Sometimes Chip's jokes is just too goddamned much. This new one, it was downright spiteful.

He made a pained face. "What I got to do to convince you?"

I shook my head.

"What I got to say? I am one-hundred-percent serious, Sidney."

"Your lips is still moving, brother."

"Tell me what I can say."

"It's what you *can't* say. Shut up." I rose to my feet, the springs of my recliner squealing. I brought my hard gaze to rest on him. I looked at his hands, at the yellowish, unclean tinge of his fingernails. "Brother, I really got to get on with my day."

Chip nodded, but continued to sit. His expression was unreadable as he stared at me. "I guess you ain't ready for it. I mean, I guess it's a lot all at once. But, hell, *Sidney*. *Think* about it. After the Falk Festival, you and me, we could rent a car and drive on over to Stettin. Since we'll already be in Europe anyway. Or we take the train, if it ain't too long."

I felt sick. The way he kept this up, it was making my nerves radiate. "And how is it that of everyone on earth, you're the only one who knows about this? Hiero alive? *Poland*? You sure you ain't going senile, brother? " I wondered suddenly if there wasn't something really wrong with him. See, five years ago Chip spent some time "resting." He wasn't just tired. Some dame found him in his PJs and slippers sitting in the Paris metro at four in the morning. He didn't say a word for three months, then come on out of the hospital perfectly normal, walking back into his life. I know, I know. We getting old.

"Chip," I said.

Chip lit right up, as if he been waiting for me to really engage with him. "I got a letter, Sid, I never told you about it. Was maybe three months ago. I'd just got back from my Italy-Greece tour, I was tired as all hell, and there it was, just this plain brown envelope, this plain brown paper. Well I opened it, and damn if it wasn't from him, something like ten sentences long, but definitely from him, and it ain't said much, just that he'd just heard all about the festival and would we visit him. Terribly spooky. It was enough to make your toenails grow backwards."

"Uh-huh."

"Then a second one come two days ago, saying basically the same thing. And then I remembered I hadn't told you about the first one."

"Letters," I said.

"That's right."

"What makes you think they're from him?"

Chip glanced up at me, looking suddenly old.

"Your cigarillo," I said.

He blinked and looked at where it was burning down between his fingers. He crushed it out in the ashtray.

"Someone's playing a joke on you, Chip. Or else you cracked again."

"I ain't cracked, Sid."

"Uh-huh. And where is these letters?"

Chip scowled. "I knew you'd ask that. Truth is, brother, I got so upset I ate them. Tore them up and ate them. Out of pure nerves."

I said nothing.

"I'm kidding," he said uneasily. "Jesus, Sid, come on. The letters, they at home. In a stack of invitations asking me to play the world over."

"You didn't think to bring them?"

He give me a nervous smile. "Well, them invitations wasn't for you, brother."

"You think this is funny?"

"No," he said. "No it ain't."

I frowned. "You know what I think?" But I didn't finish. Seeing him there I felt something like despair and just couldn't go on with it. I picked his glass up off the floor, went in, set it on the kitchen counter. Then walking on down the front hall, I tugged his coat from the hook, and stood there holding it out for him. The fabric like butter to the touch.

He rose up slow from his chair, wheezing at the effort. Coming over to me, he gathered up the coat with what I suppose he thought was dignity. "I guess you got a lot of packing to do," he said. "I guess I'll let you get on with it."

"I guess you will," I said.

"You been married how many times?" he muttered.

I said nothing. I opened the door for him.

He went out into the moldy stairwell—with its glaring red emergency exits, its carpets so worn now nothing but dirt held them together—and just stood there, as if waiting for something more. "See you on the plane?" he said.

It seemed almost sad. I closed the door in his face.

———— ▪ ————

Chip goddamn Jones. Holy hell could he beat the life out them drums. Even back in Weimar, even as a kid, the man was made for greatness. And onstage beside him, playing my upright with all the fire I could muster, what did it matter if I was merely, as the critics said, *"solid and dependable on the back shelf"*?

It's no exaggeration to say that of all the gents who played in our band, I become the least famous. I ain't never made it. Now Chip, Chip's reputation as one of the great American drummers was—to put it in the language of commerce we all so fluent in these days—it was well-earned but cost him much. The man damn near ruined himself. I only thank god he was so disciplined back then, that we got the best of his playing on that recording. That I got the best of it.

See, *Half-Blood Blues, 3 mins 33 secs*, is almost all I got out of that time. I ain't sore about it. Ain't no glory made from being *dependable*. But it started Chip's career a second time. Jolted the man awake again. And, well, it made Hiero one of the most famous jazz trumpeters of his generation.

The kid's existence might've been a fiction we'd all cooked up if that disc hadn't survived. Today you ain't no kind of horn player you don't acknowledge some debt to Hieronymus Falk. He was one of the pioneers: a German Louis Armstrong, if you will. Wynton Marsalis praised Falk as one of the reasons he started playing at all: "Hearing Falk—man, that was it. It just blew my mind out. I was just a kid, but even then I knew I was hearing genius. His brilliance was that obvious." Even fellows who ain't never played jazz understood he was the man. Punk guitarists, avant-garde cellists, even tootsie-pop songbirds was all drawing on him. I heard a riff on NPR the other day had Hiero all over it.

But the kid could've been lost to history easy as anything. That's what gets to me. The chance in it all. It all started up again in a small

French town used to be in Vichy. This dark apartment, it was being renovated, see—we're talking the early sixties here—and after days of tearing up the walls, the contractor discovered what looked like shrapnel deep inside the crumbled plaster. Just this shiny thing gleaming through, like a dark coin in dirty snow. It was a dinged-up steel box. And inside, hell, was the five discs made us so famous in Berlin, along with one warped, half-baked disc with no label. Turned out Sir Vichy, long dead but once a prominent Nazi cog, he'd loved jazz enough to hide them away. The contractor took the box to his university prof brother, who gave it to some French classical musicologist, who—out of carelessness, or contempt— left the box in a filing cabinet in his home office. It sat there five, maybe six years, until he died. Then his Berlin-based daughter arrived, a professional mime so I'm told but that don't matter. It don't flavour the story. She found the box in her papa's cabinet, and took it to a different musicologist, this one back in Berlin. And after just one listen to the unlabeled disc, he declared it the rawest kind of genius.

Well hold on to your hats. So this Berlin scholar, he starts digging. And once in the mud he starts seeing similarities between the five Hot-Time discs and the warped, genius one. In some ways it sounds like the same band, just pared down, but. Well, there's just something more torrid, more intelligent, stranger, *hotter* about that phantom disc. Not that the Hot-Time Swingers wasn't good. Once upon a time we was the *stuff*. Played the greatest clubs of Europe, our five recordings as famous as anything. We had fans across the continent, played Austria and Switzerland and Sweden and Hungary and even Poland. Only reason we ain't never gigged in France was cause Ernst, a proud son of a bitch, he held a war-based grudge. Lost it soon enough, when old Germany started falling apart. But before that our band was downright gold, all six of us: Hieronymus Falk on trumpet; Ernst "the Mouth" von Haselberg on clarinet; Big Fritz Bayer on alto sax; Paul Butterstein on piano; and, finally, us, the rhythm boys—Chip Jones on drums and yours truly thumbing the upright. We was a kind of family, as messed-up and dys-functional as any you could want.

So the scholar digs all this up. But then he gets stuck, unsure of himself. Right away he knows it's old Hiero on lead trumpet. Well congratulations, he wins a point. It takes him a couple weeks to decide it's me on bass and Chip on drums. Ooh, you on a roll now, boy. But then he can't fathom the second trumpet at all, assumes it's got to be Ernst the Mouth. Seems the old owl read somewhere that despite Ernst's preference for the licorice stick, he was also an able trumpeter. (False false false. Old Ernst played trumpet like Monet traded stocks.) And man, he can't figure for the life of him why the other Hot-Timers ain't on the recording.

Now, he wasn't all wrong. He does discover Paul was arrested in '39 and died in Sachsenhausen. He figures out Chip and me returned to America on the New-York bound SS *St. John*. That the kid was arrested in Paris and taken to Mauthausen via Saint-Denis. But where's Big Fritz? And where did Ernst disappear to after the recording? All mysteries.

The musicologist's essays caught the eye of John Hammond, Jr., that jazz Columbus who discovered Billie and Ella. Hammond was then a talent scout for Columbia, signing cats like Aretha, Bob and Leonard. He tracked down the disc in Berlin. And to hear Hammond tell it, our recording damn near made an amnesiac of him. We blown every last thought out of his mind. When he finally come to (don't you love how these exec types talk?), he known he needed to do three things. One: convince Columbia to remaster and release the recording with huge distribution. Two: track down those of us ain't dead yet. Three: tour us Hot-Time Swingers to fame, fortune and all that damned et cetera.

It was Louis helped him find me and Chip. Louis Armstrong. See, he known a thing or two, and despite hating Hammond he penned the man a letter setting things straight. That was most definitely not Ernst von Haselberg on second trumpet, he wrote, what a fool idea. If he had to guess, it was Kentucky's own Bill Coleman. He explained the recording was based on a popular German song whose name escaped him. He also told him that me and Chip was probably living back in Baltimore, check there. He ain't said nothing else, gave no details about how he might know any of this. Sure Hammond wrote him back. But not two days after posting the letter it was announced in the news that old Satchmo had died. Hammond found me and Chip in the *phonebook*.

Chip wasn't shy. He said he didn't know how Armstrong known all that. And he got me to agree to Hammond's record deal—if it proved kosher with Coleman, that is—though I told him no way in hell would the Hot-Time Swingers ever go to tour. We'd known for years that Ernst, Big Fritz and Paul was all dead. Word gets back. And Hiero, well, there just wasn't no *Half-Blood Blues* without the kid. Cause it was his piece, see—he'd been the frontman, had written the damned thing in his own blood and spit. He had that massive sound, wild and unexpected, like a thicket of flowers in a bone-dry field. Ain't no replacing that. And anyhow, Chip and me had no taste for resurrecting all that. Not after what had happened.

Of course, the recording's cult status had to do with the illusion of it all. I mean, not just of the kid but of all of us, *all* the Hot-Time Swingers. Think about it. A bunch of German and American kids meeting up in Berlin and Paris between the wars to make all this wild, joyful music before the Nazis kick it to pieces? And the legend survives when a lone tin box is dug out of a damn wall in a flat once belonged to a Nazi? Man. If that ain't a ghost story, I never heard one.

One question kept flaring up, though: who was this Hieronymus Falk? Some of the wildest stories you ever heard come out, a couple of them even true. Folks reckoned he could play any song after hearing it just once (true); they believed he was Sidney Bechet's long-lost brother (ain't we all?); they murmured that like the bluesman Robert Johnson, Falk would only play facing a corner, his back to everyone (handsome devil like Falk? think again)—and speaking of the devil (and Johnson), they reckoned he'd made a pact with hell itself, traded his soul for those damned clever lips.

I don't know, maybe that last one is even true.

Then in the fall of '81 a few more details come out. In an interview Hammond gave, he claimed the kid died in '48, after leaving Mauthausen. Died of some chest ailment that August, of a pulmonary embolism. Pulmonary embolism? Somehow that ain't struck folks as right. "What *really* happened to Hieronymus Falk" become something of a journalist sport. All sorts of nonsense started up. One article said Falk got pleurisy. Another said pleurisy of the suicide variety, implying he brought it on himself, one too many rainy walks in that frail body. Still another said forget the lungs—it been his heart that give out, cardiac arrest due to starvation. More romantic that way, I guess. No one seemed to get it right. All of this was like an old knife turning in me and Chip's guts. Leave the poor kid dead, we felt. Let him lie.

Through all of it, Hammond stuck to his guns.

"It's like I said, Sid, pulmonary embolism," he told me later. "I've never been more astonished than when everyone refused to believe it. A man like Falk, though, I guess he's got to have a glamorous death. With the right kind of death, a man can live forever."

Hell, I thought when I heard that. *A man like Falk?* Hiero was just a *kid*. Ain't nobody should have to grow up like that.

———————— ■ ————————

I stood a long time behind my door, listening for Chip's shuffled footfalls on the stairs. Then I locked the two deadbolts, rattled the chain into place.

Chip Jones, I thought grimly, as I went back down the hall. *Chip goddamn Jones. The man don't understand limits.*

Not that I believed him. Even for a second. I returned to my quiet living room, turned off the lights, stood at the window with one slat of the blinds held down, staring out into the street. After a minute Chip appeared, a small silhouette in the gathering darkness. He crossed the street, walking slowly, then turned and glanced up at my apartment. I released the blinds with a crackle and stepped back into the shadows.

After a time I sat, looked at my hands. The room darkish now, the late afternoon haze laying shadows against all the furniture. Everything looked heavier. I could smell Chip's cigarillo like the devil's presence.

Then I said to myself, be fair, just picture it for a minute. What if this wasn't some prank of Chip's, what if these letters did exist, what if somehow, like the proverbial voice from beyond the grave, the kid was reaching out to us? What would you do, Sid, if all that was possible? After what you done, wouldn't you owe it to him to go? I sat there until the room went full dark, staring through my warped living room blinds into the street.

It was no use. I did not believe it.

I knew I should get up, get back to packing, but I didn't move. An odd feeling come over me then. I could feel my hands and feet tingling like they wasn't my own no more, and then it seemed like some shadow passed over my heart. I shivered.

I must have slept. I woke with my head twisted hard to one side, a long line of drool dampening the front of my shirt. It was still dark. I got up, checked the clock, grimaced. Still a few hours yet.

Then I was packed and wrestling the battered suitcase down the stairwell and out to the waiting taxi. It idled there in the cold early light, the clouds of exhaust hauntingly white in the street. Gave me a chill, seeing it.

I got into the cab with a groan. The peeling seats smelled bad, like garlic or onions. "BWI," I mumbled. "Don't go taking no scenic routes either. I got a plane to catch."

The cabbie wore an Orioles cap turned backwards. I ain't understood how men got to keeping their hats on indoors in this day and age. He shrugged. "Sure thing, boss, BWI." He punched the meter and pulled away.

The city always struck me as dirty this early in the morning. The streets wet with the night rains, the slow scuttle of rats under parked cars, the trash and blown papers in the alleys. Wasn't always this grim.

At my age, a man shouldn't have to take a cab to the airport. Should be someone he can call, take him there, wish him a safe flight. I ain't got no regrets about it though.

"No regrets is right, boss," the cabbie said cheerfully. "Regrets don't do you no good."

I looked at him in surprise. I hadn't realized I'd spoken out loud.

"Where you off to?" he said.

I watched his eyes in the rearview mirror, drifting over to me, away.

"London," I said. "I'm going back to London. I live there." Better not to tell folks your business, I figure. Nor to let them know you're leaving your pad empty. A man's got to be careful these days.

"London?" the cabbie said. "No kidding. I used to live in London. England's alright but the food'll kill you. Whereabouts you live over there?"

I frowned. I ain't got no mind for this damn small talk. Best to shut him up quick. "Not London England," I said. "London Ontario. In Canada."

The cabbie's eyes sort of glazed over. Canada kills any conversation quick, I learned long ago. It's a little trick of mine.

I was watching the streets scroll on past. Baltimore always seems like the kind of city you're either leaving or just returning to. Ain't no kind of place to hang your hat. Even as a kid I'd dreamed of getting out. I watched the green wall of shrubbery along the freeway pour past the cab window, feeling uneasy. I ain't no fool, I known this was like to be my last trip away.

See, I was born here, in Baltimore, before the Great War. And when you're born in Baltimore before the Great War you think of getting *out*. Especially if you're poor, black and full of sky-high hopes. Sure B-more ain't *south* south, sure my family was light-skinned, but if you think Jim Crow hurt only gumbo country, you blind. My pals and I was as much welcome in white diners as some Byron Meriwether would be breaking bread in Jojo's Crab House. Things was *bitter*. Some of my mama's family—two of her brothers and a schoolteacher sister—they was passing as whites down Charlottesville way. Cut us off entirely. You don't know how I dreamed of showing up there, breaking up their parade. I ain't so sure about it now, I suppose they was just trying to get by best they could. *We* could've passed too, said we was bohunks or something, but my pa ain't never gone for that. Negro is what the lord made us, he always said. Don't want to be nothing else.

At the airport, I checked myself in and started the slow walk to the gate. Long white tunnels, checkpoints, passports. I didn't see any sign of Chip.

Even when they called for boarding, I ain't seen him.

Not a bad start, I thought with satisfaction. Hallelujah. Maybe Chip going to miss this plane.

We was set to fly first class, courtesy of old Caspars, and I'd no sooner settled into the wide seat, slipped off my old orthopedics, and leaned right back, than I saw Chip shuffling on down the aisle toward me.

"Sid," he said, out of breath. "I didn't think I goin to make it. They damn near lost my reservation." He looked crisp, sharp, perfectly attired in a black silk suit with a grey kerchief folded in the breast pocket. "I think you in the wrong seat," he said, studying his ticket.

I pulled mine out, looked at the numbers on the overhead latches.

"Ain't you in 2B?" he said.

"4D. I'm in the right seat."

He frowned. "I'm in 2A. I ain't nowhere near you. That can't be right." He ducked his head, looking around. "On the other side of the goddamned plane," he muttered. "I put us together, brother, I swear it. Hell."

"It's alright, Chip," I said, all of a sudden feeling friendlier. "Don't you mind it. I'm like to sleep the whole way anyhow."

Chip nodded, miserable. "Well. Maybe they'll let me come over once we get under way. Maybe the seats'll be free."

Then he was gone, settling in on the far side, and the stewardess was stalking up the aisle stowing bags and kits and purses. And then we was lifting up off the tarmac and tilting steeply, rising up into the ether. I gripped my old armrests and stared out the cabin windows at the clouds. It was too grey to see much of the city below. Before the seatbelt light come off I'd downed two sleeping pills and drawn the blanket up to my neck.

Well, I thought drowsily. A man ain't but one kind of crazy.

I could see Chip leaning out into the aisle, trying to catch my attention. I leaned back, closed my eyes. Berlin, I thought. Hell.

Chip looked worn awful thin by the time we set down. More long grey tunnels, checkpoints, passports and the like. Then we was sitting on a tight little bench at the luggage carousel waiting for my damn suitcase to clatter down. It didn't come. We watched two green bags turn on the slatted ramp, vanish, come back around again.

"They lost it," I said. "I fly once in fifteen years and they lose my damn luggage."

Chip nodded. "I ain't lost a piece of luggage in near forty years. Good thing, too, cause the stuff ain't cheap, boy."

I looked at his matching luggage, all monogrammed, high-end leather, set out beside him in descending order of size like a damn family of suitcases. "Ain't that something," I scowled. "How about that. You just one amazing traveller ain't you."

He chuckled. "Aw, Sid, I just saying. It's alright. I'll lend you some clothes for the premiere tonight."

"I ain't going to need your clothes. They going to get me my damn suitcase."

"Sure they will," Chip said encouragingly. And I got that funny dark feeling in my chest again, like something was real wrong. It ain't *normal*, Chip being this friendly.

At the luggage counter a man with a natty little moustache told me my luggage ought to arrive at the hotel before me. It been rerouted by accident to Poland. But it coming right back, sure.

"Poland!" Chip laughed, as we stood in line at passport control. "It just going on ahead of us, to let Hiero know we coming." And later, at the taxi stand, he said again, "Poland, Sid. Think of it. That ain't so far your suitcase can't go there and get back to your hotel before you even arrive. Hell, that's close, brother. Closer than DC to your old Fells Point pad."

I scowled and looked away.

On the drive in I told the cabbie to swing us by the Brandenburg Gate. I'd sat up front to get some space from Chip but he just kept leaning on forward, breathing his damn cigarillo breath down my neck.

"I don't know, Sid," he said. "I reckon we should just check in. We got the opening in less than three hours."

"The Brandenburg Gate," I said again to the cabbie in German. And to Chip, "It be alright. You just relax some. Sit back and see."

Sure, I admit, some part of me was just trying to spite him. But I was curious, too. The city's new hugeness shook me. It'd always been big, but not like *this*—the war opened great holes all those decades ago and I could see them even now. Green parks broke up the sea of cement, and so many concrete lots sat empty, all gone to weed. The streets looked wider than I remembered, too. As we passed the Berliner Dom, I got a vague itch all high up in my throat. My god. That vast pillared Renaissance church—it'd *shrunk*. Looked timid, apologetic, like a man brought down in the world.

Chip set one big grey hand on my seat and leaned forward as the cabbie turned up the broad avenue of Unter den Linden. "You know where we are?" he said quietly.

A weird feeling rose up in me. Last I seen Unter den Linden, they torn out all them linden trees that gave the boulevard its name, tossed up white columns in their place, sanded the pavement so their damn jackboots wouldn't slip.

All that was gone like it ain't never been. I got a shock of recognition, of half-recognition, and heaven knows why but I recalled the night I seen my ma's body laid out in her coffin. As I leaned low over her, her features seemed the same, arranged in familiar calm, but there was a trace of something not her, a watermark left by the undertaker. A whimsy to her lips, maybe. As if in dying she'd learned a whole new kind of irony, a contempt for what she'd left behind.

"This ain't our Berlin, Sid," said Chip.

I swallowed. Seemed like my damn voice wasn't working right.

Chip put his hand on my shoulder. "It's the years, brother. They wreck everything. For real."

I nodded. "It's lost something. I bet ain't nobody even remember what it was."

"Except us, brother. Except you and me."

I said nothing.

Chip leaned back. "That's what this weekend *about*, Sid."

I sort of half turned in my seat to look at Chip where he sat, his big hands pressed between his thighs, his sweet black suit utterly unrumpled. "You keep on talking," I said. "You keep on trying to sell me something."

He chuckled. "Aw, ain't no convincing you. I know that. You don't want to go to Poland, that's okay."

"You damn right."

He chuckled again.

But something was wrong in me. Even being put up at the Westin Grand on Friedrichstrasse didn't sweeten my mood. I lay in the dark room on a bed the size of a banquet table, the velvet curtains shut, a chalky dryness to the air like centuries of dust.

Hell was I tired. Too tired to sleep. Tired as laundry, my ma used to say. I been talking German again like it was my first tongue and I thought how strangely the mind traps language, won't let it go. I stretched back on the bed, let out a long breath. Room all done up in creams and beiges so pale was like you ain't actually supposed to see any of it, like you'd stepped into a great void.

The quiet just swallowed me up. It was like being cottoned by moss. Oh Berlin, our beautiful Berolina, our charcoal life. What a city this was, after that first war. And all of us poor, antsy, fetching to know what more life held. I been a latecomer, didn't hit these streets till '27, but man was she beautiful. Hundreds of gates flocked here, dragging their instruments. Hundreds of stage hens.

Every joint felt famous then. The Barberina. Moka Efti. The Scala. In the Romanisches Café, the great brains of the age gathered like grapes to trade ideas over beer. I saw Kästner there, and Tucholsky, even Otto Dix. Dix maybe dreaming up nightmares for his paintings, pausing over his glass as something new struck him. That famous one he did of Anita Berber, the dancer, her hair and dress red as torn flesh.

That Berber girl, hell. We used to flock to watch her dance at the White Mouse. She'd slither half-nude through the packed tables, bring her dance to a climax by breaking champagne bottles over fellows' heads. Broke one over Big Fritz's head, he ain't hardly noticed. I remember her working the Eldorado, too, that pansy club so dark you couldn't hardly see the stage. And her all flexing and shivering to the dry old tunes of Camille Saint-Saëns—*man*, did she ever bring it down.

In the craziest days, there was more than twenty cabarets. For real. Damn near every casting agent become a Columbus—new talent was everywhere to discover. Marlene Dietrich at The Two Cravats; Ursula Fuller at the Red Feather. Who'd have reckoned Fuller—so dainty, an angel on earth—would cut her chops in that lowdown joint? Cause The Feather, man, it left *nothing* to the imagination. We only ever been there once but I ain't never forget it. Dancers come out near naked. Sitting on gents' plates, their legs splayed, they slowly got dressed. Was like spying on your neighbour's wife. That was the idea, anyhow. Though I remember Ernst lean over to me and smiled: "Whose neighbour's wife looks like *that*?"

A knock come at the door and I got achingly to my feet. I figured it got to be my damn suitcase. Poland, hell, I thought.

It wasn't the suitcase. Some gent stood there holding a blue suit on a coat hanger under a plastic sleeve. "Mr. Jones asked me to bring this down to you, sir," he said in dignified German. "And allow me to introduce myself." With his lightning-fast speech and his humble stutter I ain't caught his name. But he seemed to be me and Chip's minder for the night, sent from the festival. If it's not too much trouble, he stammered, could you be ready to leave in an hour? Sure thing, brother. Closing the door, I was half afraid he might choose to stand in the damn hall the whole hour. I put my eye to the peephole. Well he had more sense than you figured.

Ain't no way Chip's suit was going to fit. Chip known it too. But I laid it out carefully on the bed and then went to the window and drawn back the curtains, staring out at the city. The light was already greying, the late afternoon beginning to sink away. Streetlights was coming on. I studied the line of rooftops, the glint of glass off the Reichstag and the low sprawl of trees on the boulevards far below.

A city can change without being no different. I known that. Hell, I ain't hardly recognized the Baltimore I come back to after Paris. But Berlin ain't just any city. I remembered how Chip and me was in hot demand when we first got here. German jazz bands needed us for the sex of it. I mean, toss a few honest-to-god Yankees into your line-up and wham, you was the real thing. This festival, I known, wasn't so different.

Back then, it even got so Germans began pretending they was American. *Herr Mike Sottneck aus New York* billed his band as "amerikanische Jazz-Tanzkapelle." Wasn't the only fake. Least the Krauts picked up some of what we was doing. See, we hailed from the cradle of jazz, and that gave us a feel for the music. I ain't saying it was racial. It had to do with rubbing up against jazz in your tadpole years. With the fact that back home folks of a certain class wasn't afraid to play it in their houses. Lot of the Krauts had classical training, and ain't quite broken out of the schmaltzy continental salon dance style. Was like a sickness, that style. Like a damn infection in you instrument.

I ain't saying everyone. But when you heard cats like Gluskin and Bela, with their choppy harmonic shifts and slippery percussion, well, you thought you'd died and gone to hell. Couldn't swing their way out of a playground. No feel for improv. Ernst once told me he caught Wilhelm Bosch *transcribing a Red Nichols solo from a record*. Beat that. Red Nichols is bad enough. But then Bosch let it out on stage note by stale note, reading from his sheet music. Ernst was laughing so hard he like to be sick.

Chip and me, we didn't give that sort the time of day. We was snobs, purists. And so we swung with Franz Grothe and Georg Haentzschel, Walter Dobschinski and Ernst Hoellerhagen and Stefan Weintraub. We swung with Eric Borchard, till that night when, high on horse, he strangled his girlfriend. Then we swung with someone else. It been a ride.

It was a cool night, the coppery reek of raw exhaust on the breeze. I looked across the grass of Rosa-Luxemburg-Platz, studying the glowing ochre Babylon theatre. From a distance it put me in mind of a slab of cheddar, that lustrous colour and all them angles. How strange to be standing here again, in this very square I used to tread when I was young. The building caught the last of the sunlight, bright against the grey square.

Chip stood between me and our eerily silent minder, what's-his-name. Chip was fixing his hair, spitting on his fingers then dabbing at the pale part in his Afro. Already sick with nerves, I looked past him, at the Babylon, the crowd of folks spilling out onto the plaza. Seeing just how many there was, I begun swallowing hard. My damn throat felt like it stuffed with cotton.

"Sid? You got the nerves, brother?" said Chip.

I waved him off. "I'm alright."

The square was filled with a carpet of folk rolling all the way to the theatre across, the Volksbühne, with its fearsome grey pillars. The Babylon looked packed so tight a gent couldn't sneeze without greasing his neighbour. As if every Tom, Fritz and Eva in the city had turned out. Hell. I'd banked on this being a smaller affair.

"How we even going to get in?" I said. "There ain't even room to get in the damn door."

"Aw, we'll get in. You'll see." Chip was looking at me with his thin oyster lips pressed tight. "You sure you alright? You looking a little green, Sid."

"I ain't green."

Chip grunted, patted my shoulder. Felt good having his hand there, reassuring. I was damned uncomfortable. Chip's suit hung too short on my arms, hiked high up off my wrists like I about to wash my damn face. And his shirt sagged real loose on the collar, tailored for his fat bull's neck I guess.

I thought of telling him so. Instead, I said, "I should've punched you in the goddamned mouth second you asked me to come back here."

That seemed more fitting.

But Chip, he was laughing, already leading me and our minder towards the front door. "Hitting me wouldn't of made no difference. Ain't one single tooth nor shred of sense left in this old head."

"I expect that's the truth."

He turned back to me then with a funny smile on his face. "You ready to get back into the world, Sid?"

And before I could answer, he thrown open the damn door and shoved me on in.

Just like that, everything erupted. Hordes of folks was all up in our faces, their cries clattering about the theatre like trapped birds. *Chip Jones! Mr Jones! Sidney Griffiths! Charles! Sid!* Cameras flashed like pinpricks of light on a water's surface. Our minder, the sorry runt, he just too damn scared and too damn small to make anything of his job. As he squeaked for folks to step on back, I got jostled right and left, nearly falling down the carpeted steps, the silk of my suit roughing against Chip's. A sudden urge to grip Chip's coat come over me, but knowing I'd look a fool I just held my breath. The air felt heavy and sultry as a July night in Baltimore. And everything around us glowed red and yellow: the walls, the glare of sun dying in the windows, the gleam of blouses and handbags, of shoes. I felt suffocated by the marigold brightness of it all. And some damn fool named Sidney Griffiths had his name shouted over and over, like he was lost.

"Just a little nervous, eh?" said a milky voice suddenly at my ear. Caspars' arm come up under mine.

The crowd began unbraiding around us, and I turned to look Kurt Caspars in the face. His plump cheeks all stubbly, his Scandinavian paleness a shock against his dyed black hair. He was smiling that half-mast smile of his, that awful ironic smile makes you feel something bad just happened somewhere else and what kind of damn creep you must be not to know about it yet. Nodding, he left us.

Our minder led me and Chip through the nightmare of a foyer into the theatre. I ain't said nothing to him. Cause damn if that theatre wasn't *packed*. Stuffed row on row with every damned brand of folk. All that noise in the foyer—they was the *overflow*. God in holy heaven, I thought, sinking into my seat. Why did I come.

The minder sat Chip in the front row, among the VIPs. Set him down like an old sack of potatoes between two gents we ain't known from Adam. Then he led me to the other end of the same row, taking the seat beside mine. That surprised me. Guess I reckoned he'd file old Jones and me side by side, seeing as how we was a package deal.

I sat feeling out of sorts, a weird sulphur smell coming off the upholstery, like it was newly shampooed. Seats creaking around me like Virginia crickets. The other VIPs was all older than me, wax-faced and stern. I didn't know none of them. No Marsalis, no Grappelli. I wondered where everyone was.

Kurt Caspars took the stage, smiling his cold weasel smile. "Thank you all for coming tonight," he said. His weird, angular accent somehow put me in mind of Big Fritz. Hell. Fritz. That poor bastard. There was a time I couldn't think of him without getting angry. Coming back here was a damn fool idea.

It pleased me some to see Caspars' hands trembling. "What we've managed to create here tonight," he said, "it's been the work of so many voices, of so many years. A festival for Hieronymus Falk here, in what used to be Horst Wessel Square? It's a testament to the power of the new Germany, of a people filled with the future."

The crowd, man, they ate this cheddar *up*. Cheering, clapping, banging the damn armrests on their creaking blue seats. Me, I sat frowning to myself. The thing about Caspars, see, he's a master of talking big and saying nothing. But conviction in a voice ain't like meat in a stew. It ain't got no sustenance. I knew that even back as a kid. I glanced down the row to see what old Jones was making of this. His face look empty, sharp, staring straight at the stage. I tried to catch his eye, but he didn't look at me.

All of a sudden Caspars quit the stage and a tremendous hush descended. The lights dropped, and the whole theatre sat in silence, waiting. I must've been fidgeting, cause our minder leaned over and whispered, "They're going to show the documentary first, then afterwards your row will go onstage to answer questions."

"So they're delaying the guillotine," I said.

The chap paused, silence opening between us. Then he leaned over once more and said, "They're going to show the documentary first, then afterwards your row will go onstage to answer questions."

A chill run through me. I got that odd feeling again, like something bad was going to happen. My stomach was burning.

But then the screen began to glow, the soundtrack crackled in, the audience began applauding. I drawn in a slow breath. Two hours, I told myself. Two hours. Ain't hardly long at all.

───────────■───────────

Caspars' documentary wasn't told in no straight line. Seemed like one person was still talking when another one shown up onscreen, and then they was both talking over some photograph of someone else. I don't know. But every time the kid flash up onscreen, his face eight-feet tall, that chill cut through me. It got so I felt like I was watching myself watching the picture, my eyes pried wide, my hands damp on my trouser legs. Christ, here it all was, every last piece of our Berlin life: the women we'd messed with, the clubs we'd gigged at. And ain't none of it seemed *right*.

Then this old gent come on and I known him at once. He'd been our band's first manager. Hell, he'd lost his hair, his blue eyes was hazy with age and almost colourless, but I known him alright. He looked tidy and simple and entirely unscarred by life.

"You have these four men in Paris," he was saying, "these men who've just watched the Nazis march in. And what do they do, instead of packing up to leave like everyone else? They write this song of resistance, they give their collective finger to the authorities. In this tiny little studio, where they could be arrested anytime. This studio where the equipment hasn't been used for at least half a decade, the lathe and lacquers just sitting there gathering dust. Most of the blanks had been damaged, the coating scratched. I mean, in some cases you could see straight through to the aluminum. Now, you have to understand—to achieve perfect sound on lacquer-on-aluminum, the disc's surface must be absolutely smooth. So the band had maybe nine or ten functional discs to work with. Nine or ten tries to get it right. And at the centre of it all, you've got this kid directing everything, this twenty-year-old Falk. And he's screaming in the middle of takes, wrecking them, he's grabbing the discs and gouging their surfaces with his pocket knife. Anything to stop a bad take from existing.

"And amazingly, it's on the very morning before Falk's arrest that Griffiths decides he's had enough of the kid's perfectionism. So he takes the last disc they've cut and he tucks it into the case of his upright. You know, on the off chance it's any good. And what's remarkable about this fact is that those parts of the recording that couldn't be remastered, those parts where there are actual pieces of the performance missing—those were pressed off by Griffiths' bass strings boring into the lacquer. So those gaps are missing because the thing is that fresh, that literally hot off the press.

"And it's pure genius. Which would seem impossible—I mean, it's just *four* men, barely half a band, the piece extremely pared down because of it. Minimalist. But Falk's so gifted he can single-handedly make their four instruments sound like eight. His complexity is unbe*liev*able... the piece is brilliant. Even with Falk yelling halfway through—what does he say again?—'just a damn braid of mistakes,' something like that? Even his screaming doesn't ruin it. If anything, the line's now legendary. Just a damn braid of mistakes."

That son of a bitch, I thought to myself. What did *he* know about us? He cut out on the first boat, day after Hitler was sworn in. Left poor Ernst to take his place, become our clarinetist and manager both.

More quick images. I closed my old eyes a minute. Then a scholar come on, some dry old owl I ain't seen before, looking fit for the coffin in his suit and blue bow tie. "Life for black people under the Third Reich," he said through his nose, "was extremely contradictory. This is because there were so many different *types* of black people, and their treatment depended on what group they belonged to. For instance, you had the children of the African diplomats who'd come to the country during its colonial period. You had African-American performers, the opera singer Marian Anderson and jazzmen like Charles Jones and Sidney Griffiths, who, like their counterparts in Paris—Josephine Baker, Arthur Briggs, Bill Coleman and the like—all came to Europe to get away from the overwhelming racism prevalent in the Southern United States in that era. The Jim Crow laws, in effect from the late 1800s right into the 1950s, barred blacks from active participation in society. In the twenties Europe was still a place black entertainers could come to earn a good living. Especially in Germany, whose borders were kept open to foreigners due to the Versailles Treaty. Also, the loss of the First World War had brought about a whole new artistic movement. The market for jazz had grown tremendously, and there was a decent following."

Hell, it burned me up to see it. How the sweet jesus could *he* know what drove us there? He ain't known nothing of my childhood, my thoughts, of that last-minute shrug brought me to Berlin back then. I been a hair's breadth from staying put in London, a whole other life.

"Hieronymus Falk," he went on, "now, he belonged to a rarer

group. He was what back then was called a 'Rhineland Bastard.' See, after the First World War, part of the conditions levied against Germany were that France was given control of the Rhineland, which of course borders their country."

He leaned forward, as though getting to the meat of his story. "Now, instead of sending French soldiers to occupy it, they sent men from their African colonies. As you can imagine, this didn't sit well with some of the German populace. They dubbed the soldiers the Black Shame, the Black Scourge, the Black Infamy. Women who bore children with these men, like Falk's mother Marieanne, they were assumed to be either prostitutes or rape victims. So even after the soldiers were sent home, and Hitler re-occupied the Rhineland, these children were seen as part of a significant insult to Germany. A cultural stain."

New images come onscreen: black-and-white footage of soil-dark soldiers standing in a loose file, their uniforms muddy. "Is this what France calls a man?" said the German voice-over.

The scholar's voice drifted over the imagery. "Different types of black people were treated in different and often contradictory ways under the Reich. This was in large part due to the fact that there were at most four thousand Germans of African descent in the whole country. And with a number that small, it was hard to effect cohesive legislation against them. Even so, many had their papers confiscated, making them effectively stateless."

I hadn't known most of what he was saying. You don't stop to look around when you running, and back then we was all running. I sat skeptical, and pained by it.

"In the end, Falk's fate was outlandish in that he was one of a minority of Afro-Germans who were sent to concentration camps. Now if he'd been African-American, they would probably have held him indefinitely at Saint-Denis, like they did with other black musicians arrested in Paris. But Falk was German—or by their measure, 'stateless'—and so he was transferred to Mauthausen. Of course, it's hard to get a sense of how many blacks actually went to the camps, because so many records were destroyed.

"Remember, there was no on-paper legislation against blacks, so they were often admitted to work camps on trumped-up charges and under various crimes. Some were interned as Communists, or as immigrants, who wore the blue badge. Or as homosexuals, who wore the pink badge, or as repeat criminals, who wore the green badge, or asocials, who wore the black badge. Even more obscuring is that the asocial group included the homeless, pimps, pickpockets, murderers, homosexuals, and race defilers, so that it's even more difficult to figure out who among them was black. These people are lost in the dark maw of history."

Then there was some ruined old fool up there, his dour mug peering out at us. And then I saw with shock that the fool was me.

Well, hell. Nothing, *nothing* I tell you, can prepare you for the utter wreck of your face onscreen. I looked like one of them worn-out wood houses ain't been painted in decades. My skin was thick with pores, my cheeks gaunt, my eyes like dim windows, going blond with cataracts and full of uncertainty. When my name flashed onscreen, I got that strange dark feeling welling up in me again. That sense something wasn't right in me, something bad was coming.

"Sure I played alongside the kid, Hieronymus I mean—see, we called him 'the kid' back then," I said in a creaking voice. Then Caspars interrupted me, and when I glanced off-camera to meet his eye, he whispered I should look straight ahead.

The audience laughed at this, not unkindly. I hunkered down in my chair a little. Feeling the minder's eyes on me.

"What I recall most about him, besides his playing, was his reading." I looked off-camera again, then as if remembering Caspars' last prompt, stared at the screen like a badger caught in headlights. "What I mean by this is, he been obsessed with Herodotus. All them old historical tales. Hieronymus reading Herodotus—that made me laugh. Yeah, he read all them old histories, Egypt stories, Greek stories. Like he didn't get enough of such things in the crib, you know?" I cleared my throat, frowning. Looking off-camera again.

Caspars whispered something.

"Well," I said in reply, my voice soft. "Well." I sat there staring at my lap, not saying nothing for some seconds.

Watching myself freeze up onscreen, my body went real tight, the theatre seat squeaking beneath me. I could hear myself breathing through my mouth.

I gave a taut laugh on camera and said, "Well, it been right terrifying. I mean what else could it be? We gone out for a cup of milk, gone out to quell our bellies, and we end up in Café Coup de Foudre with the Nazis. It was right terrible." I licked my lips, my eyes flickering. "Listen—nothing I could say now would get at just how terrible it was." I grown emphatic, using my hands. "I mean nothing I could say to you now could *begin* to bring home how harsh, how awful it been." I paused like a man who'd made a great point. I remembered then that Caspars hadn't reacted to what I'd said. "Only thing I can say is that being there with him during the ordeal, seeing his courage, it was an honour."

A long silence fell over the theatre as my face faded out. My heart had inched up my throat till I could hear the blood in my ears. That odd feeling come over me so strong I near couldn't breathe. Hell, I thought. What is it. The dark felt soft and hot, like an animal crouching on me.

Then Chip come onscreen, and that bad feeling in me just grew. He looked rough, old, holy in his ice-white suit, like a Mississippi Baptist spent his life preaching on the delta. Staring at his burnt-out face, his swollen cheeks and his eyes rusted from horse, I seen him with eyes afresh. He looked wrecked, and what's worse, wholly blind to his frailty.

"When Hiero got arrested in that café," he was saying, "they'd had to make up a reason for it. So they branded him a race-polluter, a stateless race-polluter and an immigrant and a Commie. All sorts of things. Hell if anyone was a Commie it was Sid. But they held Hiero for two weeks at Saint-Denis, no trial, nothing, before putting him on a transport to Mauthausen. *Mauthausen*. Very name of it give you the shivers. Poor kid was hauled off there, and no amount of money, talk, or pull could get him out. Not that Delilah had any kind of influence no more—she was even on thin ice herself.

"Sidney Griffiths," said Chip, shaking his head. Something in me died at that gesture. It seemed so contemptuous.

"A shame, the trust we all put in him." Chip took a long, deep breath, reflecting. "But he's a lesson, really. A lesson in what jealousy'll do to a man. To betray such a genius musician, and a *kid* at that, over a woman. Over the kid's talents, and over a woman. I mean, there he stood, denying his friend, pretending he didn't even *know* him, while they dragged the poor boy away. I ain't saying he pre-arranged it. I ain't saying that. But handing Hiero over to the Boots, to the Gestapo, like that..." He shook his head. "That's mind-blowing, ain't it? I don't have to tell you what a great blow that was to the legacy of jazz. I mean, here we was on the verge of that groundbreaking recording... I know, I know, we still got a pretty good take, but imagine what it *could've* been. Hell. It's a crime. It's a crime for which Sid ain't never been held to account."

——————— ▬ ———————

I ain't saying I seen it coming.

But hearing Chip onscreen, all a sudden that crushing hot feeling in my chest just drain right away. It like I ain't even there no more. Like something just finished. Just ended. This blood trapped in my head, the slow dim throb of it deep inside.

I closed my eyes.

And then I was waking in some other room, a room cool and alien to me, the windows letting onto an old Baltimore street I don't barely recognize. Lying on a bed in the damp sheets of a lady who ain't my wife. The room white as wheat with early sun, a dry smell like cinder coming off her body. I wanted to turn to her, to gather her small limbs into me way I done just hours ago, kissing the joint at her throat where her collarbones meet, her wet dirty curls. But I didn't. Something was rising up in me like bad digestion. Dust on the bedside table, a half-empty glass of water. Gulls crying outside. I lay beside that woman, thick with unhappiness, thinking of my wife.

Then I was back. The air in that theatre gone rich and hot. It was stingingly quiet. Gripping the arms of my seat, I pushed on out of it, its joints squeaking. The film was still rolling, the theatre soot-black, but even in that dark I could feel everyone's eyes on me, their gazes weighing me down like a sack of ashes.

Our minder whispered, "They're going to show the documentary first, then afterwards your row will go onstage." But I wasn't listening.

My damned old legs wasn't moving right. I could feel my heart punching away at my arteries, my whole body shuddering. Don't you damn well look Chip's way, I thought. Not one glance, Sid. I stepped hard across the minder's knees, past the legs of all these folks, past Caspars.

Caspars leaned forward in his seat. "Where the hell are you going?" he hissed.

I stood there, half-dazed, shaking. Feeling suddenly old. Shaking and saying nothing.

You a damn coward, I thought. That's what you is, Sid.

No, I ain't said nothing. I just started up the aisle, slow. The silence sharp as needles. Folks watching me leave and not the picture, and me feeling their stares. My face weighed heavy, like some great load I got to haul without dropping.

Ain't no one said nothing. But then from the darkness some son of a bitch hissed at me in German, "Shame on you."

I tripped a little. Stared at the pale faces in their seats. Then kept on moving.

I broke through the doors, through the foyer, out into the night. The coolness of the city air rushed over me. I stood there in the empty square.

Even at ten years old, Chip was a veteran liar. A real Pinocchio. I recall the Saturday I first met him: the Baltimore weather all sultry, the air stewed and stinking of sewage. Steam belched from the hot manholes, and walking through it, it stuck in your gullet like crumbs. I was sitting in the park where us blacks went, sitting with my sister, Hetty—Hetty wearing the Philadelphia hat she wouldn't take off her head for no one cause our pa give it to her. She was teasing me something awful. Calling me cross-eyed, gimp-legged. So when a kid come up in the distance, sank his tan overalls into the sandbox, I spat on my sister's shoes and ran off to join him.

He was a small, funny-looking git, a real balloon head. Getting near, I reckoned him for a strange one. Those full round cheeks, those prize-fighter biceps that seemed borrowed from an older brother. As I come up, he never even raised his face.

"You want to play ball or somethin?" I said, glancing down at his crown. His Afro had odd bald patches in it, grey flakes.

He finally looked up, and his weak sneer turned something inside me. "This look like a ball field to you, sucker?" he said. "This be a *sand*box. For makin *sand*castles." Shaking his head, he spat air through his lips. "I'm sittin in sand, and he's talkin ball games."

I felt like a blue-ribbon idiot, all right. My face gone hot, I turned and started back to Hetty.

"You live Peabody Heights way, right?" the boy called out.

I turned. He didn't look no friendlier, nope, but there was a shrewder look in his face, like his attention been filed down to a single, sharp point. "You live down on Maryland Ave."

That thrown me a little. "How you know?"

"I lives in Peabody Heights too," he said, like it was common knowledge. "Ain't you seen me at church?"

Believe me, if I'd seen this melon head at church, I'd have remembered. But I couldn't risk his sneer again. "Maybe. Yeah, I think so."

My heart sunk into my heels as he spat all disgusted into the sandbox. "You a dirty liar," he said, his thin lips riding up on one side of his mouth. "You ain't never seen me in all you life."

"Have *too*," I said.

He shook his head. But not wanting me to walk off again, he changed tack. "You know they named Charles Street after me?"

Now who's the dirty liar, I wanted to say, but I'll admit I was kind of afraid of him. "Oh yeah?" I said. "Your name Charles Street?"

"Naw, fool, who the hell's name Charles Street? I Charles Jones. Charles C. Jones."

"What the C stand for?"

"Never you mind. Just C. Charles C. Jones. And one day I be mayor of this town."

You keep counting them chickens, I thought. Here was a boy with years of disappointment ahead. Best let him have his way now, at least he'd have the memories. "Sure you will." I stood there in the dead heat, my skin prickling, wishing old Hetty would hurry up and call me so I could walk away.

"Where you goin now?" said Charles C. Jones, smiling a little. He'd sensed I'd go away any minute, and he meant to keep me as long as possible.

"Hetty and me—that my sister Hetty over there, in the stupid hat—we goin home now."

"Why don't you ditch and come on over to my house? I gots candy, chocolate."

To me, chocolate was the sole reason we on this earth. But to have to go over to *this* joker's house—no thanks, jack. "Hetty and me got to be gettin home."

Just when I said this, who starts jogging up to us but Hetty, her hat flapping as she flown over the dry yellow grass. She stopped at the swingset to get her breath, leaning against its stripped wooden frame. Then she started running again, holding her chest as she reached us.

"I'm goin over to Lucia's," she said, looking at me with a teasing smile. She could tell I wanted away from this boy, and she wasn't about to make it easy. "Mama said we could stay out till six today, so . . . you go amuse yourself, lizard boy. Spittin at me like that. You two amuse yourselves and we see you at home."

With hate in my heart I watched her jog off. Imagine spending the day with this boy, his moods and grim smiles.

Standing from the sandbox, the grit poured from his clothes like water. He punched me on the arm. "All right now, let's go see Tante Cecile."

"Who?" I said, marching all reluctant behind him.

"My great aunt. She's where all the chocolate's at."

Charles C. Jones lived in a big broken-down brownstone on the corner of Mace and East 26th. The porch was covered with ratty old couches coughing out foam, and the whole place smelled of bacon. Climbing the stairs, I said, "Nice house, Charlie."

I guess I meant to suggest mine was nicer. But he didn't catch no irony or rivalry in my voice. "Thanks," he said seriously. "But don't call me Charlie, no one calls me Charlie. Y'all call me Chip."

"Chip."

"You goin tell me your name, or I got to guess?"

"Sidney. Sidney Griffiths. Y'all call me Sid."

In the dim foyer, which reeked even worse of bacon and of sweaty leather shoes, Chip yanked me to him. "Now when we go up to see Tante Cecile, don't you damn well talk. Alright?"

I stood there, more shocked by his cussing than anything.

He scowled. "You want chocolate or don't you? Then quit you gawkin and come on."

Chip pulled me past rooms so packed with stuff it was spilling out the doors. Past the kitchen stinking of bacon fat and something sweet, past the living room with its magazines all covering the floor, past a room ladies used, their garters and stockings strung up everywhere like shed skin. Finally we reached a door cracked a finger's-width open, a stale smell drifting out. I was seized with sudden terror, disgusted at the thought of eating anything that came from the same place as that stink. Chip shoved me through.

The room was overhung with lace, the mean sun burning through, lighting up everything. Hell. On the bed by the window lay a creature so ancient I'd swore it known Cain back in the day. Its skin was so ashy it looked grey, its face so scrawny it was caving in on itself. Looked like an enormous old sea turtle.

"Tante Cecile," cried Chip in a deep voice, throwing up his arms. "It's us, Arnold and Theodore! We come to see you on you birthday!"

At first, seemed the old witch had died of fright. Then slowly, she began to sit up in bed, her nightdress crackling like butcher paper around her. Her ashy old face filled with wonder. "What a surprise! It's my birthday?"

"Yes! And *both* of us done come this year, both Arnold and Theodore."

Her face lit up. "Arnie *and* Theo? Oh, my god, I don't believe it!"

I didn't believe it either. Chip avoided my gaze. "Yes, Arnie and Theo, Arnie and Theo!" he said. "We done come to see you on you birthday!"

The old gal's teeth nearly dropped out of her head, she was smiling so hard. "Well, we better have ourselves a lil' old party," she said, her muddy Baltimore accent suddenly going all Mississippi. Leaning forward, she reached under her pillow and pulled out a beautifully carved wooden box. Setting it on her lap, she sprung it open and took out a Baby Ruth and some Chuckles.

"Both Arnie *and* Theo is here today, Tante Cecile," said Chip, winking at me.

"Oh, yes, I forgot!" She reached back into the box and pulled out some Necco wafers and Hershey's Kisses. "Both boys done come today. What a surprise!"

No sooner had Tante Cecile put the candy on her lap than Chip snatched it all up, tossing me the wafers and the Baby Ruth. He tore his wrappers quickly, stuffing everything into his mouth at the same time, chewing wildly. I stood there holding mine, astonished. Still smacking his lips, he made a crazy face at me, as if he didn't understand why I wasn't eating.

I was fetching to leave when Chip held my arm. In the same deep voice, he said, "Both Arnie *and* Theo is here today, Tante Cecile."

"Oh, yes, I forgot! Both boys done come today. What a surprise!" Tante Cecile reached into her cedar box and pulled out four more candies. Chip snatched these up faster than pulling money out of a fire. Again, he tossed me two, gobbled the rest down.

"We got to leave now, Tante Cecile. We come back some other day." Grabbing my arm, he hauled me from the room, shutting the door hard behind us.

"What on earth was *that*?" I hissed.

"Shhh, keep your pipes down," he whispered. "Tante Cecile done lost her wits ages ago. Memory like a pigeon. Only she don't know it, cause we not allowed to tell her."

"Who is Arnie and Theo?"

Chip chuckled. "Those be her sons. They both dead now. She won't share her candy otherwise. I figured I go in with you, she give out twice as much."

I stood there staring at him in the dark hallway. Here he was, cheating his own blood and grinning about it.

He give me a look. "You goin to eat that?"

I stuffed the candy into my mouth. It tasted like chalk.

I don't known how long I walked. My damn hands wouldn't stop shaking with the fury of it. Goddamn Chip. Chip son of a bitch Jones. I left that awful theatre and just turned up the nearest street, passed the hundreds of parked cars, followed the new lamps away.

I come to a rest in a small treeless park. Trudging over the trim grass, I sat down on a cold bench. Lord my knees ached. All these changes. A cold wind was cutting through the park. Construction cranes hung like broken bridges, silhouetted in the distance against the glow of the Berlin skyline. I reached down, rubbed my smarting legs. I could feel that old damn pressure on my bladder. I needed a toilet. I got back to my feet.

Ain't no good getting old. And this night, of all nights, brother, I got old.

Chip Jones was a bastard. Sure he was. But he ain't never been malicious like that before. Petty, mean, a bit on the wrong side of crazy—but they ain't the same thing. This, this was like a scald that don't give you no peace. It burned and burned and burned. Something my mother used to say come to mind, something I ain't thought of in a dog's age. Ma used to say to me, she said, "Sid, that Jones boy ain't got no light to his eyes." He ain't got no light to his eyes. That used to tear me up, cause I always reckoned Ma was calling him stupid. Now, shuffling through a dark Berlin park seventy years later, I finally come to understand what she'd meant.

The café I found smelled of dishwater and cabbages, the varnished wood cheap and the seats sticky with fake leather. I didn't care none. I come in through its brass doors grimacing. There wasn't but two diners inside, a fellow and a lady, sitting together at a shaded table by the wall. I nodded at the barmaid, a thin woman with hair like dead grass, and took a seat at the bar. I opened the menu. I wasn't hungry.

The barmaid come up, and I ordered some wurst, sauerkraut and boiled potatoes.

"Where's your bathroom?" I said.

She tapped her ballpoint pen against her teeth, as if thinking. She tilted it lazily toward the far end of the bar.

Ain't no sooner had I got back than the café chain rattled, and the seat beside mine was being pulled out by big, grey hands.

"You goddamned bastard," I said, not even looking up.

"Hell, Sid," said Chip, holding his chest from the long walk over. "That ain't right, what he did."

"You sitting down? Here? Get the hell away from me."

He opened his hands, closed them. "I don't know what to tell you," he said. "I didn't say all that. I swear."

I glanced up at his face, at its perplexed look. Like he known he should be sorry but wasn't sure just what for. "Chip, I mean it. You get the hell away from here. We done, brother. You hear me? We done."

"Sid, I didn't know," he said. "I didn't know that all was in there."

"You *murdered* me. You flew me out here and you *murdered* me."

The barmaid was looking at us uneasily.

"Aw, Sid." Chip's eyes was all glassy as he blinked at me.

And then he started to cry. The skin of his neck welled up under his chin like he'd tied a black kerchief there, his shoulders shaking with it all.

I swore, looked away.

"Aw Sid," he mumbled, "aw, hell, Sid."

I sat in silence. I ain't going to say nothing more to him, I thought. But then I could hear my old damned creaky voice starting up. "I thought, ain't no way he could do something like this," it was saying. "I thought, he brought me ties from his tours. He's a friend. He ain't that kind of mean."

"Sid." He was wiping his eyes with his big thumbs. He looked so old, so old. "Sid, you know how they edit these things. Hell, I ain't said half of that. You know how these things get cut."

"Get cut is right."

"Sid. Come on."

"What you think? You just come in here and it all go away? I should tear your goddamned head off. Jesus."

But something was already going out in me. Hell. Chip just look so damned small sitting there, his little shoulders rolled forward in that suit, his big veined knuckles raw on the counter.

"I know I did," he said quietly. "I know I got carried away. But I ain't meant it like he put it together. I swear. Caspars, he just kept asking and asking. Just kept on me. I said a lot more, all sorts of things that was real nice about you. They just wasn't in it. He known what he wanted, Sid. And that's what he took."

We was silent for a time. The barmaid come over and Chip shrugged at her and she just stood there looking at us. After a minute I blown out my cheeks, told her to get him the same as me. Chip's German wasn't half so good as mine.

"You're a bastard," I said, but without force.

He nodded miserably. "I am. I am. I feel damned awful."

"You going to feel worse, too. I'm flying back first flight I can get." He looked at me.

"Aw, don't give me that look," I scowled. "You *surprised*? You honestly *surprised*?"

"I guess I ain't. I guess it makes sense. I mean, I understand."

"Do I look like a man gives a damn?"

"You'll miss Poland, I guess."

I hissed bitter air through my teeth, not saying nothing.

"I ain't sore about it," he said, lifting up his eyes and looking at me hopefully. "If you change you mind, well. I already rented the car."

"You ain't serious."

He looked confused, unsure how to respond. I got down from my chair, slapped some money on the counter. "Eat," I said. "Eat my damned plate too. Finish it. Ain't no good leaving a thing unfinished." And I pushed on out of his life for good.

Or what I figured was for good.

I blown off the rest of the festival. Yes sir. And since I figured Caspars owed me something, I spent Saturday getting massages and eating rich, indigestible meals on his dime. On Sunday I bought ties in the Westin Grand shops, chocolates, wine I didn't even like, charging everything to, you bet, The Kurt. My only regret was not being there to see his damned face when he got that bill. Chip come to my door twice that first day but I ain't answered it. Then he stopped coming by.

I saw the old Judas at last on the Monday morning. I woke up to find my battered suitcase set just outside the door. Ain't even needed to unpack it. I was following my porter through the lobby to the taxi stand for the airport when the young fellow turned his head, stopped short. To the right a small crowd had gathered on Behrenstrasse. A fish-grey Mercedes was shuddering and inching forward, shuddering and inching back, trying to pull out from the curb. As it rolled back, it damn near hit a taxi pulling out behind it. As it rolled forward, it near hit a parking sign.

And, hell, crouched over the wheel, looking crazily back and forth, face all squinched up, was Chip C. Jones. Damn jack look frightened as a child.

"Hold up, jack," I said to the porter, who gave me a confused look. I switched to proper *Hochdeutsch*. "Could you wait one second please?"

I left him curbside as I strode up to Chip's car, rapping with my knuckles on the window. Chip whipped his head around, real nervous, his face hardening when he seen it was me. He rolled down the window.

"Leave me alone, Sid. I doing fine."

I like to have spat out my damned dentures at him. "Doing fine my ass. Jesus. You know what you look like from here? Hell, brother, can you see *anything?*"

"Go on," he scowled. "Get lost."

I shook my old head. "You like a damned fool out here."

His arms all folded up over the steering wheel, his face staring up over the dash. "I'm fine," he muttered. "Hell. I just got to get on the road and I be fine."

"Sure you will. You be fine like Tante Cecile was fine."

He looked at me then with something like hope. I felt suddenly angry again.

"Don't look at me like that," I said. "I ain't going to help you."

"I ain't asked for you to."

"No you ain't."

I stood there leaning in at his window, watching him watching me there. I could feel an old knife twisting in my guts. "If you asked for it," I said. "If you asked for it maybe you'd get it."

"I ain't asking for you to help me."

"Can you even see over that dash? You need some phonebooks to sit on?"

He said nothing. I watched him struggle to put the stick in reverse.

"You driving a standard? You even crazier than I thought."

"I ain't crazy, Sid," he shouted suddenly. He look like he going to start crying on me again.

I stood back then and crossed my arms. "Go on. Let's see you get out of this then."

He said nothing, just sat blinking ahead of him. An ancient old raisin of a man.

I could see the hotel staff watching through the glass. "Son of a bitch," I said at last. I came around to the driver's side. "Get out of the damned seat. I mean it. I ain't helping you but I be damned if you going to ruin a perfectly good automobile."

I opened the door, the bell chiming from the dash, a fragrance of clean leather like a new saddle wafting out at me. Hell. The porter was still standing at the sidewalk, my suitcase in his red fists. I lowered my window, gestured for him to bring it on over.

Chip was careful not to look at me. I glanced across at the road. Everything seemed to slow right down. The day, bright and cold in that now unknown country. I don't know. We don't none of us change, I guess.

III

Berlin
1939

I

What is luck but something made to run out.

We jogged through the street, Paul and me. Slowly, we swung up into the trolley as it clattered down the boulevard, its brittle bells chiming. Leaning down, Paul hauled me aboard after him. The late evening sun sat like phosphorus on him, lighting up his blue eyes, his pale knuckles where he held me. It was the last week of August, and the light cutting through the trolley windows fell lush and soft as water.

"You need to do more sport, buck," Paul laughed.

I nodded, gasping.

We tottered down the aisle to our seats. The trolley floor rattled and shuddered under us as it gained speed. The mahogany benches was warm from the long sun, and I shielded my eyes, looking past the tied-off curtains, the glass lamps clinking quietly. The city poured past us like something final, something coming to a end.

I sat there catching my breath, feeling a strange, vague sadness hammering at me.

Paul's mood was entirely different. With a gentle smile, he winked at a jane across the aisle. Blushing, she looked down at her feet. Hell. He was a real cake-eater, our Paul, a great ladies' man. With his wavy blond hair and his natty moustache, Paul look more like a motion-picture star than the out-of-work pianist he was. Watching him brush the street dust off his dapper blue suit, I caught a sudden glimpse of how every damn jane on the trolley seen him: handsome, athletic, with that strong jawline, those eyes bluer than Greek silk. The perfect Aryan man. And he was Jewish.

"Listen, Sid," he said. "Were you serious about helping me out tomorrow?"

"What, with Marta? Or with Inge?"

He shrugged. "I don't know. Marta, I guess."

"You got my number if it's Inge."

"Inge then. It doesn't matter so much."

The boulevards was all shady, the green lindens dark against the bald sky. The trolley pulled up alongside a stop, emptied, filled up, then rolled back out again. We was on our way to the Hound to practice some numbers with the kid, though I wasn't sure what the point was. We been banned from playing live. Which meant we was banned from playing, period. In fact, if Ernst ain't owned the Hound—a sweet little sanctuary of a club bought with his papa's money—we might've give up playing at all. Well, not really, but you get the idea. The club been closed up for months, become more a place to just mess around.

My eyes drifted to the window, watching folks out in the slow summer light, the jacks in their shirtsleeves, the girls on their bicycles. We was passing a crowded square filled with tables, folks drinking coffee, eating pastry, when I caught sight of a face I known.

"Ain't that Ernst?" I said, sitting up in my seat.

Certainly looked like him—his jet-black hair, his skin so pale it near translucent, the veins standing out like etchings under the flesh.

He was gesturing to a woman, a cigarette burning down in his fingers. I ain't recognized the woman.

"What, there?" said Paul. "No, that's not him."

"The hell it ain't. Look again, brother." We was coming abreast of them now, their small table set out on the pavement in the sunshine. The woman he was sitting with wore a huge grey headwrap, fastened with some sort of ugly brass brooch. She was thin as a garden rake, and when she smiled I seen real clear a row of very small, very crooked teeth. We clattered past on the tracks.

"Where?" Paul said, frowning.

"Over there. With that jane with the cloaked birdcage on her head. You ain't seen him?"

Paul twisted round on the mahogany bench, squinting out the window till we was long past. "It wasn't him," he said firmly. "What would he be doing with a jane like that?"

"A jane like what?"

Paul jutted out his lower teeth, gestured with one hand like he wrapping a turban round his skull.

I smiled. "You get what you pay for, brother."

"Ernst must be on damned poor footing with his pa, if he's paying for *that*."

The trolley stopped, its bell chiming before starting back up. A older jack got on, short, narrow-shouldered and wearing a party badge. We fell silent. Seeing me, his face gone grim, but then his eyes settled on Paul, and he started smiling. Good old Aryan Paul. The jack glanced at his pocket watch as he neared us.

He sat down across from us, his mottled hands resting on his knees. The sun slanted in through the windows behind him so I couldn't no longer see his face.

"If this weather persists, we'll have summer right into November," he said pleasantly.

I ain't said nothing.

After a moment, Paul smiled. "We can only hope so." I could feel him gearing up, gathering his charm. He flashed one of his startling smiles.

"You're not in uniform, son," the jack said.

"Not yet," He give the jack a knowing look.

The man seemed to think about this for a moment. Then he lowered his voice. "What do you know?"

"What have you heard?" Paul asked back.

"It's coming, isn't it?" The man leaned forward, across the aisle. "The horses are gone from the markets. My wife thinks it's nothing. But it's really starting, isn't it?"

"It's always starting," said Paul. "We always have to be prepared."

"The British won't stop it."

"The British are impotent," said Paul.

"Yes," the man said. "Yes."

There was a fleck of parsley in the man's teeth and I stared at it, feeling sort of sick. "We don't start wars," he muttered, "but by the Führer's grace, we finish them."

My mouth had gone dry. I reached up and flagged the next stop. We stood, gripping the brass railing for support. The trolley shook, shuddered to a halt.

"Heil Hitler," the jack said.

"Heil Hitler," said Paul, smiling.

Then we got off and walked the rest of the way to the Hound. Paul was shaking. I thought it must be nerves, but then I glanced at his face. He was furious.

I didn't say nothing. Ernst had secured us brown Aryan identity cards months ago, but we still wasn't comfortable. "Just don't do anything foolish," he done told us. "Don't draw any attention to yourselves. They're good forgeries, but they're not perfect."

So we passed, sure. But there was passing, and there was passing. Sometimes it seemed we'd passed right out of our own skins.

———————— ■ ————————

Ernst's club, the Hound, been shut down for its degenerate sympathies a long time ago. And by "degenerate sympathies," I mean us. It wasn't no dive, not exactly, not yet. Still got running water backstage, tiled floors, grand lighting. Jacks walked up red velvet stairs into a gallery of brass and mirrors. Or used to, when the carpet was still down, before Ernst sold it to keep us in fuel. We didn't care that rats lived in the walls, that the water come out brown some days. For us, for Ernst's Hot-Time Swingers, its stage was our home.

Me and Paul gone in to find the kid already up on the boards, trilling out his scales. Always felt spooky, playing a stripped-down session without Chip. Sure you can be brilliant without the skins, but still, never felt right. It was like waking to find someone had cut you open and yanked out you damn appendix while you was sleeping. Something was *missing*.

Half a hour later we was still up onstage, the kid and me staring over the piano's back at Paul. All three of us in our shirtsleeves, smoking and drinking the czech. The kid kept stopping, gesturing softly at me, counting me in. I finally just stopped, folding my arms over my axe with a sour look.

"Hell, brother, quit that." I wiped a handkerchief along my neck. It was *hot*. "What is you damn problem?"

Hiero looked at Paul, like he half frightened.

"Well, *say* it," I said. "What the trouble?"

The kid shrugged.

"Hiero," said Paul. "What's the problem? Sid's five minutes away from just packing up."

"I'm sorry," he mumbled. "I just tryin to get this line to go *underneath* him."

Paul smiled tiredly. "Sid, this kid's going to be your *death*."

He punched a few low ivories for emphasis.

The kid just stood there, waiting. He snuck a quick look at me.

"Alright, alright," I said. "We goin back to the bridge. You happy?"

The kid looked sheepish.

"You boys go on back," Paul said, lighting a cigarette. "I'll wait for you here."

Son of a bitch. We gone back into it alone, me and Hiero. And this time I *felt* it, I felt the kid sort of getting between my strings and pushing back against them as I walked across. He fixed his eyes hard on me. Then he pursed his lips and blasted back into his end of the song, and we played through the bridge. Paul started tickling his way back in.

But it was a damn strange feeling, the kid making me start again. I didn't like it.

We played on through into the change. Then suddenly the kid lowered his horn again, looking nervous-like out at the darkness.

"What the trouble *now*?" I barked. But then I fell silent.

Someone was clapping out there, the applause slow and loud.

"Ernst?" Paul called out. He pushed back his stool, leaned an elbow on the corner of his upright, shielding his eyes. "That you?"

Ernst come out of the shadows, his cigarette burning so low it like to scorch his fingers. His sleepy eyes look hooded and soft. "Gents, break for a minute. There's someone I'd like you to meet."

A figure come out from behind him and begun snaking between the tables. Man, it was *her*. That jane with the tiny teeth. She was wearing a tall headwrap, a sleek blue dress that poured off her like water. Hell. Tottering on heels high as dinner forks, she look tall and stiff as a birch. Something happened to my breath then, it sort of snagged in my chest. Not that she was beautiful. Her skin was a odd tawny colour, like oats. And she was rope-thin, with one a them stark bodies, like she built of planks nailed together. I could see the bones in her wrists sticking out when she lift up one hand to adjust that thick headwrap.

"You boys don't sound so bad," she said in English. "For a trio of *Germans*."

"Sid's from the States," Ernst murmured.

"Mmm. Of course he is."

Man oh man. That *voice*. It was low-pitched, cozy, full of the dark tones of my old life in Baltimore. I found myself giving her a harder look. That small, high chest. Those plum lips that turned playfully up at the edges. Even her boyish hips. She smiled, and her crooked teeth seemed suddenly sensual.

Ernst put a elegant hand on her elbow, like to guide her forward. "Gents, this is Delilah Brown. She's up from Paris. You'll have to excuse her, she doesn't speak German, but she has a few things she'd like to discuss with us."

Paul run a finger along his thin moustache, watching me. "I bet Sid here could discuss a few things with her."

"In what language?" Hiero smiled slyly.

"In the language of *love*."

"You both asses. Both of you." I cleared my throat, stepped down from the stage. "Miss Brown?" I said. "Sid Griffiths. This is Paul Butterstein. And—"

"Hieronymus Falk," she said. "Yes, I know." She was staring at the kid with this wolfish look. Her eyes was amazing—a weird pale green, translucent almost.

"She likes *you*, buck," said Paul, smiling at the kid.

Hiero dropped his gaze.

She give Ernst a quick glance. "Where are the others? The Hot-Time Swingers had six, didn't it? This isn't all of you?"

I sort of flushed, hearing that. Like we was the *stuff*.

"Where're Chip and Fritz?" said Ernst.

Paul shrugged. "Fritz said he had a meeting. Chip, hell. He's probably sleeping it off somewhere. What's she want, Ernst? Who is she?"

"They said they'd meet us later," said the kid, his voice shaking a little. "At the baths."

"First, sit," said Ernst. And then in English, "Please sit, sit." He pulled out a chair, and the jane sat at one of the blue-clothed tables under the stage. "What can we offer you? I'm afraid all we have is the czech."

She glanced across at Paul, who was rummaging at the bar. "The czech?"

Paul was already returning with a cloudy bottle gripped in one fist, five shot glasses pinched in the fingers of his other hand. He held the czech up to the light, shook it. Then he poured out a finger for each of us, set our thimbles down with a soft click. He poured one for her, too.

She held the liquid up to the dim light, her brow wrinkling. "You're kidding. You drink this stuff?"

Ernst smiled. "Chip sometimes inhales it. But generally, yes."

I smiled, took a sour swipe of it. Felt like gasoline scraping out my throat.

The kid turned his thimble in his long fingers.

"It ain't really Czechoslovakian," I said, coughing. "We used to call it the *Cheque*. Like, you drink it up now, you pay for it later."

"When the cheque comes, you pay," Ernst smiled. He put his shot back with a elegant shiver. "Go on." He gestured at her thimble.

"Hieronymus hasn't touched his," she said suspiciously.

"She says you drink like a girl," I said.

The kid ain't reacted, just looked at her.

"Go on," Ernst said again.

She lifted her thimble, give a sly little nod at the kid, punched it back.

We all watched her face.

She opened her eyes. "Jesus," she croaked. Her lips twist up, and she give a soft little shudder. We all started laughing. "That's even worse than it looks. No wonder Hitler's so angry, if he's drinking *this*."

There was water coming from her eyes.

It *was* damn wretched, that czech. I bet it ain't even legal in half the states back home. The kid, he start laughing that high, broken, hiccuping laugh of his. Then he give her a startled look from under his hat brim.

But that jane just leaned forward, the low lights catching the ghostly rye of her skin, and all at once I seen it clearly. This girl was high yella, like me. A *Mischling*, a half-blood. She got the kind of mixed-race face only a keen eye can see.

"Boys," she said, crossing one long leg over the other. I watched that blue hemline inch up, felt myself flush. "Boys, I'd like to invite you to Paris. To cut a record. We're looking for exactly what you've got."

Ernst said in German, "She wants us to go to Paris. To cut the wax."

"Paris," Paul repeated, frowning.

I was still staring at her slash of pale thigh when, glancing at her face, I seen she was watching me. I blushed. "You in the *business*?" I said. But it come out sounding sort of lewd.

There was a flash of impatience in her eyes. "I'm Delilah *Brown*."

"Oh," I said. "Of course."

"The *singer*," she said after a moment. "*Black-eyed Blues? Dark Train Song?*"

I was nodding hard. "Sure. Of course. Delilah *Brown*."

But I glanced over at Ernst, like to see if she was joking. Ain't no singer I ever heard of.

"She represents Louis Armstrong," said Ernst.

Hell. Now *that* we understood. Our whole table fell silent.

"What she want?" the kid said at last. His voice was real soft. "She a agent?"

"You his agent?" I said to her.

"No."

Paul brushed a golden lock back from his forehead, fixed his clear blue eyes on Ernst. "What are we talking about? She means Armstrong the horn blower? For real?"

I shook my head. "No. She mean Armstrong the *court jester*."

"That was Archy Armstrong," Ernst said distractedly. "And yes. It seems she's for real."

I looked at him. "There a jester named Armstrong? Really?"

He nodded. "King James the First."

"Hell."

That jane just watched us, not understanding a word. I guess she must have thought we was discussing her proposal, by the severe set of her jaw. "Well? What is it?"

At last Ernst give her a long, slow look. "You're asking us to leave our lives, Miss Brown. It's a difficult choice. If we go to Paris, we won't be coming back."

Her face tightened. "With all due respect, Mr. von Haselberg. If you don't go now, you won't have lives to leave. You're drowning here, we both can see it." She give a faint smile, like to soften her words.

Ernst brushed a fleck from his trousers. "We're surviving."

"But not *living*. You know the difference. You don't need to decide now, of course. But I'm offering you a chance to *live* again, to play your music. To walk the streets of a city not afraid of being arrested. Or worse, for god's sake. Berlin is like a locked room to you boys. I'm offering you a way *out*."

I barely caught all that. I was still looking at her thigh.

———————————— ▬ ————————————

Jazz. Here in Germany it become something worse than a virus. We was all of us damn fleas, us Negroes and Jews and low-life hoodlums, set on playing that vulgar racket, seducing sweet blond kids into corruption and sex. It wasn't a music, it wasn't a fad. It was a plague sent out by the dread black hordes, engineered by the Jews. Us Negroes, see, we was only half to blame—we just can't help it. Savages just got a natural feel for filthy rhythms, no self-control to speak of. But the Jews, brother, now *they* cooked up this jungle music on *purpose*. All part of their master plan to weaken Aryan youth, corrupt its janes, dilute its bloodlines.

We lived with that for ten damn years. Through the establishment of old Joe Goebbel's Reichsmusikkamer, his insistence that all musicians "register." Through that ugly Düsseldorf exhibit last spring. Hell, let me help you picture it. Take '37's Degenerate Art soiree in Munich, replace the paintings with posters of jungle minstrels squawking on their saxes, and flood the rooms with beautiful music, and you got the idea. We was officially degenerate.

And like a shadow running beneath all that, there was gates scrubbing cobblestones with rags, gates getting truncheoned just for sitting in a damn café, gates reduced to eating from backstreet garbage bins. And the poor damn Jews, clubbed to a pulp in the streets, their shopfronts smashed up, their axes ripped from their hands. Hell. When that old ivory-tickler Volker Schramm denounced his manager Martin Miller as a false Aryan, we known Berlin wasn't Berlin no more. It been a damn savage decade.

So, yes, Paris sounded pretty tempting.

Problem was the papers. Wasn't no way folks like us was getting the right papers to go to Paris. It ain't been possible for years now.

Don't get me wrong—I loved Berlin. I ain't saying otherwise. And for a while the Housepainter didn't even seem as bad as old Jim Crow. Least here in Europe a jack felt a little loved for his art—even if it was a secret love, a quick grope in the shadows when no one was looking. I ain't took it personal. Truth was, I didn't look all that black, and to those who suspected the truth, well, congratulations. Pour youself a drink.

Cause blacks just wasn't no kind of priority back in those years. I guess there just wasn't enough of us.

———— ▪ ————

The Jewish baths was half falling down, half broken, most of the pools already closed to the public. But it was the only baths some of us still legally allowed to use, and sometimes a jack just ache for the fragrance of boiled stones, for the hot and freezing waters. The clear green pools sunken like craters in the earth. We'd just put our heads back and glide, naked as the day we was born.

Chip and Fritz was waiting for us in the changing room. Chip had his shoes off, stood wriggling his damn toes on the stone floor.

"You ain't gone in yet?" I called. "We reckoned we smelled you from the street."

"You smellin Fritz, maybe," said Chip. He lift up his chin, waft the air from under it. "Unless you smellin Dr McMorran's Special No. 9."

Paul sniffed the air. "What is that? A cough syrup?"

"It medicine alright," I said. "For head cases."

"It's the scent drive the ladies *wild*," said Chip.

"It the scent drive the ladies out the *room*," I whispered to the kid.

Hiero grinned, thrilled to be in on the teasing.

Big Fritz sat slumped on the hard wooden bench, huge, flushed and tired-looking. He was a massive Bavarian, with thick fingers, straw-like hair, and a strong, hawkish nose. He was broad as a damn trolley to boot. He lumbered upright, breathing heavily in that hot change room.

"You alright, Fritz?" said Ernst, coming over. He set his hat down gentle on the bench, begun untying his laces.

Fritz waved one hairy hand. "I'm fine. Just worn out." His low voice boomed throughout the room—you almost felt the rafters shuddering. He blinked his slow lids, the sweat shining on his hairline.

"Old Fritz ain't built for the heat," said Chip, smiling.

"Not like you jungle monkeys," said Fritz.

Hiero give him a uneasy look.

I grimaced, even though I known he only joking. It was just his way. Fritz was rough at times, sure, but he ain't meant nothing by it.

Chip asked Paul bout his two janes. Paul been running with two ladies for a month now, sometimes slipping away from one to be with the other in the same damn *night*. One evening, he was even on a date with both of them in the same *restaurant*. And neither found it out. Chip said it was his piano hands—one ain't never doing the same thing as the other. Hell. I thought Paul got to be near exhaustion. Chip thought he was a beautiful son of a bitch. The kid, well, I think he was just a little frightened by it all.

"You're going to have to choose sooner or later," said Ernst. "If only to keep yourself from collapsing."

"Chip doesn't think so," Paul smiled. "He thinks I should introduce Marta and Inge to each other. See what comes of it."

I laughed. "Marta's a tasty little dish alright. But you be a damn fool you risk losin Inge. Girl got a chassis like, well, hell." I held out my arms like to measure a iron boiler. "Brother, you got to pull back you own eyelids just to get it all in *view*."

"I still ain't clear on why you got to *choose*, buck," Chip said.

Fritz chuckled, his enormous red cheeks juddering away. But it seem to me his eyes looked small, hard.

"What you think, kid?" said Chip. "Inge?"

Hiero shrugged shyly.

"Speak up, brother."

"Marta," the kid said, reluctant. Then he blushed. "Or Inge. Aw, they both nice."

Chip peeled off his trousers. He stood with one foot propped on the bench, his hairy bits swaying like a bell. "Marta!" he laughed. "Hell, brother, there ain't nothin on the front, and too much in the back."

"She got a nice smile," said the kid, trying not to look Chip's way.

"Old Inge, though." Chip grinned. "She get you hot behind the ears just by takin a breath. She make you *motor* smoke."

"You're making *my* motor smoke, buck," Paul called across. "Put on a towel, or come on over here and give us a kiss."

"The towel, *please*," said Fritz.

Chip ignored them. "Nice smile won't pick the locks, brother." He was leaning forward and I swear he *liked* his old calabash clapping there. "A nice smile won't get you any nearer the treasure at all. Less it's one hell of a smile. Like old Mona Lisa. Now there's a attractive jane— she got *mystery*."

Ernst hung his tie over the door of the locker. He turned, give old Chip a long appraising look. "Charles C. Jones," he said with a slow smile. He unfastened his cufflinks. "Every so often you say something absolutely astonishing."

Chip chuckled. "Sure. Wouldn't kick old Mona out of bed. She ain't got no eyebrows—ain't you curious where else the hair's missin?"

Ernst blinked. "Every so often," he said, shaking his old head. "And then you just keep on talking."

I twisted out my shirt without even bothering with the buttons, kicked free my damn drawers. I looked up to find Hiero staring at me.

"You just ain't my plate of steak, buck," I said. "Don't you get no ideas now."

Chip looked up, smiled. "Hell, Sid, you got to do more sport. I seen better legs on a Georgia chicken."

I swiped at him with my towel. And then we was running through the long corridor where the older gents lounged on benches, wrapped in sheets like they ready for burial. Wet stones slapping under our feet. We run howling past two wrinkled old jacks leaning in robes over a chess set, the mulchy smell of their wet skin, their damp towels coming off them. And then we was out, running in the dimly-lit caverns of the bathhouse, its cathedral ceilings vanishing overhead in shadows and steam. Huge and vaulted like a opera house, with its haunting acoustics, its crumbling arched galleries along the walls.

Old Chip run straight for the far pool and leapt, smacking the water with his belly.

"Hell, brother," I said, laughing. "You must have a stomach of stone."

"Man, that *hurt*," said Chip, grinning. He shot a long stream of water through his foreteeth.

I crouched down, slipped in. Our voices echoed back to us off the walls. Around us the steam rose in panes, distorting everything, making it shimmer. Felt like you was standing in a autumn field, trying to see through thick fog.

The others come out slow like, Ernst dropping his towel from his soft waist and wading in, gleaming pale and waxy. Paul, he stood like a crane on one leg before putting both feet down. Fritz's enormous gut, already red from the heat, just grown pinker and pinker, and he heaved it in both his hands as he come down into the water, his cock like a red slug under it.

Ernst splashed across to the wall. "Where's Hiero?" He wiped the water from his face.

"Aw, he just bein shy," I said.

"He all anyone care bout?" said Chip.

"He's probably going through Chip's wallet for his middle name," called Paul through the steam.

"I'll give you a middle name," said Chip. "And by middle name I mean a kick in the teeth."

Big Fritz coughed, his grunts rumbling off the walls.

And then the kid come in, clutching his towel against him. His skin look real dark against the white cloth, his skinny chest heaving a little with his breathing. Kid seemed nervous as hell, but wasn't no reason for it. I felt bad, seeing him like that.

"We just talkin bout you, kid," called Chip.

Hiero waded in, looking alarmed.

"We was wonderin if you black *all* the way down."

"You need to learn which hole the shit's *supposed* to come out of, Chip," Paul called across.

Hiero glanced over at Paul. All a sudden he laughed.

"Aw, you think he funny?" said Chip, smiling. He splashed on over to the kid, set both muscular arms over his narrow head, dunked the kid in a single violent thrashing of foam. Kid's body look like windblown ashes under that water. "Keep on laughin, buck," Chip hollered. "You still laughin?"

"Chip," I called. "Stop that."

"That's enough," said Fritz. He reached across, and gripping Chip's underarms, dragged him off the kid like he lifting nothing heavier than a sandwich. Chip squirmed against Fritz's belly. "Leave him alone, now. You're too rough with him."

I swear, the damn rafters shuddered, Fritz's low voice echoing.

A rise of water surged back, and the kid shot up, coughing and spitting snot. He shook his head to clear the water. Smiling in a way supposed to be casual, he looked embarrassed, terrified and angry.

Chip was struggling in that massive grip, making a disgusted face. "Hell, I can feel how happy you is to see me," he hollered. "Get *off*, get *off*."

"You sure that what you want, buck?" I laughed.

But Fritz let him go, and he splashed out of reach at once. "You be careful, brother," he called. "I like to slap you face, if I could just figure out which side of you to start climbing."

Ernst stood abruptly at the edge of the pool, a great wave of water slapping his pale chest. His deep black hair was slicked back. "So let's talk about it. Do we go or not?"

"To Paris?" Paul called out. "Of course we go. Why wouldn't we?"

Chip and Fritz both glanced from Paul to Ernst and back to Paul.

"Do you know what they're talking about?" said Fritz.

Chip shrugged.

"We have an offer, gentlemen," said Ernst. "A lady came by today to ask if we're interested in cutting a record with Louis Armstrong."

Chip give a low whistle.

"What did you tell her?" said Fritz.

"That we needed to discuss it. What else would I tell her?"

Chip grunted, splashed in the steam. "I can't believe you even *askin.*"

"Is that a no, Jones?"

"It a *yes,*" he said. "And I addin a *hell yes* on top of it. Paris? Armstrong?"

Big Fritz frowned. He loomed up out of the steam like a dark boulder. "How do we know this is real? Who is she? She could be anybody."

I chuckled. "What you think, brother. You think Boots goin take the trouble to *trick* us into goin to Paris? You thinkin that more *likely?*"

Fritz ain't said nothing, just shifted massively in the water.

"She's with Armstrong, Fritz," said Ernst. With his slicked hair lifting up, spiking in all that steam, he looked like a fiercer version of hisself. He stretched out his long blue arms along the wall, let his ghostly legs drift up, tilting his face back to stare at the ceiling. "I have no doubts that she is who she says she is. That's not the question here."

Fritz was still frowning. "She came down here to find *us?* She came to Berlin for *us?* With the Führer going on the way he is?"

"You mean the Housepainter," I said.

Fritz give me a look.

"She's not here for us," said Ernst. "She's down here to collect some money owing to Armstrong. We're just the butter."

"I think you mean the cream," said Paul. He floated lazily over toward Fritz. "Listen, Fritz, Armstrong's a fan. He's got our records."

"Which records?"

"Do it matter?" I said.

"We didn't ask," said Paul. "She said Arthur Briggs caught some of our shows a few years ago. And Bechet told Louis how fine we sounded when we opened for him back at Vaterland."

"Bechet?" Chip grimaced. "Hell. He still owe me fifty bucks."

"She sort of acts as Armstrong's manager in Paris," said Ernst. "I don't know. Sorts out his affairs, I guess."

"*Affairs*," whispered Chip.

Paul grinned, the tip of his tongue peeking between his teeth.

"What are you, ten years old?" Ernst frowned. "I guess Armstrong's been following us for years. When he heard we were still here, and not playing live anymore, I guess he thought maybe there'd be some incentive for us to come on over."

"What Ernst ain't tellin you," I said, "is what all she said bout the kid. Armstrong wants to play with the kid *especially*. Rumour is he the best damn horn blower this side the Atlantic. Some sayin he even better than Briggs. Henry Crowder said that. Crowder told Armstrong Hiero reminded him of King Oliver in his prime."

I don't know, I guess I reckoned we'd all start to joke about that. But ain't nobody smile at all.

"So do he even want us?" said Chip. "Or it just the kid he want?"

"She said he wanted to play with the Hot-Time Swingers," Hiero said nervously. "She said all of us."

Fritz looked over at me.

I shrugged. "She *said* that, sure."

"She called us *iconoclasts*," said Paul.

"And you ain't slapped her?" Chip smiled. "Usin language like that in front of the kid?"

"What does it pay?" said Fritz in his blunt way.

Ernst lift up his head. "What does it *pay*?"

"Hell, brother, ain't no way it goin pay less than what we makin now."

"Sid's got a point," said Paul.

"A little one, maybe," said Chip, splashing water my way. "At least, that what all the ladies say."

"Haw haw," I said.

We was silent then, all of us adrift in the warm blue light. The water sloshed against the stone walls, the soft murmur echoing high up in the ceiling.

There was a thin cough. Then the kid stood, water streaming off his bony chest. "I think we should go," he said softly. His upper lip was trembling.

"We just got here," said Paul.

"I think he means to Paris," said Ernst.

Hiero looked embarrassed, dipped back into the water.

"You think we should go?" said Chip. "You think we should go to Paris, get away from the Housepainter? You think Armstrong enough of a reason? You reckon walkin about the streets of you own damn city without bein afraid you goin get killed or disappeared be worth it? You think so?"

Hiero looked direct at Chip. "Yes," he said simply.

"Aw, kid." Chip laughed. "You priceless. *Course* it is."

"The problem," said Ernst, "is *how*, exactly."

"Slow down," said Fritz. He sounded almost angry. "I'm not convinced. I'm sorry, gents." He waded over to the shallow end, sat on the low steps, the water spilling over the walls of his thighs as he leaned on his knees. The hairs on his chest was plastered in a thick gluey rug. "I'm sorry," he said again. "But I won't jump just because she says it's time to jump."

"It's alright," said Ernst. "We're only discussing here."

"It's *Paris*, buck," said Chip. "Hell."

"Where would we stay?" said Fritz. "How long would we go for?"

Ernst shook his head. "I don't know. I don't have all the answers. I don't even know that we could go right away. We'd need visas."

"Give him a hour or so," said Chip. "Ernst always come up with something."

"Louis' jane goin be here through the week," I said. "We ain't got to decide nothin now."

"Good."

Ernst cleared his throat. "Alright, then?"

"Alright."

But something in Fritz's hesitation given us all pause, darkened the very waters we was floating in. Hell. We grown quiet then, and just splashed softly for a time. Finally Ernst cleared his throat, and with a old sadness in him, said, "Well, gents. I suppose I'll be getting back to the Hound."

"Working late again? I can't understand why you still write those articles, buck," said Paul. "No one gives a damn about jazz anymore."

Ernst paused. "I do." He climbed gleaming white from that water like it done leeched all the blood from him.

———————— ■ ————————

We ain't stayed long after that.

Outside, under the gas lamps, the square in front of the baths glowed like talcum. Folks strode dumb through the gloom. Back of my neck was still wet and I could feel the cool air across it. Chip give me a soft punch on the shoulder.

"Let's ankle, buck." He sounded gloomy.

I felt it too. I nodded.

The roads was dark. We kept our heads down, shoved our hands all up in our pockets, our hair damp in the night air. We walked slow, like we dreaded getting back. We could see Fritz, the kid and Paul some feet ahead in the darkness, and then they vanished in the shadows and we couldn't see them no more.

I always adored Berlin at this hour—the stillness, the way the shadows crowded the shop windows. We passed a toy store with swastika balls in the window, a butcher's with the iron gate dragged down. There was a thin silt on the air, a taste like dirt, and I snorted to get it out my nose. Then we heard the clatter of sharp voices, and down one hazy road we seen street crews at work in the dim light. Young urchins clutching steaming black pitchers, pouring tar between the uneven cobblestones. Vapour rising from the lines. Men in thick coveralls wiping the grime from their faces.

We slipped back into shadow, took another route.

I got to thinking how small we come to be these last months, me and Chip. Even two years ago, we like to holler through these damn streets like we on parade. Now we slunk in the shadows, squeamish of the light. I thought of the two of us listening to Armstrong's records back in Baltimore when we was kids. And I thought of my ma's family back in Virginia, fair as Frenchmen and floating like ghosts through a white world. Afraid of being seen for what they truly was.

Then we heard it. A sort of high-pitched screech. It come gusting past us like a dark wind.

Chip gripped my sleeve. "That wasn't Hiero?"

I listened for something more. Nothing.

"Hell," Chip hissed.

And then we was both running.

We come round the corner breathing hard, and I stopped. Everything slowed right down. Under the faint lamps of our building, in the middle of that alley, three Boots got the kid by his hair, like they hauling a steer by the horns. Trying to drag him off his feet. But somehow the kid ain't gone down, he just flung about like trash in the wind. A fourth bastard, tall and thick through the neck, was holding Paul by the throat. My stomach lurched, the sick inching up. Felt like a light was going out in me.

"Chip," I hissed. "Holy hell."

He already taken off his hat, was wriggling out of his jacket. He strode right on up to the nearest Boot, and leaning down low, kicked the bastard's left knee in. There was a curious crunching sound, then a high ugly squeal. And then Chip start to kicking him in the throat where he lay writhing. A second Boot turned, swung back, cracked a bottle over Chip's head. Old Jones gone down clutching his skull.

"Goddamnit," I hissed.

"Jewkikes!" the Boot start hollering. "Jewfuckers! Nigger kikes!"

I waded on in. In a flash I seen the shadows under the far building stir, begin to heave, and it was like the whole damn doorway just shuddered on out: Big Fritz. He seized the Boot brawling with Paul by the back of the neck. Lifting him clean off his feet, he thrown him down on the cobblestones like a sack of meat. Started stomping him shitless.

I was punching that son of a bitch with the bottle hard in the teeth, his face twisting up. I kept trying to get hold of his collar but he kept slipping away from me, spitting blood, clawing at my damn cheeks, at my ears. "Where's your racial pride," he screamed. His mouth was like a torn hole, filling with blood. "Niggerfucker! Niggerfucker niggerfucker niggerfucker!"

His eyes was jagged glass in the weak light.

I hit him again. And again. Then something struck me sharp in the ribs and I fell in a rush, trying to twist away from the damn boot heels I known was coming. I could hear the kid screaming, just screaming and screaming. No kicks come. I winced, glanced up. Big Fritz was standing over me, shuddering.

"Fritz you sweet son of a bitch," I shouted. "You fightin like a *bastard.*"

But when he turned his face I seen he was crying.

Footsteps echoed from far off in the dark alley. I stumbled up, groaning. I wasn't thinking clear. Three more Boots was coming hard at us, all plain-dressed but for the damn jackboots under their long pants.

I was moving slow now. I swung clumsily and missed. Got slammed in the gut once, then again. But I got a good knuckle up under the jaw and that damn Boot fell to a knee. Hell. But now the first bastard was back up and I hit him hard as I could in his face, feeling something crack wetly under my fist.

When I turned round I seen Fritz lurching after two of them, as they gone running back down into darkness. There was two Boots just writhing on the cobblestones, whimpering horribly. I just wasn't able to catch my breath, and kept bending low, gasping, spitting up some of what I et earlier. Wheezing and wheezing.

There was a low scuffling in the doorway to our building and when I lift up my head I seen the glint of it first. That broken bottle. Held to the kid's throat. "I know this Jewfucker," the Boot yelled. "You're the fuck who fronts that jazz band, that fucking nigger music. I'm going to gut you. I'm going to gut you."

But he was looking at Chip, weaving unsteadily in front of him. There was blood all down the back of Chip's shirt, like a sticky black apron. Then old Jones was crouching, like to find his balance. I blinked, wiped blood from my eyes. Then the kid was crawling away, and Chip and that Boot was punching each other against the walls of the doorway, and then all a sudden Chip was standing over the Boot and the Boot was lying across the stoop, his head lolling in the gutter.

Something black seeped from the Boot's chest, a long wet stain on the stones.

"Chip," I hissed. "We got to go."

Chip ain't moved.

Fritz was holding Paul under one arm, pulling the kid to his feet with the other. He give me a sharp look. "Sid," he called out. "Let's *go*."

"I know. *Chip*," I said quietly. I gone over to him. "We got to go *now*."

He was still holding the neck of that bottle in his fist. I watched the blood ooze out from under the Boot's body, glowing blacker than pitch, like some terrible dark maw been opened in the pavement, a portal going down.

"*Chip*," I said again.

He finally turned. We run.

II

"They goin be comin for us," said Chip. Wincing, he twisted around, glowering up at Fritz. "Hell, brother, you diggin to China or what?"

Frowning, Big Fritz leaned back from Chip's scalp, a shard of black glass in one palm. His huge fingers poised delicately on the tweezers.

"So what you sayin, buck?" I said.

Paul was holding a wet cloth to his cheekbone, where a violent red welt was rising. "He's saying we have to stay here," he muttered through the rag. "He's saying he hopes you sleep alright on the floor."

The kid sat picking at his hands, saying nothing.

I shifted on my seat, trying to breathe better. My ribs was damn sore. The Hound felt dark, utterly silent round us. We ain't known where else to go.

We sat in darkness at the edge of the dance floor, the stage in shadow behind us, the sole light shining down from Ernst's office over the alcove where the bar was. His door stood open up there, the light spilling out in a tan shaft over the stairs. Ernst sat smoking in silence at the table beside ours.

There was a quiet click as Fritz dropped the shard into a dish.

"They goin use this as a excuse," said Chip.

"Excuse for what?"

"For anythin. Beatin up folk. Arrestin gates. Who knows."

Fritz frowned. "It might not be so bad as all that. There are still laws. They don't just break them, not any more."

I shook my head. "What country you been livin in? That exactly what they do."

Chip sucked his teeth. "*Hell*, Fritz. Go *gentle*."

Fritz grunted.

There was another click of broken glass.

Ernst sat at a angle in his chair, one knee folded over the other, a cig flaring and dying out in his pale fingers. When he finally spoke, it was softly, with measure. "Chip's right. We should stay here until we can figure something out."

"Guess we ain't stickin round Berlin after all," I said to Fritz. "Better pack you spare undershorts. How you say, *Mr Armstrong you got mighty handsome calves* in French?"

"You find this amusing, Sid?" said Fritz.

"I ain't laughin, buck," I said. "It hurt too damn much to laugh."

"Hiero?" Paul said then. He leaned across, dipped his chin to get a look at the kid. "You alright?

The kid was trembling light and fast. He glanced at Paul, glanced away.

"Aw, he fine. Just dreamin of Paris."

"Course he fine," said Chip. "Kid ain't got a mark on him. Jesus *hell*, Fritz. I ain't a slab of wurst."

Fritz gestured with his free hand, then set his huge palm on Chip's scalp, angling it into the light. "None of you find it peculiar, this woman showing up with her ridiculous offer the very night we get attacked? How long have we been living here? And how many incidents have we had?"

"You reachin now, brother."

Ernst shifted in his chair. "What do you know that we don't, Fritz?"

Fritz pressed his lips tight together.

"Fritz?"

"Nothing. But I know a bad feeling when it comes."

"Alright, that's enough," yelled Chip, banging a raw hand on the table. A glass clattered. "Ain't no one sayin nothin more to Fritz until he done workin on my damn head. Alright?"

"I don't know about Paris," said Ernst. "But we can't stay in Berlin. Not now."

Fritz looked across at Ernst. "This will pass. It will."

Ernst stood, frowning. "Well. For now, you'll stay here at the Hound. At least until we find out how serious this is. Maybe the boy didn't die. Maybe no one recognized you."

"They recognized us," I said.

"You don't know that," said Fritz. "Not for sure."

"There ain't three jacks in the whole damn city you size, Fritz. Never mind takin a stroll at midnight with a couple a black gents. They known us. For sure."

That night we slept rumpled and sore in our clothes. With the club's long, narrow shape, its one strangely angled wall, felt like we was in the hold of a ship. Or maybe it was just that old sofa I was stretched out on, its cushions slanting badly. Room was lined with old chairs, a long mirror across the far wall, a mash of chipped tables set end to end. A huge copper sink like a old kettle drum stood in one corner, catching the tracelights reflected by the mirror. A high, barred window been covered with a gold curtain, but streetlight still spilled whitely through its seams.

I was roused by a steady tapping on my foot. Slowly opening my eyes, I thought, Hell. Delilah Brown was standing over me, nudging me with the toe of her high heel. Decked out in a white skirt and a white blouse and with a white headwrap twisted like gauze round her head. She held a paper sack in the elbow of one arm.

"You look awful," she said.

"Morning," I muttered, closing my eyes again. Breathing *hurt*, brother.

Paul lift up his head from under the far table, his oiled yellow hair flying at weird angles. "Mmm. I know that voice."

Hiero was still snoring away in the big armchair beside the mirror.

"Sid, where's Ernst?" Delilah ask more softly, like not to wake no one else. She crouched down in that tight skirt, her knees pressed hard together.

I wasn't thinking clear.

"Ernst," she said again. "Where is he?"

"He ain't here?" I blinked, glancing sleepily at Paul. In German I said, "Brother, where Ernst get to last night?"

Paul's voice sounded thick. "Maybe he went back to his flat. I think he said it was safer. It'd look too damn strange, him not going home." He ran a scarred hand through his hair, and sat up spastically, like a marionette. He stretched his stiff neck. The bruise on his cheek just made him look more rugged, more chiselled, like a debonair Bogart. The bastard ain't even able to get beat up without looking good.

I grimaced, rubbed my sore ribs. "So *he* get to sleep in a bed? Hell."

There was a clatter in the doorway, and Chip come in. He got a big white bandage wrapped round his head. "Ernst in his office," he grunted in German. He looked at Delilah. "You lookin for Ernst, girl?"

She looked at me. "What did he say?"

But his face was so swollen, so cut up, I started grinning and didn't translate. He look like a plate of mashed black beans, trying to talk.

"What you smilin at," said Chip. "You seen you own face, buck?"

"Sid wasn't hit in the face," Paul mumbled.

"You sure?" Chip paused, looking Delilah up and down. He switch over to English. "What, the whole damn circus in town?"

"It seems so," she said, looking *him* up and down. "Mr. Jones, I suppose?"

He started to smile then stopped, grimacing in pain. "Charles C. The gents call me Chip. But you can call me anytime, day or night."

"Charming."

"Aw, you got to excuse him," I said. "He got hit on the head awful hard."

"She ain't goin be worried bout *that* part my anatomy," he said in German, smiling.

Paul snorted. He gestured at Delilah's white headwrap, at Chip's bandaged scalp. "All you two need is a camel."

Delilah ain't understood the German, but she got the gist of it. "You can tell Mr. Jones I have some extra skirts too, if he'd like," she said curtly.

"Oh, he be interested. Chip look real cute in a skirt."

Chip come all the way into the room then, kicking the kid's armchair so that he like to fall out of it. "Rise and shine, brother," he hollered. "It a new day."

"Let him sleep, buck," I said.

But the kid was already opening his frightened eyes, staring at Delilah where she crouched beside me. She give him a wink. Flustered, he looked quickly away. Seeing his discomfort, the brutality of last night come back in a rush. I sat up, rubbed my face.

"So you the *famous* Delilah Brown," said Chip. He sat on the far sofa, propped his feet up one at a time on the stained coffee table, crossing his ankles. "All the talk since yesterday been bout the *famous* Delilah Brown. Famous Delilah Brown the singer."

A faint frown flickered across her face.

"Chip," I said uneasily.

"Anytime you're done," she said, "you just let me know."

"Aw, I just gettin started, girl," Chip grinned. "When I done, you be seein the back of my head."

"Hope it's better than the front."

I laughed.

I felt Chip's rocklike eyes on me, his sudden irritation so intense felt like webs on my skin. My heart tripped in my chest. I glanced at Delilah but she wasn't looking at neither of us no more. She was watching Hiero.

Chip gestured at the rolled paper bag she was still holding. "What you got there, Famous Delilah Brown? You got some fuel for our old engines?"

She ain't said nothing for a long moment, just studied Chip with her hard green eyes. Then she smiled. I could see her crooked little teeth. "You and me, Charles," she said, "we're going to get along just fine. I can see it already."

Old Chip wasn't sure just how to respond to that.

She opened up the brown bag, pulled out a folded morning paper, six marzipan croissants.

"Now you on the trolley," said Chip, smiling. "How'd you know we was—"

"Your saxophonist. Fritz. I met him coming out of the club this morning. He told me about last night. He said maybe you might want something to eat other than salted peanuts." She was staring across at the kid. He stood at the sink, turning on the old spigot and waiting for the brown water to run through. He start to washing his face, his arms, the water shining like beaten silver on his dark skin. "Is he alright?"

"Hiero?" said Chip. "He fine. The damn Boots beat him with *feathers*."

Delilah looked unconvinced. My old ribs started aching all over again.

"Wait—you said you run into Fritz?" I said. "Where was he goin?"

But maybe she ain't heard me.

Chip was already tearing apart one croissant with his fingers, stuffing the flaking pastry into his mouth. Paul grinned at me, gleefully showing off his bread-filled teeth. He reached for the morning paper and begun pulling it to pieces, scouring it for some word.

"I always hungrier when I ain't slept," said Chip. "Is that strange?"

"No," said Paul.

"Why ain't you slept?" I said. "What you doin awake so early?"

"What you jacks doin *asleep* be the question. Ain't that damn cat kept none of you up?"

Hiero was drying hisself with his own shirt. He turned shyly. "Cat?"

"Did I stutter, buck?"

"Did he say cat?" Paul said to me. "Cat?"

"Cat," I nodded.

Chip stared from one to the other like we was all off our nuts. "Cat. C-A-T, Cat. That damn squawlin in the damn walls from that damn feline bastard all the damn night. It ain't kept you up?"

I started to laugh. "How hard you get hit in the head?"

"Jesus, brother. It ain't shut its damn yap all night. Felt like I was sleepin in a music hall, all that wailin."

"Keep drinkin that czech, brother."

"I heard it," Hiero said quietly.

Paul raised an eyebrow over the top edge of his newspaper.

"Every damn jack in a six-block radius like to have heard it," said Chip.

Paul smiled. "I guess Armstrong's girl's not the only singer around here."

"Come to think of it," Chip said with a grin, "it sound a bit like her. She say where she slept last night?"

"Dame Delilah the Second," Hiero murmured. "She just keepin us company."

"Dame Delilah the Second, is right," laughed Chip. "Ain't no one like to get no sleep at all round here now."

Delilah cleared her throat, turning at each mention of her name. "I'm standing right here," she said, frowning. She folded one brace-leted wrist at her hip.

"Aw, we ain't makin fun," I said in English.

"It complimentary," Chip grinned.

"Mmm. I'm sure it is. Ernst is in his office?" But she was watching the kid as he picked up his horn, fiddled nervously with the plugs. I could see he was trying to look anywhere but at her. Hell.

"Ten-pfennig socks at KaDeWe," muttered Paul. "I guess we're going to miss out on those." He turned the crinkled page.

"You find anythin bout last night?" said the kid in his soft way. His eyes flicked over to Delilah, back to Paul.

"I'm looking, I'm looking," said Paul distractedly.

"You reckon that be good news?" said Chip.

I shrugged. "I don't reckon it means nothin. What it say bout Poland?"

Paul shook his head. "This is just the neighborhood rag, buck. It won't give you any news you haven't already heard elsewhere. You know that." He kept turning the pages. "Fritz would be delighted. The heart of commerce just keeps on beating."

"Go on, Socrates. What else you got?"

Hiero lift up his head, staring with sudden intensity at the paper. He blinked twice, rapidly. Then he reached across, tore a strip off the back page. Paul pull back fast, annoyed, but the kid ain't said nothing.

"What you got there?" said Chip. "Hey, *answer* me, buck. Don't make me come over there and take it off you."

Hiero looked around, nervous. In that thin reedy voice of his, he said, "Albert Basel reviews the Golden Seven in here. Listen. *Never have I heard a more loathsome example of noble men trying to embody something base. The Golden Seven is a parody of negroid drum rhythms that ends in being more despicable than Chicago jazz itself.*"

Chip whooped. "Old Goebbels startin to knock down his own damn walls. What he doin, gettin Albie review the Seven? He off his nut?"

"You got to ask that?" I said. "For real?"

"Goddamn Albie," he muttered.

Albert Basel, see, he was this critic down from Leipzig, a born-again Boot whose pen was, as Chip put it, a inch-and-a-half bigger than his sword. It so happened that in '29, he wasn't able to get enough of us. Savoured us like a fine Merlot. Wrote article after article bout "German jazz's ingeniously complex rhythms." That was me and Chip he talking bout, we his particular favourites. Then come '33. Seeing his teaching days at the Leipzig Conservatory done for, he suddenly change his suit. I remember the first day I seen him in the street and he just cross to the other side, like he ain't heard me hollering at him. We was "aural vermin" after that, "Jewish-Hottentot frivolity."

Chip ain't never forgive the son of a bitch.

But it ain't made no sense, his reviewing the Golden Seven. Cause the Seven be old Goebbels' answer to folks' hunger for jazz. See, the music refused to die. Never mind the Swing Boys up Hamburg way. There was still jacks who known their Whiteman from their Ellington. And they still hankered to swing. The wireless done totally ban jazz, sure, but Joey Goebbels was shrewd enough to offer a alternative. And the Seven was that damn alternative. Like replacing sugar with salt. Staffed with half-rates like Franz Thon, Kurt Hohenberger and Erhard Krause, they played from—holy hell, wait for it—*sheet music.*

"What else he say, kid?" I asked.

The kid turned, staring at the doorway.

I looked up. Ernst was glaring at us, his pale face blurred in the half light. He worn a plain black suit, and with his black hair and coal-dark eyes he look fearsome. "Who isn't here?" he said sharply.

Paul lowered the paper, glanced up over it.

"Say what?" said Chip.

"Who isn't here? *Who*?"

I blinked. "Fritz ain't here. You meanin Fritz?"

Ernst frowned. "Fritz uses the stage door," he said under his breath. He turned to Delilah. "Are you expecting anyone? Did you tell anyone to come by?"

"No."

"What goin on?" I said. "Ernst?"

But he ain't answered, just turned on his heel, walking fast. We was up quick, following him out onto the stage. Ernst got halfway across the boards when he froze, held up one waxen hand. No one moved. And then we heard it too.

Four steady sharp knocks on the front door. The glass rattling. A muffled voice calling out in German.

"That ain't Fritz," I whispered.

Hiero was standing with one long hand clutching his horn, his eyes flicking bout the club for some damn way out.

"Holy hell," Chip hissed through his broken face. "It the *Boots*."

"I expect so," Ernst nodded, coming calmly back towards us. All at once it was like whatever been seething in him just smooth right out, harden right up into a sheet of steel. He cupped his hands, lit a cigarette. His pale hands steady. "Go through the water closet. You can get to the cellar through there, behind the old props. Get in there and go right to the back of it. And keep quiet. All of you."

The kid, he was trembling.

"What bout the alley out back?" I could hear the fear in my voice. "We get out there, we out for *sure*."

Ernst shook his head. "They'll be watching it," he said almost casually. He gestured with his cigarette. "Go."

So we gone.

Running across the stage, down the steps, through the sound doors and along the narrow brick corridor to the water closet. Kid was still gripping his horn and I near tore it from him. Then I thought, hell, maybe it's better out of sight. I don't know.

The damn blood thundered in my head. A low panel of plaster been cut out from round the pipes in that water closet, just under the faucet, and the kid crouched down, pried it free. He bent his shoulders low, slipped through into darkness. The closet was a cramped space and there wasn't room for all of us at once. I waited in the hall, glancing back in dread at the low door up the stage.

"Hurry it up," I hissed. "Paul? Hell. Go."

I listened hard but ain't heard nothing.

"What, you worried bout you handsome suit?" Chip said to Paul. "*Go*, buck."

Paul finally slipped through, and then at last Chip was wriggling low. I stepped in, shut the door real soft behind us, leaving it unlocked.

"Thank hell old Fritz ain't here," Chip whispered back at me, half in the hole, one elbow extended awkward out. His white bandage glowed like milk in a dark room. He give me a frightened smile.

I followed him down.

The sawdust was thick, the air sour with it. I felt a cough coming, held it in. We was in a cramped space that stretched behind the prop storage, under the stage. There was all these cold, jointed pipes in the darkness, and I shifted real slow among them, feeling my way with my scabbed-over knuckles. I reached back, shut the panel behind us. It gone utterly black.

I felt a hot hand on my shoulder, heard Chip suck in his breath. My eyes was adjusting and I seen, just faint like, tiny cracks of light coming in through the nail holes under the stage. And then a terrifying sight rose from the shadows. Twin shining eyes, like brass coins, narrowing to slits in the dark. They was gone almost as quick as they appeared.

"Dame Delilah," said Chip. "I told you, brother. Damn cat *lives* in here."

"Shut up," Paul whispered. "Fuck."

Our breath filled the space. After a moment I heard a slow, heavy tread passing the boards over our heads, the soft scrape of a heel. Whoever it was stopped, like they looking out over the dance floor.

I lift up my eyes, real slow, in the blackness.

Then the jack start speaking, just real soft, real calm. It was a muffled, slightly nasal voice. I ain't able to make out the words.

After a few minutes there was a sharp crash, then another.

"That's enough. I mean it," Ernst shouted angrily.

There was another crash, the clatter of Chip's snare overturning.

The footsteps crossed back above our heads, come back again. Stopped again. The jack continued on in that same calm nasal voice. And then I thought, God, did we leave anything in the green room. Anything suggesting we slept there last night, that four men slept there. Hell. There got to be *something*.

I felt Chip's big hand gripping my arm.

The doors in the corridor behind us was banging open. The sound coming closer. The green room. The prop closet. The old dressing room. Door after door, bang, crack, bang. We heard boots kicking their way through the clutter in the closest room. There was a pause. The water closet banged open.

Ain't none of us even breathed.

I heard someone come in. They seem to be looking a long damn time in there.

The jack above us was still going on in his nasal voice. Something bout permits, hours of occupancy. I ain't heard it clear.

Whoever was in the water closet was breathing real soft. Something clicked, rolled in the sink. I heard something tap at the far wall. Then it sound like the jack stood up on the toilet seat, was tapping the ceiling, lifting the panels one by one. Son of a *bitch*.

That panel under the sink was awful damn obvious. *If he come in here*, I thought. *If he come in.*

He called out in a startlingly clear voice, like he standing just at my elbow: "My wife wanted me to ask you where you got those apples."

There was a muffled comment from the corridor.

"Six o'clock," the Boot replied. "No, sorry. Five o'clock. But not tomorrow."

There was some long damn answer from the corridor. I crouched in that darkness holding my breath, praying. Just praying.

And then the jack gone out, shutting the door behind him. I heard a clattering in the next room.

I was crying soundlessly. I dragged my damn face against my sleeve, feeling ashamed. I ain't never thought fear had a taste. It does. In that small darkness it was a thing filling my nostrils, thick as sand in my throat, and I near choked on it.

———■———

I ain't known how long we was in there. My legs was throbbing and then they just gone totally dead. And still we was crouched silent in that cellar. After a while Delilah called through for us to stay put, the Boots was gone but they might be back. And then some more time passed. Chip shifted on his haunches. The kid let out a strange strangled sound, muttering a embarrassed apology. My mind started to drift.

At last there was a rustling in the wall, and the panel was pried back. Ernst peeked in.

"Alright. Come out," he said brusquely.

Hell. We stumbled out filthy and shaking. Ain't no one talked at all. I had sawdust in my collar, plastered to the sweat, and I started scratching hard at it. Ernst led us back out, up the steps, across the cluttered stage and up into his office. The tables on the dance floor been overturned, the drum kit scattered.

Delilah sat on the leather couch under Ernst's long windows, her thin hands folded in the lap of her white skirt. Her eyes was dark.

The carpet was covered in papers from upended drawers.

"Sit down," Ernst said to us. He crossed behind his heavy desk, smoothed his tie along his shirt front. "We're in trouble, gents."

Ain't none of us sat. Our damn knees was still cramping.

"How bad is it?" Paul said after a moment. "They know who we are?"

"They think they know who you are," said Ernst.

"Hell," Chip swore. "Goddamnit. Where the hell's Fritz? What he doin?"

Ernst shrugged. The walls of his office was painted a deep maroon and the black furniture give it a gloomy feel. He picked up a silver pen, began tapping it on the desk. "I put in a call last night. To Hamburg."

We all lift up our eyes, staring at old Ernst. You like to hear the rats tunnelling in the walls, it grown so hushed.

At last Chip spoke up. "You pa? For real?"

"How can he help?" Paul said angrily. "*Why* would he help?"

"We in *trouble*, buck."

"We've been in trouble for months."

"I don't know that he will," Ernst cut in. "He might not."

My eyes drifted over to Delilah, to her long legs crossed high. In her white skirt and white headwrap she look ghostly, a phantom of other times.

The kid turned, gone out onto the stairs, come back in, like he just stretching his legs, like he ain't got nowhere to go. He set one soft hand against the door frame. He looked anguished. "And what he say?" he said.

Ernst gestured vaguely with his pen.

"What do *that* mean?" I mocked Ernst's gesture with my battered hand.

He looked at me with his heavy-lidded eyes. "It means I'm still waiting. It means he'll call me back. He might telephone back this afternoon."

Chip scowled. "Or he could buzz you in a week. Or in a month. What we goin do, just sit round here waitin for the damn Boots to come back?"

"Even if he could help," said Paul, "can we even trust him?"

Ernst run a hand white as limestone over his slicked black hair. "I believe so. Yes."

"Right," said Paul. "And then the question becomes, *Will* he."

Cause old von Haselberg was disgusted by us. One of the Fatherland's coldest industrialists, he trafficked in iron, steel, coal, in arms too. A kind of Saarland empire. Nothing so soft or pansy as jazz. His business was hard, he was hard, his world was hard. He done rode out the inflation years by buying hordes of machines on borrowed change that'd lost its shine by payback time. He wrestled the unions, stomped down luxuries like the eight-hour workday. Ernst told us during Weimar his father been beaten twice in the streets, for making blood-soaked money off the poor. Old von Hasselberg ain't minded it at all.

And *this* was the jack who written us off as degenerates. *This* was the jack we needed now. We who was the ruin of his good son. Ever since the day when a adolescent Ernst heard Ma Rainey and Rabbit Brown at his friend Paul's house and become a jazz-lover to the end.

Ernst's eyes still lit up whenever he told it. How he listened with one ear pressed right up to the speaker, like that old black-hearted jazz was talking just to him.

"So we *definitely* goin," I said.

Chip grunted.

"Fritz won't be happy," said Paul.

"Fritz will live," said Ernst.

———————— ■ ————————

Ain't nothing to be done then but wait.

Whole damn club grown subdued after that. I got to feeling uneasy, pausing in whatever I was doing to listen for noises at the door. Paul and the kid spent their time cleaning up the mess. I ain't seen Chip for some time, and then I seen his bandaged head lurking at the bar, and then I ain't seen him again. The hours passed.

It was late summer outside. But here in the club, all its lights down, it felt cool, nearly cold. I lived in my overcoat. The stage was dim, the houselights real low, and the broken chairs was piled up in the shadows under the stage. The air reeked eerily of old roses. I glanced up as I stepped into the wings and seen Delilah sitting up in the flies, at the edge of the platform, staring down at me.

Hell. I crossed the boards, picking my way between the cords and loose axes, then climbed up that creaking old ladder. My ribs throbbing as I hauled myself through and onto the rough wood platform. Delilah give me a look, then glanced away. She was balled up against one railing, her head made magnificent by a huge golden headwrap. The fabric shimmering every time she turn her face.

"You changed you hat," I said.

She shrugged disconsolately.

"You okay? We goin be alright."

"Ernst is scared. I can tell."

"Shoot, girl, Ernst ain't scared of nothin. 'Cept when Chip get goin on his licorice stick. That scare all of us though."

She looked away. "Where did he come from?"

"Who?" I said foolishly. I followed her eyes down to the kid, dragging a old trunk into the wings. He look small, vulnerable from that height. "Hiero? He from Köln, I reckon."

She turned, studying me. "But where did he *come* from? He just appeared, out of nowhere, without having played with anyone? Just showed up like this?"

I wanted to ask, like what. But I ain't wanted to hear her answer.

She shook her damn head, her spidery eyelashes down-turned. "Lou was like him. When he was young. Would you say Lou's *talented*? Do you still call it talent, if it blooms without any kind of nurturing? That's got to be something else."

She made talent sound like a damn insult. I felt something sour and gravelly in my throat. I set my scratched palms against the rough planks.

"Paul brought him down to us," I said after a moment. "Paul discovered him."

"No one discovers that."

I shifted uneasily.

"What was he doing in Köln?"

I shrugged. "Paul's aunt lived in the same neighbourhood. Paul was out visitin her when he heard Hiero playin from a window across the way. His aunt said somethin like, *Oh, that's that poor little Falk boy. He's black.* Somethin like that. Paul gone right on over, ain't even put on his damn shoes."

"The poor little black boy," she muttered. "Jesus. Imagine if he hadn't been practising just then." She give me a look. "Or maybe he'd have found his way to the footlights regardless. A gift like his, it leads, don't you think?"

"Aw, he *good*," I said cautiously. "I ain't sure he ready to lead so much yet."

She narrowed her sleek green eyes. "He's the best player I've heard since I first heard Lou. And that's the truth. He'll be famous long after you and me are forgotten, Sid."

There wasn't no sorrow in it, no regret. Just some slow-burning excitement. Hell. I felt sick, rubbed my sore ribs, stared down at the kid. He was pulling out a blond wig, setting it on his head, turning side to side in front of the costume traces. He do a little curtsey, cocked one hip, then took it off and kept rummaging through.

"What is it with you and Hiero?" I said, hearing a sourness come into my voice.

She give me a odd look. "What do you mean?"

"Nothin, nothin. Just, you watchin him a awful lot."

"Oh." She stared thoughtfully down at him.

"Like that," I said.

She looked at me, then smiled distractedly.

What I was really thinking was, maybe the damn kid *known* she up here. Maybe he was messing with that damn trunk there in the wings cause he *wanted* her watching him. The son of a bitch.

"He talk like us, you know," I said all a sudden. I ain't sure why.

She ain't understood. "He speaks English?"

"No. No I mean his German. It's this weird sort of mix. Like he catchin our old accent, mine and Chip's, mimickin it. Like he ain't got his own way of talkin. His horn playin's a bit like that too."

Down in the damn wings he'd put on my hat, was tipping it with one finger down at a rakish angle. Hell. What he doing with my hat? He slouch his shoulders in a exact imitation of me. His suit look damn filthy.

"He looks up to you so much," she said, smiling.

"Hell he do. I reckon he just tryin to provoke me."

Delilah shook her head. She put one cool hand on my wrist, and a fierce thrill coursed up through me. Holy *hell*. "There's a real goodness in you, Sid. I could see it right away. I understand why he follows you like he does."

I felt a quick surge in my chest. I stood abruptly, nearly shaking her hand off.

"Sid?" she said, startled.

"Hold up," I said. "Just a minute." I climbed down that rickety ladder, jogged over to the bar, pulled up a bottle of the czech from its sheath. Put two small glasses in my suit pockets. Then I come back up the ladder, that bottle gripped careful in one fist.

"Oh, what're you doing?" she smiled.

"Just warmin our old bellies." I grinned and poured us each two fingers. "Where I from, folks call this a Cossack Conference."

"You're not going to start dancing on me, are you?"

"Up here? Shoot. Not till we get deeper into the bottle."

We clicked glasses. I still able to feel the burn of her fingers on my wrist, like it left a sear there.

"How you get together with old Armstrong?" I said.

"We're not together. Not like that."

"No. I meant, how you and Louis meet?"

"I know what you meant. Everyone sees us and thinks it."

I could feel the heat emanating off my face.

"Lou discovered me," she said with a soft shrug. "Well, Oliver discovered me. Lou, he just was the one who knew what to *do* with me. He taught me how to sing."

"*Lou*," I said softly, shaking my head. "You call him that, for real?"

"What I call him I can't repeat in public," she said, smiling.

I give a quick laugh. "Aw, can't figure at all why folks would think there be anythin between you two. So you ain't from Orleans?"

"I'm from Montreal. I met Lou in Chicago. Before him, I was just running around Little Burgundy, singing at weddings and such. The church choir."

"Sure," I said. "Sure. Me and Chip use to play railway stations. We ain't had no axes, just made the sounds up with our mouths. We was kids though."

"You been together a long time, you two."

"We ain't together. Not like that."

She laughed, soft, unexpected. It sound a little like stepping down a river bank, through the soft reeds, like air bending and lifting some green thing.

"It been our whole lives. We grown up on the same damn block. Chip got me into jazz."

"So it's his fault."

"He the guilty party." I smiled. "So, old Chicago. When was you in Chicago? We like to been there same damn time. Eddie Condon was there? Earl Hines?"

"You know Eddie?"

"Aw, not personally," I said quickly. "He a dazzlin gate though. Chicago used to seem so damn glamorous."

She snorted. "When you weren't sleeping it off in a park, maybe."

"Maybe we was on a bench next to each other."

"I was a sixteen-year-old girl from Montreal, Sid. I slept in the *bushes*. Terrified for my *virtue*." She laughed again, real soft like. I studied her crooked little teeth, feeling this big welling up of desire in me. Hell. What was *wrong* with me? She went on, "I was sure—*sure*—I just needed to find King Oliver, let him hear my voice, and it'd all start up for me. He'd just put an arm around me and introduce me to his Creole Jazz Band. Crazy, hmm?"

"Aw, not so crazy."

"I thought, talent knows talent."

"Sure it do."

She leaned back and studied me, laughing. "Look at you. I've got you tied around my little finger, don't I?"

I flushed.

"I'm teasing." She give me a strange little smile, glanced away. "I was so young." I seen her eyes drifting over to the kid. He was still sorting through that trunk. Chip had come out, standing in his stained and grimy shirtsleeves, his old skull swaddled in that bloodstained bandage. Jesus. He pulled out a long sequined gown, holding it up to the kid like to check his size. I heard the kid laugh.

When Chip turned round I seen last night's dried blood crinkle stiffly on his back.

Delilah said, "One night I was outside Lincoln Gardens when Lil Hardin came out. Did you ever meet Lil? Oliver's pianist? Well it doesn't matter. Lou lost his mind for a bit and when it came back to him he found he'd married her. Poor Lou. But that was later. So I saw her coming out and I got filled with all this arrogant hope. I thought Oliver might still be inside. So I slipped in."

"Sure. Shy sixteen-year-old jane from the provinces think her idol be inside, she just slip on in. I can see it."

"I never said I was shy," she smiled sly like.

I laughed. "And?"

"And he was in there alright. I guess he liked what he saw." She sat back, took a sip of her drink, the bangles on her wrist clacking softly.

I watched her for a moment, then leaned forward, shaking my head. "Aw, no way, no way girl. You ain't gettin off that easy."

She laughed that dark watery laugh.

"Go on, Delilah. What you say to him?" Saying her name aloud like that felt so damn intimate, so soft, I started to flush again. I lowered my eyes, picked at a bit of dust floating on the surface of my drink.

"You want to know what I said?" she asked.

"Go on. Tell me you secret."

"You're really interested?"

"In how a girl from Canada break the bigtime? Who ain't interested?"

"The *bigtime*," she muttered, but there was a dark note to it. "My name doesn't even reach from Paris to Berlin."

"Aw, girl. We livin in a soap bubble here. We ain't get no news of the world at all. You know that."

She look embarrassed then. Looked away.

"Go on," I said again. "Tell me what happen with King Oliver."

She start smiling soft, like she remembering something from a long time ago. "Have you ever seen King Oliver? I mean, in the flesh, up close?"

"I was in his cab once," I said. "Well, he just gotten out of it one block back."

She give me a funny look. "Well he's a big fellow. Very soft in the middle, sort of like your Fritz. The moment I came up behind them all standing there I knew it was him, I could tell just by the roll of his shoulders. But my god, he was so *fat*. I thought, *Good god, he looks like a big ol' baby.*

"When he turned around and saw me there, all of sixteen, he just laughed, and asked who let the baby in. And I said, *I'd of thought you let yourself in, baldie.*"

I grinned. "You pullin my leg. Ain't no *way* you said that."

"Oh, it gets worse," she laughed. "He wasn't offended at all. Oliver? He's got a hide thicker than a kettle skin. He asked if I'd come in to eat or to drink, and I just gave him this long long look, and said, *I'd say eat, but you look like you about cleaned out the place.*"

I shook my old head.

"The gate standing there with him started laughing and laughing. Well, that was Louis. I guess it must have been funny. I was just this tiny rail of a thing, talking big to old Oliver like that. Anyhow. Oliver didn't know what to do with me, but Lou took me home with him, put some hot food in me, gave me a place to sleep. Like an older brother would do." She nodded, sort of thoughtfully, and stared down at the kid. "Old Lou saved me."

I got this dark feeling. "So *that's* how it's done, gettin in with the bigwigs." I forced a smile. "You just talk rough to em. I reckon old Chip's due for some big things."

"Chip? He'll go far alright," she laughed.

I snuck a glance at her. She ain't hardly touched her czech.

"I always liked nightclubs after hours, after closing," she said after a moment.

I nodded. "When all the folks is gone. Sure. Chip always say they feel lonely, hopeless. I sort of think the opposite. Somethin so *unexpected* bout them."

"Yes. Like something could happen any moment. It's all so *possible*." She smiled.

Then I wasn't thinking anything at all for a long, long moment. She was so beautiful.

"What you two doin up there?" Chip called up. He and the kid was standing with hands on their heads, staring up at us in the flies. Delilah give a little wave.

"We hidin from the Boots," I said. "What you think?"

"I think that ain't what you doin," Chip said.

The kid start laughing.

I glanced over, embarrassed, but Delilah ain't seemed to notice. "Why do you call him Chip?" she said.

"He hates Charles."

"Why?"

"Aw, he reckons it makes him sound like a preacher's son."

She was silent for a moment. "What does his father do?"

I grinned. "He a preacher." Then I reached across, tapped her ankle. "Hey, girl, you want a laugh?"

She give me a suspicious look.

I smiled. "For real. You want a laugh, ask Chip what the C stand for."

"The C?"

"In his name. The C. Ask him what it stand for."

"Charlie," she called down. "What does the C stand for?"

He look up, grimacing like he got a sore tooth. "Chip, sister. It just Chip."

"What does the C stand for, *Chip?*"

I shook my head. "He ain't told no one his middle name. Not ever."

"I can hear you," he called up at me. "You ain't invisible." And then, to Delilah: "Girl, a man got to keep some things to hisself."

"Some men could keep even *more* things, if they of a mind to," I said. "I ain't sayin. I just sayin."

"How bad can it be?" said Delilah. "What is it, Clayton?"

Chip stared at her in disbelief. "Holy hell. You *guessed* it. First try."

"Really? It's Clayton?"

He snorted. "*Clayton?* I ain't from *Idaho*, girl."

Paul come up onstage, lift up the lid of his piano, start working the ivories real soft. He was watching me and Delilah up in the flies.

"She askin bout his middle name," I called down to him.

"Tell her to try Cecil," he said, dropping a register.

"Paul thinks it might be Cecil," I said. "I always thought Chauncey."

"I ain't no Chauncey, buck. You know that."

"Cecil," Paul said again. "I got a good feeling about Cecil."

"Chevrotain," Hiero said abruptly, his voice cracking.

Paul hit a sour note, stop playing. "*Chevrotain?*" he laughed.

I waved them down. "You both goin wrong. Old Jones' folk ain't so fancy as all that. It like to be Christopher. Or Curtis."

"What about Carolina?" Delilah said. "Or Christina?"

Chip looked up at her blankly. "They *girls'* names."

She smiled, give him a wink.

"Alright, alright," said Chip. "We wrappin this one up, sendin it out. You bucks ain't even close. *Especially* you, girl."

"Chloe?" she called down.

Chip snorted, shook his head. "*Chloe*," he muttered. "Chloe ain't even on the right damn side of the *bonfire*."

She give the kid a crooked smile and I laughed then, sort of leaned over, nudged her gently with my shoulder. Like to flirt.

She glanced over at me, her face closing right up. Not with anger or hate or caution or none of the usual reasons a jane shut down shop in you presence. No, it was something drier, something rougher. There just wasn't no interest. Like she was wishing I get up to go, so the damn kid could come clambering up, take my place.

I smiled, looking painfully away. I was biting the inner wall of my cheek so hard I could taste the blood.

———————— ■ ————————

Next day I was shuffling through the club looking for Ernst when Chip and Paul call me over to the bar. They was sitting on the high stools, arms folded in front of them, playing a hand of dead man, working their way through a bottle of the czech.

Chip give me a drunken smile. "*There* you is, brother. Sit on down here a minute."

"I busy, Chip."

"We got to talk."

"Six of hearts," said Paul, frowning. "Or is that a nine?" He turned the tattered card this way and that, staring stupidly at it. "I'm going to call that a nine."

"We into spades now," said Chip. "What you *doin*, buck?"

Paul poured a second finger into Chip's glass. "You've got to catch up to me, or it's not going to be much of a game." He'd folded his cuffs back over his fair forearms, the stains on his collar and cuffs a dull yellow.

We was all of us starting to turn sour, ripe, without no clothes to change into. Chip been scrubbing his out in the big sink each night, but there wasn't no getting the old blood out. I could see a rip in Paul's stitching at his shoulder. We was all shaving on the same dull razor. Our mugs full of cuts. On top of it all, the club was numbingly cold. It was the height of summer, and we was trapped frozen and afraid inside.

Paul lay down his hand. "Go on. But be gentle."

Chip smiled. "Ten seconds of sack time, two hours of apology."

"Why don't we walk Sid in? He's good at showing his hand."

"You funny," I said, shaking my head. "I pass."

"You been passin since the day you was born, friend," said Chip, licking his front teeth gingerly. His swollen jowls was starting to come down some. Still looked stuffed full of cotton though. "Aw, I kiddin. Come on now, I just kiddin."

"He's just kidding, Sid." Paul was already pouring me a glass, sliding it over my way. "Sit down, sit."

Chip chuckled. "You know what you is, buck? You a blue-ribbon fool. Starin after the kid like you goin murder him in his sleep."

"What you sayin?"

"Like you goin murder him over that bearcat. Over that strip of lead."

Paul smiled. "It's okay, Sid. Don't be embarrassed."

"He damn well should be embarrassed. Goin on like that." But Chip's face, it turned all anxious then, and I was thrown a little, seeing his concern. "It just, we see what goin on here, Sid. You settin youself up for the icy mitt. Rejection, brother."

"It's not how you do it," Paul agreed, running a finger along his moustache, shuffling through his cards. "What are we starting with, spades?"

"Hearts."

Paul frowned.

"You want to get to her?" said Chip. "Really get to her? You got to run the kid off first. But not like no schoolboy, not like no sucker. Like a *man*."

"Be a man, Sid," Paul murmured, distracted. "You're sure you don't want to start with spades?"

"Hearts."

I wrinkled my brow. "Uh-huh."

"Well, you goin sit or what?" said Chip.

I sat.

"We serious, Sid. You can't stand round gawkin like a boy who missed the jitney. You can't let her see you doin it. You got to be subtle, like. Just anythin he do, you got to sort of overshadow it. Make her forget his old game before he even finished. But you got to make it look like you ain't tryin, or you *sunk*, brother. You got to do it *regal*."

I felt that old blackness rising in me. Cause it seem damn sinister, the kid and Delilah. And yet I suspected it too. I blown air through my lips. "You ain't seriously suggestin I fight a nineteen-year-old kid for a twenty-nine-year-old woman? For real?"

Chip shrugged. "Paul done broke up two marriages before he was sixteen."

"They were very youthful women," said Paul with a wide smile. But his eyes wasn't focusing quite right. He reached for his glass.

"See, there you go," said Chip. "And Delilah ain't youthful."

I shook my damn head, give them both a dark look. Then I downed the czech, shuddered, and turned to go. "You both off you nut. Ain't no way Delilah interested in the kid. No way. She feel anythin for him, it be like a sister."

"I seen some low-down dirty things in my time, brother," said Chip, whistling. "This is just the icing."

"Watch you mouth. Just watch how you talk bout her."

"Hold up, hold up," said Paul with a easy smile. "Hold up there, Sid."

Chip started laughing. "Don't go all Joe Bavaria on us, brother. You ain't a prude. Come on. So she ain't no caviar. Each man got the spice he likes. So you like old ordinary pepper."

"Nothing wrong with pepper," Paul agreed.

"It's black," said Chip.

"And peppery."

"That it is, buck. That it is."

I give them both a closer look, leaned in, seen the red veins glowing in Chip's watery eyes. "Jesus. How much you two had to drink?"

"Aw, we ain't hardly had nothin," Chip said, like he wounded by the question.

"Hardly touched the bottle," said Paul.

"*That* one, at least."

Paul laughed a weird long laugh. He lowered his cards, his shoulders shaking. Chip glance quickly over at his hand.

I scooped the bottle away. "Jesus. Ernst wants us to run through a set for Delilah sometime in the next *year*. You reckon you sober up anytime soon?"

Chip leaned forward. "How we goin through a set without Fritz?"

"Can't play without Fritz," said Paul, nodding. He kept on nodding.

I glanced across. Paul had a second bottle of the czech down by his knee, and he was refilling his and Chip's glasses on the sly. I just shook my head. "Hell. Day I listen to advice from jacks in the sauce, that be the day I hang up my old spurs."

"He's going to hang up his spurs," Paul smiled.

"No more ridin for Sid," said Chip. "You pourin us another finger? Pour one for Sid too."

"I ain't touchin it," I said.

Chip give me a tragic look. "Brother, you got old Berlin's finest genius when it come to the janes sittin right here, and you ain't goin ask him *nothin*?"

I glanced across at Paul, his head lolling on his shoulders. And then I thought, hell, ain't like there anything to lose. "Alright," I said. "For real. How you do it, Paul? How you get them to fall for you?"

"You got to clear that glass first, buck," said Chip.

I frowned. Then I punched it back, set the glass on the bar with a bang.

Chip whooped. "*There* he is. The old Baltimore Special hisself. All aboard if you gettin aboard." He slapped me on the back.

I coughed against my hand. "So what you secret, Paul?"

He lift up one shaky eyebrow. "Secret? It's no secret. You let *them* come to *you*. A jane doesn't like to be pushed."

"It don't hurt if you look like a Adonis, neither," Chip smiled.

Paul shrugged, chuckling.

"You both off you nut." But I was smiling some too, now. That was the damn czech, I guess, eating its way through my liver. "I ain't no Adonis, buck."

"Sid got a point."

"That is a point," Paul agreed. He cleared his throat, glanced up like he just realizing he sitting at a dark bar in a shuttered club and he ain't changed his shirt in two days. He run a thumb under his bleary eyes. "Okay," he said. "Okay. First thing you need to understand, janes don't make any sense. None. If they're mad at you, it means they're interested. Or maybe they're not. If they ignore you, it means they're not interested. Or maybe they are."

I nodded, blinking. "Okay. They make no sense. Got it."

Chip poured me another two fingers. "And you got to make them feel they *special*."

"Sure," Paul nodded. "You need to make them feel like you're listening to them. Like you're getting to know the *real* dame."

"And you got to buy them stuff, buck. Dames like presents. You ever known a dame not to like a present?"

Paul nodded. "Dames like presents. It's true."

"You got to get her thinkin of you before she think of the kid. *That* the trick."

"That *is* the trick," Paul said, nodding sagely. "Yes it is. Whose turn is it?"

"Pass that old bottle over, brother."

"I think it's my turn. Isn't it my turn?"

But I wasn't hardly listening. Cause Hiero come out through the heavy red curtains from backstage, the left side of his afro pressed flat like he been sleeping. His horn was hooked over his forefinger, the thing gleaming like a outrageous jewel.

And, hell, Delilah come following him through. She was laughing, teasing, batting her damn eyes at him sort of foolish like, like she ain't realized we sitting here. The kid turn up one side of his mouth, as if he got a cramp in his jaw, as if he embarrassed. Then he just pursed his lips to his trumpet, blown a huge high C, sliding down the scale hair by hair till he got to the bottom. His notes so damn hot they smart you ears.

He paused, put a hand to his eyes, stared out at us. "What you doin over there?"

Paul start to laughing. "Don't you mind it," he called back.

"We talkin bout you," said Chip with a sloppy grin.

I flushed.

I was watching Delilah up there onstage. She was wearing that gold headwrap from yesterday, its sequins glittering like a million eyes in its folds.

"Ain't that somethin," I murmured. "She look like a queen."

"More like a fortune teller," said Chip.

"A misfortune teller," said Paul, laughing silently.

"Aw, you both crazy. She lookin good."

Chip fixed me with a baleful eye. "That there look like a mound of garbage on her head, brother. You think she'd wear that if she ain't got to?"

I blinked. "What?"

"Open you eyes, buck. That dreck on her head's a gift."

"What?"

"You don't recognize that fabric?"

The bronze shimmer, the winking sequins—it hit me then. That curtain we drawn over the green room's window. I tried to still my face. But I so overwhelmed with disappointment and irritation that I could feel my old cheeks creasing up.

"What the hell," I muttered. "So we got no curtain now?"

"Kid nailed an old tarp up," Paul smiled. "It works better. Cuts out more light."

Chip belched. Then again.

He done pour the dregs into my glass when I wasn't looking—that awful grit that cling to you tongue like bayou mud—and I started gagging, coughing back into the glass. Chip whooped. "Go on, buck," he grinned. "Polish her off."

Felt so cross-eyed, it like I going blind. Holy hell.

The kid was squealing his way along them damn scales, squawling and brapping up and down, up and down again. Like to make you skin crawl. I closed my eyes, opened them. The walls was shifting ever so slightly.

Chip grunted. "I goin to the john. Don't mess with my cards."

Paul ain't even stirred.

Delilah was reaching down, taking off her heels. She stood barefoot on the boards, and I was astonished at how short she suddenly was. Like a *kid*, I thought bitterly.

"I need to talk to you," Paul said quiet like. He lift up his head, and his eyes look very clear, very pale. "Sid? Hey, Sid."

"I listenin."

"I need help."

"Damn right you do. You and Chip both."

He shook his head. "No. I'm serious. I need help."

"I told you," I said, leaning emphatically forward with each word, "I-take-Inge-but-not-Marta. Marta-ain't-my-speed-buck."

"I left something at the flat," he muttered, "something I'm desperate without. I can't go out for it. But I can't ask anyone else either."

"Ask Hiero. He the one to make you dreams come true." I scowled, staring across at him still walking up and down them scales. Delilah was leaning back on the piano, just watching him work.

Paul give me a confused look. "Hiero?"

I was thinking of that advice they give me. Of what a jack can give as a present to make a girl swoon. Hell. I ain't giving her no damn *rag* for her *hair*, that for sure. I got to make it *meaningful*.

"You listening Sid? Sid?"

My mind swum back through its fog. "You left it back at the flat." I nodded. "Sure. What was it again?"

He lowered his face. I known then he ain't said what it was.

"If it that important," I said, "get Delilah to fetch it. She goin out still. Or if it too embarrassin for a jane to see, hell, there still old Ernst. What the problem?"

Paul was nodding slow like, but his eyes was tense, unconvinced. I ain't asked why not go for it hisself, blond and blue-eyed like he is. It was fear. I known that. I wasn't sure why Paul was talking bout it and then it struck me.

"Hell," I said. "You want *me* to go for it? You want me to go, I go. Just tell me what I lookin for."

Paul's face lit up with relief. But just as quickly he fell to brooding.

Slowly he begun shaking his head. "Naw, Sid. I can't ask you to go out there." But he set a unsteady hand on my shoulder, looked at me a long time.

"Then ask Delilah. She ain't goin mind stoppin in at the flat." But I known by the set of his mouth, the way it slunk back at its corners, he wouldn't never ask her. Paul got this iron core. Ain't much ever move it. "You reckon her coat do the trick?" I said impulsively. "That it ain't too flimsy? It kind of cold in here."

Paul shook his head like to clear it. "What?"

The kid was still squawking up and down them scales. Jesus hell.

"Delilah's coat," I said. "You reckon it warm enough for her? She come from Paris in the summer and all. It look a little flimsy to me. She got to be freezin in here."

Paul's shoulders was slumped. "I don't know. I guess. Who couldn't use a new coat?"

I nodded firmly. "I been thinkin that too."

All a sudden Hiero, up there on the boards, twist into a hopping melody so fresh I ain't recognized it. Naw, I *did* know it: *Empty Bed Blues*. He was playing *Empty Bed Blues*, but doing it so coy it ain't sound *nothing* like itself. It come out flirty, girlish almost, and he left small gaps where a singer's voice should be.

Delilah looked surprised, charmed, her lips half open. She took a few lazy steps forward on her small bare feet. Staring up at Hiero, she raised her arms, hitching her shoulders to her ears.

"*When my bed get empty, make me feel awful mean and blue,*" she wailed. "*When my bed get empty, make me feel awful mean and blue. My springs are gettin rusty, sleepin single like I do.*"

Paul smiled over at me.

Holy sweet hell. Her voice thrummed like a muscle. It was low and rich, with the quiver of something mustering its strength. "*When you get good lovin, never go and spread the news. Yes he'll double-cross you, and leave you with them empty bed blues.*"

She swung the thick, strong rope of her voice round the words, coming down hard on them, cinching them together. Then she flung the notes bold up in the air, high and horn-like. But her voice was at its core a sailor's voice, rough and mannish. Her low notes bitter croaks, filled with muddy regret.

Hearing them like that, Delilah and the kid, I got filled with this weird energy, this strange aimless feeling. It wasn't the czech. I mean, it wasn't *only* the czech. I felt puckered, dry in the throat, the juices sucked out of me. Then the kid lowered his horn, smiled at her shyly. And she stood there, looking at him, filled with a exquisite radiance. I thought, *Ain't no way I able to give her that. No way.*

Then I felt someone's eyes on me, and turned. Chip stood across the dance floor, staring me down hard. He give me a dark look, shook his head.

The damn ceiling was spinning. Paul's hand was at my shoulder.

"Man, you're really loaded." He grinned.

"Like a rifle," I mumbled. "Like a rifle."

The next evening we was still drunk.

Now Delilah, she a right bone-grinder. For *real*. Ain't none of us prepared for her odd flattery, her strings of teasing insults or for the careless, distracted way she offer up her opinions. Not to mention the mysterious ending to her conversations, her sometimes just standing up mid-sentence and walking away. It intrigued a jack. Never mind what Chip protested, all his talk of her being a chunk of lead, boring as black pepper—I seen it in *all* their faces, the way they turned at a opening door, hoping it might be her.

So when Chip come up onstage, staggering just a little, and start fussing with his drum kit, I known he was watching Delilah with at least half a eye.

"You don't sing half as bad as I figured," Chip smiled. "Yesterday night."

"Why Charlie, you'll make me blush."

"Charlie a name for *horses*," Chip grunted. Then he belched, smiled proudly.

Ernst come onstage carrying his licorice stick. "Chip, you're a real gentleman. A real class act." He was in his shirtsleeves, his tie in a loose knot. "Anyone heard anything from Fritz? Anything?"

The kid shrugged.

Delilah was leaning against the exposed brick, thumbing the top button of her dress, a faint smile on her lips. Hell. I known nothing sexy was meant by it, she wasn't doing it to be seductive. I ain't got no excuse. But when she turned suddenly, seen me standing there at the edge of the dance floor, I dropped my eyes and my face gone hot.

"Hiya Sid," she said.

"Delilah," I said, trying to sound sober. Studying the tips of my two-tones, like there was a spot on them needed shining.

She laughed, lowering her hand.

I seen something dark and muscled move out from the wings, cross under the kit where Chip was leaning, slip fast behind the piano, and move toward Delilah. Holy hell, that one damn big rat. I waved an arm, called out sharply to warn her. "*Delilah!*"

Everyone froze, staring at me like I was off my nut.

That dark furred thing wound itself through Delilah's shins, and she crouched down, her dress all rising up her thighs. Still looking at me, she lift it into her arms. It started mewling in a high, spiteful tone. Hell. It was a *cat*.

"Somebody been drinkin *somethin*," said Chip in a stage whisper.

Paul tipped his thumb over his open mouth, like he pouring out a bottle.

"Hide all you aftershave," said Chip.

My whole damn body flushed.

It was a shaggy, wild-eyed, crazy-looking cat. A majestic ruff of black and white fur crowned its shoulders. Delilah lift that rank thing into the air, stare into its eyes. "Hiya Lilah," she murmured. "How are you? How are you?" She give a soft, choppy laugh.

"It a cat," I said, astonished.

"Well, she swears it is," Paul smiled. "I'm not convinced." He tripped over a cord, started laughing.

I shook my head. "Holy hell. Where that nasty thing come from?"

"Paris," said Chip. "Though she claim she from Montreal originally."

"Be nice," Ernst said in English.

Delilah looked up at that. "You boys better not be making fun of her." Her smile was fierce. "She's a warrior cat. Aren't you, sweetie?"

"Dame Delilah the Second?" Chip laughed. "She only eats things smaller than her. Hiero better watch out."

"Dame Delilah?" I said. "It from the wall?"

The cat squealed and writhed out from Delilah's grip, landed softly. Everyone laughed. My face flushed harder, and I thought, hell, ain't no one else look surprised by this. Like they all already known it.

That cat scampered over to Chip, jumped up on his lap. He stood with a clatter, dumping it onto the floorboards.

"It likes you, Charlie," Delilah laughed.

"*Chip*, sister. Hell."

But the cat was purring and weaving its way through the drum kit, rubbing up against old Chip's ankles. "Come and get this filthy thing away from me," Chip barked. "It got to be *diseased*."

"If it's attracted to *you*," said Delilah.

Ernst laughed.

But Chip, he just give me a sour look. His eyes roved slowly over to one corner, and then he shook his head.

The kid. Hiero stood at the edge of the wings, a damn radiance in his face.

So *he* done it. *He* give her the cat. Hell. I ain't able to figure it, what it was between those two. He so *young*.

I felt uneasy, weakly determined. Ain't no way a jack compete with that. No way. But he got to *try*, at least. I thought of Paul's advice.

Delilah sat on the edge of the stage, folding one long leg over the other, keying open a tin of sardines. Now where the hell that tin come from? Dame Delilah the Second drop down off Chip's kit, come running over.

"Sid?" Ernst called down. "You joining us?"

I just give him a weak smile. I walked in a weaving path, holding onto the stage with one hand, trying to hide my drunkenness. I wet my lips. I ain't figured out what to say yet.

Delilah glanced at me as I come up. "Sid?" She sounded alarmed. "You feeling alright?"

Her bare feet was dangling loose in front of me. I glanced up. Sound of my name on her lips brought a lazy smile out of me. "I feelin good," I said, thinking my voice rang a bit shallow. I cleared my throat, deepened it a register. "I feelin good." There, that was better. Then, remembering what all I meant to say, I tried to make my face solemn. "But I worry bout you."

She give a vague smile, glanced nervously round. "Me? Why?"

"You must be cold." My words sat like a wad of wet rags in my mouth.

She frowned. "It's *summer*, Sid. I'm okay."

In the dim pit of my hooch-soaked brain, I tried to puzzle out what she meant. No, I known what she meant, but I couldn't think of no clearer way to start. I mean, to make it acceptable to a dame's ears, in high-hat language, not in that gutter-talk we all rattle off in our sleep.

"Ain't you a little frigid?" I tried.

Sensing even as I said it that it ain't quite right.

I heard a sharp laugh from the stage. Shaking, Chip leaned over to the others and uttered something. Muffled laughter rang out, everyone staring my way. Even Hiero laughed his high, hiccuping laugh. I felt a twinge of panic though my daze. My brain just wasn't on the trolley, brother.

I glanced desperately at Delilah. Her face had gone savagely red.

Feeling my moment slipping away, I blurted, "I want you to have my coat, Delilah." I made to take it off, to give it to the girl. But the czech, hell. My rubber arms got all tangled in the sleeves, and I stood there swaying with one shoulder forced awkwardly back, making short, violent jerking movements to free myself, like I the biggest damn ass ever to grace the green earth.

I started to laugh. It was a weird, panicked laugh, and even as I was laughing I was thinking to myself, *Sid, what you doin, fool? Stop it. Stop it.*

"Sid?" Delilah said, puzzled. "Sid, are you okay?"

Chip almost fell off his damn stool, cackling that hard. The kid was holding his sides, gasping and gasping. I just ain't able to extricate myself. Then I felt a cool hand on my shoulder, turning me: Delilah, hauling my old arm back into my sleeve.

"I just tryin a give you somethin," I said thickly.

"You sure is, buck," Chip called out.

Oh, girl. She was practically *green*-faced, she so embarrassed. "I appreciate your concern, Sid," she said with real dignity. "I'm not cold. But thank you."

And gathering up her own coat and her calfskin gloves and her tin of fish and her foul flea-ridden cat, she nodded to the gents, giving Ernst a longer, more polite nod, and left the stage.

I stood there, feeling a vague shame drift through me. And by vague I mean like a wall of water smashing into a village, obliterating everything. I got this weak sense of nothing, filled with numbness, like everything round me was taking place underwater.

Hell, those jacks was laughing and laughing like to wet themselves. Even Ernst had a smile on his face, shaking his head like he ain't believed what he just seen.

"Aw, Sid," Chip gasped. "Holy hell, Sid, you priceless."

"Alright, ease up now," said Ernst. But his eyes was still damp with tears of laughter. "Where's Fritz? Anyone heard from him?"

"Do we still got to play if Delilah ain't here?" said Chip.

I start to leave the dance floor but my old legs just wasn't working. I thrown myself down at one of the tables in front of the footlights.

"Jesus Christ," said Ernst. "How much have you gents had to drink?"

Paul looked suddenly serious. "Not very much," he articulated carefully.

Then Chip's foot banged the bass drum. He give a start, looking down at it like it done it of its own volition. Then he looked at Paul and snorted.

And then they was both laughing their old heads off again.

I felt sick with embarrassment. All I heard banging bout in my old skull was Hiero's damn hiccuping laugh. The bastard.

They was playing a sloppy set, Paul missing his cues with a big grin at each nod from Ernst. Chip, drunk though he was, sounded tight as ever, brushing them old skins with real ease. I sat a long time at that table, feeling sick. Then I got to my feet, stumbled backstage.

She was just leaving the green room as I come down the steps, through the sound doors. Seeing it was me, her smile weaken a little. But she ain't slapped my face or scowl or nothing, which I took for a good sign.

"Listen, you got to excuse me on account of earlier," I said, clutching my hat hard before me in both hands. My arms was trembling a little and I tried to hide it by moving them. "I wasn't in my right mind. I ain't meant what I said. If—"

"If he really thought you were frigid, he wouldn't still be trying to get under your dress," said Paul, strolling out of nowhere. He tipped his hat at us and kept going.

Oh, the silence. A jack could grind his teeth on it. I stood there swallowing hard, not knowing where to look. Only thinking, *Don't you damn well meet her eye.* I lowered my gaze, but realizing my eyes was level with her breasts, I flinched and glanced up again.

She look damn uncomfortable. She was smiling so hard I thought maybe her face going to break.

I cleared my throat. "I got to ask Ernst bout somethin. I just remembered it."

"Okay," she said, nodding quickly. "Yes. Okay then."

She sort of spun round awkwardly on her heels, started walking purposefully off in the opposite direction. Ain't nothing down that way but the prop closet.

———————————————

Sick ain't even the right word. Mortified, ashamed, embarrassed—hell, I was so far deep into it I ain't even known what I was feeling. And being trapped in that damn club. Jesus.

The next night, I drifted into the green room looking round for something, anything, to rid me of my restlessness. Chip was sitting in there, brooding on the wall like he waiting for a painting to appear. Dame Delilah the Second was curled in his lap, purring away.

He give it a disgusted look. "This damn mangy rotten godawful ugly thing," he scowled. He still sounded drunk.

I sat beside him.

"Her bank still closed?" he said. "What you thinkin, courtin a dame when you three sheets to the wind. You ain't *never* go in drunk, brother. You crazy." He shook his head. "Fool fool fool. Tellin a dame you aim to sin with that she frigid."

I sort of lifted my shoulders, dropped them with a sigh. He was right. I got to get a hold of myself. Get smarter bout how I gone after her.

He give a sharp laugh. "A cat ain't somethin you can one up. It ain't." He lift up the Dame from his lap, its claws digging in hard to his suit. He grimaced and set it back. I could smell the czech on him still, coming off his breath in waves. "But it alright. Now you exactly where you want to be. Now you get to be *apologetic*, brother. Dames love that."

I scowled. "Hell, Chip. I want you advice, I ask for it."

"I serious, brother. Go on up there right now, tell her how damn sorry you is. It goin work. You see."

I studied his face in the ugly yellow lights from the costume trace. The light was pooling weirdly along his oyster lips, making him look like he leering at me.

"What. She here?"

"Where you been, buck? She been upstairs the last hour." He chuckled. " Up in Ernst's office. And she *alone*, brother."

"Where the kid?"

Chip shrugged.

Hell. Hell and hell again. I got up, casual like, turning my old hat in my fingers, then sort of sauntered out into the corridor like I just thinking of something else. But what I was thinking was: *Enough. Clear the damn air, let her see what you thinkin. Then leave it be.*

Ernst had dragged a chair up onstage, was sitting alone cleaning his licorice stick softly. He ain't even look up as I gone past, the instrument gilt as a blade. The club was dark, but there was lights on in Ernst's office. I shuffled through the tables, up the narrow stairs. The door stood open, but I stopped in the shadows anyhow before tapping on the door frame.

She stood in her blue silk dress, holding the gold scarf on her head with both hands, the fabric slipping like silty water down one ear. Her taut armpits was peppered with hairs black as scabs. "Sidney," she said, turning to me. "What a surprise."

"I come to apologize." I ain't looked at her face. I feared her irritation. But the silence, it was brutal. I lift up my eyes. She was staring hard at me, waiting.

"I ain't got nothin to give you," I said.

She stood there, blank-faced for a minute. "Is this a joke?"

"No."

"Because I've had just about enough of those from you."

I cleared my throat uneasily.

"What do you want, Sid?" Something in that sounded thin, vulnerable.

I went to take her hand but she bowed forward quick, tying that sloppy gold fabric back into place. She let her hands hang loose at her thighs. I ain't so foolish as to try it again.

"I ain't got nothin to give you, Delilah," I said quietly. "But I wish to all hell that I did."

My face gone hot, hearing myself talk like this. I ain't never spoken to a jane this way, not even in my greenest years of dating. Delilah's great intelligent face, the rough pureness in it, like both pain and happiness left their mark on her. Hell.

She stood there looking at me, her lips like a ripe bruise. She ain't said a word. I felt sick.

"Hell, girl," I muttered. "I sorry. It ain't right, puttin all this on you."

I touched my old hat with two fingers, nodded, turned back to the door.

"Sidney." She said it full of a sullen tenderness, like she irritated with herself.

I stopped. The oak flooring creaked under my heels. I felt a hot radiance in my nerves, my whole body filling with a confused, battered feeling, like a moth caught in a lantern.

"Come in," she said. "Shut the door."

She reached across, drawn the curtains shut in the office windows. That cramped awful place with its heatless heaters. Her thin blue dress so sheer I could see the hooks of her undergarments through the satin.

I moistened my lips, nervous.

Staring hard at me, she raised her arms real slow. Her gaze was full of such awful intensity I ain't known what all I should be watching—the teasing lift of her arms, or the tension in her green eyes. I glanced from one to the other, feeling frightened, excited.

She untied the gold fabric of her headwrap, unwound it slowly, then pulled it off and held it balled up in both hands.

Holy hell. She was *bald*. Her scalp was rough with tufts of hair, the pale skin shining eerily between them.

Her face was utterly still, utterly empty. But her eyes shone with defiance, water glistening in them. She put one hand on her rigid hip. "Still want me now, Sid?" she said bitterly. "You still itching to have a go at me?"

I ain't said nothing. Just stared.

In a dark voice, she said, "They said it was *stress*. It was supposed to grow *back*." But her voice sort of choked off then. She glared hard at me.

I took off my hat, blinking sort of slow like.

Then I stepped forward, leaned down. And kissed her.

She ain't even moved. But I could feel the relief through her body, the tension going. And then she was kissing me back, her mouth soft and warm on mine. I thought, Hell, this girl don't even know what she is. She the most stunning and original thing I ever known.

She pulled back, put one hand to my chest. "What're you doing?"

I put a hand on her scalp, real gentle.

"Don't, Sid. Don't. It's ugly." She turned her head away.

"Hey. Hey," I said, brushing my knuckles real soft over her wet cheeks. "It ain't. Come here. It don't matter. This goin sound crazy. You been here all of a bug's age, girl, but already I feel like I known you a lifetime. I think I fallin in love with you."

She looked quickly up at me. Then pushed me hard on the chest. I stumbled back.

"Don't you go messing with me," she said. "I mean it. Sid? I mean it."

I stood rubbing my chest.

"Say it again," she said.

"What?"

"What you just said."

"I fallin in love with you?"

"Come here," she said.

My legs unsteady, I stepped closer. Her ropey fingers, the marble wrist bones, that slender pale throat like some young birch. She was all length and grace standing there, and seeing the shadows pooled at her collarbones, like a dent made by a human finger, I wanted to put my mouth there.

She took my hand, drew me over to Ernst's old sofa. I ain't took my eyes from hers. She lay herself down, shyly drew me down on top of her.

"What you doin, girl?" I whispered. "Ernst could come in."

Her eyes narrowed teasingly. I could feel her breathing beneath me. I brought my mouth down real soft on her head, kissed the cotton-floss. She made a soft noise, lifted her face, and I kissed her again. Then I rose on one slow elbow and yanked open the front of her dress.

What I remember as I kissed my way down her ribs was the peace she seemed to be in then. The absolute peace.

Shooting out of sleep in the morning, I lifted up onto one elbow, peering through the darkness of Ernst's office. I was covered in a thin blanket, my trousers, shirt and socks strewn around me like some tentacled beast. I could still feel Delilah's warmth on me, like a shadow. Turning to touch her, I got a handful of nothing.

"Lilah?" I said softly. "You here, girl?"

I got this weird feeling in my chest, like something bad was prowling in the damn rafters. The door stood half ajar, and looking across I seen that foul cat sitting in the crack, studying me with its yellow eyes. Then it turned, slipped out.

I shivered. "Delilah? Where you get to?"

I got up, slipped into my trousers, come out onto the stairs to stare down over the club. Chip and the kid sat at a table, not saying much. The kid's horn stood upright at the table's centre, like it on display.

"If it ain't Captain Romance," Chip called, as I come down.

I smiled, blushing. I was still buttoning up my old shirt. "Where Delilah? You seen her?"

Hiero give me a long measured look. *That's right, buck,* I thought. *It ain't all bout you no more.*

"What, she missin too?" Chip run the back of his hand across his damp lips. "Is my lips bleedin?"

I give him a look.

"Feel like they bleedin. What?" He blown out his cheeks. "Paul gone out early this mornin. Ain't none of us seen him go. Ernst out lookin for him."

"You foolin."

"Ask the kid."

"What he go do a fool thing like that for? What he thinkin? Hell."

But then it felt like I not even in the room, my nerves driving me so far back into myself. All a sudden my throat felt cold.

"What is it?" said Chip. "What you ain't sayin, buck?"

I cleared my throat, sat down. I stared off at the exit, at the doors to the front lobby. "He was askin yesterday bout goin back to the flat. He said there was somethin he needed."

"What he needin so bad?"

I shrugged. "He ain't said. He was embarrassed." I fixed my eyes on his old piano, standing open and grinning whitely at the room. Dread was rising up in me. "I said he ought to ask Delilah to help him," I muttered, real soft.

"He wasn't lookin so good," said Hiero. His fingers picked absently at his frayed sleeve. "I kept askin if he sick. He kept sayin no, but. Hell. You known somethin was wrong."

I thought of how Paul was yesterday evening, his blond hair upright as quills, that slack drunken laugh of his. Chip exhaled, set his thick hands on the table.

"Hold up. Ernst gone out there?" I said. "Jesus Christ. We lose Ernst, we good as buried."

"It alright," said Hiero. "If they just goin off to the flat, they like to be back soon. It ain't far."

"Paul been gone all damn day, buck. It been *hours.*"

I felt sort of lightheaded, thin, near transparent with fear. "What time is it?"

"You missed lunch," said Chip.

"Ernst was goin check the flat," the kid said soft like. "He find them. Don't you worry, Sid. Maybe they ain't even together."

I give him a despairing look. Shook my damn head.

"If they been pinched," said Chip, "if they been pinched, we got to get out of here. The Boots be comin here next."

But if they been pinched, hell. Ain't nothing else matter no more.

"We got to stay calm," said the kid. "They could be comin back right now. We just don't know." There was a undercurrent of strength in his voice I ain't recognized. And then I did. It sound like Delilah.

Ernst come back late the next night. Our anxiety was chewing its way through our guts, we was so nervous. Ernst come in real slow, and I known it at once. Never mind his slick hair looking impeccable, his silver cufflinks shining. He run a pale hand down his tie, tucking it cleanly into his suit. Then he just shake his head.

"You're sitting in the dark," he said. "Somebody turn on a goddamn light."

I felt my heart sink.

"Nothin?" said Chip. "For real?"

"Maybe that's good news," said Hiero. "Maybe that means they're not in trouble."

"No, kid," said Ernst. "It's not good news." Then he stopped, give the kid a hard look, his dark eyes looking liquid. "What do you mean, 'they'?"

"Delilah been gone all day too," said Chip. He give a quick glance over at me.

I could feel my old head spinning. "You go to the police?" I said nervously.

"Yes."

"They ain't got them?"

"They said they hadn't heard anything about anyone fitting Paul's description." He swallowed. "I didn't ask about Delilah. But she's a Canadian citizen. She should be fine."

"And American. She both."

Ernst nodded. "Then she's even safer." But there was something soft, something pliable in his voice, made me think he ain't believed it.

"Aw, look who just in time," hissed Chip.

I looked up.

Big Fritz was slipping silent through the soot-darkened curtains up-stage. He was carrying his sax, his coat folded over the other arm. For a instant I ain't believed he real. I sat still in my chair, my eyes fixed on him. He stop to study the cat lying like a pile of rags between the footlights. Then he come forward and down to us.

He look *awful*. His brown suit damp and sallow, his ruddy jowls shadowed with stubble, his small flinty eyes studying us each in turn. His mouth sagged in his soft cheeks like moist dough. He look like he bout to speak, but then he ain't said nothing.

"Hell, Fritz," said the kid. "You okay?"

"Fritz," Ernst said with a quiet nod. But he ain't moved.

We was all watching him.

He opened his massive hands, gestured weakly. "I came as soon as I heard." He sound sad. "Poor Paul. Jesus. What was he doing out there?"

I stared at Fritz's raw-looking nose, peppered with fat black pores. Thinking, hell, he look damn gruesome.

"Not just Paul," said Ernst.

"Delilah's missing too," I said quiet like.

Fritz give me a long look. "Armstrong's girl?"

Chip scraped back his chair, stood abruptly. "Sid's girl," he said in disgust. "You been gone a long time, buck."

Fritz frowned at Chip. His tight lips gone white at the corners.

All a sudden I just wanted to screw from that place, to slit my own throat, hell, just *go*. I ain't wanted a single damn word more of this. I sat real still.

"Delilah Brown," said Ernst. "Armstrong's singer up from Paris. She was with Paul when he disappeared. It doesn't make sense."

Fritz leaned back against the edge of the bar. "I didn't hear anything about a jane. She's American?"

"Canadian. Both."

"You're sure she was with him?"

But Ernst was studying him with his very dark eyes, like he brooding on something. At last he said, "What did you hear, Fritz? How did you know to come back here?"

Fritz shook his head. "Only that Paul was arrested."

"Jesus," Chip muttered.

Fritz glanced at our faces. "You didn't know?"

"No." Ernst sat back, crossed his legs. But there was a hardness in his gestures, like he trying real hard not to feel what he was feeling.

"What you mean, arrested?" the kid said nervously.

"He was deported to Sachsenhausen. This morning. I don't know what the charges were. I expect the usual."

"The usual," said the kid, and there was a bitterness there I ain't heard before.

"Holy hell," Chip whispered. He begun running his hand down his face, staring at the scuffed floor.

The cat stood in the footlights, stretched, lay back down. Started licking the tops of its paws.

I felt something just give out in my chest, like my lungs was collapsing. I was breathing real fast, real shallow. *Sachsenhausen*. Hell. Not one of us had to ask where that was. A jack could live in a windowless pit and still know the word Sachsenhausen.

A tap was dripping somewhere back in the green room. The floor shuddered slightly, like a big truck passing in the street outside. I could hear the kid breathing.

"What bout his papers?" said Hiero. "He got his papers with him, right?"

Fritz shook his head. "I didn't ask about his *papers*."

"*Who* didn't you ask?" said Ernst. "Where did you hear all this, Fritz?"

Sachsenhausen, I thought. Hell.

Fritz ain't said nothing for a long moment. His huge red face looked flushed, but it always look like that. He fold back the doors of his suit, put his huge hands in his trouser pockets. At last he sort of sighed. "Albert Basel. I've been hiding in an old flat he owns. Hoping this would blow over."

"Albie Basel!" Chip shouted. "*Albie Basel?*"

"What you doin over there?" I snapped. "He *killed* us last year."

"It made more sense than staying here with you," he said grimly. "Than all of us being in one place. I should have said something. I'm sorry."

"Aw, he *sorry*," hissed Chip.

Fritz stood real damn still, like he made of wax. "Shut up, Chip. I mean it now."

"Sure you do. If you ain't gone out in the damn daylight maybe the Boots be less suspicious. They come here huntin for us the morning you left. You known that?"

"If you hadn't killed that poor boy, we wouldn't be in any trouble at all."

"Poor boy?" I said. "The one with the bottle to the kid's neck?"

Fritz scowled. "You know what I mean."

"Enough," said Ernst.

The club's coarse light, it sat on our faces in a way made them look like masks, shone this soft transparency over the flesh. Ain't none of us look like ourselves.

Delilah's gone, I kept thinking. And then: *Sachsenhausen*. And then: *Delilah*.

Ernst stood decisively. He run a hand over his sleeves, like out of habit. "I'll get the Horch out of the garage. I'll bring it around out back. We need to go. Now. We don't even know what Paul or Delilah will have told them. But I'm sure it'll be enough. Take what you need from here."

Sachsenhausen.

"Where we goin?" Hiero asked slowly, like from underwater.

Delilah was gone.

"Hamburg. And then, hopefully, Paris." Ernst look like he going to say something more but then he broke off, as if there too much to say.

Sachsenhausen.

"I won't be going," said Fritz. There was a strain in his voice. All a sudden I was seeing again just how huge he was, how much his own man. He crossed to the stage, gathered up his coat and his alto sax.

"You can't stay here, Fritz. It's madness."

Fritz let a long silence trail Ernst's words. He frowned. "Franz Thon has invited me to join the Golden Seven," he said calmly. "I wanted to tell you before I heard about Paul. And then, well." He sort of shrugged.

I got a strange taste in my mouth, a texture like cobwebs. Fritz in the *Golden Seven*? Hell. *Imagine* it. I ain't never heard nothing so unreal in my damn life. And all a sudden it all seemed so dreamlike, so ridiculous.

Ernst was staring at the filthy floor. "And you've accepted Thon's invitation."

We sat there in silence, all of us staring at Fritz.

After a moment he shrugged again. Then he turned to go. He was holding his chin stiff as he made his way through the tables and up toward the front of the club. I imagined I could hear his fat thighs rubbing together in that suit. He stopped halfway up. "You should come too, Ernst, while they'll still have you. They're not bad players. But they'd be so much better with you there. Think about it. Food, good money— you'd be taken care of." He glanced us over, a kind of sadness in his eyes.

Ernst bent down, lit a cigarette very carefully. I seen him shake out the match but his hands, hell, they was trembling.

"I don't think I've ever been more ashamed of someone in my life," he said. "Never." He exhaled a long slow stream of pale smoke. "Good luck to you, friend."

"You callin him *friend*?" Chip shouted. "*Him*? That fat *fuck*?"

Hiero was staring at Fritz with a unreadable expression in his eyes.

Fritz nodded, twice. He made to say something, then seemed to decide against it.

Chip stood, leaning across the table. "You sack of *shit*," he shouted. "Get out of here before I shove that axe so far down you throat it come out the other end. *Go*."

"Damn it, Chip," Ernst raised his voice. "Sit *down*."

But Fritz was already out, past the coat check, into the lobby.

Chip's panting filled the club. We heard the bolt on the front door punch back, then the glass clatter as the door opened and shut. Then nothing but silence. That dripping water from the faucet backstage, a distant rattling from outside, like the street itself was trembling, the great pavement shaking.

III

I was curled up against the back window of the Horch, my suit jacket folded under my head. Mile after mile rolled by, barren in the dark. I remember the sun coming up red in the east. Delilah, the smell of her skin, her cool fingers tracing a line down my ribs. And old Paul blind drunk at the piano, his amber laugh. I felt heavy, blank, like a light gone out in me. The Horch banged and jounced over the back roads, climbed back up onto the highway. And then I ain't felt nothing. Not a twinge of grief, disgust or anger. Nothing.

I remember the kid swearing. We was long out of Berlin when he start to cussing and banging his hand against the back of Ernst's seat, shouting that he left his horn in the Hound. I opened my eyes. My own axe loomed between us, its head pressing hard up against the canvas roof. The kid put a hand on my shoulder, murmured a apology. I just closed my old eyes.

I remember a early sky blond as ash, a warm wind smelling of coal and birch leaves. The mute road rolling out before us. Chip cracked his window open, and smelling all that dust I thought I was going to cry.

I just shut my eyes tight, buried my face in my jacket. Thinking, there got to be something we could of done. Cutting out for Hamburg ain't no kind of loyal.

Somewhere through that fog I heard Chip and Ernst in the front seat, arguing. The miles poured past, never-ending. I remember seeing Chip unwind the stained bandage from his head, peel the gauze off his scabbed-over scalp and ball up the bandages, tossing them out the window. We was nearing Hamburg. And then we was pulling over, lurching to a stop. I lift up a feverish face and seen Ernst out on the gravel shoulder talking to two armed Boots.

"It okay, it okay," Hiero whispered to me. He squeezed my arm. "Don't you worry, Sid, we goin be fine. Ernst got it under control."

One of the Boots crouched down, staring in at us with a flushed face. Ernst barked at him to step away from the Horch, like he might sully it. There was more talk, and then suddenly they was pulling away in a storm of gravel. Ernst thrown hisself back into his seat, his delicate hands on the wheel. He had a quiet, angry-looking smile on his face, and saying nothing, started the auto back up.

I slept again.

———— ■ ————

I woke feeling drained. Thoughts of Delilah and Paul rose up in my mind, and I tried to force them back down. Shadows passed by in the windows.

"Sid," the kid said quiet like. "How you doin?"

I shifted, glanced over at him. The road's holes rattling the wheel-wells, making my feet stammer against the floor. The kid's knees was folded up over my old axe.

"Hiero," I said, then begun coughing.

"You thirsty, buck?" said the kid. He pulled a canteen of water from under his seat. "Go on."

It was late afternoon. Outside, a soft green light lined the boulevard, filtered through the trees. We started passing tall, pillared gates, the arched and gabled roofs of vast mansions rising up over their brick walls. Ladies strolled the streets, maids in strict uniform walking hordes of dogs on leather leashes.

Ernst look uneasy, driving real slow. We ain't none of us talked. Except Chip, of course.

"Shit, Haselberg," he grinned. "You grown up here? With butlers and gardeners and nannies wipin you ass?"

"We don't choose where we're from," said Ernst.

Chip chuckled. "I guess you got to keep you hands clean for you clarinet."

I could smell the sea through the open window. Ernst pulled onto a leafy road, winding between pale lindens. I seen some wide green lawn just beyond the trunks. And then it struck me: this wasn't no road at all, but a damn *driveway*. Hell.

Ernst pulled to a stop on pink gravel. "We're here." With a vaguely sour look on his mug, he climbed out of the Horch, left his door standing wide.

Well, knock me over with a feather. It was a huge, white stone mansion, with pillars and twin staircases leading up to the front verandah. A stone balustrade looked out over the yard. On either side of the huge façade, long, windowed wings stretched on for what seem like forever. On the lawn beyond I seen figures working, two gents crouched in the flowerbeds, a jane carrying some sort of bucket over their way. Looked like a damn *institution*.

"You grown up here, buck?" Chip muttered. "Hell. You father ain't happen to wear a little white coat most days, do he?"

Ernst put a hand on the warm hood of the Horch, studied us where we stood on the running board staring in awe at the property. "My family—well, they aren't me. Please remember that."

Hiero nodded. "We know you, Ernst. It alright."

"And no," he said to Chip. "I didn't grow up here. Mutti bought this place two years ago."

"You got to have one damn big extended family," Chip said with a smile. "Hell, buck. Boots ain't never find us here. Even if they lived in the damn place *with* us."

A tall man had come out to the balustrade and stood watching us, his long shadow bent and stretching out toward us. Something in the way his grey fingers grasped the stone made me real uneasy. Ernst shaded his eyes, studied him.

"That you father?" said Hiero.

Ernst shook his head. "It's Rummel."

The man come down one side of the steps, moving with a stiff grace. As he approached I seen just how damn long and thin he was. He got to be six and a half feet, but thin as celery, his lean, bony face expressionless, his hooded eyes pale. He give a quick, stiff bow, the corded muscles knotting in his neck.

"Mr. Ernst," he said. "How pleasant to see you."

"Rummel," said Ernst, smiling. "This is Sid Griffiths. Chip Jones. That over there is Hieronymus Falk. They'll be staying here tonight. Would you find them a room, please. In the west wing, I'd think."

Rummel nodded. "Shall I inform your mother that you're here?"

Ernst give him a look. "Where's Father?"

"Your father, sir?"

But Ernst shook his head. He was already starting toward the house. "Leave your instruments, gents," he called back to us. "Rummel will take care of that. Are you hungry?"

Holy hell. The entrance hall we come into just gone up and up, near twenty-five feet to the moulded ceiling. The floor was pearled marble, the walls lined with leaded glass windows doused in light. In the centre of the foyer stood a single dark table, holding a glass bowl of lilies floating in water, the buds rocking softly. There was corridors off to the left, the right and straight ahead. Past tied-off green velvet curtains you could see a indoor winter garden. Curving up round either side of the entrance hall, wide steps led to the upper floors.

Hiero was staring at Ernst with a strange look on his face.

"Yes, yes," said Ernst, "it's big, I know. They don't even live in most of it. It's like a tomb. Come on. I hate coming in through this entrance."

Chip give a low whistle. "Hell, buck. It amazing."

"Yes, that's the point," Ernst said crisply.

He led us toward the right corridor and stopped at a small rounded alcove, glancing down at the curve in the hall. There was a tall window set in the facing wall, and we could see the white Horch parked far below, covered in dust. "I don't know if they'll be in the back garden, or in the sun room."

There was a low mahogany bench set against the wall, and the kid sat down with a frown. Lifting his head, he listened.

Something was coming down the hall. Sound like the shifts of a dress rubbing together, the soft click of heels. And a mechanical squeaking, like a drinks tray. I got to wondering if we was intruding on some sort of afternoon tea.

But then a elderly dame come into view, wearing a elegant cream dress. She was pushing a girl in a wheelchair. Hell. I wiped a hot hand on my thighs. That girl was so damn pretty, all dark eyes and auburn hair, her slender hands folded in her lap. She look strange in that contraption, delicate-featured, and when she smiled it was like a ripple passing over a calm lake.

"*Ernie!*" she exclaimed. "I *knew* it. I *knew* it."

"Hi Buggy," he smiled. He stood very still, waiting for them to approach. Chip give me a surprised look.

The older dame put her toe on the brake of the chair, punched it to a standstill. Then she straightened, smoothed her hands along her sleeves, give Ernst a careful look. "Well," she said. "Look at you. You look awful."

Ernst chuckled.

"Liesl *thought* she heard a motor in the drive."

The girl smiled up. "I *told* you, Mother."

Frau von Haselberg clasped her hands, turned to look at us. She was pale as spring cabbage, her face full of tiny wrinkles like the veins in a leaf. Her brown eyes the only spots of darkness on her. She looked a little sickly, strange, white as something churned up from the earth's depths. "You must be Ernst's Americans," she said. "We've heard so much about you. It's a shame Ernst hasn't brought you for a visit sooner. We of course have all of your recordings."

"Of course," Ernst said dryly. "But have you ever listened to them?"

"*Ernst,*" said his mother, like she shocked. But she was smiling.

Chip took off his hat as Ernst introduced us. I stared at his gouged knuckles, the scabs from that fight a lifetime ago. His oyster lips was still badly mashed up, split and scabbed over, and his one eye wasn't focused quite right, narrow and squinting. *Hell*, I thought, *he damn ugly. Like a Frankenstein.*

Ernst gestured at the two dames with a smooth grace. "This is my mother, Mrs. von Haselberg. And this is my sister, Liesl. We call her Buggy. She's a frivolous troublemaker."

Liesl give us a startling smile. "It's true. You'll see."

"Are you here for a long visit?" said Frau von Haselberg.

"No."

His mother seemed a little disappointed. "You drove all the way from Berlin? Today? You must all be rather exhausted. You'll stay for tonight, of course. I'll have Frieda make up some rooms."

"Exhausted, Mother? Strong men like them?" said Liesl, her smile full of mischief. "I should hope not."

"I ain't so tired," said Chip, grinning.

Liesl focused her gaze on him, her smile widening.

I looked warily at both of them.

"Rummel said Father is away?" Ernst said after a moment.

His mother sighed. "Near Saarbrücken. Working. He should be back soon, we hope. You've come to see him? Nothing is wrong, I hope?"

Ernst give her a quick look. "He didn't say anything?"

"About what?"

"You know how he is, Ernie," said Liesl. "*Rummel* knows more than we do."

"Ah, yes. The frail von Haselberg women. We mustn't tax you, must we."

"Under no circumstances," said Liesl.

Frau von Haselberg just shook her head.

I was looking out the window at the sun, low over the wide green lawns. It was so damn peaceful here.

"Let me get them settled," Ernst said to his mother. "We'll find you in a bit. We'll be hungry, if Anke could find a little something extra."

Frau von Haselberg nodded. "Anke isn't with us anymore. But the new girl will be able to find something, I'm sure."

Ernst nodded. "Yes, yes. Fine."

He led us deeper into the house, up a low flight of stairs, along a open passage with closed doors on one side, a view of a long sitting room below us on the other. Chip leaned over the railing, rolled his eyes at me, kept going.

"What happen to you sister?" the kid said quietly, as we went.

"Polio. Four years old." Ernst cleared his throat. "She's paralyzed from the waist down."

"Hell," said Chip. "Well. She seem alright."

"She's not," Ernst said curtly. "Neither of them are. They're bigoted two-faced snobs and they'd toss you into the street as soon as look at you. So would Rummel."

"Rummel? You butler?"

Ernst frowned. "Rummel's not a butler. Rummel is—*efficient.*" He slowed, give us a considered look, like he deciding something within hisself. "When something needs doing, Rummel does it. Without fail."

"I reckon you ain't talkin bout the laundry," Chip muttered.

Ernst give a bitter smile. "No. There are others who do that."

———————

That night I slept a long time in the soft bed. When I finally woke in the late morning I found a clean suit set out for me, near my size. I wondered where Delilah and Paul slept. What they was waking to.

I found Chip and the kid out in a side courtyard, where the Horch been parked for the night. Both got on clean suits too. Someone done washed the road dust off the auto, and it gleamed like a bone in the sun.

I stood just inside the French doors, looking out at them. Hiero was sitting on the stone steps, his back to me, watching Chip run a hand along the shining Horch. It seem so ordinary, this scene. Then Hiero turn round, staring directly at me though I was standing in the shadows. "Sid?"

After Berlin, something happened between me and the kid. I ain't understood it. But it was like he started looking out for me, watching over me, keeping a closer eye. Hell. He like a brother, baring his teeth at Ernst or Chip or anyone who bite too hard at me. Like we ain't had a rivalry over Delilah just days ago. But something in me just wasn't working right, cause even as it was happening, I ain't felt nothing.

As I come down the steps into the white sunlight, I seen a movement from under the alcove. Ernst's sister was wheeling herself slowly over to Chip.

"It's a beautiful automobile," she called to him.

He shrugged, said something I ain't caught.

"A Horch 853 Sport Cabriolet," she laughed. "The 1938 models were nice, yes."

Chip give her a quizzical look.

"I'm good with wheels, Mr. Jones," she said.

He stared at her like he ain't never seen such a creature. Then he laughed. "Aw, you just call me Chip."

"Chip, then. You must call me Buggy. Liesl is far to . . . comatose."

The kid give me a brooding look as I sat down.

Liesl was still laughing. She obviously one of those janes who can't stand pauses in conversation, will do anything to fill them. She seem so frail, so delicate. Beautiful like a turning season, like something you known just ain't going to last.

"Yes, it's because of this," she was saying, slapping the arm of her wheelchair with a flat report. "If you can't laugh at it, Chip, then it's a sad fate indeed."

"Sad fate," the kid muttered, scowling. "That chair cost more than folk make in a year."

"On the other hand," I said in soft rebuke, "her legs don't work."

Hiero scowled again. "Ernst ain't foolin. She seem alright, don't she. But he know his family, Sid. That girl be dangerous."

I glanced over at him, taken aback by the anger in his voice. He watched Liesl in her chair, watched her run her fingers through Chip's scruffy afro. "I never liked Hamburg," he said with a soft fury. "My mama come through here sometimes. I reckon it reminded her of my daddy. I always hated it. My mama, she from Köln."

I lift my face, hearing that. "*From* Köln? You mean she born there?"

"What else do 'she from Köln' mean?"

"So you a *Mischling* then?"

"What. It ain't obvious?"

"You looked in a mirror? Ever?"

He studied the smooth back of his hands. "Black as a starless night."

"Ain't nothin wrong with black, buck."

"My daddy from Cameroon."

"Cameroon? Hell."

The kid smiled shyly. "He been royalty there. Kaiser Wilhelm II hisself invite him to this country to be schooled here, to study medicine. He sailed into Hamburg on the Wöhrmann Line in 1899. Met my mama on a school break. That was in April. She was studying to be a nurse. Then he graduate, move on down Köln, marry her."

"Sound like you got all the facts real accurate," I said. Thinking, *Shit, you tell a tale like you don't want to be believed.* "Royalty. Shit."

He grinned at me. "For real. Hard to believe, ain't it."

"It hard to believe alright."

Chip went over to the Horch, pulled old Ernst's licorice stick out of the backseat, and brought it back to where Liesl was parked in the sunlight. He start showing her how to finger that clarinet. Then he took it from her, smile, lift it to his lips, and blown a sharp needling high C. He wiped off the reed, passed it back to her.

Hiero looked at me, lifting his eyebrows sourly. "You know what I think when I look at her?"

"What."

He studied her with his small dark eyes. "I'll show you," he said in a flat voice. "We got to drive to it though."

I run a hand over my eyes, like to shield some of that bright sunlight. I felt real tired. That heaviness in me again. "It ain't safe, kid."

"It safe enough." He studied me, set a hand on my arm. His grip was strong. "I won't let nothin happen. I swear."

I looked at him in surprise.

But we sat awhile longer in the sunlight, neither of us moving. The kid watched Chip wheeling Liesl over the flagstones.

"My middle name be Thomas," he said. "I want you to know that. I ain't keepin it a secret."

I sort of smiled at him, sad like. It seemed such a small thing to offer. "Roscoe," I said. "Sidney Roscoe Griffiths."

———————■———————

Hamburg. It wasn't nothing to me, another grim north German city. I remembered it being rainy, its skies a murky grey like a constant reflection of water. We come through here once or twice working the clubs to the damn Swing Boys. Them rich sweet-faced kids who come out to defy the Housepainter. Every last one of them got up in glen-checked suits and crepe-soled shoes, short skirts and silk stockings, their long hair so thick with grease you could roast a pig in it. Like it what you *wear* that matter. I known they meant well, known they was our audience, but man, most ain't known two strokes bout jazz, come out only cause of the ban. Kids who thought Whiteman, Gluskin, Bela was the equals of a Armstrong or a Basie. Ain't even able to cut the rug, their arms all swinging together like some hundred-legged beast. Shaking their hair or their homburgs or their closed umbrellas. I known they loved us, got beat up in the streets cause of us. And hell, I *wanted* to love them back. But I ain't never did.

I thought about it as we drove on through the town. All that Swing culture was already dying.

Kid and me ain't hardly talked on the drive. Maybe he was thinking some of the same thoughts I was. At last he tapped the dashboard with his long soft fingers, gestured for me to pull into a lot. I come to a stop, the Horch purring quietly, then stared up through the window at the big sign on the fence.

"Hell. You takin me to the *zoo?*"

"Hagenbecks ain't a zoo," said the kid. "It a animal park. It supposed to be better than zoos. They don't use barred cages, just moats to keep the damn animals in. So they free to roam wild in their own spaces."

"Kid, I ain't in the mood. For real." I folded my arms over the steering wheel, blown out my cheeks.

He give me a curt look. "You got to see somethin. *This* the Hamburg I known."

He climbed out, shut the door with a bang. I watched him through the clean windscreen for a minute. Sighing, I clambered out after him.

The gates at the entrance stood tall and imposing in the sunlight. We crossed the concrete square, stood at the ticket booth. The jack standing in there give Hiero a polite look. The kid stared him down boldly.

Going in, we passed a woman and her very young son. The boy pulled back on her hand, stared at us with frightened eyes.

Hiero ain't said nothing. A dark, satisfied smile passed over his lips.

Hagenbecks was a green, shady park. The air carried traces of shit and piss and mud, like we was moving into farmland. I seen pale birds overhead, crying like widows, and then the path wound down by a pond. I seen the backs of grazing hippos, their skin glowing like polished rocks. The kid looked uneasy, scanning the path ahead.

"It alright," I said. "We ain't got to be so nervous here."

He looked at me. "It ain't that."

Then I caught sight of a row of thatch-roofed clay huts. The kid start striding hard toward them, and I sort of trailed after. We ain't seen more than a few other folk in the park that afternoon. I paused on the path. Then I gone closer.

Wasn't no moat at this exhibit. Instead, a breast-high wooden fence stood spiked between us.

"These the dangerous animals," Hiero said bitterly.

I just stared in amazement. I wasn't even clear on what all I was seeing at first. Then I swore softly.

Cause it was *people*. Black folk. Barefoot, dressed in rags and bones. A group of jacks squatted on flat rocks in the mud, smoking crude pipes, disks hanging from their huge earlobes. Women sat in a circle farther back, leopard-print cloths tied firmly round their privates. With mortar and pestle they was pounding cornmeal, the powder of it dusting their feet. And despite all the mud, despite the filth and the flies, their skin looked weirdly shiny. All silvery black, like the zookeepers kept them buffed up like onyx.

A ache come into my chest. "They keep *people* here?"

"This just the African exhibit," Hiero muttered. "They got one for Samoans, for Esquimaux." He was trying to smile, like it ain't so horrifying. Or like it so horrifying, it funny. But the smile ain't reached his eyes.

"A human zoo," I mumbled. "Shit." I was just too damn astonished to say anything else. A old woman come out from one of the huts, carrying a baby in her arms, her shrunken gams gleaming in the sunlight. She crossed that sun-beaten patch of mud, singing something real soft to the baby. The baby started squalling.

"My daddy ain't never forgive hisself for comin here," said the kid.

I ain't said nothing.

"He a *chief* in Douala. Here he just a savage in civilized clothes. But hell, Sid,"—Hiero give me a quick angry glance—"I ain't never heard him say a damn word against Germany. Not once. Herodotus tell this story bout King Darius of Persia. The king called the Greeks to him and asked, *How much scratch I got to pay you to eat the bodies of you fathers when they die?* Greeks told him ain't no sum on earth get them do that. Then Darius called some Indians to him, jacks who eat their fathers, and asked them in front of the Greeks, *How much scratch I got to pay you to burn the bodies of you fathers when they die?* Indians said no way in hell they burn their fathers. See, a jack always reckon his own customs is the best in the world. Ain't no way you change his mind. But my daddy, he wasn't like that. He come to Germany, that be it. He make hisself into a German."

I ain't said nothing to that.

We stood a long time at that enclosure. The sun slid lower. When I glanced over, I seen the kid lock eyes with one of the men, a jack with greying hair, the whites of his eyes gone yellow. They stared a long while at each other. I could hear the birds crying overhead. Some folk come down the path, chatting, drifted on past.

Hiero ain't even blinked. There wasn't no shared curiosity in that gaze, no sense of shock. Just calm resignation, like when a man gazes at a portrait of hisself from another time.

When we left Hagenbecks, it was like something gone out of the kid then, some kind of fury. He was just wearied. We ain't drove back to Ernst's estate at once. Kid directed me down toward the piers, and we pulled in slow, got out, walked to the far end to sit in the cool sunlight. Our legs dangled out over the black water. A swell of gulls rose over our heads, screaming. Air stank of the salt and the heavy docks across the way.

A big grey ship pushed slowly through the locks.

Hiero banged the dried mud from his shoes, stared out over the long shawl of water. "Hell. Hard to believe there be Algerians at the end of this water."

I nodded, feeling depressed. "And Icelanders."

He smiled. "Canadians?"

"Indians."

"Some poor old jack in Baltimore lookin right back at us," said the kid, swinging his big feet.

I frowned. "I might even know him. Might be my Uncle Henry."

"America," said Hiero, and there was something in his voice.

"You talk bout this sea and that sea," I said. "Atlantic. Pacific. But it all one water, ain't it? Why divide it up?"

Hiero squinted up at the gulls. "You a real poet, Sid. A goddamn Herodotus."

But my thoughts done already wander, to the day the kid first walked into our lives. How Paul brought him down to the Hound one night, the kid's face half hidden by a old tramp's cap slouched low over his eyes. I remember how I grinned at Chip, thinking he look like a damn child. No more than twelve years old. Hell, Paul *couldn't* be serious. Was we really supposed to believe this Joe Diaper be a horn blower for real?

The kid come up, his jacket swaying every which way. He look awkward, all knees and elbows. He dressed like some tramp, huge khaki trousers held up with blue suspenders. Ratty houndstooth coat. And that dirty cap on his head, looking less like protection from the weather than something to hide under. Shade the world from his eyes when he ain't feel like seeing it. He might've been any nasty little street brat to look at his clothes. What got you was how he *moved* in them. Didn't strut exactly—he was too shy for that—but he moved with a rhythm got you thinking. Like he had a damn limp.

Paul kept going on bout what a dazzling genius he was, what a rare talent. A damn *virtuoso*. Me, I couldn't stop looking at his skinny wrists.

But when he lifted his horn, we give him a respectful silence. His trumpet was a cheap-looking thing, dented, like a foil-wrapped chocolate been in a pocket too long. He put his rabbity fingers on the pistons, cocked his head, his left eye shutting to a squint.

"*Buttermouth Blues*," Ernst called back to him.

The kid nodded. He begun to tease air through the brass. At first we all just stood there with our axes at the ready, staring at him. Nothing happened. I glanced at Chip, shook my head. But then I begun to hear, like a pinprick on the air—it was *that* subtle—the voice of a humming-bird singing at a pitch and speed almost beyond hearing. Wasn't like nothing I ever heard before. The kid come in at a strange angle, made the notes glitter like crystal. Pausing, he took a huge breath, started playing a ear-splitting scale that drawn out the invisible phrase he'd just played.

The rest of us come in behind him. And I tell you, it ain't took but a minute more for me to understand just what kind of player this kid was. He sounded broody, slow, holding the notes way longer than seemed sane. The music should've sounded something like a ship's horn carrying across water—hard, bright, clear. The kid, hell, he made it muddy, passing his notes not only over seas but through soil too. Sounded rich, which might've been fine for a older gate, but felt fake from him. The slow dialogue between him and us had a sort of preacher-choir feel to it. But there wasn't no grace. His was the voice of a country preacher too green to convince the flock. He talked against us like he begging us to listen. He wailed. He moaned. He pleaded and seethed. He dragged every damn feeling out that trumpet but hate. A sort of naked, pathetic way of playing. Like he done flipped the whole thing inside out, its nerves flailing in the air. He bent the notes, slurred them in a way made us play harder against him. And the more we disagreed, the stronger he pleaded. But his pleading ain't never ask for nothing, just seemed to be there for its own damn sake. In a weird way, he sounded both old and like he touching the trumpet for the very first time.

I *hated* it. It felt so damn false, so showy. I kept my face lowered, out of the footlights, as we come to a slow stop, the music breaking apart.

When I looked back, old Ernst, he got water on the eyes. He *cryin.*

Paul just leaned forward, give the kid a loose hug round the shoulders. "What'd I tell you, boys? The voice of *God.*"

I thought of it now, sitting on the pier with the kid. But all of a sudden it ain't mattered no more that the kid wasn't, in my opinion, as good as everyone claimed. Sitting here at the pier, staring out at the flat, grey waters, he looked so damn small, so vulnerable. Like he something blown in on the wind. And I known then that this was what Delilah seen when she looked at him.

I put a hand on his shoulder, felt his sharp bones moving through his shirt.

He look at me shyly, smiled. "We goin be alright, Sid," he said. Then he ducked his head, embarrassed, looking away.

———————————————————

Couple days later I was coming up out of the gardens, crunching over the pink gravel, when I turned round to see Ernst striding toward me.

"Sid." His linen suit was wrinkled in the elbows. He smoothed his hair, glanced back at the vast house behind him. "My father's returned."

"He get them? He get our papers?"

"I hope so." Ernst put a hand on my shoulder, started walking. "Come with me. I want him to meet you. I want him to see these are real people he's dealing with."

He led me into a stone courtyard, vines crawling across a old fountain, the stonework cracked. I followed him through a arched entrance hall, up a long staircase I ain't encountered before. Fat gilt eagles perched on all the mouldings, their wings crested and fearsome. Every piece of furniture was thin and gold, the walls overhung with mirrors and soft cream curtains. The air smelled of fresh cut lilies.

"This is the East Wing." Ernst smiled bitterly. "Our Poland."

Rummel stood on the landing. He give Ernst a curt nod as we come up. Sour-looking, long-faced, sallow in his black suit, Rummel turned without speaking, leading us along a airy corridor, past tall leaded windows overlooking the gardens. Hiero done told me once bout Charon, that Greek who ferries the dead to the underworld. Rummel, hell, he like our Charon. His eyes was so pale they might've been blind.

We come to the study door. Ernst dismissed Rummel, who bowed, turned and made his noiseless way back down to the landing.

Ernst put a hand on my arm. "Sid, my father's not like other men. He's very *subtle*."

"Rummel?" a man called out sharply. "Is that you?"

"Not Rummel," Ernst called. He give me a look. "Be careful what you say."

His shoulders tightly set, he opened the door and walked on in.

I followed him. The blue carpet felt thick underfoot. Sunlight from a tall window caught in the folds of drapery, casting long amber shafts across the walls. A small man sat behind a huge dark desk, writing carefully, and he ain't paused even to look up. His skin looked waxen and pale. His silver-grey suit shimmering in the light from the windows. I seen his cropped grey hair, his fine thin moustache, the etched grooves in his face.

The man lift up his eyes, frowning in displeasure. I lost my breath for a second. His irises—they was a frightening dark blue.

"Damn it, Ernst, I'm very busy. What is it?"

Ernst sat on the white sofa across from the desk. "Nice to see you too."

His father grimaced, took off his spectacles, held them dangling in one hand. "Yes, yes, of course it's always nice to see you. You're looking well. Thin, maybe."

"I've put on weight."

"Ah. Not thin, then." He glanced back down at the paper in front of him, scratched a few more lines. He looked up, lifted his eyebrows. "Well? What is it?"

"I know you're busy," said Ernst, "what with the war you're starting."

His father waved a dismissive hand. "So dramatic. My goodness."

"We've come for the documents, Father. For Paris."

"Yes." Old von Haselberg nodded. His gaze shifted over to me, and I flinched. "You must be one of Ernst's musicians."

I was still standing foolishly just inside the door, next to the heavy bookcase, its gilt tomes morocco-bound. I swallowed hard, feeling like a damn exhibit just been wheeled out. "Sidney Griffiths," I said.

"Of course, yes," said von Haselberg. "It's a very peculiar music you boys play."

"Sit down, Sid," said Ernst, gesturing beside him on the sofa. "You don't need to wait for my father to invite you in."

"Where is Rummel?" von Haselberg asked distractedly.

"On the landing. Where he always is. Looking like a corpse, I might add."

"Yes, poor Rummel," von Haselberg smiled. "I'll need him in a moment."

Ernst said nothing to this.

I watched von Haselberg slide the paper he been writing on into a drawer, locking it. He stood, and taking up his cigar, come round his huge desk. He had that sleek grace his son had inherited, that easy fluidity about him. He took my hand in a firm grip, smiling.

"What's my son been telling you about me?" he said, chuckling. "No doubt I must be quite the ogre."

I shrugged, glanced on over at Ernst. He was frowning, studying the gardens through the big window. In profile, his skin looked near translucent.

When von Haselberg sat, he unbuttoned his suit jacket, stretching his legs out straight.

The old man cast about, looking for a ashtray, then frowned, tapping the ashes onto the carpet. "That Frieda. She keeps emptying the ashtrays and then forgetting to put them back. You'd think she was trying to get me to quit."

"You *should* quit, Father," said Ernst. "It's a disgusting habit."

"Nonsense."

But Ernst had crossed the carpet, kneeled down, and with a kind of soiled dignity flicked his handkerchief from his breast pocket and palmed up the ashes.

"Leave it, son, good lord." Von Haselberg raised his eyebrows at me, like he was shocked at his son's foolishness. "We do pay the girls for that."

"Is that what you pay them for?"

"Stop it, Ernst. Honestly."

Ernst pursed his lips, folded the dirty handkerchief back into his pocket.

Old von Haselberg chuckled, his dark blue eyes creasing. "You didn't come here to do chamber service, I assume. Though it doesn't offend me in the least." He looked at me. "As long as my son is doing what he loves to do."

Ernst smiled too. "What a remarkable father you are."

Hell. I start to feeling damn uncomfortable.

But von Haselberg just sort of shrugged a weary shoulder. He ran his small hands along his thighs, like he was growing tired. "Mr. Griffiths. You've been living in the Fasanenstrasse flat? I trust you found it comfortable?"

"Don't start on that, Father."

"For heaven's *sake*," he said, losing some patience. "It is called being *polite*."

"This is where he reminds you you're living off his charity."

"Don't be ridiculous. I meant no such thing."

Ernst just lifted up his eyebrows, in a exact echo of his father's earlier gesture.

"And what do you think of this Poland business?" said von Haselberg.

"Don't answer that," said Ernst.

But there was a long silence after that, as if both men was waiting for me to speak. I sort of cleared my throat, glanced over at Ernst. He was studying his shoes. "What Poland business?" I said reluctantly.

Von Haselberg laughed a abrupt, gruff laugh. "An excellent answer. Indeed. Where did you say he was from, was it Baltimore?"

Ernst nodded.

"Yes, yes. An excellent answer for an American. Can I offer you something to drink?"

"No," said Ernst. "We're fine."

"Ah, a pity." Still von Haselberg got to his feet, and gliding over to the bookshelves, pulled down a bottle of claret. He poured all three of us glasses, brought them clinking to the side tables beside the sofa.

"I said no, Father."

"Then don't drink it," he said. "They aren't poisoned, I assure you." He smiled at me through his cigar. "I really do have a deep respect for the arts. All the arts. I don't think I understand jazz, but I do admire the passion you boys devote to it. Dedication can be genius in its own right."

I nodded uneasily, turned the glass in my hands.

"My father is a great patron of the arts," said Ernst. "Isn't that what you're saying?"

The old man sat again with a groan. "Not so great, I'm afraid. My work keeps me busy. But it would be a poorer world without them. And I have no illusions, Mr. Griffiths. I am an old man, my sense of art is old, but I know that what I love was once rather shocking to the old men then. Mozart, Schiller, Goethe. Paul Hindemith, even."

"Oh? Hindemith? Early or later work, Father? I always supposed you to prefer Kurt Eggers or Arno Breker. Hans Pfitzner. Richard *Wagner*. I underestimated your catholic tastes."

"Wagner," von Haselberg said, shaking his grey head like he filled with regret. "He's awfully dramatic, isn't he."

"You like Wagner?" I said politely.

"Good lord, no. Only according to my unhappy son."

Ernst scowled. "You thought we'd wait around in Berlin like goddamn *children*."

Now his father shifted in his chair, and there was something hardening in him, finally. I swallowed hard. His eyes was darkening. He said crisply, "I didn't care in what manner you chose to wait. But yes, you were to wait in Berlin until I telephoned you."

Ernst sort of lift up his face. "You mean until the papers were cleared."

His father rolled the blue cigar smoke over his tongue, breathed it out in a long ribbon. The ash from the cigar dropped on the carpet again. *Oh, hell*, I thought. *Don't you damn well get up for it, Ernst. Jesus.*

But Ernst sat fast, just flexing his jaw.

With a strange look on his face, almost a ironic smile, von Haselberg got to his feet. He slipped back behind the desk, withdrew a thick manila envelope from the top drawer. "All they need are your signatures," he said to me. "We took care of everything: photographs, documents, 'sponsors.' In the case of the Germans, we even paid the Reich tax. You're free to go to France." He fingered a monogrammed pen from his breast pocket, glanced across at his son. "I'll even donate the pen, Mr. Griffiths. As a patron."

He come back across to me, handed me the envelope and the pen with a smile.

I held my breath. Holy hell. Just like that, here they was. Our lives in a unmarked envelope. I slipped the papers out, begun thumbing through them. There like to be thirty pages at least, all covered with tiny typed print. I ain't sure what I looking for.

"Mr. Falk," von Haselberg said. "He's got a brand new German passport."

I glanced up, nodded.

"Let me see them," said Ernst. He flipped through the several packets. He withdrew Fritz Bayer's papers, withdrew Paul Ludwig Karl-heinz Butterstein. "These two won't be needed," he muttered.

"Ah. Yes. Your Jewish pianist. I suppose events caught up with him."

"*Events.*" Ernst stared a long time at his father. "If you'd cleared these sooner, he'd still be alive."

His father nodded. "Was he very talented?"

"He was a *person*, Father. What does it matter?"

"He was brilliant," I said angrily. "And he's not dead."

Ernst glanced at me. He passed the papers back. I counted out the three packets remaining, slid them into the envelope. Ernst was staring at his father, a tight, unreadable expression on his face.

"Thank you," he said at last. "I know this isn't easy for you."

Von Haselberg laughed dryly, as if to brush the words under the rug. "Mr. Griffiths," he said, standing. "A pleasure to meet you. I wish you great success in your music."

"Thank you."

"One more thing." He give me a careful look. "You'll want to leave immediately. Do you understand?"

"Okay. Sure."

"Ernst. Will you send in Rummel on your way out, please."

The old man was already turning from us, sliding back behind his desk, taking out the sheets he'd locked away earlier. I glanced back, then left the room.

Ernst shut the door with a soft click.

In the hallway I turned, give him a fierce look. "Where the hell you goddamn papers?" I hissed. "There ain't nothin here for you."

He exhaled softly, his shoulders buckling a little under his jacket. Then he caught his breath, a near noiseless sound, like he clearing his lungs.

"Ernst?"

But I couldn't barely look at him. In a delicate gesture, he buttoned his suit jacket, smoothed out his tie, like he packing everything in tight. His face went still as a cup of water.

"I won't be going with you," he said quietly.

"What you sayin?"

"I won't be going with you," he said again, in the exact same tone.

I swallowed. My old brain was working slow. "What you mean? It Armstrong, buck. It Louis *Armstrong.*"

He just sort of wrinkled his brow, glanced away out the window. It was the closest I ever seen him to showing any strong emotion. And then I understood.

"Shit. You *known* bout this. This how you got him to help. You agreed to stay so we could get out."

He shook his head. "No. Don't be ridiculous."

But it was like he wasn't able to think up any alternative lie. He just stood there with his head down, his long pale fingers hanging empty. At last he give me a dim smile. "Look at who I am, Sid. I'll be fine here. I will."

"Fine, hell." I felt this damn lump in my throat.

"There are maps under the front seat of the Horch, as well as an envelope full of francs—enough to last a long time if you're wise with it. Also all the details about how to reach Armstrong in Montmartre."

"We ain't goin without you. Jesus, Ernst."

"Stick to the back roads. You'll see on the map where to cross. Be careful."

I shook my head. "There won't be none of us left." I thought maybe I going to start crying right there. I bit my tongue hard.

And so we left him.

Pulled the long, ghostly nose of the Horch round on the paving stones, needled out through the gates, turned into the oncoming darkness. The headlights cut through the dusk. We drove west in silence with a weight in our chests, all of us brooding, mute with our own denials. Deep into the night. We ain't hardly stopped, except to refuel from the extra gas tanks we packed in with us, to slip away into the grasses to relieve ourselves.

The sun was still low on the horizon, the early shadows long over the uneven asphalt, when we seen the border crossing a couple miles ahead.

I thought Chip and the kid was still asleep, when all a sudden the kid cleared his throat and said, "He ain't comin. For real he ain't comin."

Chip turned round, studied the kid, but ain't said nothing.

The yellow countryside was unravelling, and far ahead in the cool morning light we seen the dark forests of France. We was passing the tall signs printed in black paint, the Achtung and Achtung and Achtung, each underwritten with instructions I ain't read. Then I seen them sawhorses strung with barbed wire, and I kicked at the brake. The car jolted and lurched, slowing down.

"Shit, buck," muttered Chip. He run his hands over his face, yawned.

I tapped the gas again, and with the smoothness of a thoroughbred, the Horch passed between the sawhorses, winding slowly. Through the dusty windscreen I seen two armed Boots standing in a guard hut off to the left, their machine guns trained on us. Their murky green uniforms clean-collared and pressed, like they just come on duty.

"Shit," Hiero whispered. His eyes was real small.

"Don't you say nothin," said Chip. "You hear me? Nothin."

My eyes was fixed on a armed Boot who come out from a sheltered alcove with his palm up. A rifle was looped over his shoulder. I tried to make my damn face neutral, unassuming, but my heart was clattering away in my chest. I come to a careful stop.

That Boot was standing between two sawhorses, and he stepped forward then, approaching the auto with a frown.

My knuckles was going white on the wheel. I was afraid to let go, afraid my hands just start trembling away. I cleared my throat. "Give me you papers," I whispered, my voice all high and crackling like a fire.

I leaned forward, rolled down the window. The late summer air smelled of dirt and smoke.

The Boot's green fatigues was reflected in the Horch's chrome. I sort of squinted up at him, nodding. He was young, brown-haired, tanned, his raw lips chapped from too much sun. There was a hooded look to his eyes.

"Papers," he said brusquely.

I passed them out to him. My hands was shaking like a pensioner's, like I eighty-two damn years old.

He grunted, begun thumbing through them. His eyes was very black, like Ernst's. He walk slowly round to the front of the Horch, studying the grill and silver headlights there like he ain't never seen nothing like it. Then he come back.

"What is your destination?" he said flatly, still flipping through the papers.

"Paris," I said, and coughed. I cleared my throat. "Paris," I said more firmly.

He peered in at me, then ducked his head, give old Chip and Hiero a good long look. His eyes alighted on the bass propped in the back seat.

"We American musicians," I said nervous like. "We just passin through to play in Paris."

He glanced up at that, stared across the canvas of the car roof at something on the other side. Then he said, "Wait here. Don't move." He walked away, over to another guard, begun talking in a low voice.

The morning sun slanted in through the dusty windshield, heating up the old leather seats. I felt a line of sweat inching down my ribs.

Chip set a dark hand on the dash, like to feel the warm sun. "It ain't nothing. Don't you crack, Sid. They just tryin to make you nervous. They probably talkin bout the damn football scores."

I wasn't so sure. It looked pretty serious to me. Hell. What if Ernst's old bastard of a father given us false papers? There got to be something odd bout Hiero's at least. The kid been stateless for years now. I tried not to swallow.

The Boot turned, shielded his eyes, glanced back at us.

Directly ahead of our car, behind a low mound of sandbags lying like shot dogs, crouched a Boot at a heavy machine gun, watching us. His helmet shaded his eyes.

That first Boot come back to us then, still thumbing through the papers. He squatted down at the window, give Hiero a long slow look. *Don't you crack boy*, I was thinking. *Don't you damn well crack.*

He handed the papers back to me with a dismissive nod. He stepped away from the car, gesturing to the soldiers standing in the ditches. They come forward, drawn back the sawhorses, the weight of it straining the slender Boot on the right.

That Boot was still backing away from the Horch, waving us through.

It was a trick. They pretend to let you through, then they start shooting. They wait till you between the lines, so it ain't no country's fault. Sure, we heard the stories. I put a nervous foot on the gas, glided slowly past the dusty sandbags, past more barbed-wire sawhorses, past the jack behind the machine gun.

"Easy," Chip murmured, "just go easy."

We rolled real slow over to the French side. A Frog soldier step forward, waving with two hands for us to stop. The kid twisted round, staring back at the Krauts behind their guns. Chip snapped at him. "Turn youself *round*, boy."

There was another machine gun set just off to one side, atop a small rise, fixed direct on our windshield. I could feel the hairs on the back of my neck prickling.

The Frog soldier who come forward stared at us with real animosity, like he eager to send us back over the lines. His eyes was old, shifty, jaded. In his hefty paunch and greying moustache you seen all the awesome slaughter of Verdun.

"*Papiers*," he snapped. He held out one meaty red hand.

I fumbled at the dash, pulled them out a second time.

"*Vouz-allez où, là? Votre destination.*"

I sort of looked at Chip, looked nervously back at the soldier.

"You ain't speak English, I reckon?" I sort of lifted one hand off the wheel, towards him. He stepped swiftly back, leveling his rifle at me.

"*Tes mains—dans la voiture, mains dans la voiture,*" he barked.

I froze. I held my old hands up, terrified. "No, no. I ain't meant nothin."

He shook his old grizzled head, handing the papers back in to me. "*Non,*" he said, frowning. "*Non, vous devez retourner. Ce n'est pas correcte, ça.*" He waved his gun back at the German lines, gestured with his hand for us to turn round.

"Aw, no," I said. "Please."

"We Americans," Chip shouted at him. He leaned across me, over the seat. "Goddamnit. We Americans. We goin to *Paris*. Don't you turn around, Sid. Don't you do it."

That grizzled soldier was glowering at me, like he wanted nothing more than to haul me out by the collar and line me up against a wall. I was shaking.

"*S'il vous plaît,*" Chip called out at him. "*Monsieur, s'il vous plaît.* American." He picked the mess of papers off my lap, started waving them at the soldier out through the window. The soldier refused to take them, just stood shaking his head.

A second French soldier come across through the barricade, shouting something harsh. I start to sweating. Holy hell, I thought. This is it. This is it.

That second soldier leaned forward, yelling something at us I ain't caught. He seized the papers from Chip's hand, begun snapping through them fiercely.

The grizzled soldier with the hard eyes shook his head, muttering comments every few pages. "*Oui, oui,*" the second soldier said, frowning.

I wet my lips. Don't do this, I thought. Please god, don't.

All a sudden that second soldier hand the papers back to us, and turning swiftly, gestured at the soldiers behind him. And then the barricades lifted, and we was being waved on through, into the black forested hills of France. I looked in amazement at Chip. Gripping the wheel, I couldn't get my breath.

"Go on, buck," he hissed. "Get us the hell out of here."

I tapped the gas, and we moved forward, gliding on into the free west.

IV

Berlin
1992

After a minute, Chip said, "You still mad, ain't you. You still thinking about it."

I ain't said nothing, just shifted grimly from second to third, that Mercedes purring under my hands. We was pouring like syrup along those sleek Berlin roads, the bad white sun cut by the tinted glass. That seductive new leather smell around us.

Chip slipped out his old titanium cigarette case, flicked it open with a click. I gave him a long brooding look.

"You ain't smoking those in here," I said. "And put on you seatbelt."

"Aw, Sid. Don't be like that. You allowed to be just a little excited, you know. Ain't no law against it."

"Seatbelt," I said again.

He slipped an elegant cigarillo into his mouth, then reached up, pulled the old belt on. Then he turned to me and gave me this uneasy, hurt look. "Just so you know," he said. "Just so it been said. I ain't got no hard feelings."

I damn near bit my bridge in half, hearing that. I started coughing.

"Sid?" he said again, after a moment.

"What?"

"I said I ain't got no hard feelings." He shifted his hips and the ribbed leather squeaked under him. "Ain't you got something to say too?"

"What is it I supposed to say to you? What exactly?"

"Aw, I don't know." He sort of brushed this fleck of lint off his sleeve. "This the part where you tell me you ain't got no hard feelings neither. Hell, brother. Come on. You my oldest friend."

"You a son of a bitch, Chip. That's what I got to say to you."

He was silent for a minute but then he looked at me and gave me this sly old grin. "Most likely I am," he said. "I most likely am that. But I just wanted you to know. In my books you still golden, brother."

Chip goddamn Jones. Like a damn bull terrier, when he got something in his teeth.

I pumped the brake and the car almost stopped, got up on its rear wheel, took a bow, and rolled over. I mean, that's how responsive this sweet ride was. An angry driver bore down on his horn, screaming at us as he roared by. We hardly heard him with the windows up. But when Chip rolled his down the whole roar and whine and clatter of the city rushed in. I could smell this singe on the air, like burnt oil. So much exhaust, I thought. So much grit.

Then Chip gave this low whistle through his teeth and I looked over at him.

"Hell," he murmured.

Cause there it was. The Wall. Or what had been the Wall. Sprawled and broken and cleared away. Along the pitted concrete still standing in Potsdamer Platz, a kind of bazaar had sprung up. A Polish market, it looked like. Dour plump men with fast hands hawking bright oranges, portable radios, sweaters knit so damn tight they looked like armour.

The air smelled peppery. I stopped at a traffic light just as a Trabi raced past, its plastic rattling.

"There ain't no going back, I guess," said Chip, tapping his false teeth together.

I wasn't sure if he meant to the festival or back to the old days.

"No there ain't," I said to both.

"Sid," he said, suddenly very serious. "I *am* sorry, brother."

I was silent a long minute. At last I said, "You got to make it right, Chip."

"I will. I'll make it right."

I nodded. And then I said, gruffly, "Roll up you window." It seemed indecent, somehow, us coming through here. I don't know.

So we cut out again, me and Chip. Don't know what it is about that man. He's like a weakness for me, even seventy years later. I ain't a stupid man, no more than most. And he ain't that damn charming. But it seems we is friends to the last. Why, I don't know. The best I can say is that it's like some rundown part of me. See, I got this torn rotator cuff, makes me favour my right arm. It's like that. I just got this broken switch in my brain, can't say no to Chip Jones.

We was just pulling slow off a roundabout, into the long vacant roadways leading into the airport, when Chip opened his eyes, his face going all suspicious.

"We're at the airport," he said.

"Look at those damn bifocals working away," I said. "You sure got your money's worth on them, boy."

"Sid? What're we doing here?"

"What do folk do usually? We catchin a boat." I shook my head.

But he wasn't having none of it. Just looked out at the rows of taxis and tour buses and the sliding glass doors we shuttled past. "I thought we was going to Poland, brother," he said. And then: "You know your flight to Baltimore's already gone?"

I pulled on into the rental lot, gave him a hard look. "I know."

He looked nervous at me. Hell.

"Chip, ain't no damn way I'm driving this rig through to Poland. Size of a damn . . . Why a man so small rent a car so big, huh? What you thinking? Anyhow I don't know that it's even legal take a rental car over the border to another country. You want to get to Poland, we going to have to fly."

Can't tell you how relieved he looked.

"I thought maybe you wasn't coming," said Chip as we checked our luggage, his old family of monogrammed brown cases, my one battered never-unpacked bag. And then, later, as we moved through the security gates, he said again, "I thought maybe you was going to duck out on me, brother."

"It ain't too late," I said.

"Hell," he said with a grin. "It's early yet. It's always early, while you still alive."

"You going to print that one up? Get yourself a bumper sticker?"

Chip chuckled. "Sid, Sid, Sid. Look at this. You and me, it's like old times. Hiero going to be so damn surprised he like to eat his old trumpet."

I wasn't really listening. We was making our slow shambling way toward the gate. "He going to be surprised?" I said.

"Sure, brother. Like a fat girl opening a full fridge."

And then it hit me. I stopped walking, put one damn hand on the top of my head and blown out my cheeks. I stared up the corridor, looked back at Chip.

"Chip," I said.

He was still smiling, sort of half turned toward me. "Let's go, man. What is it?"

"Hiero knows we coming, right?"

Hell if he ain't stopped grinning right quick. I could see him looking at me, trying to decide something. I felt the little hairs on my neck prickle.

Then Chip clear his damn throat and hold out his big hands at me, as if to wave me down. "Course he knows. I mean, he don't know exactly when. But he knows."

"He don't know exactly *when?*"

Chip sort of blinked at me, confused.

"Chip?" I said.

"You forgetting, brother. He *invited* us."

"Don't mean you don't *tell* a man before you come to *visit—*"

"You right, you right," Chip cut in softly. "But how you write something like that? What do you say? *Dear Hiero, we coming up now to see you ain't a ghost? We sorry your life been so disappointing? We glad you ain't dead yet?*"

"How about, *Hiero, we coming to visit second weekend of October. See you soon.*"

Chip cocked his head, gave me a quick grin. "That ain't half bad."

Some folks was passing us, giving us a royal look, but I didn't give a fig. I just stood there shaking my head like it ain't got no neck muscles left, like maybe with the right amount of shaking I could just loosen its screws, and knock it right the hell off.

"But Sid," Chip said after a minute, looking genuinely baffled. "He going to be *happy* when he sees us."

———————— ▪ ————————

I felt *sick*, brother. I got to thinking all about showing up at Hiero's damn door and him slamming it in my face. Or him grabbing my old lapels and hurling me off his porch. Hell, even grabbing an old axe from the woodshed and cleaving my skull in two. Maybe me crying, begging for my life. I don't know. Hell.

But I got on the damn plane. My knees shaking. Chip ain't seemed to notice. Was a short flight into Stettin's airport, and then a long damn taxi to the bus station. I ain't seen none of it. Stettin just seemed very dark, and cold. I kept rubbing my old hands together but couldn't stop them trembling.

Our bus wasn't parked with the other coaches but off back by a chain-link fence, under a gloomy concrete building with cracks cobwebbing up its walls.

"You ain't serious," I said, when I seen it.

Chip put a hand on my shoulder. "Hell," he said. And then, with a smile, "Well I guess it'll get us there. It look like it been getting folk there for fifty years at least."

"That ain't going to get us out of the *parking lot*," I muttered.

It was a damn *relic*. An old transport bus, bleached white with dust. It sat high on its huge military tires, its joints rusty, its chassis pocked with dents like it been in a battlefield. Its weird Soviet hood looked insectoid, creature-like, and with its luggage doors lifted like wings I got to feeling distinctly uneasy. I couldn't see nothing through them grimy windows. Bus looked damn abandoned, I thought.

Chip was already stowing our suitcases underneath.

"Chip," I said, still studying the bus.

"What?"

"How long this trip supposed to take?"

"Half a day, I think," he said.

"Twelve-hours, half a day? Or have-a-catnap-then-you-there, half a day?"

He shrugged. "It don't matter now. You coming?"

"You get on that bus, ain't nothing *else* going to matter."

But Chip pushed on past me, grabbed the guardrail with one hand and hoisted himself awkwardly onboard. The bus stood so damn high off the ground, I wasn't sure I'd be able to pull myself up and in. Should be a damn ladder.

It was dark inside. I started up the short steps, blinking and peering about. The driver sat at his huge steering wheel, looking scarred and rough. I couldn't see his eyes. Through the shadows I nodded hello. He looked away.

"Ain't he going to take our tickets?" I asked Chip as we sat down.

Chip shrugged.

My eyes was starting to adjust. It was yellow as a toilet inside, the seats foamless and reeking of old piss. There was others huddled in the chill with us, pale and grim and avoiding eye contact. I shivered a little. Folks with strange bundles gripped in their hands, scarves and hoods pulled down low. Their faces blurred and indistinct. A woman was coughing in some row farther back.

Was like they been waiting for us. No sooner had we sat down than the driver got out, banged shut all the baggage doors, and come back on board glowering. He yelled some words in Polish, but no one seemed to pay no attention. Then he sat down, pulled out some levers, started the old engine with a roar, snapped his dusty window open. The brakes groaned, the axles hissing under us like asps.

And then there was a sound like an enormous pressure releasing, and that huge rusted bus started shuddering on its big tires, rolling slowly out into the dead road.

We pulled out through the gloomy streets of Stettin, passing grey facades of chipped concrete, shuttered windows, folks dressed in dark coats carrying bags of groceries. The streetlights was on even though couldn't be much past noon. The roads looked windswept, bare, as if readying for winter.

We wasn't but ten minutes out when the bus slowed to a stop. An old man lumbered up the aisle and, climbing down, started walking out into the dark fields. He carried a sack of onions over one shoulder and I watched him trudge off into the gloam and disappear.

We pulled away again. The asphalt on these roads was bad and the old bus shuddered and crunched and banged its way onward. The city was now far behind and we was driving through the blasted countryside, past desolate fields, long swathes of dark forest. I started thinking all this was real. Hell. I ain't quite believed it and then I was sure I ain't believed it and then I didn't care if I believed it or not. But here I was, no longer really doubting Hiero would be where Chip said he was.

"Half-Blood Blues," Chip said suddenly. He was rubbing the stubble on his cheeks like he sharpening his old fingers. "You know I always figured it was about himself."

"Don't start, Chip. Let's just leave it for a bit."

"But it ain't. I reckon he named it for Delilah."

I closed my eyes. Suddenly I didn't want to talk about none of it, not now, not later.

"We should've brought him something," said Chip. "A gift."

I snorted. "Like what. Wine? A keychain?"

"I don't know. Something. It ain't never good showing up empty-handed."

My eyes was still closed. Now I opened them, gave him a look. "That's what you worried about? Not having a gift for him?"

Chip seemed unruffled, though. "Doesn't hurt to be polite, Sid. That's all I'm saying,"

The hours passed. After a time Chip slept. I slept and woke. Glanced over at him, dead as winter beside me. His face looked real smooth there, the wrinkles slipping back like water so that you almost seen the purity of bone beneath, his essence.

But then Chip cracked one eye open, his lean wet lips drawn down. "Hey."

I gave him a sleepy old look.

"Hey," he said again. "Sid."

"What?"

"Hey, you remember Panther Brownstone?"

"Mmm."

"That old gate who give me my first go at the skins?"

I grimaced. "First go at the skins is right. What was that gal's name?"

"Shit." Chip smiled a little, but thoughtful like. He sat up, started grinning for real. "I forgot about that. Hell. Yours had a chassis made you want to buy the whole damn car."

"She was my first love, that girl," I said.

"Best damn trombonist you like to meet."

I chuckled. "Anyway, what brought back that memory?"

He shrugged. "I don't know. All this, I guess." He gestured at the strange greyness passing us by. The long wide stretches of field and farmland. "Something about it gets you to thinking."

I nodded. "What about him?" I said after a minute.

"Who?"

"Panther Brownstone. What about him?"

"Nothing. I was thinking he seemed like a son of a bitch, but he wasn't."

"No?"

"No."

But he *was* a son of a bitch. I remembered it clear. A rainy Tuesday, Baltimore all sultry and stinking of piss. I was shaking like crazy, following Chip down into that club. I ain't never seen nothing like it. Thirteen years old. That joint stinking of rubbing alcohol, dark as my shirt, with cheap wood tables set crazily over the checkered floor in the shadows. And Panther Brownstone, lean and bony as a broom, got up from a table in the back and stepped up onstage, winking at old Chip.

"We got a special guest tonight," he announced. "Ladies and gents, just in from the Village, put your skin together for Charles C. Jones!"

"Chip," I remember hissing at him. "What's going on?"

But he just gave me that old grin. "Lower your pipes and mind me," he said.

Then he'd bounded onstage, shaking out his legs and arms as if trying to get the rain from his clothes. I tell you, I almost hit the floor.

He sat himself down at the kit. Couple of folks laughed from somewhere in the smoke, he seemed so crazy, so coltish. But with a nod from Panther, he hit his sticks together, and they kicked off into the set.

Hell. I known he played the drums a bit, but nothing like *this*. I watched in awe as Chip skipped gently on the cymbals, worked his skinny thigh into a rhythm on the bass. Holy hell, my boy could *wail*. Limbs all twitching, his very skin seemed to peel back on the harder hits. Was one of those moments someone comes unclothed, you see this whole other life in them. I was trampled flat.

After the set, the audience was like to tear off their clothes, they so damn delighted. They roared and slapped the tables, ladies flapped their stained drink napkins. When Chip come down off the stage, I flung my arms so hard around him he damn near fell down.

"How you learn to play like that, Chip man?" I yelled. "Where you learn?"

Panther come up then, in his plum three-piece suit, and put one big hand on Chip's shoulder. He wore a big gold watch on his skinny wrist, and his nails was perfectly manicured. And so damn *clean*. I ain't never seen such clean hands on a grown man before.

"Boys," he said smoothly. "I'd like to stand you a drink."

I was in love. Pure and simple. This place, with its stink of sweat and medicine and perfume; these folks, all gussied up never mind the weather—this, *this* was life to me. Forget Sunday school and girls in white frocks. Forget stealing from corner stores. *This* was it, these dames swaying their hips in shimmering dresses, these chaps drinking gutbucket hooch. The gorgeous speakeasy slang. I'd found what my life was meant for.

Panther Brownstone, he led us to a corner table he emptied just by his presence. Man, I thought, that's power. We sat at the knifed-up chairs, while he snapped a tan handkerchief out of his front pocket and whisked the nutshells and cigarette butts to the floor. His eyes glistened like carpenter beetles.

"A scotch, neat," he said to the barmaid when she come over. "Two lemonades for the boys here."

She smiled at us, looking like my mama's sister. Hell.

"I'd stand you boys some real drinks," he said smoothly, "but I ain't no Socrates. I don't corrupt no kids. Just everyone else."

And he grinned this gruesome toothy grin.

"I'll get right to it. Charles, you ain't half bad. You ain't half good, neither. Not yet. But that old crowd loved seeing you up there. Like a dog driving a automobile, I guess. If it was up to me, I'd have you in here gigging with us every Saturday. How that sound to you?"

Chip's old eyes was near wet with excitement. But his voice sounded steady.

"Saturdays?" he said, as if checking his schedule in his head. "Saturdays? Well, I guess that could work. Okay. I guess it sounds pretty good, Panther."

Panther's eyes flicked to me, then back to Chip. He got this little old smile creeping up under that pencil moustache. "How old're you? I don't mean in dog years."

"Sixteen," Chip said.

"Thirteen," I said.

Chip kicked me hard under the table and I gave a start, reach down, rub my damn shin. But Panther wasn't looking at me.

"Thirteen," he said quietly. "Thirteen. I figured you just a bit younger."

"Younger!" Chip shouted.

Panther started to laugh then, from deep in his chest. "Easy there, son. Ain't no way you boys coming in here regular anyhow. Even sixteen. We get shut down for sure, we got kids in here. You understand?"

Chip said nothing. His eyes got real small, real mean.

"Look, kid, don't be sore. You hit them skins good for you *age*. But playing good for you age don't mean you playing good for the ages. 'Less you a Bolden, or a Jelly Roll or something. And they don't come along but maybe twice a *century*. Listen, jazz, it ain't just music. It *life*. You got to have experience to make jazz. I ain't never heard no one under eighteen even sound like he know which end of his instrument to hold."

"I know what I'm doin," Chip said.

Panther held up his hands. "I know you do, kid. I know."

The scotch and lemonades arrived.

"Here you are, sugar," the barmaid said, giving Chip his glass.

He ain't said nothing.

Panther gave him a long appraising look. Then he lifted one long bony arm and snapped his fingers. A lady walked up, her friend lagging behind her. They looked old, man, maybe even old as twenty. Their chests popping out the tops of them dresses.

"Gals," said Panther. "You be sure to take care of these boys here."

"Sho thing, Panther," the first one said. She gave a sort of seductive smile, her upper lip hitching up.

I couldn't believe it. I couldn't think of nothing to say.

Panther looked at Chip with this suddenly cold, ferocious glint in his eye. "I see you around, kid," he said. "You keep at it, now." And then he stood from the table, took his glass, was gone into the smoke.

"*Ass*hole," said Chip loudly.

"Honey, I thought you played real fine up there," the first woman said to Chip.

He gave her a look.

"What's your name, sweetie?" the second one said to me.

"Sidney Griffiths, ma'am," I said.

"I was the one played," said Chip, giving me a look. Staring at his tiny smug eyes, I wanted to slam my heel down on his toes.

"And you was real fine, honey, real fine," the first one said again.

"I bet you be just as good, you gave it a whirl," the second one kept on at me. Well holy mother. I seen I'd scored the prettier of the two, with her slanted seed-like eyes, her toffee skin, her lips like split fruit. Wasn't one piece of her didn't remind me of food.

"What you boys drinking?" the first one said.

"Lemonade," I said.

"*Strong* lemonade," Chip cut in.

The second one giggled. "Why don't you get us some drinks, sweetie? Two sidecars."

"Now you on the trolley," grinned Chip, like he'd thought of it himself. "Sid, go on over the bar get us somethin put some hair on you chest."

"Why don't you go?" I whispered at him.

"Go *on*," he hissed. "They *lookin* at us."

Took me three weeks' allowance to buy them drinks. And the bartender near laughed himself stupid, pouring them out for me. I was stumbling through veils of smoke back to the table when my cat-eyed girl met me halfway. Taking the two drinks from me, she set them on the nearest table, so that half the liquor splashed out.

"Aw, what you doing?" I said. "Ain't you going to drink it even?"

But she just grabbed my hand, led me through humid bodies to a stairwell dark as a heart chamber.

"Where's Chip?" I called ahead to her. "We got to tell Chip where we going."

She waded through groups of groping couples, to the first landing, where she thrown open a door and pushed me in. Well, knock me down with a feather. It was a *bedroom*. I stared at the yellow satin sheets, torn and stained in places, the windows dimmed with what looked like grey paint but was probably just years of tobacco smoke. My heart begun stuttering in my chest.

"You live here?" I said in surprise.

She closed the door, then come around and grabbed my front collar so hard she almost choked me.

"Hey," I shouted. "Hey, what you doin? Don't you try nothing or I call Chip."

"Aw, sweetie," she smiled.

And then she leaned down and kissed me.

Well, son of a bitch. It wasn't no sort of ordinary kiss neither. Her tongue got in my mouth, sent blood rushing to every damn pocket of my body. Her lips was hot, like the ridge of a cooking dish, her breasts all pressing up against my chest. She smelled just like almonds, even her hair.

Then she pulled back, gave me this sly look.

I didn't know what to say. "You real pretty," I whispered.

She smiled. "Think so?"

I nodded.

I didn't understand when she sunk to her knees. I started to drop down too, but she stopped me, pushed me up again. She kissed my button fly, then tugged the buttons open, yanked my pants down, my drawers. Before I known what was happening, she had me in her mouth, all hot and moist and velvet. My skin tingled all over at the impossible softness, like being hit with hot and cold water all at once. It almost hurt.

Afterwards, I didn't know what to do. I felt sort of embarrassed, ashamed. Breathing hard, I kneeled before her on the floor, putting my hand up her dress, wanting to please her.

She pushed my fingers gently away. "That one be a freebie, cause you so cute, honey. But you want to jass, you got to pay up."

I ain't understood. The truth come to me slow, as if through layers of smoke. "You a *whore*?" I said.

She frowned, leaned back on her haunches, gave me a cold look. "You going to use that language in here? After what all I just done for you?"

I blushed. I ain't known what else to call her.

"I'm sorry," I said.

"You real young, kid. I thought you was older than that."

"I'm sorry," I said again, trying to make it better.

Frowning, she got to her feet. "Call me a whore and I sure as hell gonna act like one. Cancel that freebie. Pay up. Pay me now or I callin Vaughn."

Hell, where'd this come from? Everything turned suddenly ugly. I ain't never in my life been in such a fix. Panicked, I scrambled into my pants, dove wildly across the room for my coat.

"Don't you bolt, fucker," she said, her wet lips all twisted up.

"I got to get my wallet," I said, knowing damn well that while my wallet may be in my coat, wasn't no scratch left in it.

I buttoned my fly, straightened my shirt. She watched me with a hawk's eye. Reaching into my pocket, I got hold of the door at the same time and thrown the goddamn thing wide open. Scrambling down them stairs, my heart slamming in my ears, I heard her yelling, "Stop that nigger!" But I could be a real jack-rabbit in a crisis, and I was too quick to be caught by no one, even that meathead Vaughn. Knocking folks down right and left, I burst outside, my breath catching on the muggy air. I run down South Broadway, turning onto East Pratt then zigzagging back to South Bethel and Eastern Ave. Only when I stopped to get my breath, cars all blaring in the streets, did I reckon I'd forgot poor Chip. "God*damn*," I hissed under my breath. Sighing hard, I started running on back.

Lucky for me, Chip done already left the club. Unlucky for him, he lay out on the pavement of South Broadway.

"Shit, Chip," I said, fixing to help him. His nose been bashed up real good, blood messing up his two-tone jacket. I helped him up. We sat side by side on the pavement, panting.

"Well I known *mine* was a whore," said Chip, smug like.

I begun laughing. A long, loud crackling laugh. Chip, he tried to look all serious, all adult, but he couldn't help it and started laughing too. There we sat on South Broadway, howling like two escapees from Spring Grove's local asylum. The jazz life. I was hooked.

In time we passed through dead fields. Passed makeshift barriers tangled with rusted barbed wire. Passed ancient wooden houses left to rot like so much garbage. I known places like that. Reeking of harsh soap and cheap tobacco, their living rooms full of doilies, cobwebs, widows.

Every hour or so we'd stop at some abandoned crossroads, some dusty old driveway, and another passenger would climb down and drag their old luggage from the undercarriage and disappear off into the landscape. Already, it seemed like half the passengers had got off. Ain't no one else climbed aboard yet.

"Poland," I murmured.

I nudged Chip. He grunted.

"Why you reckon Poland?" I said.

"What you saying?" Chip was trying to prop his feet on the seat across from ours but his legs was too short. His face looked like slack leather, the skin exhausted, the mouth drooping. "Why Poland what?"

"Why'd he come here? Of all places?"

Chip just sort of grimaced. "Hell, brother, ain't nothing of his life make sense."

"I know. I know. Just seems sort of strange to me."

"Halelujah and praise the damn powers that be. Of course it's strange, brother."

We sat for a while in silence then. But I ain't stopped brooding over it. The rhythm of the tires thrummed up through my legs. I could see an old lady in a scarf delicately peeling a hard-boiled egg across the aisle, holding its white globe between one thorny thumb and finger. She ain't had but three fingers. I tried not to stare as she sucked the whole damn thing into her mouth and started to chew.

I guess Chip ain't stopped thinking on it neither, cause after a few minutes he said, "I think only Hiero can answer that. The why of it, I mean."

I gave him a look. "Think about it. Kid just come out of internment, why ain't he headed west? Why go east? You a black man arrested for sticking out like a second head—wouldn't you go where you less visible? DPs was all over the place back then. Why go east? Don't make no sense."

"I don't know, Sid. I guess you got to ask him."

"He could have gone back to France. He *known* France. Could have gone south. Ain't never been south. But east? Toward the damn Soviets?"

Chip shook his head.

"It don't make no sense to me," I said.

He shrugged. "Maybe he was a Communist."

"Hell, is *everyone* suddenly a damn Communist to you?"

He looked sheepish, remembering the documentary.

I paused. "It's like he *wanted* to suffer."

"There's easier ways to suffer, Sid."

"I know."

Chip sat there frowning. "What's weirder to me is that he *could* stay here. After the war, like. The Poles was real eager to rid their country of Krauts. Couldn't be quit of them quick enough. Even before the Potsdam Conference."

"Ladies and gentlemen, Charles C. Jones, Human Encyclopedia," I said.

Chip reached down into his pocket and pulled out a slim little guidebook. "One thing I learned in my life, Sid: sightseeing ain't but a waste of time 'less you know what you looking at, 'less you know the history."

I barely heard him. "Maybe we assuming too much. Maybe he only just moved to Poland now. Last year, like. Maybe he spent all his life living somewhere else, somewhere west. But then why ain't we heard he was still alive?"

Chip shrugged, suddenly uninterested. He tucked the book away, settled back, closed his eyes. I watched him awhile, then turned to the window. All that Poland rolling by. Its cliffs and rivers. I couldn't stop thinking about the documentary, and all of what I'd heard about Hiero. How he'd lied about his pa being royalty, how he been out of place his whole life. Growing up in Köln, folk used to tease him something awful. Called him all sorts of things. Chimney Sweep. Monkey's Son. Blubber Lips. Black-Eyed Chinaman, because of his squint.

Hell. And to go back into all that, after the war. It didn't make no sense. But then he ain't never done what you expect, even as a kid. He'd just go to some cold place inside himself to wait out the teasing. I seen it myself, I remembered how it was. Never struck out. Rarely talked back. Like a shadow.

A shadow of his father, maybe. Florian—that was his father, the blond Florian Falk, if Caspars' film wasn't *all* lies—he wasn't the kid's real pa. No, sir. Typical war story, but with a kink. Florian, see, he come home from the Great War to find his sweetheart married to another man. So old Florian ends up marrying the sister, Marieanne, who was pregnant by another man. She sweet as dates, sure, but a little touched. From birth she been odd, they ain't known what was wrong with her. Anyhow. Her sister gone and told Florian that Marieanne been raped by a French soldier, and would he step on in, do the right thing. Well, his heart was broke anyway. What did it matter. I guess he probably thought he'd take the kid on as his own. Ain't no need to complicate things with the truth, see.

But eight months after the wedding, sweet dark Hieronymus come into the world.

Who the real father was, Caspars claimed to know. Almost seven feet tall and blacker than a power outage. He ain't been a rapist at all. He was a colonial soldier from Senegal, one of them sent to occupy the Rhineland by the French government. And apparently, Marieanne Falk had loved him.

———————————

The old bus was slowing down, turning, its tires crunching into the mud-crusted lot of an old restaurant. Or what I reckoned for an old restaurant. I watched a small boy sitting with his grandpa at the front of the bus, the old man shaking and swaying along with the turn. The boy kept twisting around, staring back at us, like we was something from another world entirely. Go on, boy, I thought. Get yourself an eyeful.

Wasn't no other passengers left now, just them two and us.

The driver stopped with one last shudder, punched open the folding doors. He leaned far back in his seat, barked out some raspy word in Polish.

"What do you figure, brother?" I asked Chip.

He chuckled. "Rest stop. How hungry are you?"

Outside there was rickety wood tables under a blue tarp awning, and peeling posts standing off-kilter in the mud. We shuffled on over, our legs stiffer than wood, sat down. A paper menu, all in Polish. I seen Chip's soft leather shoes was smeared with mud, and smiling, I shook my head. Serves him right. There was a few weathered wood buildings, with wood arcades set out front. I set my hands on the table and looked at Chip. He smiled back.

"Lovely spot for it," he said.

The flies was huge, armoured things, they swarmed in the cool air. There wasn't no sun in the sky, just a white haze. I slapped weakly at my neck and wrists. I could see the spots of blood where they already got at me.

"Aw, they got to eat too," Chip chuckled. "Just leave em."

"This a restaurant for folks too? Or just for the flies?" I stared at the driver who sat with his back to us at the farthest table. "You think he deliberately keeping away from us?"

Chip shrugged. "No. No, I reckon he just don't like folk much."

"So what is this place?" I said. "Is this an old Soviet commune?"

"You got me, brother. Ain't much now, whatever it was once."

There was a big red sign hanging over the door of the far building. It been scratched out with what looked like a blowtorch. "What you reckon that was?" I said, nodding toward it.

Chip didn't even turn around. "Hell, Sid, I told you. I ain't got no idea."

I said nothing then. We was both tired, I known it. I didn't see the old grandfather and the boy. Turning in my seat, I caught them making their slow way back down the road, carrying a sack each.

"It's just us now." I felt depressed somehow.

"What?"

"It's just us now. All the other passengers is gone."

Chip shrugged. "Long as this bus keep going, I don't care if even the driver decides to get off."

"Hell, brother. Don't it feel to you like they all know something we don't?"

"You mean, like rats on a sinking ship?"

"No. Maybe."

"Sid, they getting off cause this is their stop. Ain't nothing more than that."

But there *was* something more. I could feel it, though I wasn't able to explain it. You get old enough, you start to trust your damn instincts sometime. Or, least, you start to listen to them. I stood up unsteadily.

"I be on the bus for a bit," I said. "Don't mind me."

Chip looked at me. "You want me to order something for you?"

"I don't much feel like eating."

"It's alright," he said. "I'll get you what I'm having. Go get away from these damn flies."

The bus felt lower somehow, longer, the ribs of its chassis leaner. I climbed back onboard.

Then it was like something guided my eye, drawn my old hand down towards Chip's carry-all. I dragged his bag out from under the seat, running a finger over its print of interlocking Ls and Vs, its precious leather. I unzipped it.

It didn't take but a minute to find the envelope. The stationery Hiero had written on was brown as dishwater. *Mr Charles C Jones*, scrawled in bad handwriting across the front above his address. That handwriting—I known it right away. With shaking hands, I fumbled open the flap, the paper rough as newly sanded wood. *My Dear Friend*, it began:

I hope this letter does not come as too much of a shock. If it is any consolation, it is probably just as much of a shock for me to write it. You see, until recently, I did not know you were alive. Please do not take offense at this. Last week someone told me about a Falk Festival taking place in Berlin sometime this year—imagine it!—and that you were one of its featured guests. I was also given some of your press. I must tell you, I was delighted to see how well you are doing—as we both know, yours is not an easy vocation. Congratulations on your continued success, your President's Medal and the Hall of Fame citation. I am genuinely proud, if that is not too presumptuous to say.

I have a favour to ask. Seeing as how the festival will bring you to Europe, if it is not too much bother, I would very much like to reconnect with you. As you can see by the envelope, I live a little off the beaten path now. As I cannot travel—my health will not permit it—I would like to ask you to visit me here when it proves convenient for you. Actually, ever since I learned you were alive I have felt the urgent need to see you.

I eagerly await your reply.

Yours,
Thomas Falk (Hiero)

PS—I would appreciate if you did not pass on my contact information to anyone. My life is a quiet one; I could not bear it any other way.

I sat there, the paper's grain harsh against my fingers. My god, he was really alive. Surely and truly alive. I'd believed Chip while at the same time not believing him.

My throat going dry, I glanced back down at the paper. *Thomas* Falk. He'd dropped his first name. And he didn't *sound* like the old Hiero: his praise detached, his invitation to Chip warm but not boyish.

His invitation to *Chip*. Like that, it hit me.

The kid hadn't asked for me.

And then it was like the bus tilted sideways and I couldn't breathe. I felt dizzy, hot, sick with it. I stood up, the bag falling from my lap. The air coming in from the windows stank of mud and horses.

The bus creaked and rocked as I sat down. Chip was climbing slowly up the steps, his huge hand on the greasy rail.

"You grub's getting cold," he called in. "Sid?"

You right bastard, I thought. You old son of a bitch.

"Sid? What you doing?" He stopped when he got a look at me.

My voice was shallow. "Hiero didn't ask for me. In the letters. He didn't mention me."

Chip was looking down the length of the bus.

"In his letters," I said, louder now. I shook the envelope at him. "The kid didn't ask me to visit him at all. Everything was addressed to you."

"Oh, hell, Sid." He seemed to relax. "Of course it was addressed to me. He didn't have your address."

I was near tears, frustrated beyond myself. "You don't know that. You don't know nothing about it. All you know is what's in this letter."

He ain't understood none of it. "It don't matter, does it? Of course he wants to see you. Hell, Sid, he probably don't even know you still alive." He come slowly down the aisle. "Sid, you got to relax. Why wouldn't he want to see you? Think about it, brother. We was all friends back then."

I wasn't able to look at him. "What have you done?" I muttered.

"Sid." Sitting down on the seat in front, he stared over the back of the headrest at me. "Sid, you got to calm yourself down. I mean it."

I was shaking.

"What are you worried about? The documentary? Hell, Hiero was *there*, brother. He knows the *truth*."

"I *know*."

He grunted. "Right. Good. Now, we going to eat? Last I checked that driver was wolfing down some goulash mess and I reckon when he done, we done. His bus don't wait for no one."

"No," I said, barely listening. "No I reckon it don't."

I looked out at the shabby grey hamlet we'd stopped in. It seemed to me we'd left something behind us, something essential, and we just kept getting farther and farther from it.

V

Paris
1939

That first night, we slept dreamless in the freezing car. In the early hours Montmartre looked sick, exhausted. I wasn't half awake before the street-lamps gone out, one by one, the street cleaners clattering on past. I could see Chip's head hanging at a bad angle in the seat beside me. Hiero whimpered in his sleep. Shivering so hard I could hear my damn teeth, I slept again.

In the morning Chip's neck was stiffer than cold molasses.

"Hell," he said, squinting over at me. You could see his breath. "Don't it never end?"

I looked in the rearview mirror. "Kid?" My mouth felt thick with cotton. "Kid, you awake?"

He lift up his head, grimaced.

"Hell," Chip said again, rubbing his hands together to get warm. "Paris, buck. City of lights. We got any scratch?"

"Some," I said, yawning. "Ernst give us some."

"Good old Ernst," Chip smiled, his teeth chattering. "Good old goddamned Ernst."

Hiero was fumbling around in the back seat, working his arms into his heavy overcoat, folding up his damn knees into the seatback with a thump as he did.

"Hell, kid, did you have to bring your elephant?" Chip grunted.

Hiero stopped, looked at him.

"Yeah, you heard me," said Chip, turning to him. "Now come on. Let's get some of that famous French cuisine."

"Dejeuner," I said distractedly. "Breakfast is dejeuner."

"You goin be a gentlemen yet, brother. Damn. Since when you croak Frog?"

I shrugged. I was thinking of Delilah, some of what she'd taught me, but thinking of her suddenly stripped away any good feeling I'd had. I shook my head, wrestled open the door, got out. I felt dark, depressed. I kept seeing old Ernst in his brown suit, his pale brow furrowed as he turned from me to look uselessly out at the garden. I kept seeing the quiet pain in his face, like he known for weeks the end was near, but was paralyzed now that it had finally arrived.

We found a small outdoor café that was serving at this hour and settled under a green awning. It was empty but for a old gent reading the paper, dressed all in grey with a grey fedora set stiff on his grey head. Like a damn wax statue. The hard metal chair felt cold through my trousers, and though the chill was burning off some, I ain't seemed able to get warm. As a car passed in the street, I lifted up my eyes, seen pigeons scattering like blown paper in the abandoned square.

"Where everybody got to?" I said. "Ain't it a weekday?"

"Brother, ain't nobody work in Paris," said Chip. "Paris the city of *love*."

Then a waitress come on up. Clearing his throat, Chip gestured for three coffees. He watched her hips as she walked back to the bar.

"I always liked France," he said with a smile.

"Get you mind off it," I said. "Hell, brother. After what all we just been through?"

The kid was leaning forward, setting his wrinkled coat sleeves on the table. "You think Ernst goin get out?" he said soft like.

"You don't got to whisper, Hiero," I whispered.

"He ain't comin kid," said Chip. "No chance. His car is *parked*."

"He said he goin try."

"Don't matter."

"He said when his pa gone back to the Saar, maybe then. Maybe he goin use his own contacts."

Chip just give him this withering look.

"Hell," I said, all a sudden tired of it. "Leave it alone."

Then the waitress come back, set down three cafés au lait. Chip turned this dazzling eighteen-carat smile on her. "Bon*jour*," he said. "Al*lô*."

She laughed.

I closed my eyes. It sounded damn mournful, that laugh of hers echoing off the square.

"Now *that*, brother," Chip murmured as she sashayed away, "*that* is the *real* French cuisine, right there."

"She got to be old as you mama, Chip."

He give me a long thoughtful look, as if absorbing this. "Aw, that be the grateful type. Makes the sweetness all the sweeter."

Hiero cleared his throat. "So what we doin?"

Chip was still staring after the waitress. "Somebody got to call Louis. Who it goin be? Sid?"

My damn foot gone to sleep and I stood up, started to shake it out. That old jack reading his paper glance over in alarm. He turn in his seat, fold one leg over the other, rustle his pages. I been dreading this hour. Louis Armstrong? Hell, I known this was it, this was our moment, our lifetime. Folks think a lifetime is a thing stretched out over years. It ain't. It can happen quick as a match in a dark room.

Hiero was eyeing me. I known we both thinking the same thing. Louis was like to ask about Lilah.

"Aw, I'll do it," said Chip. "Where's the number?"

"I reckon Sid ought to," said Hiero. "Ain't that why Ernst left him in charge?"

"Hell, brother," said Chip, scowling. "Sid ain't even in charge of his own *bowels*."

I fumbled in my pocket, pulled out a mess of francs, crumpled notes, soft paper wrappers. I smoothed one out, slid it over the table to Chip. Like that, he was up and asking for the phone.

I looked at the kid. Seemed like something was seared inside him. Like all certainty been peeled back, torn off, leaving just teeth and sinew. He had his face down, studying his hands, and he ain't said nothing to me as we waited.

After a time Chip come back out, lean over the old counter to smile at the waitress. Hell, that boy got thicker skin than a tomcat.

At last he saunter over our way, sit down with a satisfied flourish. His metal chair scraped on the bricks as he pulled it close. The shadows seemed to deepen in the square.

Hiero looked at him. "So? What he say?"

"Who?"

I laughed angrily. "What you mean who. What he say?"

Chip smiled then, like he just swallowed the damn canary. "Boys, you just stick with me. That old gate like to sit on his hat when he get a earful of us."

"So he ask to see us? For real?"

But Chip only turn to the kid, give him this long, slow smile. He stirred his cold café au lait, set the spoon carefully down on the saucer, took a sip. His eyes met mine over the rim of the cup. "I reckon I might get a chance with that waitress. What you think? Worth the effort?"

Hell. Kid like to have chewed his own arm off from the nerves.

"It ain't funny, Chip," he burst out. "Come on, what he say?"

"About what, now?"

"*Chip*," I said.

He look at me, give a reluctant sigh. "Fine, fine. Louis say Montmartre."

"Mont*martre?* We *in* Montmartre. What about it?"

"Keep you shirt on, kid. We got to *stay* in Montmartre. Just a few hours." He lifted his eyebrows at me. "You goin find this one hell of a day, brother."

I felt a lurch in my chest.

"What you sayin, Chip?" said Hiero. "Louis say somethin bout Sid?"

But Chip, he just give this low cackle, like when we was kids.

———————— ■ ————————

We climbed the broken-stoned slopes of Montmartre, the morning already brightening. I felt frail with nerves. Got so my damn hands was shaking in my coat pockets. Louis goddamned *Armstrong.* We sort of fell into exhausted silence, and I glanced over at the kid. Hope eats at you like a cancer, I guess. If we just left Berlin sooner, I was thinking, if we just tried harder for old Ernst, for Paul. If we just been better men.

The steep streets was quiet and I wasn't able to shake my feeling of being in the wrong city. There was crowds gathering in the cafés now, haunting the doorways of shops. All of them reading newspapers, muttering among themselves.

"What's goin on?" said Hiero, nervous.

Hearing him speak, a man look up, watch him with cold eyes. We gone on past, drifting toward the buildings, away from the open streets.

"Almost like bein back in Berlin," said Chip.

I frowned. "Not quite."

He led us up toward a tall church outlined against the overcast sky. Its spire sharp and fierce, like a thing out of nightmare. We cut through a dark, treed park, up a narrow set of steps, Hiero gripping the railing and grunting behind us. Chip looked back at him, grinned.

"I thought them horn players got the good lungs," he laughed.

The kid just lean right over when he reached us, gasping and coughing.

I wasn't fooled. I known it wasn't the hike making him dally. Watching him, I thought, *Sure you all that back in Berlin. But you about to meet genius, buck. You about to learn what you* ain't. *Scary, ain't it.*

Kid hacked like crazy, spitting the mess onto the cobblestones.

"Hell, kid, ain't that a bit of you appendix in there?" said Chip. "Look, Sid. You ain't never seen nothin like it. I think it's got its own teeth."

But I ain't felt much like clowning. I drifted over to the rail, set both hands on the cold steel, looked down at the steps below us.

"Go on, kid," said Chip. "Go find youself a pew. We like to be a while."

I ain't known how long we stood above that street. I watched a dark cat mince across the cobblestones. Someone dumped a bucket of wash water out a window. Then a lone figure come around the corner, start making its way up the road, its legs and arms looking grey and thin in the watery daylight, its head all bloated with a wrap. And, like that, I felt my heart suck itself down into this real deep hole in my chest. She stopped at the foot of the steps, folded her arms. She looked leaner, more worn and threadbare, but, hell. It was *her.*

It was Delilah.

I started shaking. Like that, I just started trembling real light and fast, like a bird's heart in you fist.

Chip come up beside me. "Told you this was goin be a day," he murmured. "You just goin stand there? Or you goin down give her some sugar?"

I ain't understood. I give him a helpless, frightened look, feeling the cold air coming in at my collar. Delilah was glancing across at a café, that huge blue wrap on her head like something from a far-off land. She was a mirage, I swear it. Suddenly this huge wave of meanness start pushing against me from the inside.

Hold on Sid, I thought. *You don't know nothing yet. Just hold on.*

But Chip was already slipping past, starting down them steps. "Well look who risen from the dead," he called with a smile. "Lilah, girl, you forget what we look like, you got to look so hard?"

She turned, and I seen her face clear. Was like my blood just stop. I couldn't move. I stood above her at that railing and I couldn't move a inch.

"Charles," she cried with a sharp squealing laugh. "Charlie Jones!"

"It's Chip, sister. You know it." But he was smiling too.

She just lift up her skirts and run on up the steps, her long heels like gunshots on the cracked stones. She catch him in this savage hug before he even a half dozen steps down. I bet Chip ain't been held like that even by his own mama. Then, over his shoulder, she lift up her eyes, and seen me.

Hell. I ain't said nothing. I didn't think I be able to say nothing.

She let Chip go and stood there breathing hard.

"Delilah girl?" I could feel myself gripping that cold railing.

She looked at me shyly. "Hi Sid."

Neither of us stirred, made any move to come closer. And then, hell, there was a high whooping cry, and a cloud of pigeons exploded behind me. I jumped a little. Sweet Lilah lifted her beautiful face away from mine, following the line of birds, and catching sight of the kid some steps up, she start to running. She held him to her chest in this ferocious damn embrace like she ain't never held nothing she loved before.

———————— ■ ————————

We ain't lingered long. Delilah led us into that old church, along the wood pews, out some back door into a small, grassed courtyard. Wasn't no one around. A spiked iron fence behind a hedge, a wood bench under a apple tree, a table with three rickety cane chairs. She led us to a gate in the far corner, unlatched it. It opened onto a steep alley incut with stone steps going down.

"Come on," she said. "It's not far."

"We goin to see Louis?" said Hiero in German.

I was too distracted to answer. I felt slack, strange, not quite in my own skin. It wasn't nerves I was suffering now. Every time I sneak a look on over at her, hell. De*lilah*. It ain't seemed possible. Watching her start down those steps, with her bird's bones, with that oaky smell of outdoors on her like she just been walking the countryside, like it any damn day and not miraculous at all— everything rose up in me. I caught a glimpse of her scrawny ankles under them skirts, then they was gone.

It ain't been but a week and a half, but she seemed a complete stranger. The stress of these last days, the grief—twenty years might have passed.

"Tell me everything," she said. "I want to know everything." She put her slim hand to the back of her neck, like to check that her wrap was on just so.

Chip was running his fingers over the iron railing. "You supposed to be dead, girl. How come you ain't dead?"

She smiled. "Careful Charlie. You're going to rumple your suit."

"Don't start with that Charlie business. I mean it."

Hiero trailed behind us, about as far from Delilah as that gate could get. She turn around, give him a wink.

"I think he's afraid of me again," she laughed.

"You a ghost," said Chip. "We all afraid of you."

"So where's Louis?" I said, irritable.

Delilah, she ain't hardly lift up her eyes at me at all. We come to the gate at the bottom and she lifted the latch, held it open for us. When she answer me, her voice gone different. "He's just down here a way. He still isn't well."

Chip swore. "He sick? Louis been sick?"

"You know that," she said.

I turned as we went, said to Hiero in German, "Lilah says Louis been sick."

"We still goin see him?"

"Kid wants to know if he well enough for visiting," I asked.

"Yes," she said simply.

She led us down a narrow street, past patisseries steaming with blond bread, past hidden bistros and fish stands stinking of guts and coquilles Saint Jacques.

"You boys look awfully tired," she said.

"Not too tired to scratch the old skins," said Chip.

"You're ready to play again?" she smiled. "Already? You all are?"

"Except Hiero lost his damn horn."

She give me a look. "Is that the truth?"

I shrugged.

Armstrong was staying in a small hotel top of Rue Lepic. We push on through the big glass doors. The lobby like to blind us, it so damn brassy and gilt with mirrors and white tile. Hell. Smoked-over glass on the inner windows, a shining brass elevator standing along the far wall. The doorman nodded to Lilah as we gone on past, lifting up his cap with one white glove.

As we come through I took her arm. I surprise myself, how hard I held it.

"Sid," she said. "Not here."

But I ain't hardly heard her. "I thought you was dead," I murmured. "Lilah? Girl, we thought we lost you."

But Hiero was already pushing through the glass door, staring nervously around at all that damn opulence. She pulled away.

Chip stood near the elevator, turning his hat uneasily in his hands as we approached.

"I didn't want to ask." Lilah swallowed hard and looked at him. "Where are they? Where's Ernst and Fritz?"

"Ain't you forgettin someone?" I said.

She give me a hurt look. "I know about Paul," she said quiet like. "I was there."

Hiero watched us, nervous.

"Ernst still in Hamburg," said Chip. "He with his family. He goin be alright, his pa awful damn powerful. Ain't got him no visa to get out, though. I reckon the old bastard got us visas just to clear us out of his boy's life."

"He could've just had us pinched," I said. "He ain't done that."

Chip shrugged. "If you seen Ernst's face," he said to Delilah, "if you just seen Ernst's face. It like to have broke you cold Canadian heart, girl. You seen everything he wanted just gone, just scraped out of him. You know, he love old Louis. And he give that up when he say good-bye to us."

"You wasn't even there, Chip. What you know about how he looked?"

"You told me bout it. Hell. I just sayin what you said, Sid."

I shook my head.

"And Fritzie?" she said.

Chip's face closed over. "That damn Judas gone over to the Golden Seven. He ain't one of us no more."

Delilah look real sad.

"If it up to me I'd scrape his damn name off every record we ever cut. Erase his fat sound off it like he ain't never been born."

"That's awful," she said. "It's so awful. Poor Ernst. Poor Fritz."

The elevator light come on. Its car start to descend.

"Fritz can fry in hell with them Nazi bastards," Chip hissed. "Don't waste you worry over him."

We was silent then. I felt scoured out, gutted.

But Chip, he just looked round, give a little grunt like he changing dials on the wireless. "So Louis sick? He goin see us in bed?"

"There's that," she said. "And I figured his room would be safer for Hiero."

"Safer than what?"

She furrowed her brow, looked at Chip like he was off his nut. "Than a café. Aren't you worried about him?"

We ain't understood.

"Hiero?" said Chip. "They got a problem with blacks here too?"

"Not blacks," she said. "Germans."

But she sort of stopped then, stared at us like we some downright incredible sight. "You haven't heard? For real? You really don't know?"

The elevator door banged open, the mesh gate clattered back. I ain't hardly noticed. I was watching Delilah's lips.

"We're at war," she said. "We declared war on Germany. Yesterday afternoon."

——————— ■ ———————

Ain't made one shred of damn sense. Yesterday afternoon we still been rolling through the French countryside, past slumped barns, brindled cows on the roadside, folk cycling slowly by with groceries wrapped in cloth in their baskets. Hell. It was heaven on earth, damn pastoral. We been half blind with relief, bringing our guilt with us like a packed bag we all stowed under our seats. Thinking we'd outrun the dark trains moving at night. The papers scrawled thick with lies, the wireless and its frightening speeches. The shadows of Berlin. But you know, even with the madness miles and miles behind us, we ain't felt no safer. Maybe we known, even then, what was coming.

We step on out of that elevator and Delilah pull Chip aside, wave us on.

"What you two doin?" I said.

"Go on," said Delilah. "Lou's waiting for you."

But my legs wasn't working right. Hell. *Louis Armstrong*. I caught sight of my face in a brass fixture and damn near died. Poor damn gate looked long in the jaw with terror.

The door to 301 was cracked open. Hiero come to a abrupt stop, stood just outside the door, staring at it. I felt the dread rising up in me. Like something coming I wasn't ready for.

"Sid," Hiero whispered.

I stopped, looked at him.

"I need you do me a favour. Before we go in."

"What?"

"Don't laugh."

"I ain't goin laugh. What is it?"

"Will you pinch me?"

He was already rolling up his sleeve. I thought I ain't heard him right. I looked at his sweaty forearm. It like a side of glazed pork.

"I ain't touchin that," I said.

"Go on," he whispered. "Tell me this real."

"Uh-uh. Tell it to youself."

But he just stared at me with that damn frightened look he gets. I glanced at the door, glanced back to where Chip come into view. Hell.

I pinched him.

He pull back his arm quick like he been stung.

"So?" I said with a sigh. "You dreamin? Or we get to go in now?"

He grinned, rubbed the sore skin. "Aw, it a damn lifelike dream if I am."

"They the best kind, buck," said Chip. He come on up, put a big hand on the kid's shoulder. He eyed the open door. "Especially when they got a jane in them."

"If they lifelike for you, ain't no way there be janes," I said.

"You funny," said Chip.

"Maybe there be a gent or two," the kid said.

"Aw, you just a regular Laurel an Hardy. You goin show that act to Louis?"

"Three oh one," Delilah called, striding up the corridor. Seeing us, she slowed. "Oh, you found it. Well go on in, don't be shy."

Ain't none of us moved.

"You reckon he got any French nurses in there?" Chip smiled, but he look nervous.

There was a dry cough from the room. A voice called out, "Who that? Who out there, now?"

Man, that voice—it was like gravel crunching under tires.

Delilah shook her head at us. "He likes to think he's sicker than he is. Don't mind him. You know exactly who it is," she called through the door. "Just be glad it's not your wife. You can't afford her *and* the doctors."

Delilah, she just push on past us, kicking open the door with one sharp heel.

Hell. That room, man, it was so vibrant, drenched with the light coming in those big windows. We stood blinking like damn fools. The peach curtains, all etched in lace, been drawn back, tied off. Fat ivory chairs been set along one wall. A blond brass vanity—so old-looking seemed to be pining for the powdered wig—glinted by a second door. Whole place smelled vaguely of damp flowers. And there, by a big window frosted like a cataract, his skin dark as weeds against the sheets, lay Louis Armstrong.

He give a hot laugh. "Come on in, all a you," he said. "Let me get a look at you proper. Come on now." And then, to Delilah: "I thought maybe you wasn't comin back."

She snorted, all scarves and clicking beads. "I wasn't gone an hour, Lou."

Armstrong drawn a deep rusty breath. "*Sweeeet Delilah Brown,*" he sang. "*My sweet Miss D. Brown, she is my flower, my rosest of the roses. My Isle of Delisle, I goin be your Samson...*"

She just whipped the blue tassels of her turban in his general direction. "Hush, you. Just cause you sing so pretty doesn't mean you *should*. Now. What'd the doctors say?"

Armstrong sat hisself up a little in bed. "Oh, it ain't good, girl. It ain't good."

"Mmm. It never is." She give us a look.

"Everyone," she said simply, "this is Louis."

A man ain't never seen greatness till he set eyes on the likes of Armstrong. That the truth. Those hooded lids, that blinding smile: the jack was immense, majestic. But something else, too: he looked brutally human, like he known suffering on its own terms. His mouth was shocking. He done wrecked his chops from the pressure of hitting all them high notes over the years. His bottom lip hung slightly open, like a drawer of red velvets. He lift a handkerchief to his mouth, wipe off a line of spittle. I seen something in him then: a sort of devastated patience, a awful tiredness. I known that look. My mama had it all her life.

"I be a sight I know," said Armstrong, grimacing till his eyes wrinkle up. "But the King of Spain I ain't. Now stop you gawkin and come on in here."

Man, his voice! It was huge, glass-shattering. Full of rocks and splinters, rich as cream. One by one, we all start smiling.

"You gents hungry?" He gestured over to the vanity. "I got matzos."

"Matzos, Lou?" said Delilah. "Really?" She ain't sounded happy.

"You get a taste for them yet," he chuckled. "You just ain't et enough of them."

She wrinkled her face up.

Matzos? I shared a glance with Chip. Did he get them cause one of our gates was Jewish?

"Louis likes them for a late night snack," said Delilah. "Always has."

"Since ever I got teeth to eat. Now who we got here?"

Delilah cleared her throat. "Louis, this is Sid Griffiths. The bass player."

"This ain't *the* Sid Griffiths?" he chuckled. He give me a look. "Oh, I heard some things bout you. Things I ain't like to repeat to you mama."

Delilah blushed.

I couldn't find my voice. Hell. "It's a honour to meet you, Mr. Armstrong," I said uncomfortably. "You been a mentor to me my whole life."

"*Louis,*" he said, narrowing fierce eyes at me, like I offend him. "Call me *Louis.*"

"Louis," I repeated, swallowing hard.

"Aw, I just foolin with you." He laugh from deep in his chest. "You look like you cat just got run down by the milk truck."

I just smiled and smiled, like I too damn simple to speak.

Delilah was putting her hand on Chip's shoulder real gentle, like to start next with him, when he thrust hisself forward, his hat angled like a sail on his head, and sat hisself down on a chair at Armstrong's bedside.

He said, "We heard you been feelin bad, Louis, real bad."

Armstrong looked at Delilah. "Oh, nothing a few matzos ain't like to fix."

"We glad to hear it, glad to hear it."

"You must be the other rhythm boy."

Chip sort of cleared his throat at that. He set his hat back on his crown, put out his massive hand for Armstrong to shake. Then just as quick he pulled it back. "You ain't contagious, are you?"

Armstrong laughed. "Ask Delilah. She been sayin I sick ever since I known her."

Chip seemed to think about this a minute. Then he put out his hand again. "Well I reckon that's alright. Charles C. Jones, Louis. You just call me Chip."

"Chip?"

"Yes sir. Ever you lookin for percussionists, ever you want to class up you rhythm section, you know we you men. Me and Sid."

I stared at Chip in horror. What was the damn fool doing, talking like this to *Louis* goddamn *Armstrong?* That cat got his pick of geniuses and here Chip was offering him our talents like we doing *him* a favour? I felt sick.

"Alright, Chip," Delilah said quickly. "You're going to tire the old man out."

Armstrong started laughing, all gravelly, like he clearing his damn throat. "Old is right, girl. Old as the moon."

"Louis?" said Delilah, catching his eye. "Isn't there something you want to ask?"

Armstrong cleared his throat. "What the C stand for, Jones?"

Chip, who been getting up from his chair, froze. "The C?"

"Sure. In you name. What it stand for?"

Man oh man, I ain't seen this coming. I smiled at Hiero. "He askin what the C stand for."

The kid got this crooked smile on his face.

"Aw, Louis," Chip was saying. "It don't really matter, do it?"

But I was watching the kid. His face, it was all twisted up, like he was holding his damn body too tight, like he got to go to the damn toilet.

"Kid?" I whispered. "You alright?"

I figure he ain't took a breath in a long minute.

"Kid?"

And then, *hell*. He give out the weirdest damn laugh I ever heard.

I started to laugh.

Delilah looked over with a smile. "Hiero? You alright?"

"Hell, buck," said Chip. "Come on, get youself under control."

Kid put a hand over his mouth, hiccuped again.

Armstrong narrowed his eyes, smiling. "You sure he alright?"

"Aw, he be fine," I said. "It happens."

But the kid was mortified. He turned to face the door, clutching the handle, his shoulders shrugging every few seconds.

"Now Chip," Armstrong said in his low scratch, "you still ain't answered my question." He looked around, making like he stymied. He pulled his cream bedspread higher up his chest.

Delilah smiled, faint like. "Charlie—*Chip*—is very discreet about his middle name."

There was a weak, muffled hiccup from the corner.

"How long you been swinging with these cats they don't know you name?" said Armstrong. "Give you head a shake. Out with it now, come on."

You might've heard ice cracking in Alaska, it got so quiet then. Chip look off at the window, like he trying to find some way out of this. Like maybe it wasn't such a long drop down. I seen him glance at Armstrong, glance away, his fingers fidgeting with his cufflinks. Then his face fell, and he just sort of deflated. He lean in and mutter something real soft only Armstrong could hear.

"Say what?" said Armstrong.

"You got to speak up, Chip," said Delilah.

Chip give Delilah a sour look. "Chippewah," he said, louder. "It Chippewah."

"*Chippewah!*" Delilah cried.

Old Hiero, he damn near fell out the door, yanking so hard on the knob it swung open. Embarrassed, he banged it shut, the whole wall shuddering. He give me a look of astonished pleasure. Hell if that name ain't killed off his hiccups.

I shook my head. All these years he been a *Chippewah?*

"Well, Charles Chippewah Jones," said Armstrong. "My condolences."

That got Lilah laughing harder.

But Armstrong was already looking at the kid, a different light in his eyes. "I known you the minute you walked in here," he said. "You is Falk."

The kid stopped smiling, glancing at me, his eyes flaring wide.

Delilah said, "He doesn't speak English, Lou. But he speaks your language. I can tell you the rumours weren't wrong, he's the real thing. One of the greatest players I've ever heard in my life."

Oh, girl. And I was almost yours again. Suddenly I was struggling to keep that smile on my face.

"Lookin forward to hearin you swing, Pops," said Armstrong, grinning.

Hiero ain't understood. He let go of the knob, give a shy little nod.

"*Sid*," said Delilah. "Tell him."

"Louis wants to hear you play," I said numbly.

The kid nodded, give a little grave bow to Armstrong. Thing was, it ain't seemed ridiculous at all. It seemed, I don't know, dignified.

Armstrong laughed. "You and me, sure, we got some *talkin* to do. We surely do." He look over at Delilah. "Say it again?"

"Hieronymus. We practised this."

Armstrong chuckled, shook his head. "Again?"

"*Hieronymus*, Lou. What, you losing your ear now too?"

"Hurronnious," he said. "Herro... hell, that's Little Maestro. That pup over there be Little Maestro. Ain't heard him play yet, but I'll take the world's word for it till I do."

"You'll take *my* word for it," said Delilah. "You need more than that?"

"No ma'am." Armstrong smiled. "Now when we goin to swing?"

Chip give a happy shrug. "Anytime, Louis."

"Hiero needs a trumpet, Lou," said Delilah. "He lost his in all the fun getting out of Berlin."

Old Armstrong, he just shrugged. "Aw, ain't goin be no problem. I got a old one the boy welcome to. If he want it."

No damn *way.* I stared at Hiero.

"Well, tell him," said Delilah impatiently.

"She say you can use Armstrong's horn till she get you a new one," I muttered.

Hiero sort of ducked his head, smiled.

Delilah caught my eye like she just done *me* some favour. Hell. I was smiling so hard I like to split my damn face, trying to ease that burning in my gut. Little Maestro? Armstrong's *horn?* Sure the kid could play a sharp set, but on Armstrong's level? I smiled and I smiled, smiled, smiled. If all this damn jawing meant anything, it was that the kid still got borders to cross to get to where Louis was standing when he cut *West End Blues.*

─────────── ▪ ───────────

Oh but Delilah, sweet Delilah. Sweet like lemon in a wound.

The dead don't just stumble back into a life, like the grief ain't been real. I could feel that old sickness in me I thought been carved out. I thought: *Sid, you just let it be. It ain't goin happen with her again. Not like it was.*

Afterwards, we was standing out on the grey cobblestones in front of Armstrong's hotel. I looked down at the narrow streets of Montmartre, hardly believing we was here in the flesh. Chip clapped me on the shoulder, give me a gentle shake.

"You awake in there, buck?" He slip a address into my hand. "That be her flat. You goin over there to help move our stuff up."

"Whose flat?" I said foolishly.

"I got to spell it out for you? Go on over there."

"Aw, hell." I shook my head. "We stayin with *her*? No way, brother. No."

But a hour later I was parking Ernst's dusty Horch up on the curb and wrestling a big metal trunk out of the cab, banging it hard down into the street. When I glance on up, there she was, staring down at me through warped glass with dark eyes.

It was a shabby old apartment house. The street door was propped open with a cinderblock and I dragged that thick trunk through. Inside, a tile courtyard stood open to the sky and there was a checkered path leading across it to the stairwell. Stone lions crouched on the outer lintel posts. A fountain in the corner stood dry, its bowl stained by the pigeons. I dragged the trunk through the small foyer, set it down at the edge of the tile floor. The walls was yellow, chipped and peeling, and I leaned up against them as Delilah come out. She bent over the balustrade and called, "It's up here. Second door on the left."

I give her a grim look. It going be like *that*? She ain't even coming *down*?

"Where's Hiero?" she called.

Hell.

"What?" she said.

I shrugged. "I ain't said nothin," I called up.

"What? I can't hear you. Come up."

I blown out my cheeks, lifted that damn trunk up by the leather strap. I was determined not to ask her bout Berlin. Not to start nothing up with her. No damn way. When I come through, the apartment surprised me with its calm pale tones, the cream walls with their mouldings, the grey ceilings, and the long row of cold windows behind the furniture. Dragging in that trunk, I called out to her. But Delilah wasn't in sight. Frowning, I gone back down and begun to wrestle our old instruments up the stairs. I set everything down on the gleaming oak floor of the living room.

Then, the glass doors of the dining room opened, and Delilah come in, holding them open with a hand on each door. She wore a blue dress that hugged her hips and a purple wrap on her head, and her skin looked soft, bruised, velvety in that pale light. A faint scent of sugared almonds, like she just been baking, reached my nose.

"Hi, girl," I said, all at once shy.

"Don't mind me." She smiled, distracted. "I was just changing. You'll all be alright out here? We can put one of you on the sofa, I think." She glanced round. "I sleep just through here." But she ain't met my eyes as she said it.

I sat down, stood up. And then, hell, it ain't mattered what I'd told myself.

"Lilah," I said. "Listen."

She cleared her throat, put one uneasy hand on her wrap. She ain't come no closer. "I know it's not much, but—"

"It ain't the flat," I said. "The flat's fine."

She give me a puzzled half-smile.

My head felt thick, strange. "Aw, Lilah. You goin tell me? Or I got to ask?"

"Ask what?"

"What you mean 'what.'"

She clasped her hands before her thighs, stood there looking at me.

I swore. "If you was to tell me you Lilah's twin sister, I'd believe it. If you was to say you just blinked you eyes in Berlin and was transported here on the back of a *pigeon*, I'd believe it. You ain't real, girl. You ain't. Not to me."

At the mention of Berlin, her face darkened.

"You get picked up by the Boots," I said, "and then you just disappear? End up back in Paris like it ain't nothin? You know how that look?" I turned, walked over to the window, walked back. "You ain't got nothin to say to that?"

"I had a *ticket*, Sid. I wasn't arrested. Hiero didn't tell you?"

"Hiero?"

"Hiero. Your *friend*. He didn't tell you I was leaving?"

"The kid *known*?"

"Of course he did. You think I'd just run off like that?" She give me this sudden sad look. "Oh, Sid," she said, sort of quietly, like she only just starting to understand.

I shook my head. "The kid *known* you was goin?"

All a sudden I sat down hard in her wicker chair. Kid known my grief. He known it, he seen it, he lived it alongside me. And he ain't done nothing to soften it.

I wasn't sure if maybe something was wrong in all of it, if there been some mistake. But then I thought back to his shifty looks, his worried frowns, his sudden brotherly protection of me, and I thought, *Hell, brother, he a cold old Kraut after all.*

"Sid?" said Delilah. "What're you thinking? Sidney?"

She was still standing there, looking at me. Something gone dark in me then. Something I ain't able to explain. It wasn't jealousy, it wasn't betrayal. It wasn't even a lack of trust, exactly. I don't know. It was like I been sick from Lilah too long to just start back in.

I pushed back the chair, made to get up and go.

But Delilah come over to me, laid one cool long hand to my throat. I froze. The light seemed to slow right down. "Sid," she said, as if from a long way off. "Where're you going now, hmm?"

And then she leaned in, real slow, and kissed me.

Hell.

——————— ▬ ———————

It was then I started to hate his damn face again. Hiero. Little Judas.

I ain't said nothing to Chip, I don't know why. Maybe it just felt too delicious, knowing what the kid was really capable of. That night we rolled up in them blankets and lay ourselves out on Lilah's living room floor. Everyone but the kid. For some damn reason he gotten the couch. But no sooner he fall asleep than Chip rose up and dragged Hiero off that sofa by one ankle. The kid hit the floor like a sack of vegetables. Yawning, Chip sprawled out there hisself.

Hiero call over at me. He was standing, clutching his blankets to his belly. "You goin let him do that, Sid?" he complained. "It ain't right. You goin let him just take the couch?"

"Eat it up, kid," I said coldly. "Eat it up and try not to choke on it."

Chip cackled to hisself. "You young yet, kid." You could almost hear him smiling in the darkness. "You can take the stiffness. I only got one bone can take that kind of stiffness."

I rolled over onto my back, folded my hands under my neck.

"Hey Sid, where's you sweetheart?" said Chip. "*She* got a sweet old bed."

"Shut up, Chip."

"Aw, she ain't home yet," Hiero whispered, confidential like. "She out paintin the town, brother. Left our boy to his own *devices*."

"His five-fingered device, maybe."

There was headlights cutting up through the window as a taxi pulled past, the cold beams sliding over the ceiling, down the far wall. Some jack was hollering in the street below. I listened for the scrape of Lilah's key in the lock, feeling something real black rising in me.

"Or after that sweet old kiss, maybe she got what she needed," said Chip, a smile in his voice.

"Maybe she scared she goin get more of it," said Hiero with a squeal.

Chip was laughing so hard he like to wet hisself.

I sat up on one elbow, stared over at the kid's dark form. "You say another word and I'll shove that fuckin horn down you throat. You hear me? Kid?"

There was a thick silence.

"You alright, buck?" said Chip. "We just foolin with you."

I scowled. "Don't you start on nothin. I mean it."

"Hell. I ain't startin. You like this girl, you got to give her space. You keep on her this quick, she goin to lose interest in you, like that." Chip snap his damn fingers.

But I was thinking of that soft cool kiss she give me. Of her fingers on my throat. I lay awake a long time, thinking of that. Then I was thinking of old Berlin, and Ernst, and Paul. The kid started snoring soft like.

"Chip," I whispered, after a long silence. "You awake?"

"No."

"You ever think about that Boot? The one you stuck?"

He grunted, rolled over in his sheets. "What you mean. You mean like, I ever sorry bout it?"

"I don't know. Yeah."

"No," he said. "Never."

We lay on in silence, Chip finally dropping asleep with a loud snore. I stared at the grand high ceiling, feeling anxious, angry. Goddamn kid.

Lilah, she ain't come home at all. Not the whole damn night.

———————————■———————————

Delilah had promised us that Armstrong be set to play in two days. Two days—*hell*. We all known it was a lie.

But it seemed all Paris was waiting too. Anxiety hung over the streets like clothes on a line. When we walked them cobblestones, we seen families huddled in their apartments, crouched over the wireless. Waiters was bent over counters, listening to static. Hell, in those first tender days it seem like everyone was just hunched on up over some radio somewhere, it ain't mattered where, staying put, like if they moved they might miss the war. First it was the Frogs advancing into the Saar. Then it was the Frogs and the Limeys advancing on the Maginot Line. Then the Krauts was advancing too. Chip, he just shook his damn head. Delilah told rumours of food shortages, but after the darkness of Berlin, all that damn butter and wine in the cafés told us different. It was just fear, we known. Only thing we trusted in all we heard was the *static*.

Hiero stopped talking in the streets, in the cafés. A damn relief, I thought, the little bastard. Then even the skies drained out. I wished to god I'd just go to sleep and wake up in another reality. Cause I seen what the Krauts was capable of, I ain't no fool. They like to eat old France down to her crusts. Other days I'd go down to the Seine, lean out over the brown water, think of Paul and Ernst. There was posters going up, shabby gents pasting them along the walls with huge sopping rollers: tots in gas masks, flames, blond mothers herding children into bomb shelters. I watched shop clerks hooking blackout curtains in the windows, and I ain't felt nothin but nerves.

Cause nothing seemed to happen neither. The Krauts kept on in Poland and the Frogs just waited. It was the beginning of the Phony War, and it was set to drag on through that bleak winter and into spring.

We kept close to Montmartre, to Delilah's flat, lurking in the Café Coup de Foudre, or drifting aimlessly in the grey streets with our collars turned up. We walked sometimes twenty miles in a day. These was jazz streets, after all. That music done hung its hat here once, drawn near *everyone* to gig. We passed cheap pensions, abandoned flats where jazz men used to swing. Passed a rundown Le Rat Mort, saw the Big Apple's narrow door nailed up, drifted past old Bricktop's where Bechet and McKendrick had spilled out into the street, shooting at each other, both drunk as gulls. Along Rue Pigalle and Rue Fontaine only our own echoing footsteps kept time. We grown lean as greyhounds, our bodies all hope and bone.

And then I just wasn't thinking of Ernst and Paul so much anymore. My mind turned to Armstrong, to playing with him, and to Lilah too. Wasn't that my fear left me, it was still there. But a jack just worry and worry and worry, then it dies out in him. Guilt don't enter into it. I guess folk just ain't built to be faithful to nothing, not even to pain. Not even when it their own.

Delilah and me was set to have dinner but now I was dreading it. Sure, wasn't none of my business where she been on her nights away. But, hell. That kiss.

Worse, seemed she start in on the kid again, fussing over him, paying him all kinds of attention. Luring him from the shell of his damn silences. And he come crawling out. Chip told me all bout it over lunch. How that morning, in the market, the kid been buying her trinkets, cheap tin rings, headscarves and such.

I was grinding my old teeth down to their stumps, hearing him tell it.

"She was lookin for you too, brother," he said.

"She was there? At the market?"

"In the bony flesh."

"Ain't that a wonder," I said, scowling.

She caught up with us at last that afternoon. We was in Jean's old music store, where all the gates in Paris gone for the sweet sound, looking for some damn obscure record Chip wanted. It was a dark basement shop, dusty and unswept, and the weak daylight filtered in through high, filthy windows. There was brass horns strung up all about, hanging like a curtain of dead game.

The door banged open, and there she was, descending the stairs in her long heels, laughing, clinging to the kid's skinny arm. Hell. Something turned in me.

Chip ducked to see round the horns. "Hiero, brother, you got a little somethin on you sleeve."

"Ooh, boys," said Delilah, "I'm still shaking."

"Hiero's that good, huh?" smiled Chip.

At the mention of his name, that scrawny Judas untangled his arm from hers, drifted over. He look embarrassed. I moved away, toward the piano.

Lilah laughed. Her crowded teeth shining like rice in her dark mouth. "We were just down at Place Pigalle, and who do you think we—"

"Aw, what you two doin down there?" I chuckled, forcing a grin. It come out sounding sort of choked. I start to plink nervously on two of the keys.

Chip give me a look.

She furrowed her brow. "Who do you think we ran into?" she finished.

Chip shrugged. "George Washington. No, wait. Abe Lincoln."

"Jo Baker," she said. "Josephine Baker."

Well ain't you grand, I thought with unexpected bitterness. *Ain't you special.*

Delilah was fussing with the jangling bangles on her wrists. She worn long white gloves. Give me a pang of tenderness, seeing how self-conscious she was. But I dragged it back. I *wanted* to be annoyed.

I closed the lid of the piano with a heavy thud and she glance over, quick, then look back at Chip. "That Jo Baker can put a girl right off her day. She can make you feel like you're nothing but fluff, just Lou's bit of fluff."

"Aw, girl," said Chip. "You a lot of things, but you ain't fluff."

She looked at him to see if he was mocking. "And her sashaying all about town with those ridiculous swans and leopards and god only knows what else all following behind. She puts on such airs. Looks right through you. You ever heard her sing, Chip?"

"I *seen* her sing," he smiled. "It ain't the same thing."

"What'd you think?"

He chuckled. "Very talented, what all I could *see*."

Lilah made a sour face. "She's just a cheap copy of Addie Hall. You ever heard Addie in person? She's been doing what Jo does for years. Jo can't hold a candle to her."

Then, slow like, she lift up her green eyes and look at me with real hurt.

Hell. This was my cue. I was meant to say, *You know you ten times the woman she is, Lilah girl. You know fame's comin you way any day now, it ain't lost you address.*

But I ain't said it. I don't know, I guess mercy is a muscle like any other. You got to exercise it, or it just cramp right up.

———————◼———————

That was the day the consul ordered us home, all Yanks who couldn't "prove they had important business in France." It was on the radio, in the papers, on the lips of grocers and delivery boys. Seemed every damn American in Paris was buying souvenirs for the voyage west. But, hell. Ain't nothing more important than backing old Louis.

I met Delilah for a late dinner, just the two of us, at a underground bistro down by the Seine. It been a wine cellar once, and the soft smell of smoked casks come up through the creaking floor. Rickety tables, candlelight, a trellis overhead hairy with vines. The air felt cool in the darkness. First thing she asked about was the consul.

"Aw, I ain't goin back," I said. "Neither's Chip."

"You should," she said. "Staying can't help anyone. There's no point in it."

"Louis goin?"

She shrugged. "I'm sure he will be. He won't go just yet. But he'll go."

"You goin with him?"

"I always do."

I give her a hard look. "And what about the kid? You just goin leave Hiero here?"

She frowned. "I'll come up with something. I don't know what."

"Sure you will, girl. You ain't the sort to just disappear."

She flinched.

I regretted it at once. But my guts was all knotted up. I was still brooding on her and the kid linking arms in Jean's that afternoon. We was sitting at a small table set against the cellar wall, and I leaned one shoulder against the cold bricks and stared at her. The hard angles of her cheekbones in the candlelight. Her long graceful throat. How beautiful she was.

She lowered her face, turned the glass of wine in front of her in slow lazy circles. She looked away.

"I didn't want to go," she said soft like. "You know that, don't you?"

I fidgeted with the knife and fork beside the plate. That basket of bread sat steaming between us, and though I was starving, I ain't cut so much as a slice.

"We don't need to talk about it, you don't want to," I said. "I mean that."

"It was awful, Sid."

"I know."

"You don't know."

I said nothing.

She give me a dark look, took a breath. "We'd gone back to the apartment for his medicine," she began, in a flat voice. "I don't know what for. Paul didn't try to explain it to me—the language. But I think even if I did speak German he wouldn't have explained it. It seemed a private thing. Anyway, we were heading away from my hotel—"

"*Your* hotel?"

"For my suitcase. It was on the way back."

"Listen, you don't got to tell me," I said. "You don't got to go back there."

"No," she said, "I do."

I give her a grim, exasperated look.

"We were on our way back," she continued, "when I heard someone shout his name. I don't know why he looked back. But then he was running into the crowd. I stood there holding my suitcase and then two men shoved past me, hollering at him. I didn't know what it was about. I mean I didn't know it then. But then they were shouting *Jude*, and I knew that well enough. Oh, Sid, they threw him up against a window. There were people in there, looking out. I tried to get in front of Paul with my suitcase but those men knocked me down."

"They was Boots?"

"I don't know. I don't think so."

I ain't wanted to feel anger. I ain't wanted nothing but sadness for her. But I could feel myself scowling. "Hell, girl. You walkin round Berlin with a Jew, carryin a damn *suitcase*? What you thinkin?"

She blushed, looking off up the street in the dying sunlight.

"What you *thinkin*?" I said again.

She started to cry. "I didn't know, Sid. I didn't know."

She was crying, real quiet, her thin shoulders shaking. I sat very still, staring guiltily at the tablecloth. All a sudden I wasn't angry with her no more. If they called his name, I was thinking. If they called his name, they *known* him. Suitcase ain't got nothing to do with it.

A long shadow hovered suddenly above us. I glanced up. A handsome black gent stood there wearing a fine black suit, his shirt ironed so sharp its collar look like folded paper.

"Lilah?" he said. "You alright, girl?"

She give a angry laugh through her tears, looked up. "Oh, hi, Billy. I'm fine, I am. Jesus." She sniffled. "I thought you were gone."

"Aw, I been tryin to call you, girl." He smiled to reveal gleaming white incisors. Like a damn wolf. "You one impossible lady to reach. I only got the one number."

"Well, I only have the one phone. So that's not the problem." She give him one of her sad smiles, wiping the water from her eyes with her thumbs.

"I ain't meant to intrude," he said.

"It's alright, Billy. Really it is. I'm up on Abbesses now, in the count's old flat. Drop on in, anytime."

The jack's eyes slid over to me, his shine fading a little.

"Oh, I'm sorry." She folded her napkin. "Bill, this is Sidney Griffiths. Sid, Bill Coleman. I believe you're both in the business."

Bill *Coleman*? I rose from my seat. "Sure I know you, brother. You out of this *world*. You got to be this city's second trumpet."

"You kind," he said.

"It ain't kindness. You that good, brother. You know it."

"Used to be maybe. But who's this damn kid come in on the tide? I heard he plays like wildfire."

"The new generation," I said. "We gettin our comeuppance."

"Figure it near time to clock out, ship on back to the island."

Delilah give him a look. "You're going back to New York?"

"Chicago, girl. Ain't no other island."

"Chicago's not an island, Billy."

He smiled. "It be a island in the sea of *mediocrity*."

"You sure it ain't this old war runnin you out?" I said.

"Brother, I done already lost that one. Germans overrun me."

I ain't said nothing to that.

"You bring that Chip Jones with you?" he said.

"You know Chip?"

"Aw," he said with a sly grin. "Everybody know that son of a bitch. Give him a brass hello from me."

"When're you sailing?" said Delilah.

Coleman shrugged. "Ain't got no plans yet. It got to happen though, surely. What you doin? You ain't stickin round?"

She smiled. "Where Louis goes, there go I."

Our dishes arrived then, and Coleman muttered some excuse, already backing away from our table. "I goin drop by one a these days, Lilah. I see you then. Sidney." He give me a nod.

But Delilah called after him, "So you'll be here for a while? Even with your consul shutting down the party?"

Coleman shrugged, his smile light and boyish. He bumped into a table, turned around, turned back. "Lady, I *am* the party."

Then he was gone.

We et in silence then for a long while. It ain't seemed right to start in on it all again. She seemed real cold, real calm. I felt uneasy. The fish I'd ordered tasted dry, thin, like sawdust sprinkled with lemon.

"Well, he seem grand," I said at last. It come out sharper than I meant.

She frowned, stared past me at the swinging door to the kitchen. "I'm not sleeping with him, Sid."

I give a bitter laugh. "I wasn't thinkin it."

"Yes you were."

"Delilah, you ain't got to—"

But she put her gloved hand on mine, her eyes bright and sharp. "Sometimes," she said, then paused, as if the sound of her own voice made her forget what seem so straightforward just seconds ago. She wet her lips. "Sometimes life just leaves no room for what you want. I'm sorry." She sighed. "You don't know how sorry I am."

Heat rushed to my face. "Sure. It all done now anyhow."

"Yes. It is."

"I just glad you got out."

She stared a long time at me. "I didn't say goodbye because I didn't want it to end like that. It wouldn't soften things. I was afraid anything I said would sound empty, which would've been worse than saying nothing. At least that's how it struck me at the time—you'd hear these shallow words, *I'll think of you every day* and whatever, and think, man, she is goddamn empty."

I watched her face dim, her hands soft against the wine-stained tablecloth. She started fussing with the top button of her suit jacket.

I felt sick, disappointed, somehow. "You want to go?"

"Yes. I'm done." She folded her fork and knife on her plate with a click. Girl ain't hardly touched her food.

We made our way out into the dusk of emptying streets. There was so much running through me, so much I got no intention of saying or couldn't even think how to express. I looked off down the avenue, at the bright brasserie teeming with people, the plaza with its thin traffic, the awnings under electric lights with their soot and birdshit.

We walked a while, not touching. Then she took my arm. I felt the old electricity running along my elbow and through the muscle, and I shivered, everything going quiet in me. We was crossing the bridge over the water when she slowed, glanced over the stone railing.

"Whatever happened to Dame Delilah the Second?" she said.

"The Dame? Tossed her back in the pit."

"For real?"

"For real. Kid dumped her back in the wall. It was either there or in the streets."

"Sid," she said abruptly. "I can't be with you. Not like before."

"It alright." I felt sick. "I understand."

But she let go my arm and stood staring me down. "You *understand*? You'd let it go? Just like that?"

All a sudden I wasn't sure just what I supposed to say.

"No?" I said.

"No what?"

I was watching her for some clue as to what the right thing was.

"No I wouldn't?" I said at last. And then, in a softer voice: "I thought you brung me out here to say goodbye, I thought that's what you been sayin all night. Ain't it what you been sayin?"

She was silent a long time. The streetlights over the Seine slid over the oily scum and we watched a long, dark barge drift past, cut across the lights, vanish again downriver. A man was walking across the far bridge, his footfalls in three-quarter time. I took off my jacket, draped it over her shoulders.

"You cold, girl? You want to be gettin back?"

She looked up at me. She was shivering. "Tell me you love me."

"No."

"Tell me."

I smiled, sort of sad like. "Aw, girl. You goin break my heart."

She rested her head against my chest, looking out at the slow waters, and I thought, very suddenly: *Sid, brother, anything true got to always be this simple, this clear.*

That night we made love in her room. It was only the second time. Afterwards, I slept uneasily in her narrow bed, her hot back pressed up against me. In the morning, when the cold light poured in through the dirty glass, I couldn't remember my dreams.

‖

The day finally arrived.

I come in late, banging my old axe through the door like I already into the rot.

"Hell, brother, you ain't too tired for us?" Chip called from the stage. He turn to Armstrong. "Poor boy ain't been sleepin well."

Hiero was smiling at me slyly. The son of a bitch.

"It must be catchin," Armstrong laughed in that low rumble. "All I hearin bout be this awful damn insomnia Delilah been sufferin. You know anything bout that?"

I flushed. "Where all the other gates? It ain't just us?"

Chip give a little soft shoe shuffle. "It just us. Just the stripped-down set."

"I thought we'd just start out clean," Armstrong rasped. "Thought we'd just get to know each other in a intimate way."

"Sid likes intimate," Chip smiled. "Sid likes stripped down."

"I'm sure he don't know what you talkin bout," Armstrong grinned back at him. "I'm sure he just don't have a clue."

I come on up that stage filled with dread, my old shoes dragging. Louis Armstrong, brother. That gate cast a shadow even lying down. And here he was jawing with Chip like their mamas used to knit together. Hell.

It was a small basement lounge, with the houselights up in the back and the floor unlit and the tables shoved aside, the chairs balanced upside down on the white cloths. The floor done been swept, and small piles of rubbish and dirt stood along one side of the room.

Chip drawn out a few quick taps, testing the snare. I give Hiero a savage look. He was holding Armstrong's second horn loose at his thighs, his long thin pinky sharp out at a angle from the pistons.

Armstrong give us a look. "*Old Town Wrangler?* B-flat?"

Hiero shrugged.

"You ready, Sid?" said Armstrong.

All a sudden my throat went real dry.

"Aw, he ready," Chip smiled. "Count us in, brother."

And with just a casual nod of the head, without even saying a word, Armstrong bring us slowly in. And then we was off. Chip's kit was crisp, clean, and I could feel the lazy old tug of the bass line walk down into its basement and hang up its hat, and I begun to smile. Then the kid come in. He was brash, sharp, bright.

And then, real late, Armstrong come in.

I was shocked. Ain't no bold brass at all. He just trilled in a breezy, casual way, like he giving some dame a second glance in the street without breaking stride. It was just so calm, so effortlessly itself. Give me a damn chill.

Cause he done completely shift his gears. No longer the high-C hitter, that crazy showman fluttering so tight on the high register he sound like a flute. He'd calmed down, grown up, bleeding a lyricism so pure it like the voice of a old, old gate—burned of excess, holding nothing but just what he needed for each single note.

I ain't hardly believed it. Hiero, Chip and me was so harmonious, so close in tone colour, it sounded like the same gate squawling on three different instruments. Man, it was smooth.

But then it started.

I wasn't sure what it was, at first. A late buzz on the bass, maybe, a sluggish tap of my old toe. But there just wasn't no crackle in the gut, the bass just walking real flat-footed along them lines. I start messing it up, trying to find some blood in it.

Chip give me a sharp look from behind his kit, like to say, brother, you playing like you got twelve thumbs. And I was. I could *hear* it. Then I was back in time and holding the colour just right, and all of it gelled again. Armstrong lift up his horn, look at the kid, trill lazily away. Hiero punch out a brassy reply. Chip, he was brushing them skins so sweet it like he talking to a jane.

And then, just like that, my damn fingers stumble again.

"What you *doin?*" Chip hissed at me over his kit. "Get yourself together now. Hell."

I could feel the sweat dripping into my eyes. I give my head a slow shake. Armstrong give us a look, then just keep on going.

——— ■ ———

When we broke, Armstrong walk over to us wiping his forehead with a white kerchief. Turning to us, he grunted, giving us a sharp look-over.

The blood rush to my face.

"Now that was OK," he said, breathing hard. "That was good. I reckon we got to reshape it a little though." He turn to Hiero. "You, though—man oh man. Little *Maestro?* Can that. You Little *Louis*, pure and simple. Little Louis, boy. And don't you change a thing. You the *stuff.* You perfect."

"Kid was swingin alright," Chip smiled.

"You was swingin youself, Pops," the old titan said. "Like you rubbin you own belly over there."

"Aw, when we good, we good," I chuckled.

But Armstrong just grunted to hisself and stepped off the stage, over to the bar.

Hell. I was smiling this sick smile and just wasn't able to stop. I leaned over my old axe. But my hands was trembling.

"Now tell me, boys," called Armstrong from down at the bar. He was holding a cold glass to his forehead. "Tell me bout this caveman with the clam moustache been barkin speeches all over Germany."

Chip was wiping down the skins. "He askin bout Hitler," he said to Hiero, without looking up.

"Hitler," Hiero nodded, with a dark expression.

"What you want to know?" said Chip. "It real bad over there, real bad. Folk too frightened to open their mouths."

"What you know of it, Griffiths?" said Armstrong.

I come down off the stage, feeling grateful he even ask. "Sure," I said. "Dentists be pullin teeth out through *noses*, the mouths is shut so tight. Ain't no law over there."

"They still got a ministry for it though," Chip called.

Hiero was looking at me, but I ain't bothered to translate. I was feeling stung, bitter, and seeing his damn face staring in that half-darkness ain't helped me none.

"You boys got through it alright, though."

"We didn't," I said. "We lost a gate."

Armstrong nodded. "Mmm. I heard bout that. Your pianist. What was his name?"

"Butterstein. Paul Butterstein."

"I'm real sorry for you," he murmured.

We all sort of shrugged. It was still raw.

"Ain't it been strained here, though?" Chip asked after a minute. "Lilah was tellin us bout the ten-percenter."

Armstrong nodded. "The Frenchies got their share of nightmares.

We only just one of them. I ain't worry bout it too much now. Was a time though we had to count our black gates before we climb a stage. Still, it a sight more decent than where we from."

"What, Chicago?" I said. "Try Baltimore."

"Try Orleans," Armstrong said.

Chip pour hisself a finger of gin. He turn around, lean back with his two elbows perched high on the bar like a damn bird. "It's a odd thing though. Till recent, Krauts got some kind of ladder when it come to blacks. Not like what been goin on with the Jews. If you a black American, well, you treated alright. If you a foreign student or singer or somethin, sure. They ain't want you goin back home talkin bad bout their little utopia. But if you a black Kraut, a *Mischling*, like our boy here—" He glanced at Hiero. "Well. It get real ugly."

"The music's just dyin," I said. "Ain't nothin left but Wagner."

"Wagner and the Horst Wessel," said Chip, scowling.

"Horst Wessel," Hiero said, frowning. He waved his horn dismissively.

"The Horst Wessel?" said Armstrong. "That a song?"

"It a damn *anthem*."

"He was a Boot," Chip said. "A Nazi thug. He run into some trouble with his landlady—she want more rent, or he won't keep holin her, somethin. Wessel's girl was a street hustler too, I think. I forgot the details. Anyway. This landlady be the widow of a Kozi—"

"A Communist," I said.

Chip nodded. "So some old comrades of her husband's go up to Wessel's flat, shoot him dead. And that's how it starts. Kozis, they try to make Wessel look like a pimp and a criminal. They just cleanin the streets, see. But the Nazis, hell, they turn the old thug into a martyr. A idealist who sacrifice his life for the Fatherland. They give him one hell of a funeral."

As Chip spoke, the kid was opening the valves on his horn, blowing it clear. He give me a dark look. I looked away.

"The anthem, it about this jack?" said Armstrong.

"Not *about* him," said Chip, "*by* him. It a poem he wrote, but set to music. How do it go?"

I shook my head. "Flag's held high."

Chip cleared his throat. Tapping the bar to keep the beat, he start to sing in German:

The flag's held high! The ranks are tightly closed!
SA men march with firm courageous tread.
Together with us, marching in our ranks in spirit, are those
Comrades Red Front and Reaction shot dead!

And then Hiero raise up his horn, real soft, and start playing a uneasy nervous beat under the words, against the words, like he just slyly mocking them:

Clear the streets for the brown battalions,
Clear the streets for the Storm Division man!
The swastika's already gazed on full of hope by millions.
The day for freedom and bread is at hand!

Armstrong ain't said nothing. He just walked over while Chip and Hiero was playing, pulled down his own horn, and lifted it to his broken lips. He caught Hiero's eye, then, soft like, his whole face puckered up. He come in on the loose beat.

Hell. It wasn't nothing like before.

It was the sound of the gods, all that brass. It was the old Armstrong and the new, that mature distilled essence of a master and the boy he used to be, the boy who could make his glissandi snap like marbles, the high Cs piercing. Hiero thrown out note after shimmering note, like sunshine sliding all over the surface of a lake, and Armstrong was the water, all depth and thought, not one wasted note. Hiero, he just reaching out, seeking the shore; Armstrong stood there calling across to him. Their horns sound so naked, so blunt, you felt almost guilty listening to it, like you eavesdropping. After some minutes Chip stopped singing, left just the two golden ropes of sound to intertwine.

It was then that I finally heard it. I heard how damn brilliant the kid really was.

I hated it.

"Now *that*, friends, is *music*!" barked Armstrong, breaking off. He whipped his white kerchief from his pocket to mop his gleaming brow.

"Is it ever," I said, sounding sour.

"I swear to you, Little Louis, that horn you usin ain't *never* sound so good." Armstrong's eyes was wrinkling up. "Well tell him," he said to me, "tell him what I said."

"Louis says you soundin good," I told Hiero.

The kid smiled, shrugged.

"Tell him he just a little slow between the verses," said Armstrong.

Holy *hell*, brother.

Thrusting his hand down the neck of his shirt, Armstrong pulled out the chain he was wearing. "Come on over here," he said. "Come here, all a you."

We drifted on over to him.

It was a Star of David on a gold chain. "I always worn this for luck. Always. When I's a boy, I worked for this family, the Karnofskys. They come over from Lithuania. I was just seven years old but I wasn't blind, I could see the shit these folk was handlin. And yet they was always, always, kind to me. I was just this kid could use a little word of kindness, just this kid needin a little niceness as he made his way in the world. And they give it."

We ain't none of us spoke. Hiero was looking at Armstrong like he understood.

"We goin to *do* this," said Armstrong. "We goin to *do* this, brother. It ain't right what's goin on over there. We goin to burn this Horst Wessel to the record. Lay it down, a late track. What you think? Twist it up, make it pretty. Say somethin with it to the world, to the Krauts, that only us cats can say. We goin do this for your gate Paul."

His gaze was fixed on Hiero.

Then he turned to me, his eyes bright. "Go *on*, Griffiths. Tell him what all I said."

————————————————— ■ —————————————————

Afterwards, out on the chilly street, leaning my old axe up against a bench, I seen Chip approaching like I sick with plague.

"What happen to you in there?" he said, long-faced and grey. He give his cufflinks a grim twist. He ain't sat down. Like maybe it was catching.

I laughed angrily, looked up at him. "You think he goin give me another listen? Ever?"

Chip give me a long, sad look. "I don't know, brother. I think you hurt his old ears. What happened?"

"What, you ain't never choked before?"

Chip shrugged, put a hand on my shoulder. All a sudden his eyes was two hard black stones. "You make me look like shit, buck, and I'll gut you," he said softly. "I will."

He turned, punched his fists into his pockets, and wandered off up the street into the cold afternoon.

I was shaking with anger and embarrassment the entire walk back through Montmartre. The flat was empty, and I come in banging my old axe. I sat down with a grimace, just sat there staring at the moulding on the walls.

There was a soft thump down the hall.

"Lilah?" I called out. "That you?"

"I'm in here," she called. "I'm in my room."

She was rolling on a dark stocking when I come miserably in.

"So?" she said when she seen me. "How'd it go?"

I shrugged bitterly. I just ain't able to start in on it.

She come on over, wrestle me out of my old coat. She led me over to the window seat, sat me down in all that white sunshine, run a finger light over my temple like she brushing away cobwebs. "It can't have been that bad," she murmured. "Come on. It can't have been like that. How was Hiero?"

I frowned, leaned away from her. "Hiero? Hell."

She pull back then. "Sid. What happened?"

"It was bad."

"What was bad? You were bad?"

"I wasn't bad, girl. I was *awful*."

"I doubt that."

"You ain't seen their faces, Lilah. Chip—he look *ashamed*."

She arched a eyebrow.

"What?" I said.

"I didn't say anything."

"But you goin to. You goin say somethin that'll make me mad, girl. I know it."

She stood up.

"Where you goin?"

She snorted. "When you're done feeling sorry for yourself, then we can talk." But she stopped by the vanity, and turning to me, give me a long careful look. "Well? Are you done?"

I sort of picked at my old calloused fingerpads. Shrugged.

"Good." She sat back down, took a breath like she got something to say. But then she just put her hand on my wrist. It felt cool, soft. "I know Louis," she said at last. "He can spot a gate like no one I ever met. He'll know how good you are, Sid."

"I wasn't good, Lilah. It was like I was steeped in the rot."

"But you *can* be good."

I shook my damn head like it wasn't of no consequence.

"Did Louis say you weren't going to be on the record?"

"No."

"Then stop with all this," she said, but gentle like. She pulled my fingers toward her top button, slipped it real leisurely through its eyelet. "Now *I* need *your* help with something," she said with a faint smile. "Something I *know* you're good at."

"Aw, Lilah," I said, "I ain't in the mood, girl."

But she was already undoing her blouse, slipping my hand inside it.

———— ■ ————

Louis ain't said nothing more bout the record. Not to no one. Weeks bled by, soon the light in the alleys begun failing, and then we was crunching through a crust of snow on the cobblestones of them same dark streets. It was damn near November. The trees along the Seine gone to glass, shining white and delicate. And I got to thinking, maybe I had a chance yet. Maybe he like to forget what I'd sounded like.

The months, they felt like nothing. All Paris seemed drunk and sleeping it off, that slow false war that was like no damn war at all. The Frogs was still camped behind the Maginot. Their soldiers, pencil-moustached, natty in fatigues, had taken to playing football and breeding roses hardy enough to shake off the cold. Soldiers on leave drifted through the streets in the morning haze, shivering and grim like poets out of wine. Sometimes we seen them sleeping on park benches, huddled figures in the grey light. We slept like the dead those days.

Wasn't no word from Poland. It was blanketed in darkness. I supposed the Krauts was devouring the west but we ain't heard of no savagery. A cold wind was coming out of the east, and soon we was all shivering when we come in, huddling up together on the couches. The kid looked sort of haunted these days, hollow in the cheeks, his eyes yellow with weariness. Chip and me laughed uneasily, or not at all. We was all of us stretched too damn tight with nerves. And still Louis ain't said nothing.

When word come over the wireless of a Russian assault in Finland, Hiero just shake his sorrowful head. "It winter," Chip said with a scowl, "they all like to be slaughtered." All of us huddled over the fireplace, its soft popping heat, our fists shoved up in our armpits, the wireless spitting and crackling in the corner like a second fire. And Delilah, with her beautiful head in my lap. None of it seemed real.

—————— ■ ——————

Then Louis, at last, was calling up his gates.

I sat at a table on the Bug's patio, tearing off the crusts of a day-old twist, brooding over whether I ought to start in on the gin or the rot, when Chip come striding up out of the afternoon crowds.

He looked agitated. "*There* you are," he said, out of breath. He got this feverish glint in his eye. "I was just bout to give up on you."

"What you on about?"

"We got to go, brother. Louis just phoned. He wants to talk bout the record."

I felt something surge in my chest. "What—now?"

"Aw, not if it *inconvenient* for you," he said, smiling.

I was already standing, counting out some damn francs. I had a foolish smile on my face. "And he ask for me? He said I was still in?"

"Why wouldn't you be in?"

I stopped fidgeting with my dough. "What you mean. Louis ain't asked for me?"

"He ain't asked for no one. He just phoned and said it was time. To get over to the damn Coup to meet the other gates."

All at once that good feeling just drained right out of me. I squinted at Chip in the dark afternoon light. "But did he mean just you?"

"Sid," said Chip, frowning. "I ain't asked him. He ain't said. Now you comin or what?"

"Son of a bitch," I muttered.

"Brother, he heard you on our damn records. He know how good you can play."

"What he say? Tell me what he say, exactly."

Chip give me a sour look. "Alright. And this is a exact quote. He said, *Chip, get on over to the Coup. Oh, and be sure and tell old Sid his mama is one damn honey in the mornin.* Man, you a ass. Come if you comin."

Then he was rushing off and I couldn't do nothing but follow.

They was at Café Coup de Foudre, sitting in the window. Two of the damn tables been shoved together to fit them all. I seen them through the dirty glass even before we done crossed the boulevard. We punch open the glass door, wade in through all that smoke, breathing hard from the walk over.

Armstrong give us a odd look as we come in. He was waving us over. I thought, *Hell, Sid, don't you be crazy now. That look wasn't nothing.*

But I wasn't crazy. It *was* a odd look.

"Hi Sid," Armstrong said to me in that gravelly voice.

He turned to the gates leaning up among the tables. All of them grim-faced, etched, like gangsters in a moving picture. "Boys, I want you all to meet the Fifth Column. This here Chip Jones, the hide hitter. He look and sound American, sure, but he straight from Berlin. His friend is Sid Griffiths."

"Aw, I know some of these boys already," Chip said, grinning. "I taken their money at dice."

"You keep talkin, brother." A tall dark gate with a thin moustache laughed.

"Bertie. How you wife? She still tired from last year?"

I ain't joined in. My mouth like to be stuffed with dry crackers.

"Where Little Louis?" Armstrong asked me.

I shrugged.

"We ain't seen him," said Chip. "But if he get you message, he goin be here."

One of the other gates, a short thick fellow with blond hair, muttered something in Frog to Louis. The others laughed.

"Aw, you boys will have to excuse me," said Armstrong. "Let me introduce you. Chip, this Jacques Painlevé, the trombonist. Bertie here goin tickle the keys for us. Herve be damn hot on the licorice stick. I reckon you know Jean. He goin crack the bass for you in the back line."

Son of a *bitch*. I felt my face flush. I look down at my hands. My fingernails was cutting into the flesh of my palm.

Chip ain't even seem to notice. He was messing with the trombonist's gin and the other gates leaned in, laughing. It was then that Armstrong turn to me, put a big hand on my shoulder.

"Sid," he said quiet like. "You goin sit this one out, if that okay. It ain't but the first one. We got other discs to press. Jean just got the fingers I want on this one."

I give a funny little shrug, like it ain't no trouble.

"Aw, it alright Louis," I said. "It alright. Sure. It alright."

———————————————— ▬ ————————————————

It wasn't alright.

When I wandered back into the flat, everything felt strange, a shadow of itself, like I was seeing it all for the first time. All that dust, the shabby, dented end tables, the creaking floorboards. I trudged past chairs sheeted like corpses, past grimy windowsills. Delilah's bathroom door stood open. I watched her lean over the basin, wet her thin fingers under its stream, reach up under her gold scarf to scratch her head. She heard my breathing and turned, alarmed.

"Oh, Sidney Kidney, it's you," she said.

"What you doin here?" I said. "Ain't you got some place to be?"

She smiled, shrugged. "It gets awful hot sometimes, this helmet. Even in winter. I'm like a draft horse, I just need to be wetted down sometimes."

"I'm sorry you uncomfortable." My voice, it was hard and awkward, a right plank of wood.

She stood there staring at me, water dripping from her fingers. "You sound angry."

"Well."

"A well is nothing but a hole filled with water. What is it?"

But my voice, when I finally spoke, wasn't steady. "I ain't on it. Chip and the kid are on it, but I ain't. Louis got some other gate supportin Chip."

She froze, her hands half lifted to her head, her face turned toward me. "Oh, Sidney. Oh, I'm so sorry. I am."

I said nothing.

"What're you going to do?" she said quietly.

I shrugged. "There ain't nothin else. This was it. This was my shot at doin somethin real. There ain't nothin else."

"Oh, Sid."

"Don't look at me like that. I mean it."

"Sid, I'm sorry. I'm sure it isn't you, I'm sure there's some other reason Louis skipped over you."

I give a sharp laugh. "It don't matter. Kid's on it, ain't that all that matters?"

"No, Sid, it isn't. Though I'm glad for him."

"Of course you glad for him."

"What's that supposed to mean?"

"You need me to say it? You wink and tease and flirt with the kid like you got designs or somethin." I ain't looked at her, glancing instead at the sink's rusted gullet, the clean water thrumming against it. I ain't believed a word of what I was saying. But I ain't cared. Felt like everything being torn from me.

I said, "You keep on like this, kid goin to get ideas. Like you mean it or somethin."

Silence, filled with the drumming of water on steel. She turned off the tap.

"Like I mean *what* or something?"

I felt a twinge then, like I should just shut my damn mouth. But seeing her stubborn face, its righteous frown, hell, the heat just rose up in me.

"Way you carryin on, girl, it ain't right. It ain't goddamned right. *I* know you just teasin, *I* know you wouldn't never do nothin. But other folks, what *they* goin think? And Hiero hisself—you can see he half in love with you. It cruel, makin him think you love him back."

Slowly, Delilah wrapped her fingers round the back of a wrought-iron chair. Her face darkening. She drawn back the chair and sat.

I stood there staring, the skin hot all along my hairline. I watched her watching her hands. What a face she got, smooth as the surface of milk.

"Delilah?" I finally said.

She raised her hand like to say stop. Let it fall in her lap. After a minute, she look up at me, her green eyes filled with some strange subterranean feeling.

"If I have made him think I love him," she begun, then broke off. "I hope to god I have. I've tried. I've tried everything I could think of. Someone has to. Have you even seen that kid out there, Sid? Have you taken one goddamn look? He's a sunk little boy. Lost as a stray cat. You're always so worried about you, so damn worried about yourself. He's just a *child*. And he's got no one."

She was staring at me from a cold, unnerving distance. The light in her eyes gone out. "You have some very sick ideas in that head of yours." She paused, raised her face. "Hiero's like a little brother to me."

I known that. Course I known that. I done said the words myself to Chip months and months ago. I felt a heaviness in my gut made me want to curl up and clutch my ribs. Man, the *shame*. My jaw started twitching as I stared down into her face, its utter emptiness. And I seen clearly and sharply just how much she did not love me.

"Lilah," I said.

"Close the door on your way out."

I watched her face. Nothing, no water on her eyes—nothing.

I turned to go. Even as I shut the door with a click, I was listening for her voice, thinking she might call me back.

She ain't.

———— ■ ————

Did that scrawny Kraut bastard mean to take *everything* from me—the band, Armstrong, the recording, even Delilah? Ain't he like to leave me *no* scraps? Is that what genius does—entitles a gate to claim whatever pieces of others' lives he want?

Cause I admit it. He got genius, he got genius in spades. Cut him in half, he still worth three of me. It ain't fair. It ain't fair that I struggle and struggle to sound just second-rate, and the damn kid just wake up, spit through his horn, and it sing like nightingales. It ain't *fair*. Gifts is divided so damn unevenly. Like God just left his damn sack of talents in a ditch somewhere and said, *Go help youselves, ladies and gents. Them's that get there first can help themselves to the biggest ones*. In every other walk of life, a jack can *work* to get what he want. But ain't no amount of toil going get you a lick more talent than you born with. Geniuses ain't made, brother, they just *is*. And I just was *not*.

I was drinking alone at one of the red tables in the tobacconist's down near the flat when Hiero ankled in. The tobacconist leaned out over the counter, her shirtsleeves turned up, one scrawny arm propped under either cheek. We called her the Bug cause of her thin, masticating face, her bulging eyeballs.

She come over here from Switzerland after the first war. "What'll it be, Hiero?" she called out in that cracked German the Swiss talk.

I looked up at that.

The kid seem confused a second, like he a actor done wander onstage at the wrong cue. He stood staring at her, then shrugged. Turning his face, he seen me in the corner.

"Aw, I ain't so thirsty," he mumbled to her.

"On the house," she said. "Whenever you're ready for it."

Hell. Why everyone got to be so damn *nice* to him all the time?

Hiero seen the graveness of my face, and stopped where he stood. I was thinking bout Delilah's words. Thinking, you can be damn young and not be a kid. You can stop being a kid at any age, it ain't got nothing to do with years. And Hiero, hell.

"You a fraud," I said, sort of soft like. "You a damn fraud. You hear me?"

"Sid?" he said.

I spat on the Bug's filthy floorboards.

But then his expression, hell. I wanted to take back all of it. I ain't never seen a jack look so crushed. You could see it in his face, something inside was wilting, a slow closing over. His eyes gone real dark.

"Aw, I kiddin Hiero." I kicked out the chair across from me. "Come on, bring you ass on over here and split this drink."

He just stood there a second more, looking at me with a hardened face.

"Hiero," I called out angrily.

He just turn and walk on out of that shop and into the street, the door banging behind him.

The Bug watched me with a sour twist of her mouth, but she ain't said nothing.

And so that dreamlike winter begun.

Even awake I was sleeping. Dumped in a foreign city, where I ain't known hardly a soul, the language a constant door in my face. It weighed on me, the loneliness, the jealousy. I took to avoiding Delilah when I could, leaving late or early, eating in strange cafés no gate like to turn up in. I blocked out the kid entire. I ain't certain he even notice.

The streets of Paris turned white as mould under the cold blare of gas lamps.

The kid and Chip, they gone out at strange hours, the kid dragging Armstrong's old horn with him as they went. I just turned over in my blankets, stared at the wall with dulled eyes in the darkness. I ain't asked after the record. They ain't said. Armstrong grown sick again, grown healthy. He vanished for a time to tour in some other country and then he was back and they was working again. That venom in my gut ain't eased none.

What surprised me was how easily time begun to pass. A week gone by, then a second, a third. Christmas come and gone without celebration. I marked January by the vanishing of red bows, of tree-shaped sweets from patisserie windows.

It was a damn dark winter, made darker by nothing to do. I took to spending my afternoons walking all of Paris, my toes smarting from the cold, and in my head, over and over, the ugly beauty of Hiero's horn.

One other thing happened that dreamlike season.

It was noontime, the sky entirely white. I'd just stumbled across Pont de la Concorde, my hands shoved deep in my pockets, when I felt a shadow cross my path. I looked up, and there he was again. Louis god-damn Armstrong. Standing in front of me, holding a bag of groceries, his breath clouding the air.

I flushed.

"Griffiths," he said in that rich crunching voice. "You goin this way?"

"How the disc comin?" I said.

"Oh, slow. Real slow. We just feelin our way in the dark."

I wasn't sure what to say to that. We started walking over the snow.

Armstrong give me a sidelong look. "Delilah been worried bout you. You alright?"

"She tell you that?"

He nodded.

"We ain't together no more," I said. "She tell you that, too?"

"I heard."

"She ain't even talkin to me. I come in a room, she go out of it. She tell you that too?"

Armstrong jostled his bag of groceries into the elbow of one arm, put a soft gloved hand on my back as we walked. "I know how it is, when it ends like that. I know how it hurt the heart."

I was still half-cut from the gin that morning and I sort of swayed back, give him a funny look. "I ain't *got* no heart," I said bitterly. "Ain't that why I ain't worth a damn on my axe?"

There was a old man sitting riverside, his pole drifting in the current. I reckoned it was too damn cold to catch anything. But there he was.

Armstrong's voice got real gravelly, real deep and soft, like a pelt carpet. "There is a whole lot of talents, Sid. You a mighty fine rhythm boy."

"But I ain't got the stuff."

"You know what you got. Ain't no one tell you otherwise."

I shook my head in disgust.

"It don't matter much bout all that anyway," Armstrong added. "You think it do, but it don't. A man ain't just his one talent. Little Louis needs you. And Jones look to you like you his brother. You got the talent of making others your kin, your blood. But music, well it's different. I reckon it got its own worth. But it ain't a man's whole life."

Aw, hell, Louis, I thought. *Ain't nothin else I want.*

Something gone out of me, after that. Some of that fury I been feeling. The hurt just sort of evaporated off, and I felt lighter, sadder, but less alone. I ain't saying we started being friendly again, not like that. But we circled each other, me, Chip and the kid, with a kind of restful grace. Every morning I watched them shuffle out to cut that record, and every night I seen them return home dog tired, and it seemed with each coming and going I begun to feel less bitter. Like I finally understood we was in this life together.

Delilah, hell, I still couldn't look at her without feeling brutally sick. But I wasn't angry at anyone, not no more.

And the Phony War continued. One night in February I was ankling home when I seen the sky flash like a camera, then die again into stillness. The silence was frightening. In the morning Lilah translated from the paper that it been one of the Frogs' own shells, crashing down across the river, in the Fifth, near the Censier station on Rue Mirbel. Punched a hole a foot and a half wide, wrecked a café. Two janes died. A jack got his leg cut right off. There ain't even been a damn siren.

Then the restrictions begun. Bread was cut back, twists forbidden, only basic loaves and croissants permitted. Some days the butcher shops closed. Other days, no candy. What gnawed at us, though, was Tuesdays, Thursdays, Saturdays, days when the liquor was corked up, and a jack couldn't find a hard shout to drink for all the damn francs in the city.

But even that ain't woke us up. We just brought our own rot when we gone out, toting the bottles along with us like we going on a damn picnic. It was a hazy age we slept through, and slowly it passed.

In the spring, with the rains, come the war.

III

It arrived in Paris on a bright morning in May. The air was warm, the Seine beginning to stink in the rising heat, the trees on the boulevards greener. Pigeons hobbled all about the cobblestones.

I was already drinking gin with Chip in the Coup, neither of us talking. We was both heavy-lidded from a damn air siren that morning, and the punch of tracers from battery guns in the dawn sky. It been the first daylight raid we could think of. I'd got to thinking maybe the good life was over. Maybe these years of being a gate, of late nights and women and grand friendships and, damn, that *music*, maybe it was done. Maybe fate was telling me, *Brother you get on out now.*

All winter Chip and the kid had slunk in late most nights after working on the disc, their shoulders drooping. But it been weeks now since Louis left to tour down south, and that record still wasn't finished, far as I could tell. I known it wasn't depression I was seeing in them, just a kind of weariness, the long exhaustion of working on a thing you believe in but can't see the end of.

Café Coup was crowded at that hour. All a sudden some jack twist up the dial on the wireless, damn thing crackling so loud some janes put fingers to their ears. With smoke still streaming from their cigs their hair looked on fire. It was all in Frog, the talk, we ain't understood a damn word of it. But we could see in the strained faces, the shocked grunts, the sudden sobering silence that something real dark was coming.

"What you reckon?" I said to Chip.

He just shrugged. "*La guerre, la guerre,*" he muttered.

But the gent beside us grabbed my arm, shushed us. The radio was still broadcasting. Then all a sudden it was like everyone just come to, just snapped out of it, and the crowd start shuffling and muttering. A jane in the corner stood up from her table, started shrieking some damn gibberish. Folks begun pushing in at the doorway, hollering for what they couldn't hear. Whole damn café felt like a crowd waiting for a parade to appear round the corner, filled with a dread and excitement out of all proportion.

Someone broke a bottle in the roar. Then another. Folks was pressing up against our table, jostling us.

Chip smiled tiredly, raised his glass of gin. "To the end of the world, brother."

We drank.

It was the beginning of the western offensive. The Krauts hurtled through Belgium, Holland, Luxembourg. Every hour the lines of the map was changing. Day after the Coup, Lilah reported to us the British ain't got a government, that some damn joker named Churchill taken over. Then the Frogs sent their armies north, and the Limeys opened a front against the Krauts. Then it was the Krauts landing parachutists in behind our lines. Hell. Every night the air raid sirens rung out, searchlights scarring the darkness. We'd bustle on down into the cellar to lean cold and weary against the walls.

A few days later we got news of the Krauts bombing Rotterdam, burning twenty-five thousand civilians in the streets. All of Paris gone mad hearing that, everyone's faces pale like they already dead. It was happening quick and startling as lightning. One day Holland fell. We could hear bombs thumping in the background, listening to the RAF correspondent broadcasting from Flanders. Next day word come that the Limeys run a bombing raid in the Ruhr.

Day after that we heard the French armies was in retreat, fleeing Belgium, and the Krauts marched into Brussels. Next night British bombers struck Hamburg. The Reeperbahn was chewed to mulch. I thought of Ernst. Then I tried not to. The entire damn French 9th Army was captured in Le Cateau, and Antwerp fell. And just like that the Krauts was swimming along the Channel coast, washing off their boots in the cold salt, and in a panic the Limeys start sailing away from Dunkirk by the thousands.

And then our own war begun.

———————————————

It was a Tuesday morning when Delilah come bursting into the flat, dragging Hiero by the wrist. She rushed to the big windows, wrenched back the curtains and turned to stare round the flat like she looking for something particular.

"What you doin now, girl?" said Chip, all irritable. He lift up his head from the mattress where he been sleeping.

I rolled over, crushed the pillow over my damn face. That sun was *bright*.

"They've been rounding up the Germans in the city," she said. The curtains fell back; a cool darkness descended. "Who knows Hiero's living here?"

"Ask Sid," said Chip, yawning.

I give a sullen shrug from where I lay on the floor. "No one. Just us gates."

"The Bug knows it," said Chip, rubbing his jaw. "But she ain't goin tell."

Delilah set to brooding over that. The kid ain't said nothing.

"What bout the rest of the building?" I said. "Ain't they like to remember him? He been goin to the cellar every damn night there a siren."

She frowned. "They'll think he's Senegalese," she said, after a moment. "I'll tell them he's Senegalese."

I felt a soft tremor run under my skin, just real soft, like I taken a hit of the rot straight. Cause it was the first time Delilah spoken to me directly in weeks. Hell. When it bite you, them teeth go deep.

"What they doin with them?" said Chip.

"Who?"

"The Krauts. They arrestin them? Deportin them? What?"

She shook her head. "I don't know. But they're being asked to report to the stadium at Montrouge."

Hiero splayed his gangly legs out before him, his arms crossed glumly against his chest. Lilah turned at the window, staring towards where he sat, brooding.

"Well, ain't that the party," said Chip, with that tiredness in his voice. Something done happen to him these last months. All that fire and brutality, the sharp words and surgical instinct—it had all dimmed in him. He sat up in his blankets, shirtless, his hairy back looking rolled and muscular.

Delilah turned to him, her green eyes dark. "Did you see this?" She lifted a corner of the curtains, the dust drifting off them like pollen. She gestured out the window. We could see a vein of black smoke rising from the Quai d'Orsay. The sky above it grey as lead, plume after plume of tar-dark wisps feeding the shadow. It was like I could smell them, their awful char.

"They're burning documents," she said. "Germans have crossed the Meuse. They're on their way here."

After some seconds, Chip said, "*Now?*"

"Now, in three weeks, in three months." She shrugged. "Half the city's in a panic. I suppose the other half just hasn't heard yet. Paris is going to be a war zone. They say the fighting will go street to street."

"It goin be a massacre."

She said nothing.

"Krauts are comin," I said to Hiero.

He just nodded darkly, started picking at his long fingers.

"Lucky old Louis," Chip said in a bitter voice. "Wish to hell *I* was tourin down south right now." He grabbed a tangle of his sheets, held it tight at his waist. Standing, he crossed to the window.

Frowning, Delilah took a seat beside the kid. "We've got to get visas, get out of France," she said.

"What bout old Louis?" Chip turned from the window. "You goin leave him down south?"

"It's not Louis I'm worried about."

I shook my head. "Ain't no way, girl. Everybody tryin. And the kid is a damn *Kraut*." I looked at Hiero. "Lilah sayin she goin get us visas. To get out."

He glanced at her, then back at me. "It ain't goin happen," he mumbled. "Ain't no way I goin get out. I be the *enemy*, Sid. Ain't she realized it?"

I shrugged. "She ain't listening to me."

"They comin for real then? The Boots?" he said.

I nodded.

"And Louis still down in Bordeaux?"

I nodded again. "I guess so. I guess he ain't comin back."

Hiero give a angry shrug, and all a sudden his face closed right over. "So the record dead then," he said flatly. Just like that. It dead.

I felt a surge of vicious pleasure at his disappointment. I forced it back down.

Delilah was rubbing a nervous hand at the nape of her neck. "We'll need to get to Lisbon. We can sail from there."

"You ain't getting the damn kid into New York," I said. "Lilah? Look at me, girl. Not a *chance*."

"Not without papers, no. He'll need something to get him through."

Chip snorted. "Where you goin find these magic papers?"

She frowned. A thin crease appeared between her eyes. "I know some people. They know some people."

"It soundin like a lot of damn people all a sudden," said Chip. "Why don't we just take out a ad in the damn paper?"

"It goin cost us," I said.

"What, the ad?"

I looked at him as if to say, There is just too many kinds of stupid. He just shook his damn head. Delilah, she was looking real tired, like she ain't known rest in a lifetime. Just seeing it made me sad.

And so begun her plan.

She figured the kid be safest with us, back in the States. I ain't like to disagree. All of Europe was on fire. But the first step was to get the kid a acceptable passport. Then we all be needing visas, to get the lot of us through France, into Spain, into Portugal. There was vessels setting out from Lisbon for New York every day, she said. We got to be on one of them.

She set up a rendezvous with a shadow some days later. We made our way through the city's summer streets, past folk sitting on the terraces, sipping their mineral waters, chatting like there wasn't nothing damn happening, like the war was some far-off mirage. I stared at Lilah. She had this sunken look about the eyes, dark sockets. Her thin arms swaying hard to her quick strides. Hell, I felt for her.

Feeling my gaze, she turned dark eyes on me. I glanced away, took to studying the patient, ornate buildings. "Be a lot of places to hide guns round here," I said. "If it come to that."

She laughed. It sounded angry. "They're slaughtering the French *armies*, Sid. What do you think they'll do to the *civilians*?"

I sort of blushed. Girl had a way of making you feel a fool.

"You sure you wouldn't rather Chip be here?" I said.

"Chip doesn't exactly blend in."

I blushed some more.

She led me down across the Seine to a big picture house where they was showing *Pygmalion* in a matinee. Folks drifted in real slow, like they ain't passionate about the picture but what else they got to do. I shielded my eyes from the sun, the sweat already trickling down my spine as I paid up at the ticket window. We slipped inside.

The theatre was crowded, smelling of cigarette smoke and roasted nuts. I was nervous we might not find three seats together, but Delilah strode straight down the aisle, sliding into a velvet chair. Ignoring me as I took my seat, she set her shawl and purse down on the vacant seat beside her, the brown paper envelope holding our passports and money sticking clearly out of her bag.

"Is you contact here?" I whispered nervous like. I glanced back at the faces, at the men with their tired eyes. The houselights was going down.

"Jesus, Sid. Turn *around*."

Then the newsreel started, a sharp blue light cutting through the smoke in the darkness. And all at once the theatre filled with jeering, shouts, catcalls. It was footage of Frog infantry crouched in their damn trenches, filing past with rifles slung. I ain't understood none of the damn narration, but the images was clear enough. Kraut soldiers with their hands held high in surrender. British fighters taking off in long fierce runs toward a frighteningly empty sky. Images of Krauts fleeing the battlefield, pulling away from outbuildings and barns. There was shots of old King Leopold glowering, and damn Petain standing firm.

"What they sayin?" I whispered.

Lilah scowled. "We're holding the Germans in Belgium. We're advancing."

"Advancin on Paris, maybe." I smiled bitterly.

"Hush."

But glancing at her purse, I give a start. "Holy hell." I gestured at the seat beside us. "It *gone*. Lilah. The envelope's gone, girl." I twisted in my seat, stared deep into the smoky theatre.

Lilah hauled me round, give me a cold glare. "Just watch the screen, Sid. Jesus."

I felt uneasy, my knee going up and down. I wiped my hot hands along my thighs. "So that's it? So now we just wait?"

She wasn't hardly listening.

"Okay. So let's ankle, girl."

But she grabbed my arm, held me in my seat. Her wrists looked damn thin, like she ain't been eating enough. There was that old clean lake-water scent on her. "Watch the screen, Sid," she whispered again. "We came to watch a movie, remember? Enjoy it."

Pygmalion, hell. Now that was one damn foolish picture.

———————■———————

And so we waited. Days passed. Every last one of us damn anxious and lying about it.

Then, overnight, the kid just stopped eating. Already lean from a diet of water, rot, gin and roasted street nuts, he now seem unable to take nourishment from nothing. The best cuisine in the world wouldn't help him; even small meals made him ill. Was like he was feeding on that fury running through Paris, that steady fear beginning to build.

Sure, butter, sugar, bread, eggs, all that got real damn scarce. We ain't got no coffee at all in the flat, taken to drinking some gruesome boiled chicory juice Lilah brought home, sweetening it with saccharine. But kid refuse everything we scrounge up. He grown thinner and thinner, his trousers slouching off him even with the belt pulled to the last notch, his shirts dragging off his bony shoulders, coming untucked. Seeing his throat rattle in his collars, I shook my head, thinking, boy, you skinny as a gut-string. He got the look of something hunted.

And then one morning he just collapsed. He ain't even got the strength to haul his thin body up out of them blankets. There was a darkness blooming in him, and hell if it ain't scared all of us.

I found Delilah in her room, grim, her worry etched in her face. I known what was troubling her. "He just ain't been eatin," I said. "He just weak."

"It's like what happened to Louis," she said.

I frowned. "It ain't nothin like that."

She was sitting at her vanity, staring at herself without really seeing. "Louis stopped eating, too."

"Louis et matzos."

Her smile got something of a sadness about it. "Yes. He did."

"You thinkin he picked this up from old Louis?"

She shrugged, disconsolate. "I don't know. But Louis got through it okay. So if Hiero's got what Louis had, he should be all right."

But she sounded real tense about it. I stood there at the vanity, watching her reflection as she unwound the wrap from her head. The silence felt so delicate, so intimate. I held my breath. Her scalp looked smooth, pale, near blue. She run a hand along it absently, her eyes drifting over to the window where the blackout curtains was bunched up and tied off. I gone over to her, put a calloused hand on her bare shoulder, the thin birdlike bones there.

"It's serious, Sid," she said quiet like. "We need to get him out of here." Then she lowered her hand, lifting my fingers one by one off her skin.

"Don't, Sid," she said. "That's done. That's over."

I blushed. "Aw, Lilah, I wasn't tryin to . . . I mean, that ain't—" But then I just gone silent. I felt damn foolish. Cause it was true, somewhere in me I was still thinking it. A thing like we had, it don't just *cease*.

But seeing her then, without no anger in her, just this enormous sadness, I known for real whatever we had once was just ash and dust now.

———————————— ■ ————————————

Still, something softened between us after that, some kind of tenderness come back. We was all of us sick with fear that we wouldn't get them visas. Being stuffed into a small flat together didn't help none. We grown frayed, thin, listless.

And then, at last, word come in from Armstrong. Ain't heard from him in weeks. I seen it troubling Lilah, seen how careful she was to not go on bout it. But she'd comb the papers each morning with a cold eye, them papers reduced to a single sheet, double-sided, with all them vast white blocks where the text been censored out. The war was here, even if the Krauts wasn't.

That day a letter come in the mail. From the look of it, it been delayed some while. Armstrong, it seems, done sailed out from Bordeaux on the fourth of June. Headed back stateside with his gates. He wrote urging Lilah to come on down to him before he set off, for all of us to get out right quick. Said not to worry bout his *furniture*. Son of a bitch. Lilah set her jaw reading this, her eyes hardening.

"Long as *he* get out," said Chip, scowling. He spat and got up from the table.

Hiero, it was like he just woken from a sweet dream to find hisself in a cold room. He hitch up one shoulder, turn his face aside, close his damn eyes.

So that was it for the recording. It finally come to nothing. I thought I'd feel pleased about it, relieved at least. But things ain't never what you expect. I looked with pity at the kid.

We all of us felt abandoned. And the war, it was just getting worse. Every day in the long southerly boulevards refugees streamed past, pushing carts, wheelbarrows, even baby carriages filled with luggage. Dutch and Belgian families, walking their bicycles, all of them exhausted, dragging on like they ain't got nothing left in them. I seen a woman in a black evening dress and boots, huddled on a curb on the Champs-Élysées, not even lifting her damn face when the taxis honked at her. No one even give her a glance.

The city buses vanished, near overnight. Everyone was talking bout parachutists, bout Kraut spies, the fifth column. Then the façade of Notre Dame was sandbagged, even while the book stalls on the quai stayed open. Was a damn strange time. We seen garbage trucks with mounted machine guns parked in the squares, steel girders set up near concrete blocks along the Champs-Élysées, in Place de la Concorde. One day the Bug pried her old telephone off the wall with a shrug. From now on all public phone calls in Paris was banned.

And still we waited for some damn word.

Then, one sun-drenched morning, Delilah burst into the flat barefoot, holding her heels by the straps, panting.

I scrambled to my feet.

"They're through," she said in a fierce rush. "Our visas. They're *here*."

Time ain't no steady thing. The speed it move at depend entirely upon the speed you moving at youself. It is a *changeable* thing, brother. And in those days we was all of us hurtling forward at a ferocious speed.

Delilah took me down to the Tuileries that afternoon, those vast public gardens drenched in June's easy sweetness and coral light. Hell, it might've been any summer, any Sunday afternoon, the bees drifting drunkly from bloom to bloom, the trees fat with green. Delilah walked at a easy pace, her shoulders loose, her face looking smooth and untroubled, like I remembered it. She was wearing a thin cotton dress that snapped like a flag in the wind. I thought, hell, if no other days exist beyond this, so be it.

The grass was ragged in the Tuileries, like it ain't been mowed in weeks. A policeman strolled by, a rifle slung over his shoulder, his helmet held half-hearted in one hand. Hell. And all at once I understood what felt so damn strange.

"Where the kids?" I said. "Ain't no kids nowhere."

Delilah shrugged. "You don't read the papers? They got evacuated to the countryside. Weeks ago."

Felt damn unreal. I eyed a jack reading the one-sheets near a ice-cream booth, looked uneasily at him. He got these huge thick hands, red and raw, like he work his whole damn life in a soap factory. Even from here I could see how he limped.

"So you contact down here," I said, "what he look like?"

Delilah ain't said nothing. Then she turned, give a little grunt. "That's Simone." She gestured at a bench along the path. "Did you ever meet Simone?"

"We ain't got time for this, girl. What you doin?"

Simone was a tiny bespectacled jane, dressed in tweeds, her brown hair cropped bluntly at her cheeks, like she done cut it herself. She looked like a damn *schoolteacher*. She sat dour-faced on that scarred bench, watching us approach without even so much as a smile. There was a magazine rolled up in one of her hands. With the other she pulled birdseed out of a brown paper bag, showering it over the pigeons in the grass.

"She look real friendly," I said. "A right chorus girl. How you know her?"

The pigeons cooed and parted as we come up, then closed in behind us. Delilah just sat right down next to that jane, saying something to her in Frog.

"Speak in English," said the schoolteacher. Damn if her voice wasn't lovely.

"Sorry." Lilah blushed. "I forgot."

The schoolteacher shrugged. "You will be traveling on your American passport. Keep your Canadian one very safe. It is always better to be a noncombatant in these matters."

I stared at her in astonishment. I suddenly felt real nervous.

"You are Sidney Griffiths?" said the schoolteacher.

"I sure as hell ain't Chip Jones."

She give me a look. Her spectacles was thick as wine bottles and her eyes ain't seemed to focus right, her left staring hard off to one side of my head, her right looking at the other. I glanced away. She handed her rolled-up magazine to Delilah. It was a old copy of *Life*. "Check each carefully. My people are good. But sometimes mistakes are made. You will remember to attach your birth certificates."

The pigeons was swarming the long grass, pecking like mad.

Delilah opened to a clipped page and there was our papers. She stared at them like she didn't believe what all she seeing. Slowly, her hands trembling, she begun thumbing through them. *Delilah Natasha Fummerton Brown. Charles Chippewah Jones. Sidney Roscoe Griffiths.* All typed and retyped in standard red ink. Our passports was fixed to each packet of papers. "Jesus," Delilah murmured. "Oh my god."

"Falk's is not in there," the schoolteacher said flatly.

I give her a quick look. There was voices on the path, then two janes bicycled past in the sunlight. They ain't glanced our way.

"Where's Hiero's?" I said.

She sighed, the edges of her mouth turning down. "His is a little more complicated, I am afraid."

"How much more complicated?"

She reached over, and closing the magazine, rolled it tight before arranging Delilah's hands back over it. "Keep those safe," she said. "Complicated. It will take a bit longer. He needs an identity as well as visas. And passports are harder to come by. We have been working with some people on this though. It will happen."

"*Make* it happen," I said. "It *got* to happen."

"It will." She turned those unsettling, unfocused eyes direct on me. I wasn't sure where to look. "Keep him safe until we bring them to you. You are nervous. You should not be, we will find you."

"I guess we just got to trust you a little longer," I said, feeling a old bitterness in me.

"Yes. You do."

"And we *do*," Delilah said quickly. "We do, Simone. We're just nervous."

"You must wait three minutes after I have left. Leave by the east entrance." The schoolteacher stood without another word, smoothed her long wool skirt, and turned her spectacled face to the sun. "Good day." Very casually, without looking at us, she walked away.

Delilah leaned over, give my shoulder a squeeze.

"It's starting," she whispered. "Sid? It's really going to happen."

But a strange sensation seemed to hover over everything in that garden. A sad feeling, maybe. I watched the sun-streaked heads of the young janes, strolling in their summer dresses through the heat. I stared across at the wrought iron tables on the patio, at the elderly jacks laughing there in Sunday shirtsleeves. It all seemed so slow, sad at that languid hour. Bitterness passed over me like a shadow of days half remembered. Hell. All of this, I known, was fated to ruin.

We come back up our street to catch old Chip leaning in a doorway across the way. Like he just getting some damn air.

"What you doin, brother?" I called.

He stood up straight, knocked the dust off his trousers, come over toward us. "Any luck? You get them?"

I slapped my jacket pocket. "Hand in glove, buck. Hand in glove."

"Well, well."

"Not Hiero's though," said Delilah soft like. She looked up at her windows and I followed her gaze up. The kid was standing, a dark figure, behind the far pane, his eyes on us. I shivered a little. I ain't even felt him looking at us.

"What's he doing up there?" said Delilah.

"Ernst's Horch been stolen," said Chip.

I couldn't damn believe it. I turned round, glanced up the street. "But there ain't even any damn gas. What the hell. They goin *push* it to Bordeaux?"

Delilah frowned, shaking her head. "We've got to get out of here, I mean it. In a week Paris will be a wasteland."

"Tell it to the kid," said Chip. "He the one holdin us up."

"It's not his fault."

"No. But it his doin."

She give him a dark look, crossed the street, gone inside. I stared up at the flat, but I couldn't see the kid no more. Cupping a hand over my eyes, I looked round the street. Wasn't no automobiles in sight, not a one. The buildings loomed hugely, deserted, dark.

"You get the feelin folks know somethin you just don't?" I said.

Chip shrugged. "I guess so."

We could see smoke pouring up over the city to the south.

"Someone's burnin somethin," Chip muttered.

———————————

Next morning Chip got it into his head to report Ernst's old Horch. Wasn't no damn way to dissuade him. But we no sooner step inside the government offices than I known something was wrong, our footsteps echoing over the polished marble. The halls was silent, the chandelier sparkling darkly above that mahogany reception desk. We gone past the big elevators, made our slow way up to the third floor. There was papers stacked in the halls, filing cabinets standing open in the offices. Not one damn official in sight.

"Hello?" I called.

"Holy hell, buck," Chip muttered. "Somethin goin on."

"It already *gone* on, brother." I swallowed hard. We ankled on through the gloomy halls, glancing into offices, all of it looking ransacked, overturned, abandoned. At last we found a clerk in a small outer boardroom, standing before a untidy table. With the care of a gent testing silk, he was holding a sheath of paper in his hand. Chip stiffened in the doorway, knocked twice.

"We lookin to report a stolen car," he said.

That damn jack just frowned, jerking his pencil towards the clock on the far wall. In rushed English, he snapped, "I will come on work in ten minutes. You will wait over there." He glared pointedly at a row of chairs.

"Hell." Chip scowled. "Their whole damn civilization comin to a end, and this jack still mindin his damn *clock?*"

The clerk look up then, give Chip a long, appraising frown. "You are American, yes? Why your country don't send us planes?"

I just shook my head. Everything done gone to hell, and here this jack ain't got nothing to do but nag some Yanks. I dragged Chip away by his sleeve.

When we got back to the flat, it was empty. I banged through the rooms, hollering for the kid. No one hollered back, and I found a note from Delilah on the sideboard, next to a envelope holding our papers:

The Germans are coming. The government left Paris last night. We are going to the gare d'Austerlitz to secure passage on a train. Meet us there when you get this. Don't delay.

"She took her damn visas," I said.

"She left us ours. That got to be tellin you somethin."

"What?"

Chip give me a look like I was all kinds of stupid. "What you mean, what? That she wants us to get out. Whether we find her or not."

"Kid still don't got a visa."

"I know," Chip said grimly.

You could hear the low stream of voices from blocks away. But even that ain't prepared us for the sight of the gare d'Austerlitz. The chaos was stunning. A horde of terrified folk writhing in a wild crush of bodies, scrambling over each other and hauling trunks, cases and crates as janes fainted, kids screamed. All of it washing up hard against the spiked iron gates of the station. The stink of that wretched crowd like to knock a man down. And always the wave of shouts, screams, cries, the high shrieking of kids agonized by the savage heat. When I lifted my eyes, I seen the clouds roiling overhead in long plumes of yellow smoke, like the air done turn to poison up there. A jaundiced light filtered down over everything. I felt my heart lurch in my chest.

"Aw, hell," I said.

Chip give me a sharp punch. "What is it, brother? You ain't never been to a Orioles game? It just a crowd."

"A crowd with *teeth*. We ain't never goin find Delilah in all that."

"Folk got a way of findin each other. You see. Now stay close."

He plunged right in. We was jounced and shoved and dragged apart, and then Chip was grabbing my damn shirt front and popping the buttons as he hauled me close. The heat streamed over us in sharp waves of foul air, and I breathed shallowly, trying to catch even the smallest piece of oxygen in all those fumes. Sweat run down my temples. Chip dragged me forward.

All a sudden a man was shouting in my damn ear. "Senegal, from Senegal," he hollered. He grab old Chip by the back of the neck, shouted some damn thing in Frog. Chip like to rip the old bastard's arm from its socket. I seen a hard fist hit the jack's kidney, and then he was crumpling.

"Get the fuck off," Chip shouted in English. "Goddamn son of a bastard. Get *off*."

In the madness we was jostled and shoved and pulled away from him. I seen the blood on Chip's collar where the old git torn his shirt.

"You alright?" I shouted.

"What?"

"You alright?"

He just shrugged, like he still ain't heard, and pushed farther in.

We ain't seen no sign of Lilah or Hiero. None. There was *thousands* in that crowd, and we wasn't nowhere near the big iron gates. We come to a halt, unable to jostle no deeper in. We stood there in the brutal heat, sweat glistening on our necks and arms, not looking at each other. I was blinking my stinging eyes when I felt a hand on my shoulder, and turned.

I don't know, I guess I was hoping maybe it be Delilah. But it was a young woman, holding a child high up over her head. She shouted something at me in Frog.

"English?" I called at her. "You speak English?"

"*Le bébé*," she said, "*passez-lui aux portes.*"

"What?"

A tall man in a blue shirt was looking at us. He shouted in Frog.

"*Le bébé*," she said again. "*Ils les laissent passer à la salle d'attente. C'est trop dangereux pour eux ici.*" And she ain't even waited for me to understand, just dumped this soft wet thing in my arms and gestured over my head to the next jack. It start to squalling. I handed it along.

"Hell," Chip shouted after a minute. "We ain't gettin nowhere in this."

He started dragging me again through it all, rolling past all them damp shoulders. I stumbled on something soft underfoot. Glancing down, my stomach wrenched at the sight of a woman just lying there, trying to protect her face with mud-caked hands. Before I could reach down for her, some other jack hauled her up and we was shoved onward. A sea of panting faces, women in shawls clutching bundles in raw hands, men with suitcases grasped hard against their chests. The heat was strong and moist, and with every step a new smell rolled over me like a strong current. A stink of onions, boiled eggplant, something riper and fouler than pungent leather. And hovering over everything, the sharp, acidic reek of piss.

We finally climbed out of it. Shaking Chip off, I leaned over in a doorway and begun retching. It was disgusting, all that fear.

"Come on, brother." Chip was breathing hard. "We got to find another way. Ain't goin be nothin when the Krauts arrive."

Once we got away from the station, the sudden silence was near overwhelming. Wasn't another soul in the street. We started making our way toward boulevard Saint-Michel, where all the damn refugees from the north been streaming through these past weeks. We known we get south of the city that way. We heard the crowds before we seen them. An incredible roar, as thousands of damn Parisians pushed on southward. Crowds thick as a river, dragging boxes, wheelbarrows, bicycles piled high with suitcases. Cars clogged the roads, going slow, mattresses tied to their roofs like to stop bullets from Stukas.

You couldn't hear none of the cannon fire now, only people. The crowd poured out through the city gates, streaming up round automobiles run out of gas, round trucks with punctured tires, a singe of rubber on the air. Car doors stood open, their backseats loaded down with broken wall clocks, soup spoons, boxes of salted herring. There was a overturned cart, its axle snapped, a dead horse already stinking in the heat. In folks' faces you read this quiet terror, a fierce, single-minded desperation as they trudged onward.

Chip and me, we stumbled into that storm. We ain't brought nothing, no water, no food, and I already seen the foolishness of it. My skull throbbed. Chip squinched up his eyes, grimacing. I felt this grand helplessness go through me. A old jane passed by us, her back crooked as a hat hook, wheeling her crippled old husband in a cart. I just looked away.

Chip seized my sleeve, gestured across the boulevard. A old man ran his damn wheelbarrow hard up against my thigh, shoved on past.

"That the kid?" shouted Chip.

"Where?"

"There. Under that damn tree. On the grass. There."

I looked and looked. "No," I shouted, "that ain't him. Now come on."

But Chip started pushing through that mass of folk.

"Chip," I called. "Hell. Chip!"

He ain't stopped.

Cussing, I waded on after him.

But, hell, it *was* the kid. He was sitting with his head slouched down between his knees, his hands clasped loose before him. Delilah was crouched in front of him, her back to the crowd. His clothes hung slack, like he just stolen them from some damn laundry line, and sitting there in that pool of fabric he looked totally shrunken. There was other folk, families, destitute men, sitting up under that tree. The yellow light shone on Delilah's cheekbones. Her face look sharp, angular, grim.

"Hi girl," said Chip. "How the view from here?"

"You got my note," she said tiredly.

Chip scrunched up his small eyes. "Yeah. And Sid here was especially damn glad to get one this time." His oyster lips widened.

I just looked away. It was too damn hot, just awful. "You give up on the station too I guess." It wasn't a question.

Delilah run a hand along Hiero's smooth neck.

"Kid's sick?" said Chip. He crouched on his haunches.

But when Hiero lifted his head we seen the blood. Someone had smashed his damn nose in, split his lip.

"Son of a bitch," Chip muttered. "Let me see that."

"He's fine," Delilah said sharply. "I cleaned it already. As best I could."

I just stared at him, at his head lolling on his shoulders there, like he been into the damn rot all day.

Chip got a strange look on his face. "What happen? Someone take him for a African?"

Delilah nodded. "A Senegalese soldier. Thought he was abandoning the city."

I kept staring out at that mass of fear, at all them damn folk shuffling on with their crazy belongings. Thinking, *A Stuka come, you ain't got a chance. You all just be mowed down like grass. Like a comb pickin out lice.*

Chip give me a thoughtful look. "How damn hopeless you reckon it be?"

The crowds surged, swelled up round a foundering cart, poured steadily past. All that shouting, the screaming of children, folk wheeling the damnedest things. And that nasty yellow light glinting off it all.

"We ain't gettin nowhere in that," I said.

Chip nodded. "We goin get just far enough ain't no one like to bury us after the Stukas chew us up."

"That what you worried bout? Bein buried?"

He smiled a dark smile. "I ain't worried bout *nothin*, buck."

"We're going back," said Delilah quietly. "Hiero and me. We're going back."

We both of us turned, stared at her where she sat with one arm round the kid's frail shoulders. He started coughing.

"Krauts goin be killin every damn jack they find." Chip's voice was cold. "You goin back to that? For real?"

She was staring sadly at the kid. "This was foolish. You can't panic. You lose your head, you're in real trouble. I don't know what we'll do, but this isn't any good at all. The Germans will come through here with their planes and clear this road in a matter of minutes."

I looked at her. Was like she was reading my own damn thoughts. Chip shook his head, but I known he thought it was useless too. A jack don't run away from a war. It move too damn fast for that.

And so we started back for Paris. Trudging along the sides of the road, wading against the press of refugees. The crowds ain't even hardly seem to notice. None of us spoke. The yellow light felt thick, oppressive. We gone back in, through the city gates, walking along abandoned, boarded-up streets till at last we was shuffling back up to Montmartre, the buildings dark and deserted.

Passing the Bug's shopfront, I caught a glimpse of our reflections. We seem to drift instead of walk, our faces blurred in the glass, ghosts.

The next day the sun ain't risen.

All was darkness over that empty city, the dawn sky black as char. A pelt of ash dusted the cobblestones, lampposts and boarded windows. Streets felt battered, desolate. We walked through that unnatural darkness, listening to the steady thud of heavy guns in the distance. Every once in a while a window would rattle from the recoil.

Our shoes rung hollow in the empty squares. Storefronts was all boarded up. Apartment windows was dark. Wasn't even no pigeons to be seen.

"Hell," muttered Chip. He run his hand along his face. It come away black.

"What is it?" said Delilah. "Coal? Are they burning the coal deposits?"

"They givin up on us, girl," I said. "They ain't plannin on defendin nothin. They gettin out while they can."

Chip grunted.

The kid, he ain't said a word. Trudged along behind us with his head low, his face steeped in darkness. Every block or so he'd lean up, shudder, hack some molten black sludge up from his lungs. Like the darkness had gone through to his core.

We walked in the middle of the Champs-Élysées, among the stained steel girders, the tangles of barbed wire. We stared out through the gloom. Ain't no other soul stirred, no electric lights visible.

Delilah slowed after a time, give us a sombre nod.

"What is it, girl?" said Chip.

"I need to go meet with some people. I'll see you back at the flat." She give the kid a long look. "Be watchful."

He ain't said nothin. Just stared at her with his hollow eyes.

"You want someone with you?" I said. "It ain't safe out here."

"She a tough old bird," said Chip. "She goin manage. Right, girl?"

"I'll manage." She begun slipping away into the dark.

Ain't one of us asked where she was going.

We ain't had no place in mind. But we circled down over the Seine and made our way back east. Then we was standing again at the edge of boulevard Saint-Michel, watching the refugees moving south. Ain't no one spoke. The quiet creak of axles, the rattle of carts over the pavement. A horse, its ribs jutting like forks, snorted, stamping nervously. The steady, soft shirr of footsteps shuffled by, like water, like wind rippling through grass.

These folk wasn't from Paris, we known. They was from farther north, from the fighting. I ain't made out their faces, just the pale blur of the sullen, the wretched, in their defeat. Hell. I hitched up one shoulder, stuffed my hands deep in my pockets.

After a time we trudged back, drifting toward the Bug's. Her windows was boarded up now, and there wasn't nothing but candles burning on the tables, but she was still open.

I folded my elbows on the counter. "Three cafés au lait."

She give me a weird, fierce glance, nodding hard. Her hair was loose, standing in frayed grey strands at her temples. She scratched a infected-looking rash on the back of her hand, studied me like she was weighing something.

"What?" I said.

She frowned, cleared her throat. "You pay first."

"You kiddin me? Hell, lady, it *us*. You *know* us."

She shrugged. "Different times."

I swore. Digging into my pocket, I felt around for a while. Ernst's money, which we'd divided evenly between us, wasn't so even now. Chip seem flush while the rest of us was counting every last damn *centime*. After a minute I drawn out some crumpled francs, slapped them down on the counter.

"Double it," she said.

"Now I know you shittin me."

She held my eye. One of her bulging eyes look glassy, grey. I ain't noticed it before, but now it seemed distinctly sinister. I counted out more francs, scowled, made my way back to the table.

"You ain't goin believe what this just cost," I said.

"Twice what it used to," said Chip. "And you paid up front."

I stared at him.

He held out his hands. "Don't look at me like that. Hell. Why you think I ain't ordered the drinks?" After a moment he give a angry smile.

"Don't matter anyhow, brother. Krauts get here, francs ain't goin be worth *nothin*."

Through the slats of wood I could see the light in the street shifting, glowing a paler grey. "It burnin off," I said. "Guess it wasn't the Apocalypse after all."

All a sudden the kid leaned in quick, almost tipping his chair. "Fuck this," he hissed. "Let's do it."

Chip smiled his bitter smile. "Buck, you just ain't my type. Now Sid, here…"

But just then the Bug come over with our cafés au lait, set them down hard, and the kid shut up again, his face closing. He ain't even give her a look. But once she was gone he looked up at us again, his eyes still burning.

"Let's do it," he said again, softer. "Let's cut that disc."

I was reaching for my cup. "What disc he talkin bout?"

The kid just stared sullenly at Chip, like he waiting for a answer.

"The Horst Wessel," said Chip. "I reckon that what the gate be on about. Am I right?"

Now Hiero turned his fierce eyes on me. There was a radiance in his face, a kind of feverish luminosity coming off his skin like heat. I swallowed nervously. It wasn't safe, talking like this in Kraut. We huddled in close, whispering.

"It like Armstrong said," said Hiero. "We got to *do* this. We all goin be dead in a couple days anyhow."

"Ain't no second trumpet," said Chip.

"Coleman," I said before I even thought it. It was so obvious, no other damn answer made sense. "Billy do it for sure. If he still here."

"We ain't got nowhere to record," Chip added. He took a sip of his coffee, but I could see the old gears turning behind his eyes. "But Delilah might know somewhere. Hell. What you think, kid? You ain't too sick?"

Hiero scowled at that.

And all a sudden I could feel this lightness coursing through me, this real soft excitement. Like a echo of something I felt once, in another lifetime. "Okay, Pops, let's do it," I said, imitating old Armstrong's gravelly voice. "Let's make history."

Chip grimaced. "Cut that out. You sound like a damn fool."

———————————■———————————

The sunlight splayed out across the streets. Delilah walked along the lee of the far buildings and, crossing over, come up to our flat. She moved slowly, like she got bad news for us. But when the kid give her a anxious look she just pulled out a old rusted ring of keys, set it down on the sideboard.

"The studio's not far," she said. "It's old though. Pretty primitive."

Hiero was shivering in his blankets.

"It be fine," I said. "Long as it works. You talk to Coleman?"

"Billy's in," she said.

She done already taped up a American flag in the front window of the flat, in front of the blackout curtains, to warn off the damn Krauts. The neighbourhoods all across Paris done empty out, the crowds still swelling at the stations. Though ain't no trains coming no more. We could hear the steady punch and shudder of artillery all day now, getting closer, and well into the night. We lay awake, all of us, listening to the war and to Hiero whimpering. To our shrunken stomachs groaning under our hands. We was hungry, brother, nothing but onion broth in the bistros, nothing but wizened carrots dug up past the Bois de Boulogne in the markets. That was the day the post offices dragged down their heavy iron shutters for good. Telephones ain't reached beyond Paris limits. We was finally cut off from the world.

"They shoot the hell out of us, ain't no one ever know," said Chip. "We just disappear."

"We start recordin tonight," the kid whispered through his clenched teeth.

Delilah barked out a laugh. "You keep telling yourself that. Go on. You're going to *rest* tonight, and we'll see how you're feeling tomorrow."

"Hell I will," Hiero scowled weakly. "Ain't no time left to wait."

"You think the Boots are going to care if you're sick? They're going to come through the city shooting anything that moves. You want to be sick out in that?"

The kid shivered.

Chip stood brooding at the window.

"It alright, brother," I said softly. I'd hauled out my old axe, was double-checking the action in the strings. I looked up at the kid. "We goin do this. We really goin do this. Let the damn shellin start when it want. When you ready, we goin do this. But you ain't goin lay nothin down if you can't hardly breathe."

We was all of us scared. But the next day, hell, we woke to the news on the wireless, to posters plastered all over the damn streets: Paris was a "open city." Ain't no one fighting for it at all.

Now if you lift you hand to the Krauts, you breaking the *law*.

———

Half-Blood Blues. That what he going call it, our Horst Wessel track. It wasn't true blues, sure, ain't got the right chord structure, but the kid ain't cared none. "Blues," he said, coughing roughly, "blues wasn't never bout the chords."

I figured, hell, ain't nothing else these days what it claim to be.

So the next evening the kid banged our door shut, double-checked the lock, and then we was off. A light rain was falling as we made our way along the cobblestones, through the abandoned squares. Hiero got Armstrong's case tucked up under one arm, his head down, shoulders shrugged up high. We could hear the steady thud of explosions to the north. That was the Kraut artillery. The streetlights ain't come on, and we trudged through the gloom feeling heavy as wet sheets.

"Where we goin, kid?" I said at last.

But Hiero just half turned, blinked his eyes to get the sooty rain from them, coughed. His eyes was feverish. "We goin to work."

Chip spat. "You mean we goin to *play*."

"Well hurry it up, brother," I said. "Cause I ain't walkin round all night. Unless one a you like to carry my case for a bit."

In the gathering shadows I could see the damn posters announcing Paris a open city. They been plastered in the shuttered doorways of shops, or hung already tattered off the unlit lampposts, coming softly apart in the wet drains. Hell, I thought. What coming be coming fast.

We come round a corner, stuck to the shadows. A figure was leaning in a doorway across the alley. Chip give him a nervous look until he step forward in the drizzle. It was Bill Coleman.

"Brother, I thought that was a gun," Chip breathed, nodding at the horn held loose at that gate's thigh.

"Aw, I known what you *wanted* it to be," said Coleman, smiling. "How you boys all doin?"

We give Coleman relieved nods, then all stood watching Hiero pull out that ring of ancient keys, trying them one by one in the lock of a narrow white door. I glanced across the alley at the curtained windows in the blackness. Thinking, length of time this taking, this can't be good. But then the kid dragged the door open. With the light of the evening sky, we could just make out a narrow brick corridor, then darkness. The air stunk of rat shit, of sharp toxic soap. I give the kid a hard look. He shrugged.

"Go on in," he said. "What you waitin for?"

He closed the door with a crunch behind us.

Chip fumbled for a damn switch. "Hell, kid. Lights is out."

"Not just the lights," said Coleman. "The power's been cut."

Chip let go with a string of foul curses. I started to smile, hearing it. Then there was a sudden bang, and Chip swore again. "Who put the goddamn chairs in the goddamn middle of the goddamn floor?"

I wiped the rain off my face with both hands. "How we goin record without no electricity?"

"It a war, brother," said Coleman. "What you goin do?"

There come the scrape of a match, then light flared up in old Hiero's bony hand. His eyesockets deep in shadow. "We goin play. Ain't nothin else to do."

"But we ain't goin record *nothin*."

The kid turned away.

"Aw, it goin come back on eventually," said Coleman. "We'll lay it down then, Sid. Don't you worry."

Someone had found a old candle stub and set it on a upturned glass on a chair in the middle of the studio. I got a glance round. The studio was narrow, cramped, the ceiling oddly high. The soundproofed walls looked scarred, like there been a damn gunfight. The floorboards under us been painted white, and they rattled loosely as we shifted round.

"That goin sound just beautiful on the disc," said Chip, frowning.

The kid stood in the corner, staring out at us through the darkness. He looked right creepy. I couldn't see his eyes.

I shrugged my axe down against the wall. "Come on then."

I was feeling the nerves, see. I ain't picked up a axe since that damn morning with Armstrong, in that other life. I run my fingers down the sleek strings in that flickering light, feeling sort of sad, like I been lying to myself bout something a long damn time. I thought, *It don't matter now, do it? It don't matter if you stumble. Ain't nothin to be proved no more.*

There was a kit in the corner. Coleman started blowing out his valves. I looked at the kid, he looked at me, and then Chip was counting us in. It was that sudden, brother. Ain't no talking at all. Just all of us clambering aboard that music like we all got the same ticket for the same damn train.

And it felt *right*. I just fold right back into Chip, climbing up and down the ladders of sound he lay out for me. Coleman follow us in with a bold, lurching cry on his brass. It felt full, rich, pained in some leggy way. Both bright and grave.

All a sudden Chip give me a look of surprise from his dark corner.

Kid wasn't even hardly listening, it seemed. Handling his horn with a unexpected looseness, with a almost slack hand, he coaxed a strange little groan from his brass. Like there was this trapped panic, this barely held-in chaos, and Hiero hisself was the lid.

I pulled back some as he come in, fearing we was going to overpower him in that narrow closet. But he just soften it down with me, blurr it up. Then he blast out one pure, brilliant note, and I thought, my god.

I might've been crying. It was the sound of something growing a crust, some watery thing finally gelling. The very sound of age, of growing older, of adolescent rage being tempered by a man's heart. Yeah, that was it. It was the sound of the kid's coming of age. As if he taken on some of old Armstrong's colossal sadness.

It made even me sound solar. Hot in a simmering, otherworldly way. And all at once I understood what the kid was to me. That only playing with him was I pulled out of my own sound. Alone, I wasn't nothing. Just a stiff line, just a regular keeper of the beat. But the kid, hell, his horn somehow push all that forward too, he shove me on up into the front sound with him. Like *he* was holding *me* in time.

Maybe I was just finally forgiving myself for it. For failing. Maybe that was the sound of forgiveness I heard in my old axe. Cause that night, swinging by candlelight in that cramped room, everything warring in me settled down.

I known without a doubt I ain't never be involved in no greater thing in my life. This was it, this was everything.

We was all of us free, brother. For that night at least, we was free.

———————

Next morning, we woke to a low thrum coming up through the floor, the windows rattling. I thought at first it was just the dream of all that jazz we done play. But then I woke for real, my blood thundering. I got up quick, pulled back the blackout curtains, stuck my drowsy face out into the sunlight. Streets was empty, the cobblestones dull in the light. But echoing off the buildings, through the squares, that steady rumble come clear. Boots. Thousands of boots marching on pavement.

"Hell," said Chip, yawning. "Tell me that ain't my head."

"It ain't you head." I cleared my throat, spat down at the gutter. Then I leaned back into the flat. "Krauts."

It was the fourteenth of June.

The kid was shivering hard in his blankets.

"How he doin?"

Chip pulled the sheets higher on him. Kid ain't even crack a eyelid. "All that damn playin last night run him down. It ain't good, buck. What you think?"

I didn't know. I could feel my old fingers still throbbing with the night past. I felt jumpy, a strange, thrilled feeling cutting through me. Hell. I gone over to the light switch, flicked it on. The electricity was back up.

"Ain't all bad then," Chip grunted. "Lights workin now that it *daytime.*"

"Trust the Krauts," I said, extending a salute. "*Heil!*"

But he ain't smiled. Not like he used to.

"We got to get out of here, Sid," he said, his voice low. "We can't stay. You know it."

But I was still hopping from our session the night before. "We *Yankees*, brother. We can damn well stay. It ain't our war."

"You ain't never heard of no one gettin shot, just cause they a ass?"

"Chip," I said. "Come on, brother. They ain't goin hunt you down. They ain't even known who you was back in Berlin."

"I said ass, brother. I wasn't talkin bout me." But he wasn't reassured. He just stared miserably out the window at the blue sky. "The smoke cleared off in the night."

"Sure. It a perfect day to invade a city."

Delilah come out then, tying off her silk dressing gown. She stood in the doorway, studying us. Her face looked ashen. "They're here," she said simply.

We was up then, getting dressed, slipping on our old shoes and leaving the flat, Delilah, Chip and me. Leaving the kid to sleep off some of his sickness. We made sure to bring our papers with us.

"What we goin eat?" said Chip as we stepped out into the still street.

I glanced at the windows across the way. I didn't reckon anyone still living over there.

Delilah said nothing.

Chip scowled. "Aw, what, ain't we goin eat *nothin?* Krauts might be here but my old belly don't know it. Come on. Least just stop in at the Bug's."

But we wasn't walking that direction at all. We made our way down toward Place de la Concorde. Folks dotted the street corners, a few vendors setting up their Friday stalls. We wandered past, feeling odd and lightheaded like we in a strange dream. A jane rode by on her bicycle, weeping. I heard Chip swear.

I suddenly realized I ain't heard a single cannon firing all morning, the air still except for that thrumming under the cobblestones. We went on, past the boarded up bistros, past the shuttered pharmacies and cafés, the blue sky overhead awful in its emptiness.

We come out at Place de la Concorde, onto the back of a gathering crowd. I could see a German tank, shining like it just been washed, a helmeted soldier in grey standing in the turret. Such harshness and such beauty under that June sun. There was big guns placed on the roofs of the nearer buildings. And there was thousands, brother, *thousands* of Boots filing past.

Hell.

We pushed our way through the crowd till we got a clear view of what was happening. I kept swallowing, but my damn throat was dry as toast. The Boots was clattering down through the gates and across the stones of the square, their heads snapping fiercely to the right as they passed their officers. Giving that damn angular salute. Scurrying all around, Kraut photographers knelt here and there, trying to catch every unholy angle of that parade. The Boots poured past in a steady stream of grey and green uniforms, jackboots gleaming, the sound of them making the pillared walls of the palace echo. The buildings, they looked filled with blame.

Then a old woman hissed from somewhere just behind us: "Senegalese, Senegalese."

Chip lift up his face, turned suddenly in anger. "American," he shouted. He held up his passport as if to prove some point. "U S of goddamned A. You hear me, sister? Christ."

"Hell, brother, you want to make any more noise?" I whispered.

Delilah just shook her head.

Chip looked at Delilah in disgust. "You reckon it time to run yet? We got our damn visas. You want us to wait round still? I ain't exactly *invisible* here."

Her face darkened. "Hiero's visa should be here any day. It's coming. It is."

"Like hell. You damn contact ain't even stuck around I bet."

She bit her lip, turned away.

The damn Boots kept filing by, hordes of greys, greens, greens, greys, more damn greys. Their sharp heels ringing like gunshots.

Some gent shoved on up beside us, staring out at the columns. He started hollering in relief. I ain't understood a word. He had one trembling hand pressed to his heart.

Delilah looked at us, shook her head. "He thinks he's saved. He thinks it's the British army." She turned to him, said something curt in French.

"Aw, Lilah, leave him alone," I whispered.

But it was too late. The old jack just opened his damn mouth, stared at her in horror. His eyes slid back to the Boots, back to Delilah. Then he stared round at the grim faces of other folks. All a sudden, he gasped out a sob. He walked a few paces away, then stood just staring across at a deserted building.

There wasn't nothing to do but watch. I could see the damn blood banner rising across the skyline: Hotel de Ville, the Palais Bourbon, all over the Place de la Concorde. Even the Eiffel Tower was draped with that dancing black spider.

"You had bout enough yet?" I said in disgust.

"Hold on, buck. They like to start throwin the candy soon."

I swallowed and turned away.

I felt a cool hand on my wrist. "Sid," Lilah said. "You don't want to go now. You don't want them to see you leaving. *Sid*."

"I can't watch no more of it. I won't."

Chip give me a hard look. "You want to get shot, brother?"

I shook Delilah free. "Hell. They goin shoot everyone got to go to the damn toilet? I ain't stickin round here. See you back at the flat."

It was over. It was all of it over. I turned and pushed my way back through the gathered crowd. It felt like pushing through soft wax, those folk ain't hardly moved at all.

When I come in, Hiero was still sleeping. He lay on the antique sofa in the living room's half-light, his skin glistening with a cold sweat. Frowning in his sleep, he drawn his legs up into a fetal curl. Sofa creaking under him. I kneeled beside him, took up a old jar of balm, begun rubbing it onto his hairless chest.

"Easy there, buck," I said. "You just go easy there. You alright?"

He just coughed a sharp, bloody cough, ain't even opened his damn eyes.

I set a second pillow under his head, got his breathing clearer. I felt damn hopeless.

And then I heard it. Three sharp raps at the door.

I sat very still, listening.

It come again, unmistakable.

Holy *hell*. My heart started pounding. I glanced real careful over the windowsill at the street outside, but I ain't seen no Boots, no tanks, nothing. I put a finger on the kid's cracked lips.

"Be real damn quiet, brother," I whispered. "Don't you make a sound."

And I got up from the floor, walked real careful down the hall. Each floorboard creaking under me like fireworks.

The knock come a third time, impatient, sharp.

I stood at the heavy oak door, listening. Nothing. The only damn peephole we got was a heavy iron latch in the middle of the door— nothing subtle, nothing safe. My hands was trembling. But then I thought: *Brother, if that the Boots they like to call out at you. Or break down the door. They ain't goin just to knock like they got all day.*

Still I ain't moved. I ain't moved for what seemed a lifetime.

At last, I called out in English, "Hello? Who there?"

Nothing. No answer.

I took a breath, drawn back the bolts, opened the door.

The landing was empty.

I give a quick glance down the hall, stepped out and looked over the rail at the courtyard below. There wasn't no one. But I ain't heard no one leave, and something in it all made me real nervous. There was a smell on the landing of dust, wet rubber, and under that a sharp reek of boiled onions.

It was then that I seen it. Tucked under the doormat, a single brown corner poking out. I pulled it clear, give a quick, uneasy look round before slipping back inside.

Papers. Even then, even before I torn it open, I known what it was, what it got to be. And sure enough, there in red ink: *Hieronymus Thomas Falk*. The name crisply printed on a French exit visa, transit visas, a entrance docket into Switzerland.

A high feeling come over me, everything suddenly bright, like we got some sort of golden pass out of hell. I leaned against the sideboard, trembling. A damn lump in my throat like I going to start weeping. I blinked hard.

Then it hit me. I thumbed through the papers again, held open the envelope, felt around inside. There wasn't no American passport. There wasn't no visas through to Lisbon. Hell. Whatever else he was doing, the kid wasn't coming with us back home. This was the end of our life together. This was the end of waking up to the kid's half-scared, half-sarcastic face. Shit.

It was the end of our recording.

I glanced back down the hall, into the living room. The kid was whimpering softly in his sleep. I wasn't even thinking. I slid his visas back into the envelope, walked to the kitchen, staring all around. I pulled the icebox away from the wall, tucked the envelope behind it. Shoved everything back into place. And the whole time I was telling myself, *Don't worry, Sid, you goin figure this out. Just got to get the kid back on his feet. We just need a few hours, just one good goddamn take.*

When I come into the living room, Hiero was awake. He turned his thin face up at me. "What was all that racket?" he said, drowsy. "Is the Boots here?"

"Aw, ain't nothin. Knife fallin off the counter. You thirsty?"

"I thought the Boots done got in. For sure." And then he closed his eyes.

A few minutes later the front door banged open like a rifleshot, and Delilah come tearing through. Ain't even closed the damn door behind her. "Where are they?" she said, her heels cracking on the boards. "Sid? Where are they?"

"Hell, girl. You near killed me. Where's Chip, he alright?"

She stopped, breathing hard. "What? No. Yes. He's fine. I was just coming to see you were okay. Where're the visas?"

My mouth gone real damn dry. "Visas?"

"The visas," she said, nodding. She glanced round the room.

I give her a blank look. "You mean our visas?"

"Now's not the time, Sid. Jesus. *Hiero's* visas. Let me check them. I ran into Giles' boy in the street, he said he just dropped them off. Just a few minutes ago."

I sort of shrugged my shoulders, like I ain't got one damn clue what she on bout.

Hiero start to muttering from the sofa. She looked over at him, troubled. "You didn't get the visas? For real?"

"You think I lyin to you, girl? Did the boy say he give them to me?"

She frowned, looked back at the open door. "He said he knocked. He said he left them under the mat." She was already rushing back to the mat, kneeling, peeling it up, running her hand along the old floor beneath like maybe those old visas be invisible.

Then she lift up her face, staring at me with this curious dark expression.

"What?" I said. "Don't go lookin at me like that. Hell. Maybe he got the wrong damn flat. Maybe he knocked at the wrong door."

She was gone then, her long heels clattering across the landing. I could hear her pulling back the doormats outside the other flats, running down the stairs, crossing the courtyard. Hell.

"Sid," Hiero said quiet like. "Sid?"

"Yeah, kid, I'm here," I said. "You alright? Lilah just losin her mind, don't mind her."

"Don't let them take me," he said all a sudden, real clear. "Don't let them."

"Sure," I murmured, "I won't. I won't let no one."

The door closed behind me. I turned. There stood Delilah, breathing hard. She was studying the two of us with a haunted expression.

"What's going on, Sid?" she said softly. She sort of cleared her throat, come closer, leaned into the door frame. "Don't lie to me. You didn't get Hiero's visas?"

"I told you already. I ain't got nothin."

"And you didn't hear anyone knock on the door?"

I scowled, exasperated like.

"Then why didn't you come check the other flats with me?"

I could feel my face flushing. "How you know this damn boy ain't a rat?" I said. "How you know he ain't lyin to you? You ever seen him before?"

"He's the nephew of one of my contacts," she said coldly. "He's not lying. What's going on here, Sid?"

I opened my arms, like to protest. "Lilah, hell. Maybe they was stolen. These days? Some jack even made off with Ernst's damn Horch, for Christ's sake. Ain't no gas, they take it anyway. The boy should never left such a sensitive thing just sittin out there in the hall. Hell."

"No one's living here, Sid, just us. Who'd steal it?"

I turned to her in the half-light, those shrewd green eyes cutting right through me. The room was calm, the only sound Hiero's damp breathing in his sheets. I wet my lips. "What you sayin, girl?"

Delilah's face looked severe in that light. Very soft, she said, "If you do anything to hurt him, you will pay for it. I swear that to you."

I gone cold all over, hearing her say it.

Then she was gone, the front door closing. I listened for the clack of her heels on the stairs. When I turned away the kid was looking at me with wet eyes.

"You alright, kid?" I said.

"Don't go, Sid," he said. He started to cry. "Sid, don't go. Don't go."

I put a cloth to his hot forehead, wiped off the sweat.

"I ain't goin let nothin happen to you," I said firmly. "You hear me, kid? You like my own brother. Nothin. We goin get you out of this safe."

The June light come in soft through the curtains, the streets still as death outside. All was calm, peaceful. I run the cloth over his forehead. He was wrapped up in those white sheets like for the grave. I gripped his hot hand.

VI

Poland
1992

I woke. Opened my eyes to all that brightness, the yellow walls of that bus burning with it, dazzling and sharp. I cast all about, looking for Chip, but I ain't seen him. The doors at the front was open and I stumbled over to them, down the steps, into that strange white light.

"Chip?" I shielded my eyes, squinting. "Where you at, brother?" My voice come bending back at me, sounding weird, like it was underwater.

My suitcase been dragged out of the hold under the bus; it stood in the dirt.

"Hell," I muttered, blinking. "Welcome to damn Poland."

We'd come to a stop in a small dusty clearing just off a dirt road. There was dark oaks and larches looming up all around, dense and grim. The air smelled of wood smoke, everything fresh and crisp, sharply outlined. As if all this land, all these bleak trees had stayed untouched by man.

I rubbed my old legs to get the blood going again, and then I seen Chip, standing out at the road, his beautiful suitcases lined up beside him.

"We here?" I said, shuffling over. My eyes stinging something awful. "Our driver ain't stuck around, I guess."

Chip shrugged. "He was gone when I woke up. Probably getting himself something to eat."

I glanced around. No signs of anything.

But Chip gave a little nod across the road. I thought I could see, strangely veiled by all that light, a sloped grey roof in the trees. White smoke rising from its stack, near invisible against the white sky. I looked down the road. Huge empty sky, a low plain stretching forever onward.

And what could I do but keep going. Hiero ain't asked for me, but wasn't no turning back now. I was irreparably here.

Then something occurred to me. "What if Hiero ain't here? Where we going to sleep, brother?"

"He's here," Chip said. "We ain't wrong."

Something in the way he said it, hell, my old heart started stuttering.

Chip began walking, and I trailed behind, dragging two of his damn suitcases along with my own. Not a soul in sight and the light in the sky glowing ivory, radiant. Something felt wrong but I wasn't sure what. Then I known. It was utterly silent, utterly still. Like there wasn't nothing living in them oaks, no birds, nothing. It was like the outer edge of the world.

As we trod through all this grand light, passing through bright, vacant fields, I started really thinking about the ones we'd lost, about Ernst, Paul, Big Fritz. About Delilah.

I thought of Ernst, getting it into his head the only way to take revenge on his pa was to kill himself. How he'd enlisted in the Wehrmacht, pleaded to be sent to the Russian front. Anything to stump that man who'd already gutted him. Not five weeks later, on a mission near Orel, he was shot through the eye and killed.

And I thought of Paul, trying to get back to our old flat. How he'd been after his epilepsy medication, a condition he ain't never mentioned, and one we ain't never suspected. He was walking the streets with Delilah when some ex-rival of his, a one-time jazz pianist turned Gestapo toady, caught him ducking down an alley and went hollering in after him. Hell. They arrested him on charges of treason against the regime, of race pollution. He was trucked out to Sachsenhausen, just outside Berlin. He ain't never come out.

We was all so *young*. Even Fritz, Big Fritz, who'd stayed in Berlin when we fled. Wasn't long before he nearly got arrested as a jazzman himself, had to flee to Hamburg just after we'd left for Paris. In Hamburg a friend got him a job playing jazz at the Regina, a scuzzy St. Pauli brothel. There he was protected by the whores, who'd warn him ever the Gestapo turn up. He was rushed underground, tucked behind some damn barrels. He even survived the bombings in that deep cellar. After the war, homeless and hungry, he wandered the countryside, utterly alone. Son of a bitch died of starvation in the German wood.

Did he regret leaving us? I reckon he did. He wasn't no Nazi, just a damn kid trying to save his skin. It hurt to think of him.

But Delilah, my lovely girl Lilah. Hell. I thought of how, after Hiero got picked up, she hid our discs in all different bags before quitting Paris, all the Hot-Time Swingers' old records. Even went so far as to sew *Half-Blood Blues* into a secret pocket on the inside of her coat. We wasn't an hour in Marseille when some old Vichy bastard confiscate them, even *Half-Blood*. Look on her face—hell, it *hurt*. Sure we was all upset, but Lilah—you seen in those wronged eyes she wouldn't never get over it. Who can say exactly how the pain of it played out in her life. She ain't spoken to me since parting ways at New York harbour. After kissing me coldly at the dock, she gone back to Montreal and disappeared entirely from my life. Again. I got word soon after that she had married, and then two years later I got word she was dead. Seemed to happen that quick. Blood cancer. Her husband said she gone peaceful at least. At least there was that.

Ain't no exaggeration to say I never got over it. Sits like a burn in my mind, a darkness at the edge of my thoughts. Every day of my life.

Chip turned off the road onto a narrow grassy path. Walking up it, both of us winded, I began to get the strangest feeling, like we was being watched.

And then we come around a corner onto a bald patch of grass, and seen it.

I thought for a minute it was a ravaged scrap of machinery. Standing seven feet tall at least, hammered out of twisted iron. Its hollowed eyes was staring in horror at something overhead. It was a monstrous human face.

We stood before it, astonished. Chip gave a low whistle, dropped his luggage, waded out through the grass.

"Aw, what you doing, Chip," I called. "Leave it."

"What you figure it is?" he called back. He ran his hands along the iron. "Look how it's pitted and scored," he murmured, as I come on over. "That ain't from the weather. You know how much damn work this got to be?"

"I don't," I said. "Neither do you. We going now?"

But Chip stood back and gave it a long hard stare. "You ain't going to believe this. I mean, you going to think I'm crazy. But what do it look like to you?"

I ain't said nothing.

"It don't look just a little bit like the kid?"

"Except it ain't got no eyes," I said.

But damned if Chip wasn't right. It *did* look like Hiero.

"Come on," I said. "It's creepy. Let's go on."

Chip sort of shook his head, walking back to the path. "You think it's creepy?" he said. "I don't know. Seems more sad to me."

But a few yards ahead loomed another rusted sculpture, this one of a human body, a good ten feet tall, its legs bent in submission, its arms twisted out like terrible forks. It didn't have no head, just a long stumped neck.

"You sure we got the right place?" I said.

Chip kept going. And there was more of them. Decayed iron chairs, faces melted and folded over themselves, gnarled iron hands the size of windmills. Monolithic shovels with hands still attached. All of them leaning into the long grasses, or already fallen over.

Then we broke through a last stand of larches and there was the house. Hell. I ain't never seen such a place. It was rusty looking, like those nightmarish sculptures, but beyond the long wooden porch— nearly obscured under browning papers, rubber boots, old tables—the house's grey walls was all plastered with mounted steel shovels and ladders propped against it. There was three front doors, every ten feet or so. All stood open.

"He *lives* here?" Chip muttered, looking at me.

I shrugged. "We just go on in, do you reckon?"

Chip cleared his throat. We left the luggage in the yard and shuffled closer. Old Chip stepped up on the porch, the boards creaking beneath him. He leaned through the nearest doorway. "Hello?" he called in. "Hello?"

No one answered.

With a glance back at me, he wiped his shoes and gone inside.

"Hold up, Chip," I called.

But when I stepped forward to follow him, all a sudden it was like my legs gone dead. I couldn't feel a damn thing. My hands, they just started shaking. I was filled up with some strange sensation. This enormous heat just going through me. And then it was over, and I started to shiver.

I stumbled after him, into a kitchen. It was all pale wood, everywhere: ceilings, floors, walls, tables and chairs, the huge shelving units at the centre of the kitchen, even the cooking implements strung above the old stovetop. Like I'd walked into a birch copse. And there wasn't no clutter at all. I could see through an arch into the dining area. Framed mosaics hung on the wall, along with bright paintings of geometrical shapes, and African masks. There was just one small dining table, one small chair.

Whole house smelled sweet, like brandy.

Chip was standing at the counter, looking at the door. "Hello?" he called again. He gave me a questioning look, the two of us just listening.

I shook my head. "Maybe he gone out," I said.

But Chip held up his hand.

And then we heard it. A faint thump from somewhere in the house, like a door closing. And then a sharp voice called out: "*Kto tam jest?*"

My throat froze. It was older, filled with rust, and I couldn't understand a word. But I known that voice.

It all seemed so slow then. Dreamlike, like we was gliding through all that light the way you push through lake water. Chip drifted over to the arch, passed on through, and I followed. We stepped into the brightest room I ever seen, lined with vast tall windows just pouring with daylight, and all that light radiating back up off the blond wood.

We both come to a stop. Across the room, seated in a cracked leather chair, his hair and beard completely white against his dark skin, was the man I'd reckoned dead all these years.

"*Kto tam jest?*" he said again, frowning. "Ewa?"

"Hiya kid," said Chip, real soft.

That old man ain't seemed like he understood. He turned his head directly at Chip, his eyes staring right through him. And then I seen his face open right up, just start to bloom.

"Chip?" he said. And then, in rusty German: "Is that you, Chip?"

My god. I seen his old milky eyes, the cast of his face toward us and then away, the sharp tilt as he listened for some reply, and I understood.

The kid was *blind*.

Chip walked up to the chair, crouched down before him. "It's me, it's Chip, brother." But then he just put one damn arm around the kid, and then the other, and then he was hauling the old kid out of his chair and they was both embracing.

"Up you get." Chip was laughing, his voice thin. He stood back, staring at the changes in Hiero's face: the even gaunter cheeks, the beard white as pure ash. Still got that frightened twist to his mouth. "You look *good*, brother," he said. He gave a little grunt. "*Damn* good. Like Sidney Poitier."

"You ain't the only one hasn't seen my face in years," said Hiero, smiling. Then he lifted his chin, tilted his face to the wall. "Who you brought with you?"

And all a sudden my mind gone white with panic.

Chip let him go and come over to me. "Come on, brother. Go on say hello."

It was the strangest thing. I gone over to Hiero then, unable to say a word, and just put my old hand on his shoulder. He raised his sightless eyes almost right on mine and said, real soft, "Sid?"

His rough palm touched my face, the fingertips passing over my closed eyes, my nose, my chin. I was nodding like a fool.

"You crying," he said.

"I ain't crying," I said.

And then he pulled me into a rough hug. All I could feel was his damn thin frame shaking.

———————————— ■ ————————————

"Used to be the old Ironworks," Hiero was saying in his deep, cracked voice. "For years it produced all the steel round here. I trained as a blacksmith. When the cooperative finally shut down, they let me stay on, me and a few others. Used the space as a house. Well one by one the others moved on, but here I am, still. I ain't never going to leave."

"Those your sculptures outside?" I glanced out the brilliant windows, tried not to meet his eyes.

Hiero smiled. "No."

"They ain't done by you?" Chip said, smiling. "Those old monsters out there?"

"No," said Hiero. "They was here when I come."

Well, son of a bitch. He was older, frailer, but the kid still couldn't lie for nothing. It was clear as day he done them. I looked over at Chip and could see he known it, too.

"Well," said Chip. "They really striking, whoever done them."

Hiero looked pleased. "You like them?"

"I ain't likely to forget them," said Chip.

"Sid?"

"I don't know," I said. "It ain't about liking them, is it."

"No," said Hiero, "it ain't. Let me show you the rest."

We trailed behind him. He walked through the house without hesitation, like he wasn't blind at all, moving down hallways, opening doors for us.

"You sure you blind, brother?" said Chip.

"I been living here for years, Chip," said Hiero. "But you just go moving the damn furniture on me and you'll see it get ugly, quick." He led us outside, along one wall of the house, to huge cellar doors. He pulled them back, dragging them through the grass. The interior was dim, musty like wet clothes. "They had a hell of a time renovating all this," he continued. "They was in far too much of a hurry. I wanted the cellar converted into storage, but they said the only way I could get more space was by digging down into the old floor. Fifty centimetres down. It liked to have killed me, the news. Meant getting rid of the old concrete, casting a new base with under-floor heating cables beneath it. Was a hell of a job—for months the house was full of folks. But it's done now."

I watched his face as he spoke. Waiting for a flicker of something—bitterness, resignation. Anything that would tell me where we stood after all these years. But there was nothing. Just his pleasure, his joy. The poor man didn't know a thing, ain't got no inkling of what happened all those years ago.

We went in then. The bulb was out and he ain't troubled to replace it, so the only light we had was what come in with us, through those big doors. In the shadows I could see dozens of strange shapes. And staring at those monolithic statues, the vast broken faces, their grotesque bodies, I got to thinking, maybe he *did* figure it out. Maybe he known right off, after his arrest, maybe he'd spent these long decades making peace with it.

"Sid," Chip called to me. "This one sort of look like you."

My shoes scraped as I walked over.

It was big, thin, lean in the jaw. It was clutching a second figure to itself, as if to protect it. The second figure was big in the belly, like a woman heavy with child. Then it hit me: it wasn't a woman, but a double bass.

"I don't think so," I said softly.

I looked over at Hiero's face, and known then without any doubt he didn't know what I'd done to him all those years ago. I stared at the figure.

"So he blind and now you deaf?" said Chip.

"What you say?" I said.

"Hiero just asked if you could eat now."

Hiero smiled, but tightly, his lips almost closed. "Please. It's Thomas now."

"Thomas," said Chip, glancing at me. "Sorry."

The kid's sightless eyes seemed to meet mine. "Sid? You hungry?"

"I could eat," I said.

Dinner was pickled herring and salad with store-bought sticky buns for dessert. We sat on stools pulled out from a closet, the table having only the one chair.

"Apologies, gentlemen, for the spread," Hiero said with a precise flourish of his knife. "I'm down to the last of it. I have a girl who comes in, Ewa, she comes every three days with fresh groceries, changes the lights, cleans up. She be here tomorrow. I can do most things, but some things do get beyond you."

Chip and I looked at each other, then looked guiltily away. You known we both wanted to ask about his eyes. Wanted to ask about his whole past, how he survived the camps and what had happened to him after, how he managed to make his way east and why he started going by Thomas—everything. But Hiero ain't started in on none of that. He was witty, pleasant, full of good talk on just about every subject. But he ain't gone *near* those years.

After dinner, he drawn out three glasses and a bottle of scotch.

"I been saving this," he said. "A special occasion. Got to worrying I wasn't going to have a chance to drink it."

Chip chuckled. "Hell, brother, now we talking. Give me two knuckles."

The day was failing but Hiero ain't thought to turn on no lights. We said nothing, just sat in the gathering dark, drinking.

At last Chip cleared his throat. "I ain't going to try to talk you into it. I mean, hell, brother, I *thought* about it. I did. Of coming up here, dragging you back, getting you some of what you deserve. It be a story for the ages. But I ain't going to push."

What a damn fool I am. A damn blind fool. Cause all a sudden I understood why Chip been so eager to come. I shook my head.

"You pushing now," Hiero smiled gently. "But there ain't no point, Chip. All that's another life."

Chip poured himself another glass. "You saying it ain't still in you? You telling me that?"

"Do it even matter?" said Hiero. "You famous, Chip. You don't need me."

Chip looked sort of sad at that. After a while, he said, "Is that why you didn't write all those years? You thought I'd try to get you to come back?"

Hiero shrugged.

"And you don't miss it? You don't miss it for real?"

"No."

"You don't miss the kind of purpose it give you?"

"A man's purpose ain't in what he do, Chip."

"Ain't it?"

Hiero turned his face toward me. "Ask Sid. He give it up."

I sort of shrugged. I ain't said nothing in a long while.

"Sid?" said Hiero. "I know you still here. Sid?"

"I'm here," I murmured. And then, since he seemed to be waiting for it, I said, "Aw, I ain't no kind of talent. Not like you two. It's different."

"You think that makes it easier to give it up?"

I blushed. "Not easier. Just different. After the war, after all that, I just sort of ain't wanted to play it no more."

"Why not?" Hiero pressed.

"I don't know." I opened my hands uselessly, glanced over at Chip in the falling darkness. He said nothing. "I don't know," I said again. "It was supposed to be this joyful music. And I just couldn't find none of that joy in it no more."

"I don't understand that," Chip interrupted. "I don't understand that at all." He sounded frustrated. "The music *is* the joy. That's how you find it again. By playing."

Hiero looked sort of sad at that. "There's all sorts of ways to live, Chip. Some of them you give a lot. Some of them you take a lot. Art, jazz, it was a kind of taking. You take from the audience, you take from yourself."

"But what it gives, it gives in spades."

"What do it give, Chip?" I said. "You a great artist, but you a miserable man."

Chip was quiet, turning his drink in front of him.

Hiero said nothing.

At last Chip said, "I tell you what I know. The world's damn beautiful. But it's an accidental beauty. What we do, it's *deliberate*. It's the one damn consolation you can offer not just you own life, but other lives you ain't even met." He gave Hiero a long, thoughtful look. "You don't owe the world nothing, Thomas. I know it. And you a good man. But it sure as hell breaks my heart, missing your music. There been this one brutal emptiness I been hauling around my whole life, and it's that damn beautiful music of yours. I ain't never stopped being lonely for it."

Hiero, with that unnerving precision of the blind, reached across and grasped Chip's big hand in the darkness.

"It's an old life," he said. "It's an old life."

I felt desolate, sitting there. I cleared my throat, stood unsteadily. "I reckon I got to turn in. Ain't getting no younger."

"You welcome to," said Hiero. "But you know we just going to spend the night talking about you."

I glanced sharply at him. He was smiling though, just making an innocent joke.

"Go on," I said. "It like to put you both to sleep fast enough."

Hiero got up from his chair, rapped the table with his knuckles. "Pour me another, Chip. I won't be a minute."

He led me down a dark hall smelling of sweet breads, into a narrow, simple bedroom. I could see the dark sky of the fields through the window, the billion stabs of the stars.

"Bed has fresh sheets," said Hiero, his hand on the brass doorknob. He shrugged, as if to say, What more could you ask of life.

"Thank you," I said. "Thank you, Thomas."

He was still looking where I was standing just a minute ago. "I'm glad you came, Sid. I thought . . . well. I'm glad."

This awful weight come into my throat then, I almost couldn't breathe. I swallowed it down. "What a thing, finding you like this."

"Like what?"

I shrugged, then seen he couldn't see it. "Alive."

He gave a sad smile, nodding. "Well. You get some rest. Any luck, we'll both still be that way in the morning."

He shut the door behind him. And then I known, sitting on the edge of the bed in that dark room, sure as anything in my life, that I had to tell him about the visas. That that was why I come. Not to find a friend, but to finally, and forever, lose one.

I slept. But it wasn't a dream, what I seen. There was this gap in time, an absence, and then I was thick into it again. I could see Hiero being forced to line up in a row of rusted iron statues. I seen him called out of that lineup, the SS men so astonished by his colour they rubbed his skin, like to see if the black come off. They pegged him for an athlete, like Jesse Owens, like Joe Louis, threatened to keep an even sharper eye on him, in case he used that fitness to run away. I seen an SS man follow him to the effects room, tell him to strip down—everything: coat, hat, pants. Stuffed all of it in a sack with his new number on it.

It wasn't a dream. I seen them feed him saltpetre until his limbs begun to swell. To keep that raging African libido in check. Day after day until his face between his hands felt like a slab of waterlogged bread.

And I seen the kid shaved, every last part of him, him standing in a cold room, raw as caught game, his thin legs shaking. Except it wasn't the kid he been, but the old man he'd become, so that it was his shining white beard on that dirt floor, his milky eyes troubled as he got handed a striped uniform, a tramp's cap. And I heard him say to them, "It's an old life. It's an old life."

I seen him unable to sleep. Hell. I seen him staring at his bunkmates, their limbs like twisted forks, their eyes like everything been burned right out of them. Even empty like this, they give him surprised looks, amazed at his black skin. And I seen Hiero hardly notice. These men are like smoke, you could move right through them. He even feared them a little, as if just being near might leech the muscle from his bones, carve the light from his eyes.

And I seen his days creeping by. I seen him forced into an orchestra. There's no shortage of instruments folks have brought with them, maybe reckoning they'd play when they got to where they was going. I heard Hiero playing Wagner's *Lohengrin* as new trains pulled up. I heard him playing *The Threepenny Opera's* Cannon Song as bodies was rolled by on lorries and folks was marched off to be hanged. I seen him playing in a brothel of female prisoners, their screams tearing the air as he stood there, lips working, his notes brassy and bright.

It wasn't a dream. And then I slept.

———————— ■ ————————

The sun rose, and that overwhelming light returned. I got up in the same rumpled clothes I gone to bed in, went outside, sat on the lip of Hiero's porch with my legs dangling over the edge.

I'd poured myself a mug of coffee but was drinking it black—wasn't no milk in the fridge. Thinking of that startled me. Three of us together again in a house with no damn milk? All a sudden I known there wasn't no way I could tell the kid the truth. None.

About an hour earlier Chip had stepped out, yawning, asking me to go for a walk. But my old legs wasn't feeling quite right. I watched him trudge off alone, heavy with his eighty-three years. Seemed sad, seeing the age on him.

I was just thinking of going inside when I suddenly felt a presence behind me. Glancing back, I gave a start. Hiero stood there, silent, turning his face into the sunshine.

"Good morning," I said, studying him. It still ain't seemed real, his being alive.

"Morning Sid." He was dressed in an ill-fitting T-shirt, raggedy jeans, tennis shoes so old looked like he run ten marathons in them. Trampish and shabby. Yet somehow, despite all of it, dignified.

I made to stand up, to help him.

"Lord, Sid, sit down, sit down." He gave me a gentle smile. "I been in this old house so long I could run through it backward and not hit a thing."

He felt for the lip of the porch with both hands, sat carefully.

"How'd you sleep?" he asked, a little winded.

"Aw, you know. Strange bed." I looked at him, then added, "But I thank you for everything. You a mighty fine host."

"Got some mighty fine scotch, at least."

I chuckled. "I made up a pot of coffee if you interested. Ain't no milk that I could find."

Hiero smiled.

"All these years," I said. "All these years, you been living here. And I ain't had no idea of it."

He ain't said nothing to that, and we sat in silence. I stared at his profile, his skin so rich-looking against the white sky. His eyes like opals, staring into an unseen country.

And then, I ain't known why, all a sudden I started to say it.

"Hiero, I got to tell you something. I don't want to tell you but I got to."

"It's Thomas," he said.

I blushed, cleared my throat. "What I got to tell you, it's bad."

He frowned. "What is it?"

I flung out my coffee into the weeds, shook out the mug and looked away. "Hell. All those years ago in Paris. It was my fault you didn't get your visas."

He paused, like he still waiting to hear me out. Looked like a rusted statue. Ain't no reaction at all.

My throat was dry. "My whole life," I said. "My whole life I wanted to tell you about it. I been so damn sorry, Thomas."

When he turned to me, he had a puzzled smile on his face. "That's just it. That's just what I invited Chip up here for. I ain't wanted him thinking I blamed him for what happened. I don't blame anyone, Sid. I don't."

"You're not listening. It *was* my fault. I hid your visas."

"But, Sid, I didn't even *get* my visas."

"That's what I'm *telling* you. You *did* get them. Day or two before you was picked up. They got delivered to our flat by hand, one of those days you was lying in sick and I was watching over you. They was left at our door, and I hid them."

He was shaking his head. "It don't make no sense," he said, "it don't. Why would you do that?"

I sat there trembling, not wanting to say it.

And then he said, as if to himself: "The recording."

"Thomas," I said. "I'm sorry, I'm so damn sorry. I'm sorry."

But he made a cutting gesture with one hand, like I shouldn't touch him. He sat there in that sunlight for a minute, his face turned away. Then he got real slow to his feet, shuffled to the second door, stepped inside. He closed the door behind him.

The porch felt so damn quiet. My skin, my chest, every part of me went heavy with the light. Almost blind in it, my eyes blinking, a pressure whiting out the yard. I was clutching that mug like it was my life.

It wasn't about doing the right thing, I understood then. It wasn't about compassion, it wasn't about giving comfort. Hell.

Chip come trudging slowly up, breathless from his walk. "What was all that about?"

"Nothing," I said. "Wasn't nothing."

Chip sat with a grimace where Hiero been just a minute ago.

"I don't think I should stay here," I said. "Chip? I think I got to go."

"Aw, Sid. What you tell him? What you say?"

But I couldn't say it again. I glanced at him, feeling scoured out, emptied. And then it didn't seem to matter if he known it too. "It was me hid Hiero's visas all them years ago. In Paris. You and Lilah was out of the flat, and they got delivered to the door when the kid was sleeping." My chest was giving me strange, anguished pains. "I wanted to finish the recording."

Chip glanced sharply at me, as if to say, *You did that?* But no sooner did he look surprised than his face quieted down. He stared out at the field, at Hiero's massive iron sculptures.

The silence was so painful between us I finally rose to go.

Chip put a hand on my arm. "We all done things we ain't proud of, Sidney. Especially back then." He turned to me, frowning. "It wasn't your fault the Boots picked him up. You couldn't have known what would happen."

"He wouldn't even been there if it wasn't for me. He'd of been in Switzerland."

Chip ain't said nothing for a minute. "What you done was inexcusable, Sid. Absolutely wrong. And I say this as someone who has profited off that record. But I know damn well you'd have given you whole life to spare him if you could. That kid was *blood* to you. Don't tell yourself it was any different."

I felt sick. I made to stand up but Chip put his big hand on my shoulder.

"Where you going?" he said.

"I got to go tell him something. I got to say something more."

"Aw, just give him time. News like that, it just take time."

———— ■ ————

Chip led me back into Hiero's living room, its wall of light. "This is what you missed last night, turning in so damn early." He smiled gently at me. I still felt sick, said nothing. But Chip folded open a closet door and kneeled down with a grimace. He drawn out an old milk crate filled with records. He started pulling them from their sleeves.

"What, he got your records?" I muttered.

"Aw, ain't no jazz at all," said Chip. "No. I ain't never heard of this stuff. Look at it. Adamo Didur. Miliza Korjus. Georg Malmstén. Marcella Sembrich. Kid says it's mostly Polish, some of it Finnish, Swedish. But you ain't going to believe what it sound like. Hell. Listen."

He set the needle into the groove of an ancient record player. And slowly, crackling, like from some great distance, a golden thread of voice started up. She sounded very old. Her voice rose and slipped a register and then rose again, like it was filling with this easy brightness, singing in a language I ain't known. It might have been Polish. Her voice was pale and splintered, raw, and then it was just a single, stunning wholeness, and closing my eyes I felt like so much was still possible.

Then it was over. I opened my eyes. Hiero stood in the doorway, his face strangely calm.

Chip began rising from his seat when Hiero stopped him.

"I don't need your help, Chip."

"I wasn't offering it," said Chip. "I got an urgent call. Hope you got a full roll in there cause I'm like to be a while." He gave me a look, slipped past.

The record was still turning in its grooves, the static from the old speakers hissing in the sudden silence. Hiero stood there in the doorway some moments, his eyes downcast. Then he stared right at me, his gaze like a blade.

He shuffled forward, sat himself down in his heavy leather chair. I had the feeling of being forced to go back, to confess again. With a soft grunt, breathing hard, he turned toward the fields beyond the glass, the twisted sculptures there. "This sky, Sid. It's the sky of the great epics. The great Polish epics. Of *Pan Tadeusz*." He pursed his lips a little. "That's the one thing I miss, the sky."

I nodded.

"I *have* seen it, you know. The sky was what decided it for me, all that gorgeous light. I followed it here. It's why I stayed."

I known what he was saying, what he seemed to be saying. His blindness wasn't due to the camps, and he wanted me to know it. I hadn't cost him that. I stared at him, those eyes so pale they might've witnessed the ruin of a world, the ruin and rebirth of a world.

He brought his palms to rest on his knees. "What was that just then? Was that Marcella Sembrich? I ain't heard that in years. Her voice, that's what the light was like."

I cleared my throat. "I guess so."

He turned his sightless eyes directly on me. "I see you, Sid," he said from out of his darkness. "I see you like it was fifty years ago. Exactly like that."

I ain't said nothing.

The vinyl crackled as the needle hit the centre.

"Turn it," Thomas said, without smiling. "Play it again."

Acknowledgments

Jane Warren and everyone at Key Porter Books; John Williams & everyone at Serpent's Tail in London; Jacqueline Baker; Anne McDermid & all her excellent associates; Hannah Westland at RCW; Marie-Lynn Hammond; Todd Craver; Sarah Afful; Michelle Wright; Jack Hodgins; the Prices; the Edugyans; Jeff Mireau; Frances Hwang; Richard Hess; Graham Newton; Art Schiffrin; Andrew Hamilton; and especially Patrick Crean and everyone at Thomas Allen.

Akademie Schloss Solitude; The Canada Council for the Arts; The British Columbia Arts Council; Stiftung Kuenstlerdorf Schoeppingen; Fiskars A-I-R program; Collegium Budapest/JAK; Het Beschrijf/Passa Porta; Hawthornden Castle; Klaustrid; Fundacion Valparaiso.